THE RAVEN'S EYE

ALSO BY BARRY MAITLAND

THE
RAVEN'S
EYE

A Brock and Kolla Mystery

BARRY MAITLAND

MINOTAUR BOOKS
NEW YORK

THE RAVEN'S EYE. Copyright © 2013 by Barry Maitland. All rights reserved. Printed in the United States of America. For information, address St. Martin's Press, 175 Fifth Avenue, New York, N.Y. 10010.

www.minotaurbooks.com

The Library of Congress has cataloged the hardcover edition as follows:

Maitland, Barry.
    The Raven's Eye : A Brock and Kolla Mystery / Barry Maitland.—First Edition.
        p. cm.
    ISBN 978-1-250-02896-9 (hardcover)
    ISBN 978-1-250-02897-6 (e-book)
    1. Brock, David (Fictitious character)—Fiction.   2. Kolla, Kathy (Fictitious character)—Fiction.   3. Great Britain—Metropolitan Police Office—Fiction.   4. Murder—Investigation—Fiction.   I. Title.
    PR9619.3.M2635R38 2013
    823'.914—dc23

                                                                2013024717

ISBN 978-1-250-05467-8 (trade paperback)

Minotaur books may be purchased for educational, business, or promotional use. For information on bulk purchases, please contact Macmillan Corporate and Premium Sales Department at 1-800-221-7945, extension 5442, or write specialmarkets@macmillan.com.

First Minotaur Books Paperback Edition: November 2014

10 9 8 7 6 5 4 3 2 1

To Margaret

*With special thanks to all those who helped me with this book,
especially my wife, Margaret, Dr. Tim Lyons, Lyn Tranter,
Keith Kahla, Ali Lavau and the team at Allen & Unwin, and
the unknown lady on the Regent's Canal who inspired
my interest in narrowboats.*

Then, upon the velvet sinking, I betook myself to linking,
Fancy upon fancy, thinking what this ominous bird of yore—
What this grim, ungainly, ghastly, gaunt, and ominous bird of yore
Meant in croaking "Nevermore."

—EDGAR ALLAN POE, "THE RAVEN"

THE RAVEN'S EYE

ONE

A DARK WHITE FOG hung over the canal and spread out through the bare branches of the trees that lined its banks to blanket the tall terraces of houses beyond and creep away down the side streets.

Detective Inspector Kathy Kolla and Detective Sergeant Mickey Schaeffer paused for a moment on the bridge, taking in the scene below: the dark boats moored along the towpath like a line of ghostly coffins fading into the gloom; the pulse of lights from an ambulance on the street beyond the trees; the huddle of figures beside one of the boats, their voices muffled by the fog. Kathy and Schaeffer made their way to the stone steps and went carefully down to the quay, where they were met by a Paddington Criminal Investigation Department detective, Detective Constable Judd. He was apologetic. "False alarm it seems. Accidental death. No need to bother you lot."

Kathy glanced at a middle-aged man in a tracksuit sitting hunched on a bench further along the towpath with a uniformed police officer and an ambulance man bending over him.

"Guy from the next boat, Howard Stapleton, made a triple-nine call at six twenty this morning to report finding the body of Vicky Hawke in her boat here on the Ha'penny Bridge reach of the canal. Ms. Hawke lived alone apparently. No suspicious circumstances."

Judd led the way to the stern of the second boat of the line, on whose dark green flank the name *Grace* was painted in ornate gold and scarlet letters.

"There's been a small crime wave along the canal recently," Judd explained as they stepped aboard. "Burglaries, muggings, a stabbing, a couple of arson attacks, and we've been under pressure to do something about it, so when the report came in of a suspicious death someone pressed the panic button and called Homicide. Watch your head."

They ducked through the doorway and descended a short flight of steps into a low-ceilinged living space sparsely furnished with a built-in couch and a threadbare armchair.

"Narrow, isn't it?"

Judd nodded. "That's why they're called narrowboats. Just two meters wide, maybe twenty long."

The claustrophobic effect was exaggerated by the fact that the upper part of the side walls, punctured by a few small windows, tilted inward.

Kathy sniffed the air and coughed, tasting acrid fumes.

"Yeah, that's what did it. Pathologist's with her now."

They moved on down the boat, through a confined galley, past a tightly planned bathroom and closet, and came to the bedroom at the bow, where the forensic pathologist was packing up his bag at the end of a bed on which a young woman in a nightdress was curled up as if fast asleep. The three detectives squeezed into the confined space and stared down at her, taking in the bright pink complexion, the impression of deep untroubled rest. Kathy introduced herself and Mickey: "Homicide and Serious Crime."

The pathologist gave her his card. "Not likely to be of interest to you, I think. She passed away peacefully in her sleep some time in the early hours. I believe tests will confirm carbon-monoxide poisoning."

"She looks so healthy," Kathy said.

"That's what carbon monoxide does, turns the hemoglobin cherry red."

She would be in her mid-twenties, Kathy guessed, a plain face with a slight frown of concentration that made her look studious. Her body appeared unblemished apart from a sticking plaster on her right hand. On a small shelf beside the bed lay a pair of glasses and a book, David Foster Wallace, *The Pale King*.

"Not as common as it used to be," the doctor went on. "Modern cars with their catalytic converters don't produce much carbon monoxide any more, so the old way with a hosepipe from the exhaust isn't so effective. Unlike that old beast." He nodded over his shoulder at a squat little stove in the corner of the room with a metal flue up to the ceiling.

"Diesel," Judd said, pointing out the black smears made by gases leaking from joints in the flue. "She closed all the windows and blocked off the ventilators to keep the cold out, left the heater on and took some sleeping pills." He indicated an empty foil and glass of water.

"Suicide?"

"Nothing to suggest it," the doctor said. "Careless or incompetent, I'd say."

The face on the pillow didn't strike Kathy as either, but how could she know?

Judd shrugged. "No note." His phone rang and he listened for a moment. "Yeah, yeah, okay, boss." He rammed it back in his pocket and muttered, "Fuck."

"Problems?"

"Yeah, I'm wanted."

"That's all right," Kathy said. "We'll follow up here."

"Thanks, I'd appreciate it. I've called for a photographer and more uniforms to go door to door. I didn't ask for SOCOs, given the FP's assessment."

3

"Right. Give me your number." She took it down and he left with the pathologist. Kathy put on latex gloves and went back through the boat, opening closets, the bathroom cabinet, kitchen drawers. The woman seemed to have few possessions, all of them neatly stowed away, surfaces clean. Kathy saw only one thing that wasn't strictly utilitarian, a framed print on the wall of a rather sinister-looking black bird. She felt as if she were intruding on a completely unfamiliar life. What sort of people lived like this, nomads afloat in the heart of the city? She had encountered the Regent's Canal on another case, a missing girl whose mother had drowned in the canal farther east from here, but this was the first time she'd been inside a canal boat. There was something of the submarine about it, the long tube low in the water, something surreptitious and stealthy.

When they reached the stern door again, Kathy turned to Mickey, who was thumbing through a copy of the previous day's paper, the *Guardian*. "She got the crossword out. Not dumb then."

"Where's her handbag?" Kathy asked. "Her phone, laptop? Take another look, Mickey, while I speak to the neighbor."

"Sure."

On the way out she checked the lock, seeing no sign of tampering, then maneuvered around the tiller and stepped down onto the towpath, again noticing the elaborate lettering on the boat. It seemed to evoke the spirit of old-fashioned fairgrounds and circuses, of antique gypsy caravans setting off along dusty highways. From here the Regent's Canal led eastward to the Thames and west to the Grand Union Canal, which continued north to the Midlands, and from there to a thousand branches into the most remote corners of the country, and Kathy felt a momentary pang of envy for the life of freedom which that curli-cued name promised.

The uniformed PC was still with the witness, and they had

been joined by a woman wearing a padded jacket against the damp chill. Kathy went over to them, showing them her police ID.

The woman constable said, "Police Constable Watts, ma'am. Mr. Stapleton here was the one who found Ms. Hawke."

He didn't look well, face pale, a large dressing on his forehead.

"You're hurt, Mr. Stapleton?"

"It's nothing. Bumped my head on the door frame coming out of Vicky's boat. Not looking. In shock, you see, after finding her."

"Yes."

He was trembling, and the other woman put an arm around his shoulder and said, "I'm Molly Stapleton, his wife."

"It's cold," Kathy said. "Go back to your boat and get warm. I'll come and see you in a moment. Maybe make your husband a cup of tea, Molly?"

As they turned to go Kathy drew the constable aside. "What did he tell you?"

"Not much. He's pretty shaken up. I tried to get him to go back to his boat, but he insisted on waiting to speak to you. I asked him for details of the dead woman's family, but he doesn't know."

The name on the Stapletons' boat was *Roaming Free*, and on its roof were a small herb garden, a stack of sawn logs, a pair of solar panels, and a TV aerial. Kathy knocked on the rear door and went down into a snug living room. Howard Stapleton was sitting in one of the plump armchairs, his wife visible over a counter in the galley at the far end of the room, and beyond that Kathy could make out a bay set up as a small office, with a computer and printer. The boat was filled with possessions—pictures hanging on the freshly varnished timber walls, floral curtains bunched around the portholes, china ornaments on shelves, magazines in racks, flowers in small vases—as if all the creature comforts of a family home had been crammed into the confined space. In its cheerful busyness it made Vicky Hawke's boat seem even more spartan and threadbare.

Stapleton made to rise to his feet, but when Kathy told him not to get up he sank back into the cushions with a sigh. His chair was facing a blazing wood-fired stove with a stainless-steel flue.

"You'll have a cup of tea, Inspector?" Molly Stapleton called from the galley. Her accent was Yorkshire, voice brisk.

"Thank you."

"Howard's not very well. The ambulance man said he may be concussed."

"I'm all right," her husband grunted, though his face looked as gray as his hair. "Stupid mistake."

"Do you feel well enough to tell me what happened this morning?" Kathy asked.

"Yes, yes, of course. I got up as usual at six for my run with Vicky—we've been doing that for a few weeks now. She's usually limbering up on the towpath when I emerge, but not this morning. I tapped on her window but got no response. I couldn't see in, and I noticed that the windows were steamed up."

He paused and took a deep breath as his wife came out of the galley with a tray of mugs. His speech was fastidious, almost pedantic. A retired headmaster? Lawyer?

"Um, anyway, I went to her stern door and knocked, still nothing, so I opened it to make sure she was all right."

"The door was unlocked?"

"No, no. Vicky had given me a key."

Kathy saw Molly's hand hesitate for a moment as she raised her mug.

"For emergencies," Howard added. "We're a pretty supportive community, we narrowboaters, look out for each other."

The explanation was too insistent, and Kathy noticed a frown pass briefly across Molly's face. "Go on."

6

"Well, I opened the door to call to her, but immediately the smell hit me, the fumes. It was awful. I called out and panicked a bit when there was no reply. So I held a handkerchief to my face and ran down the length of the boat looking for her and found her in the bedroom. I threw the bow doors open and made to lift her outside, but as soon as I touched her and felt how cold she was, I knew . . ." He stared at his feet. "Dear God," he said, and Kathy saw a glimmer of a tear in his eye. There was the shock, of course, and the bump on the head, but still, she wondered if there was something more personal going on here.

His wife was keeping very still, head bowed, and Kathy said, "How long have you two known Vicky, Molly?"

She looked up. "We came here . . ." she thought a moment, "eight weeks ago, and Vicky arrived a few days later. Being moored right next to us we got to know each other very quickly. Pleasant girl, new to boating, wasn't she, Howard? Her boat's old, though, a bit of a tub."

"Yes, inexperienced. I think the dealer took advantage of her. Apparently she didn't have a lot of cash to throw around."

"And were you aware of problems with the heater?"

"Only that it was an old model and a bit smelly at times. I did help her give it a clean a few weeks back. Wouldn't have said it was dangerous, exactly."

"But she'd closed the ventilators and windows in the boat."

"Yes, I'd warned her about that. But she said she felt the cold keenly."

With each new personal insight from her husband into their neighbor, Molly Stapleton's frown deepened.

"What sort of a person was she?" Kathy asked, and they both spoke at once.

"Moody," said Molly.

"Bubbly," said Howard.

Their eyes met for a moment in surprise, then Molly turned

to Kathy. "I thought she was a rather serious-minded and determined young woman."

"Well . . ." Howard objected, "but also full of . . . vitality, you know? Effervescent."

"Not with me, she wasn't," Molly said firmly.

"I'm interested in her frame of mind," Kathy said. "Did she seem depressed lately?"

"Suicide, do you mean?" Howard stared at her in surprise. "No, certainly not. On the contrary, she was excited by how things were going."

"I wouldn't be so sure," Molly countered. "I watched her the other day . . ." She pointed to the windows in the stern doors. "She was sitting in her bow, smoking a cigarette. She seemed quite agitated, gesturing, as if she was having an argument with herself about something. I went out and said hello and she immediately put on this cheery act. But it was an act, I could see that. She was worried about something."

"Well, I certainly wasn't aware of anything like that," Howard protested.

"You said she seemed excited," Kathy said. "Did she say what about? A relationship maybe?"

"No, she didn't explain, but I got the impression it was to do with her work. A new job maybe, something like that."

"Where did she work?"

"An office. Somewhere nearby, within walking distance, in Paddington."

"Doing what?"

Molly shook her head. "We could never find out. She didn't seem to want to talk about it."

"Marketing," Howard said. "I think that was it." Then he added hurriedly, "But look, I think you can discount suicide. We've been through that, haven't we, Molly?" He looked with an appeal to his wife, whose shoulders sagged.

"Yes," she whispered.

"Our son," Howard explained, "took his own life two years ago. Eighteen, he was. After that we found we couldn't live in the house any more. Then I was offered an early-retirement package and we decided to sell and live our dream. We had *Roaming Free* built to our specifications, and we set off."

Roaming free of the past, Kathy thought. Was that what inspired people to live like this? Was it Vicky Hawke's reason?

As if reading her mind, Howard said, "Of course, it's also an economic solution for some people. That boat probably cost Vicky no more than ten thousand, and yet here she was living in an up-market area of West London just a stone's throw from her work."

"Can you tell me who else is living here?"

There were five narrowboats currently moored on this section of the towpath, he told her. The one closest to the bridge was *Aquarius*, belonging to Dr. Anne Downey.

"I didn't mention that I tried to get help from her when I found Vicky, but she wasn't there—must have left early for work."

"What sort of doctor is she?"

"General practice. She acts as a substitute for doctor's offices that are short of staff."

"Is she Vicky's GP?"

The Stapletons looked at each other and shrugged, unsure.

"I suppose that must be a problem when you're moving around, finding a doctor?" Kathy asked.

"You get to know the ropes," Molly replied. "But Anne did prescribe our medications last week, so she may have done the same for Vicky, if she needed something. We've got Anne's cell phone number if you want it."

Kathy wrote it down. "What about Vicky's number? Do you have that?"

They didn't, and couldn't remember ever seeing her with a phone. "But she must have had one," Molly said.

"And she and the doctor would have known each other?"

"Oh yes, we all know each other on this side of the canal."

The other two narrowboats belonged to a man in his thirties, Ned Tisdell on *Venerable Bede*, and a young single mother, Debbie Rowland on *Jonquil*, with a three-year-old boy.

"That must be tricky."

"Yes, but it's amazing how you adapt. Debbie is a website designer, and works from her boat."

"How about Ned?"

"He's a waiter in the restaurant on the other bank. We don't have so much to do with the people over on that side, the houseboats." They couldn't give Kathy any information on Vicky's family, except that, from her accent, they assumed she'd grown up in southern England.

As she left their boat Kathy looked across the canal and was struck by the difference between the two sides. Farther along the far bank, hazy through the fog, was the restaurant Molly Stapleton had mentioned, its white tablecloths visible through plate-glass windows suspended over the water. Next to it was a row of what she had described as "houseboats," a strange mixture of structures that looked as if they had grown permanently into the canal bank. They ranged in style from one that looked like a timber suburban house, complete with broad veranda and glass french doors, to its neighbor, a ramshackle arrangement of tarpaulins and tarred panels.

"The boat of horrors."

Kathy turned and saw that Howard Stapleton had followed her out.

He nodded across the canal at the tumbledown houseboat. "Mad old bloke lives there. They've been trying for years to get him to clean it up. Look, I've just thought of something, about where Vicky worked. I remember she had a stack of brochures in her cabin one day when I looked in. They were about security cameras and alarms. I think she may have been working for a company which sold that sort of thing."

"Right, thanks."

Kathy went back to the dead girl's boat and joined Mickey Schaeffer, who was completing his search. Kathy took some photographs on her phone while he finished up. He had found Vicky's handbag in a storage compartment beneath the bed, and he showed her the contents: some make-up and perfume, a hairbrush, a pair of earrings, sunglasses, tissues, a wallet containing a credit card and a small amount of cash, and a receipt from British Waterways for mooring fees inside an envelope marked to an address in Crouch End, North London.

"Maybe her parents' address," Kathy said. "But no driving license, no phone."

"I couldn't find one anywhere, or a computer."

"Is there any twenty-something woman in London who doesn't have a phone?"

Mickey shook his head. "You're wondering if she was robbed?"

"What do you think?"

"I couldn't find any sign of a break-in, and nothing looks disturbed. There's so little of it, as if she arrived here with nothing—no photos, no documents, no history. I did find this . . ." He held up a plastic bag containing a thick roll of twenty-pound notes. "About two thousand pounds I reckon, hidden under the kitchen sink. It's like . . ." Mickey hesitated.

"Yes?"

"I'm thinking maybe she was on the run from someone, a violent partner perhaps."

"Yes, I was thinking the same thing," Kathy said. "Let's take another look at that stove."

They peered at it without much enlightenment, then examined the flue and the signs of gas leakage that DC Judd had pointed out. Kathy looked up at the dark corner of the ceiling into which the flue disappeared, then pulled a stool over and stood on it to get a closer view. There were much larger dark stains up there, and what looked like a gap where the flue had separated. She stepped down, coming to a decision. "We need an engineer to look at this, and a scene of crime team to check the boat."

"You sure?" Mickey looked doubtful. "There's no evidence of a crime, and you know how tight they are just now."

"I know, but we should do this properly."

He shrugged. "Your call."

More uniforms were arriving in a white van as they emerged. Kathy left Mickey to organize a door-to-door search of the area and set off for Crouch End.

TWO

Near this place is interred
Theodore King of Corsica
Who died in this parish Dec 1756
Immediately after leaving
The Kings Bench Prison

DETECTIVE CHIEF INSPECTOR DAVID Brock studied the inscription on the stone slab as the other mourners filed out of the church. Overhead the red disc of a weak autumnal sun had failed to disperse the morning fog, water dripping from dark branches onto mossy gravestones, the muffled notes of the organ adding to the crepuscular gloom. The brash lights of Soho on the other side of the churchyard wall might have been a hundred miles away.

"*The grave great teacher to a level brings,*" he spoke aloud the next lines, "*Heroes and beggars, galley-slaves and kings.*"

"Not to mention police officers," a voice at his shoulder growled.

Brock turned and saw Commander Sharpe standing there, uniformed, drawing on his gloves. "Dick was very attached to this place," Sharpe went on. "He cornered Charles Hammond in here after he'd disembowelled Mary Chubb—over there by

Hazlitt's tomb. Those Soho years were Dick's happiest. Never seemed to smile much after that."

Dick "Cheery" Chivers' sudden death had been a shock to them all. For several hours he had sat there at his desk undisturbed, assumed to be deeply absorbed in the thick report lying open in front of him: The Way Ahead for the Metropolitan Police in a Time of Challenge. "The excitement was too much for him," the office wit later suggested.

"This is the last time I shall be wearing this uniform," Sharpe went on, his voice hushed, though whether from regret or relief Brock couldn't tell.

"We'll miss you, sir."

"Yes, I rather think you will, Brock. Not for my engaging management style . . ." he allowed himself a little smile, ". . . but because after what you are about to go through you will look back on my tenure in the same way that Dick looked back on his Soho days, as a golden age."

"Is it going to be as bad as that?"

"Oh yes. Have you met my replacement yet?"

"He gave the team leaders a briefing last Thursday."

"What did you think?"

It had been reasonably impressive as these things went. The new head of Homicide and Serious Crime Command, Commander Fred Lynch, had been direct and forceful, his message tough but not despondent: the harsh budget cuts would require fundamental change, would encourage radical innovation, and lead eventually to a stronger and fitter police force.

"Police *force*?" Sharpe queried. "Not *service*?"

"I believe force was the word he used."

"Hm. A hard man for hard times was what I heard. It's the evangelists I can't stand, Brock, the ones who rush forward to embrace the hairshirt. But then, when you've been through more management restructures than you can remember, as I have, you know it's time to get out. You should have done the same."

That thought had certainly occurred to Brock. Superintendent Chivers's death had disturbed him more than he would have expected, and Dick and Sharpe weren't the only ones to go. In recent weeks Brock had become increasingly aware of the serious possibility that he would be marginalized by the new management.

Sharpe was watching the other mourners, huddled together in dark clusters. "I suppose he offered a carrot and a stick?"

He had. The carrot was an IT specialist from the Directorate of Information who talked about emerging technologies that would surely transform front-line operations. The stick was a civilian management expert, a "task auditor," or TA, a title previously unknown, who bore an unfortunate resemblance to Heinrich Himmler.

Sharpe laughed. "But, Brock, you were probably the only one left in the room who was old enough to remember what Himmler looked like."

Brock assumed it was impending retirement rather than Dick Chivers's death that had brought on Sharpe's unprecedented levity.

"You'll join us in a farewell drink for Dick?" Sharpe asked. "Or will Heinrich not allow it?"

Brock's phone buzzed. He tugged it out and read the message. "He must have heard you. He wants to know why one of my officers has asked for a SOCO team to attend a leaky flue. I'd better get back."

"Ask the cheeky bastard how many frontline officers his salary would pay for."

THREE

KATHY PARKED OUTSIDE A semidetached house at 62 Carnegie Crescent, Crouch End, and took a deep breath. How many times had she done this now, bringing the bad news home to a shocked family? It didn't get any easier.

She got out of the car and walked up the drive, past a Golf with a baby seat in the back, and pressed the button on an answerphone at the front door. She noticed a security camera up in the angle of the porch.

"Yes?" A woman's voice.

"My name is Detective Inspector Kathy Kolla of the Metropolitan Police. Can I have a word, please?"

The front door clicked open. Kathy pushed it and saw an empty hallway ahead. She stepped in as a young woman came out of a side door. Kathy couldn't see a family resemblance.

"How can I help you?"

"It's concerning Vicky Hawke. Are you a relative?"

The woman looked puzzled, then turned away as a baby started crying in the room she'd come from.

"Do you want to come in here? I'm just in the middle of a feed."

Kathy followed her. An infant sat strapped into a high chair next to an office desk with a computer and telephone. The young woman took a seat behind the desk and raised a bottle to the baby's face with one hand and poised the other over the keyboard. "What name did you say?"

Kathy took in the wall of pigeonholes behind her, many of them stuffed with envelopes. "What is this place?"

"This is North London Virtual Business Services. I'm Mandy."

"Hello, Mandy. You're a mailing address?"

"Mail holding and forwarding is one of our services," Mandy said brightly. Beside her the baby paused its sucking and gave a burp.

"Pardon. The name?"

"Vicky Hawke, with an e."

The keyboard clicked. "Yes, we do have a client by that name. What's the problem?"

"She's had a fatal accident. We found some mail with this address."

"Oh dear." Mandy scanned the screen. "She's paid up to the end of the month. How can I help you?"

"We're trying to trace her next of kin."

"Oh, I see. But we don't keep that sort of information."

"What do you have?"

"Name, email address, credit-card details."

Kathy took a note of the numbers. The credit card was the same as the one they'd found in Vicky's purse. "She was living on a boat moored down in Paddington. Ring any bells?"

Mandy shook her head and turned her attention back to the baby, which had begun to whimper.

"Would she have called in here to collect her mail?"

"Yes, or given someone else authorization."

"But you don't remember her?"

"Sorry."

Kathy asked her to look at a photograph of Vicky that she'd taken on her phone, and Mandy turned back and paused, bottle in the air, as she took it in.

She made a face. "Oh, that's her dead, is it?"

"I'm afraid so. Are you sure you don't recognize her?"

"Actually . . ." Mandy stared wide-eyed at the image for a moment. "I think I do remember her." She got to her feet and went over to a pigeonhole at the end of one of the rows. "That's right, she was F1. I don't remember their names, just their slot. She was about thirty? Came in once a week usually. I thought she was nice."

"Is there any mail there for her now?" Kathy asked hopefully, but there was nothing.

"She never got much." Mandy returned to her computer and checked. "End of August she signed up with us. Three months ago."

"Do you remember anything about her mail, who it came from?"

Mandy looked up at the ceiling with a frown. "I remember the first letter she got, because it was from a security company, and I was interested because we were thinking about upgrading our security at the time."

"I don't suppose you remember the name of the company?"

She pondered. "Paddington, you said? I think Paddington might have been in the name."

A few minutes on the internet produced a company, Paddington Security Services, which she thought might have been the one.

MICKEY SCHAEFFER RANG AS Kathy was getting back into her car.

"We're done here. Didn't find anything."

"That was quick. The SOCOs have been and gone?"

"They didn't come. Our request was denied."

"What? Who by?"

"D.K. Payne, our new TA."

"What's a TA?"

"Task auditor. Haven't you been paying attention? He's monitoring our use of resources."

"Oh, that. I can't believe he would override us."

"He phoned me up and asked if I considered it essential that we have a scene-of-crime team on this job. I couldn't honestly say I did. And Borough Command have withdrawn the uniforms. Same thing. Everyone's got better things to do, Kathy, face it."

Kathy felt a bubble of anger rise in her gullet. Finally she said, "Who's the senior investigating officer here, Mickey?"

"As I understand it," he said calmly, "it's DC Judd. We were just helping him out." Then he added, placatory, "I did get Borough to agree to get an engineer to do a report on the heater, for the coroner."

Kathy hung up before she said something she'd regret. Mickey had been on their team for over six months now, but they hadn't worked closely on any case together. Now she felt as if she were seeing him for the first time. She wondered if he had some agenda of his own. Perhaps he saw the new atmosphere of cuts and stringency as a personal opportunity.

She looked again at the address of Paddington Security Services. So far it was their only lead to tracing Vicky Hawke's family. She had been intending to pass it over to DC Judd and return to the many other things piling up on her desk, but now she changed her mind. There was something troubling about this death, something that didn't smell quite right, and it wasn't just the fog.

THE FOG HAD CLEARED by the time Kathy got back to Paddington, the sky a chilly blue. Paddington Security Services occupied the tenth floor of a sleek new glass-clad office block near the rail terminus. When she got out of the elevator she was presented with a sunlit panorama across West London, the swath of railway tracks, the elevated highway of Westway, and beyond it the canal basin of Little Venice and the Regent's Canal. From here Vicky Hawke might almost have been able to see her boat, a tiny capsule tucked away among the endless jumble of buildings stretching away to the horizon.

The receptionist said she'd get Mr. Budd to see Kathy, and she sat down to wait. Looking around, she noticed several security cameras, and keypads on each of the doors. After some time one of the doors burst open and a man appeared. His face was flushed, his stance belligerent, and Kathy thought that if she'd seen him coming like that out of a pub she'd have been reaching for her ASP baton.

He glared at the receptionist. She nodded at Kathy, who got to her feet and held out her ID.

He glanced at it. "Steve Budd, manager. What's the problem?"

"Do you have an employee here by the name of Vicky Hawke, Mr. Budd?"

"Vicky? Yes, in marketing. Is something wrong?"

Kathy, aware of the receptionist listening, said, "Is there somewhere we can talk?"

He showed her into a small meeting room and closed the door.

"I'm afraid Vicky's had a fatal accident."

He rocked back. "Fatal? Hell . . . Where was this?"

"On her boat."

"Boat?" He looked confused. "I don't understand. What boat?"

"She lived on a boat on the Regent's Canal."

He shook his head. "No, no. Are you sure we're talking about the same person?"

"Do you have a picture of her on file?" Kathy asked.

"Sure." He went to a computer at one end of the table and passed his open hand across the screen, which came immediately to life. He tapped for a few moments and a picture appeared, the same girl Kathy had seen lying on the bed, but suffused now with life, smiling at the camera.

"Yes, that's her. Could I get a copy of that? We don't have a decent picture."

"Okay, but she lived in a crummy apartment in Haringey somewhere . . . Crouch End." He did a bit more typing and said, "Yes, here we are, 62 Carnegie Crescent."

Kathy had the feeling that Budd had been quite familiar with that address, and she was wondering if he might be the reason that Vicky was living anonymously in a canal boat. He had appeared genuinely shocked at the news of her death, but she'd been fooled before. "What I'm after is an address for her parents, or next of kin. Can you help me with that?"

"We should have something . . . yes, here . . . Mr. and Mrs. Geoffrey Hawke, address in Islington."

Kathy took down the details.

"Jeez, marketing'll be upset."

"She was popular, was she?"

He hesitated, considering his words. "She was pleasant enough, but to be quite honest, she wasn't really suited to our work, and the others had to step in to help her out."

"How long had she been here?"

"Just coming up to three months, the end of her trial period. Frankly, we wouldn't have been renewing her contract. Shame, she had such a great CV, but when it came to performance . . ." He shrugged. "She didn't seem to have much of a clue. I wanted to get rid of her before now, but she persuaded me against my better judgment."

Unfortunate choice of words, Kathy thought. "Could I have a copy of her CV, please?"

"Don't see why not."

Budd printed out a copy and she thanked him and left, wondering why he hadn't asked how Vicky had died.

THIS TIME, KATHY THOUGHT as she pulled up at the Islington address, one of a row of tall, thin, redbrick Victorian houses; *then I have to get back.*

Her knock was answered by Mrs. Hawke, who blinked with concern when Kathy told her who she was.

"Not bad news, I hope? Is it about the accident at the end of the street?"

"Could I come in for a moment? Is Mr. Hawke at home?"

"Yes. Does it involve him?"

"Both of you. Thank you."

She was shown into a sitting room which opened through to a dining room with a view over a back garden. A white-haired man was sitting reading a newspaper at the dining table, on which stood a pot of coffee. He rose to his feet.

Kathy shook hands and they sat down. "I'm sorry to be the bearer of bad news. It concerns Vicky. I'm afraid your daughter has met with a fatal accident."

Mrs. Hawke gasped, covered her face, and turned away. Her husband groaned, "Oh no," almost as if, for all the years that he'd been a parent, he'd been waiting for just this moment.

"I told her," Mrs. Hawke said, shaking her head. "It's a dangerous place. Those drivers."

"How . . . ?" her husband asked. "What happened?"

Kathy began to explain about the boat, the heater, but as

she spoke she was aware that their expressions had changed to incomprehension.

"Just a moment," he said. "What boat, what canal?"

"In Rio?" his wife said.

Now Kathy was mystified. "No, in Paddington, the Regent's Canal."

They looked at each other, baffled, and then Mr. Hawke said slowly, "Are you quite sure that you've come to the right place? Our daughter, Victoria Sarah Hawke, is currently living with her partner, Fabio Mendes, at their home in Rio de Janeiro, Brazil. We spoke to her there just yesterday evening."

Kathy stared at them both, then said, "I have a picture of the Vicky Hawke I've come about. Perhaps you could tell me . . ."

She took out the copy of the photograph she'd obtained from Paddington Security and showed it to them. Mrs. Hawke gave a sob and cried, "Oh, thank God."

Mr. Hawke raised his eyes to the ceiling and drew in a deep breath. Finally, having composed himself, he looked at Kathy. "This is not our daughter. Have you *any* idea what you have just put my wife and me through? I really think you might have the decency to make sure of your facts before you come blundering—"

"Wait a minute," his wife said, taking the picture from him and staring at it. "Isn't this Gudrun Kite?"

He paused, irritated. "Who?"

"Gudrun, Geoffrey. Don't you remember? Vicky's best friend at school. The hair is different, but I'm sure it's her." She turned to Kathy. "We used to live in Cambridge, that's where Vicky went to school, and she and Gudrun were inseparable. Kite and Hawke—the teachers used to say they would be highflyers."

"I think you're right," her husband conceded. "I think it does look like her. But then . . ." he turned on Kathy, "how the hell did you mix her up with our daughter?"

"Because this woman was living on a canal boat in London using your daughter's name. She had given her employers your names as her parents and next of kin. That's why I'm here."

"Why would she do a thing like that?" Mrs. Hawke said.

And at the same time her husband, looking horrified, said, "She'd stolen Vicky's identity? Dear God, what else had she stolen? Her money?"

"That's something we should take up with your daughter immediately," Kathy said. "She needs to check with her bank and credit-card companies. What sort of work does Vicky do, Mrs. Hawke?"

"Marketing. After school she went to the London School of Marketing and then got a really good job in the city. She met Fabio and they moved to Rio, where they've set up their own consultancy."

"Did Gudrun also go into marketing?"

"Oh no, she wasn't really a people-person like Vicky. As far as I remember she went on to study science of some kind. She stayed in Cambridge and got her degree at the university there. It was about then, when the girls left school, that we moved down here to London."

Kathy thought about that. "I could be wrong, but it's possible that Gudrun used Vicky's CV to get the job she had in Paddington. And if that's the case she may have gained access to other personal information. Could we get on the phone to Vicky now?"

It was four hours earlier in Rio, breakfast time, and Mrs. Hawke got through to her daughter at her home. Vicky sounded incredulous as her mother explained what had happened. She and Gudrun had lost touch when they left school eight years previously, she explained, Vicky to study marketing in London and Gudrun staying in Cambridge to take up computer science. There had been no contact between them—not a phone call or a Christmas card or a message on Facebook—in all that time. And Vicky wasn't aware of any irregularities in her banking or credit-card accounts.

Kathy asked her to check these, and also to email her CV so that Kathy could compare it to the one Gudrun had used at Paddington Security Services. "I need to contact her family urgently, Vicky," she added. "Can you tell me where they live?"

"The Kites? Yes, of course, they'll be devastated. Mrs. Kite is a lovely person—please give her my love and tell her how sorry I am. I didn't know Gudrun's father so well. He was a rather remote figure, a bit intimidating and scary, a professor in something obscure at the university, like Icelandic history or something. There were two girls, Gudrun and an elder sister, um . . . Freyja, that's her name. Super bright. I mean Gudrun was smart, much smarter than me, but Freyja was supposed to be practically a genius. They lived in a big house on Harvey Road, just off Parker's Piece. Can't remember the number I'm afraid."

After they'd hung up Mrs. Hawke said to Kathy, "I remember Gudrun's mother, Sigrid Kite, very warm, unflappable motherly type. She will be devastated. You'll go and see her, won't you? I mean, not just tell her over the phone?"

"Of course. And I'm sorry to have given you both that shock."

"Well, that was Gudrun's fault, wasn't it? I wonder what the poor girl thought she was doing?"

FOUR

BROCK HAD BEEN CALLED before the Strategic Review Tribunal. They faced him, arrayed down a long table: in the center a woman from Finance Services, whose rapidly spoken name Brock had missed, ostensibly taking the role of lead interrogator; flanked by the group task auditor, D.K. Payne, on her left; and, so far ominously silent, the new head of Homicide and Serious Crime Command, Commander Fred Lynch, on her right.

From rather broad reflections on the current realities of budget cuts and diminishing resources, they had rapidly focused in on the operational procedures—"habits," the chief interrogator called them—of the twenty-three teams of Homicide and Serious Crime Command, of which Brock's was one, and had ambushed him with a case study.

"Which," D.K. Payne said with a prim smile, staring through his Himmler-style glasses, "took place just this very morning."

An erroneous logging by a local CID unit of a domestic fatality as a homicide had resulted in officers—*two senior officers*—of Brock's team attending the scene, where they were advised that the forensic pathologist had concluded that death was accidental and the dispatch had been a mistake. Despite this, the senior of the two H&SC officers had insisted on demanding full-scale forensic and manpower resources appropriate to a major homicide investigation.

Brock said calmly, "I have complete confidence in DI Kolla's judgment. She is a very experienced officer, not given to making rash decisions. If she wanted those resources she should have been given them."

D.K. Payne gave a thin, barely suppressed grin, the sort of curled lip that a wolf might have on seeing its quarry trotting blandly into an impasse from which there was no escape. But it was the woman from Finance Services who replied, in a severe monotone. "This small incident is exemplary as a catalog of the errors which are, it would seem, endemic and hugely wasteful. The first is that it is not H&SC's role to duplicate, countermand, or critique the work of Borough Area Command CID teams; the second is that investigating officers, no matter how experienced, must not assume levels of technical expertise they do not possess—DI Kolla is not, I think, a qualified forensic pathologist; and third, investigating officers must gain clearance for significant resource outlays."

"Mm." Brock frowned and scratched his beard as if seriously considering these weighty points. Finally he said, "We could debate the particular case—the CID officer was called away before a decision could be made; the pathologist, although an expert in medical matters, was not qualified to assess certain dubious features of the scene, and so on. But the most important issue is surely your third point: to what extent can we afford to have an administrative assessor, remote from the scene and inexperienced in criminal investigations, duplicate, countermand, and critique the decisions of an investigating officer on the ground?"

This was not her third point, of course, and she shot Brock an angry glare. "The *real* point, Chief Inspector, as you well know, is that we have twenty percent less resources with which to do the same job. So are you and each of the other H&SC teams going to make that saving? Or do we have to close down five teams? It's as simple as that."

Into the silence that followed, Commander Lynch finally spoke. "It's a matter of holding the line, Brock. This is an opportunity as well as a threat. It will make us leaner and smarter. The crisis will force the introduction of new technologies that will transform policing, but until that happens we have to be tough enough to hold on. Are you tough enough?"

When he was dismissed, Brock found a message on his phone from Kathy. He called her back and listened to her account of Gudrun Kite's deception.

"So what do you want me to do?" she asked. "Shall I give it back to CID, let them follow it up?"

"If you do, they'll just get someone from Cambridge police to call on the family and break the news, and we'll be no wiser about what Gudrun was up to. No, they've washed their hands of it. Are you sure you want to go?"

"Yes. If necessary I'll keep it off my time sheet, so the secret police don't know."

"They're probably listening to this call," Brock said, only half believing it was a joke. "It isn't just the false identity that's bothering you, is it?"

"No, I felt something was wrong before that—the absence of a phone or a computer, for instance. The place felt as if it had been stripped clean."

"Okay. Good luck."

"There's one thing I'd appreciate. Do you think you could speak to Sundeep and persuade him to do the postmortem? I'd feel more reassured if he says there's nothing to worry about."

"I'll do that."

Brock put down the phone, frowning into his mug of coffee,

still replaying in his mind his interview with the tribunal. What were these new technologies anyway? More cameras? More computers? Nothing to compare with a smart detective with a sharp eye.

FIVE

BEFORE LEAVING, KATHY PHONED the number she'd traced for a Professor Desmond Kite with an address on Harvey Road, Cambridge, to make sure she wouldn't have a wasted journey. His voice sounded distant and suspicious, but when she told him that she was a police officer he immediately became animated.

"Is it about my daughter?" he demanded.

"Yes, sir, it is."

"Do you have fresh information?"

Kathy was surprised. "Perhaps it's best if I tell you in person, Professor." She quickly made arrangements to come to his house at about six that evening and hung up.

What did he mean by fresh information? She checked to see if he or anyone else had previously reported Gudrun missing, but could find nothing. She shrugged and headed her car out toward the M11.

When she reached Cambridge she found the darkened streets shrouded in fog. The effect of gothic gloom was heightened on Harvey Road by the ranks of Victorian gables seen through a screen of skeletal trees. The Kites' house appeared forbidding, no lights visible in the windows, and Kathy checked the time again—ten minutes past six.

She mounted the steps to the shadowy porch and found a

brass button that she pressed. Somewhere inside a buzzer sounded, then silence.

Kathy pulled her coat tighter around her against the chill night and reached for her phone, but just as she began scrolling through her contacts list for his number a dim light showed through the glass panel above the door and she heard footsteps.

As soon as his figure appeared in the doorway, Kathy thought of Vicky Hawke's description: remote, intimidating, a bit scary. He was tall, slightly stooped, gaunt, and with what appeared to be an unyielding expression of disapproval on his bony features. "Come in."

Kathy followed him to a small study at the back of the house, where an old cat lay curled up asleep on a pile of manuscripts on a cluttered table. There was a gas fire, and this room at least was warm. She unbuttoned her coat and sat down, taking in the old prints on the walls, showing scenes of what looked like Viking warriors and maidens. Kite sat down opposite her, and she noticed that he seemed to be wearing gardening trousers, stained and frayed, and an odd pair of shoes, one black and the other brown.

"So," he said, "you have information about Freyja."

Freyja? It's happening again, Kathy thought, this sudden plunge into confusion. She said, "Is your wife here, Professor? Perhaps it would be best if she—"

"My wife died two years ago," he said, stony expression unchanged.

"Oh, I'm sorry."

"Your information," he said impatiently. "What have you discovered?"

"I haven't come about Freyja," she said carefully. "I've come to see you about Gudrun, Professor Kite." She took out the picture of the dead girl and showed it to him. "This is your daughter Gudrun, is it?"

"Yes?" He looked puzzled. "What about her?"

"I'm very sorry to have to give you bad news. Gudrun was discovered dead this morning on her boat. It seems she suffered a fatal accident during the night. We believe she suffocated as a result of a faulty heater."

His eyes widened, fixed disconcertingly on Kathy. "I . . ." He stopped, then tried again, "That . . . is not possible."

"I'm afraid it is. I saw her myself. We believe she died quite peacefully in her sleep."

"Orgg . . ." The choking sound of protest seemed to fight its way out of his throat of its own accord while he continued staring at Kathy, who began to think that he was suffering an attack of some kind. Then he lurched to his feet and stumbled across the room and out the door.

Kathy went after him and found him standing in the hall with his back to her. She could hear his breathing, like the labored gasping of old bellows, and he was shaking his head.

"Professor, please, let me get you something . . ." she began, but he lifted his hands up as if to cast her away and strode into a room opposite, slamming the door behind him.

Kathy returned to the study and waited. There seemed to be no one else in the house, which was completely silent. After a while she got to her feet again and went to his door and knocked and tried the handle, but it was locked. There was no response to her appeal to open it, and she began to get worried. Standing there in the hallway she noticed signs of neglect everywhere: dust, wallpaper peeling from a damp patch near the ceiling, a jumble of notes and lists around the telephone, some lying crumpled on the floor. Above the phone, taped roughly to the wallpaper, was a note with a penciled name, *Harris*, and a telephone number and address on Harvey Road. A neighbor, she assumed. Kathy dialed the number and a woman answered, "Hello?"

"Mrs. Harris?"

"Yes?"

"I'm a police officer, and I'm with Professor Kite at his home on Harvey Road at the moment. Are you a friend of his?"

"Well, yes, you could say that. We've known Desmond for some time. Is anything wrong?"

"He's had some bad news and I'd like to contact a friend or relative who could be with him. Do you know how I might get hold of his daughter Freyja?"

Kathy heard an intake of breath at the other end, then the woman said, "Freyja died a year ago."

Kathy groaned under her breath. This just got worse. Mrs. Harris was going on, "He has another daughter, in London . . ."

"Gudrun, yes. I'm afraid that's why I'm here."

"Oh no, don't tell me something's happened to Gudrun too?"

"She died last night, Mrs. Harris. Professor Kite is very distraught."

"Dear heaven. Wait . . ."

Kathy heard a muffled conversation, then a man's voice, brisk.

"Hello? I'm Andrew Harris. I don't think Desmond has any other near relatives, not that we know of anyway. And I suppose we're the closest friends that he has. I'll be right over."

"Thank you."

Kathy went to the front door and saw a figure emerge from a house farther along the street, pulling on a coat, and come hurrying across. They shook hands.

"This is terrible," Harris said. "What happened exactly?"

Kathy told him and he shook his head. From his few brief questions Kathy guessed he had some medical knowledge.

"I'm a doctor," he said, "at Addenbrooke's Hospital." He gave Kathy a card, *Dr. Andrew Harris, MB ChB FRCA, Anesthetist.* "I was on duty the night Freyja was brought in. I gather you didn't know about that? She was knocked off her bike here in

Cambridge one evening earlier this year. Hit-and-run, the driver was never caught." He looked around. "Where's Desmond?"

"He locked himself in there when I told him what had happened. There's been no sound."

Dr. Harris rapped his knuckles on the door. "Desmond? It's Andrew. Open the door, there's a good chap."

After a moment they heard a shuffle of feet and the click of the lock. The door opened slowly and Kite stood there, sagging on his feet. "Andrew," he mumbled. "It's Gudrun . . ."

"I know, the inspector's explained. You're coming back to stay with us tonight, so get your coat on."

"No," Kite protested, but Harris took him firmly by the arm and led him out into the hall. Kite looked befuddled, unable to resist the doctor's grip.

"It's a cold night," Harris said, looking up and down the hall. "Where's your coat, Desmond?"

"Study," Kite muttered, and shambled off in that direction.

Dr. Harris watched him go with a physician's assessing eye. "Poor chap. God, this place is freezing. Such a change from when Sigrid was alive." He turned to Kathy. "We should talk."

"Yes, I'd appreciate that."

"London? You're with the Met? Went to university with a Met detective—well, that's what he became, wouldn't have guessed it then. See his name in the papers from time to time: David Brock. Maybe you've heard of him?"

Kathy nodded. "Oh yes. He's my boss."

"Really? How fascinating. We were great friends. Small world."

He turned at the sound of Professor Kite returning, wearing a scarf and a heavy old tweed coat.

"Good. Got your keys?"

They waited while Kite rummaged through the papers beside the telephone and found a wallet and a bunch of keys, then they set off.

Mrs. Harris met them at her front door, taking Kite's coat with a look of concern on her face, and leading him through to the kitchen from which a rich smell of cooking pervaded the house. They gathered around the kitchen table and commiserated with Kite, who sat, ashen-faced, saying little. Dr. Harris poured a glass of whiskey for him, and he had some difficulty raising it with both trembling hands to his mouth. When Harris offered Kathy a glass she said no, that she had to drive back to London.

"Do you really have to?" he said. "There are things we should discuss, and you'll have to sample Deb's wonderful steak and kidney pie. Why not stay here the night and return tomorrow? Right, Deb?"

His wife gave Kathy an encouraging smile. "Of course."

Kathy thought about it. She'd already spent too long on the mystery of Gudrun Kite, but the offer was tempting and the next day was Saturday, and theoretically her day off. "That's very kind of you. If you're quite sure it's not an inconvenience."

It was settled, and Harris opened a bottle of wine, saying, "I want to persuade Inspector Kolla—may we use first names? Kathy then—I want to persuade Kathy to bring her boss up to see us, Deb. David Brock and I were on the same staircase in New Court, Trinity, in our third year. You never met him, did you, darling? Great fellow, splendid cricketer, solid batsman, eye for the girls."

It was the first Kathy had heard of it. She wondered what else Harris could come up with about Brock's youth.

"Will you set the table next door, Andrew?" his wife asked, but he said they should stay in the kitchen, which was warm and comfortable, and he cleared spaces and set out cutlery and Deb produced plates of steaming comfort food. Kite seemed barely conscious of them, gulping the pie down as soon as it was placed in front of him, as if he hadn't seen hot food for a long time.

What with the meal and the whiskey and, Kathy suspected, something that Dr. Harris might have given him, his eyes were closing as he finished wiping up the last traces of gravy.

When Harris led him away to bed, Kathy helped Deb clear the dishes.

"I can't believe this has happened to Desmond," she said. "These last few years have been a nightmare for him."

"He said his wife died not long ago."

"Yes, Sigrid was ill for over a year, and Freyja came back from America to look after her. They were such a close family, the three women so bright, so full of life, and Desmond quietly in the background. But since Sigrid died he's turned in on himself and then Freyja had her accident and they couldn't find anyone to blame, and he became more and more bitter. I don't know how he'll survive this."

Kathy imagined what he must have thought when she'd phoned him and said she wanted to talk to him about his daughter. He must have expected news of a breakthrough, and instead she'd brought him the worst news of all.

Andrew Harris returned. "He's settled down, for now at least. I really think he may be losing his mind. He seems to think that he's living in one of his sagas—he mumbled some unpronounceable name—about a man whose two daughters were taken by a monster."

"That's his field," Deb explained to Kathy. "The Norse sagas. He met Sigrid in Sweden when he was doing his research."

Andrew poured himself another glass of wine. "When he was only thirty-four he was appointed Scheving Professor of Old Norse Literature and History, the youngest ever. For thirty years, sheltered by the university and his family, he's been able to immerse himself in a world utterly divorced from reality. Now reality has given him three hard blows, and I don't know that he'll be able to cope. Maybe his college will take him in, and he'll become one of those old dons we used to see puttering about with a pair of shears, pruning the roses."

"What's made it harder for him is that he's never accepted that Freyja's death was accidental," Deb said.

"I'm afraid that was partly my fault," Andrew said. "When I first saw her in A&E she was so badly battered that I thought she must have been beaten up, and I said something to that effect. A nurse heard me, and when Desmond arrived she unfortunately told him that his daughter had been attacked. Later we realized that it was a hit-and-run road accident, but Desmond had the idea of an assault fixed in his mind. When the police couldn't find those responsible he began to talk about a conspiracy."

"And then there was the witness," Deb added.

"Yes. It happened late at night, Freyja cycling back into town from the Cambridge Science Park where she was working. An old man living in one of the houses along Milton Road heard the squeal of tires and looked out of his bedroom window. He saw a car and two men bending over a bundle on the street, and a bicycle. Then the men got into the car and drove off and he went outside and found Freyja and called an ambulance.

"The thing is, in his first statement to the police he said that one of the men was holding a club in his hand. Then later he changed his mind."

"There was a postmortem?" Kathy asked.

"Of course. I know the pathologist well, sound man. He considered the injuries consistent with a bad smash. She'd gone under the car and was probably trapped beneath, and they'd reversed off her—that was his interpretation, which was consistent with the police examination of marks on the road. Don't worry, it was all looked at very carefully. And of course there was no motive for anyone to want Freyja dead. But it was Desmond's second family tragedy within a couple of years, and his head was full of dark Viking sagas of murder and revenge, and he couldn't be persuaded to accept the coroner's finding.

"And now . . ." Harris fixed Kathy with a glint in his eye, "his second daughter is found dead, and Scotland Yard sends a detective from the Homicide and Serious Crime Command." He saw Kathy's raised eyebrow, and smiled. "I just looked Brock up on the web after I tucked Desmond in. So Brock sends a detective inspector, no less, up to Cambridge to inform the grieving parent. Something's up, isn't it?"

Kathy said, "Actually, the local CID got their wires crossed and called us out by mistake. I just agreed to follow up with tracing next of kin."

Harris chuckled and topped off Kathy's glass. "Come on, Kathy, you'll have to do better than that."

Kathy was silent for a moment, considering, then she said, "There is something you may be able to help me with, but I haven't mentioned it to Professor Kite yet, so this must be in confidence."

"Absolutely."

"It seems that Gudrun was living under an assumed name in London, in fact using the identity of someone else, a girl she was at school with here in Cambridge by the name of Vicky Hawke. Does that mean anything to you?"

"That's very strange. The other girl didn't know?"

"No, she's living overseas now and had no idea. So I'm wondering if Gudrun was trying to hide from someone—a former boyfriend perhaps?"

"Ah yes, I see. And he may have had a hand in her death."

"No," Kathy said firmly. "We don't know that such a person even exists, and I don't want Professor Kite or anyone else getting hold of an idea like that."

"No, no," Harris said quickly. "Of course not."

"So are you aware of her friends?"

"Freyja was the one who always attracted the boys," Deb Harris said. "She had very striking looks, and she was extremely bright—too bright for them, they never lasted long. Gudrun was rather plain, and not as outgoing as her sister, and I can't really remember her friends. Desmond never mentioned a boyfriend in London, but he probably wouldn't have known anyway. After Freyja died he became obsessed. It was all he thought about. He had no time for poor Gudrun."

They talked on into the evening, Dr. Harris liberal with the wine, explaining that since he was not on call that night he was therefore free to anesthetize himself. They spoke about Cambridge and London, briefly about Brock, a little about Deb's job at the botanic garden, but inevitably the conversation returned to the Kites' tragedy and, somehow central to it, because of her great promise, Freyja's unresolved death.

"She was a magician," Harris said grandly, and his wife gave him an odd look.

"A what? She was a mathematician, Andrew."

"A mathematician, that's what I said," and it was true that his words were now becoming slurred. "That was the funny thing. Brilliant father, brilliant daughter, but he couldn't understand a bloody thing she did."

"And what did she do?" Kathy asked. "You said she worked at the Cambridge Science Park?"

"Yes. One of those high-tech companies out there. She told me once what it was—something very obscure and scientific, can't remember what."

They showed Kathy upstairs to a spare bedroom, and when Deb went to find her a towel Andrew Harris suddenly turned on her, eyes bright, and Kathy had the awful thought that he was going to try to kiss her good night. But instead he said triumphantly, "*Quantum mechanics*. I knew it'd come back to me. That was Freyja's field."

Kathy was none the wiser.

SIX

THE FOLLOWING MORNING PROFESSOR Kite appeared at the breakfast table wrapped in a dressing gown that was too small for his gangling frame, his gray hair sticking up at odd angles. He mumbled a reply to Deb Harris's concerned "How are you, Desmond?" and immediately began eating the bowl of porridge she put in front of him. In the middle of this he paused suddenly, spoon pointed accusingly at Kathy, and said, "You're wrong about the boat. She must have been visiting a friend. Gudrun lived in an apartment not a boat, in Crouch End."

"Did you ever visit her there, Professor?"

He frowned, resumed eating his porridge, and when he finished shook his head. "No. Very pleasant apartment, she told me. Lucky to get it at such a reasonable rent. I've got the address here."

He pulled his wallet from the dressing gown pocket and opened it to show Kathy the address of the mail holding service. Next to it was a cell phone number.

"Is this Gudrun's number?"

"Yes."

"You spoke to her on it?"

"Of course."

Kathy found it hard to gauge his mood. He seemed strangely

unaffected now, talking about Gudrun. "What about her work, did she speak to you about that?"

"Some computer business. Boring, she said, but it paid the rent. She was looking for something more challenging. Now look, while you're investigating this accident of hers it's imperative that you reopen the case of her sister Freyja's murder."

"Do you have any reason to think they might be connected?"

He looked puzzled, as if it hadn't occurred to him. "No, no, of course not, but now you can bring a fresh pair of eyes to Freyja's case. Andrew tells me you specialize in that sort of thing—murder investigations."

"Only in London, Professor. Cambridge is a separate jurisdiction. But if anything occurs to you that might link the two cases, you should let me know." As she said it and watched his mind working, she realized that she'd made a mistake, offering him a way to try to get her involved in investigating Freyja's death.

She rose from the table, thanking the Harrises and making ready to leave. There had been rain during the night, washing away the fog and leaving the trees dripping, and when she reached the highway it began again, and she drove through heavy traffic back to London with wipers beating. On the way she phoned Brock and gave him an outline of what she'd learned.

"Not much then," he said. "Where did you stay?"

"His friends across the street offered to put me up. Thanks to you, I think. He knows you, says you were friends at Cambridge together—Andrew Harris, an anesthetist."

"Andy . . . oh yes, I remember Andy. Cocky little bastard. Useful spin bowler, eye for the girls."

Kathy laughed. "That's him."

SHE STOPPED AT HER apartment in Finchley for a change of clothes, then continued in to Central London. The offices on

Queen Anne's Gate were quiet, and she settled down to work through a backlog of paperwork that had come in on one of her other cases, a three-year-old murder for which new evidence had just surfaced. In part it related to the use of a cell phone, and as she worked through the old phone records it occurred to Kathy to check on the number that she'd got from Desmond Kite. She found that it had been registered three months before to Vicky Hawke, at the Crouch End address, and she put in a request for the record of calls, wondering as she did it whether she was making too much of the missing phone. It was probably tucked away in some cubbyhole on the boat that she and Mickey Schaeffer had missed. If it was turned on they could get a fix on it, but that would involve a paper trail which, with the task auditor breathing down their necks, might not be a good idea. It would be easier to go to the boat and call the number on her own phone and listen for the ring.

And so, when she left the office in the late afternoon, she decided to drive over to Paddington. It was raining again, the afternoon sky dark with heavy rainclouds as she pulled up the collar of her coat and hurried down the steps to the towpath beside the canal, where the stone of the quay and the steel hull of Gudrun's boat both shone slippery and wet. She put one foot carefully onto the boat's stern and made to transfer her weight on board when suddenly *Grace*'s rear doors flew open in front of her and a man burst out. As she stepped back he barged past her and jumped down onto the towpath and turned to run off, but she reached out and grabbed the sleeve of his coat, spinning him around so that his momentum swung him back against the side of the boat.

"Hang on," she said, gripping his coat. "I'm a police officer. What were you doing on that boat?" The man stared back at her with red-rimmed eyes, his face deeply lined, unshaven, half covered with wild wet hair.

He gave a hoarse cough. "Vicky's."

"I know whose it is. How did you get in?"

"Key," he muttered. "Vicky gave me a key."

"Show me."

She relaxed her grip and he pulled a key on a lanyard out of his pocket. Kathy took it. "What's your name?"

"Tisdell," he barked, drawing himself up to attention, and she wondered if he'd spent time in the army, or maybe prison.

"Ned Tisdell?" Kathy remembered the name. "You have a boat, don't you?"

His head jerked down the line. "*Venerable Bede.*"

"And what were you doing on Vicky's boat?"

"Nothing."

Kathy noticed an angular lump in his coat and put her hand to it, feeling something hard beneath the fabric. "What's that? Show me."

She stepped back a little as he reluctantly opened his coat and produced a paperback book, *The Pale King*, and the framed print of a black bird which Kathy had noticed before. "Those belong to Vicky," she said, taking them from him.

"They're mine . . . lent them to her."

"Can you prove that?"

He shrugged, all the time keeping his eyes fixed disconcertingly wide on her face.

"Well, they're going to have to stay here for the time being."

"What are *you* doing here?" he said suddenly.

It seemed a strange question, and Kathy was now more than a little suspicious that Tisdell wasn't quite right in his head. "I'm investigating Vicky's death."

"Hah!" he laughed, incredulous. "But you know who killed her."

"What do you mean?"

He laughed again, shaking his head.

"Why would anyone want to kill Vicky?" she asked, keeping her voice level, as if his words had made perfect sense.

"Because," he said, eyes bright, nose twitching, leaning forward as if to smell her, "she carried the mark of the beast. But *you* know that," he said dismissively. Then a thought seemed to strike him. "Are you trying to pin it on me? Is that what this is about?" His brow furrowed and he rose on the balls of his feet, becoming agitated. "Yes, you bastards! That *is* what this is about, isn't it?"

"Calm down, Ned. No one's trying to pin anything on you."

"Liar!" he roared and drew back his arm, fist bunched.

"Ned!"

The voice made him freeze. They both turned and saw a dark-haired, sharp-faced woman approaching on the towpath.

"Put your hand down at once, Ned," she said sharply.

He glared at her. "They're trying to frame me, Anne."

"No." As the woman stepped toward him Tisdell abruptly grabbed her arm and swung her into Kathy and charged off along the towpath. By the time the two women had found their footing again he was fleeing up the stairs that led from the towpath to the street and vanishing into the darkness beyond.

"Are you all right?" Kathy said.

The woman nodded. "He forgets to take his medication and gets overexcited. I'm sorry. He'll calm down. He's harmless really."

Kathy pulled out her phone. "I'm going to have to call this in."

"No, please don't do that. Look, I'm Anne Downey. I own *Aquarius*, over there. I'm getting soaked. Can we talk inside?"

Kathy followed her onto her boat, the same size as the others, hers tastefully functional with fittings that might have come from IKEA.

"You're the doctor, aren't you?" Kathy said. "The Stapletons mentioned you."

"Yes, that's right. And they told me about you. I'm sorry I'd already left for work when Howard found Vicky. I might have been able to do something."

She was asking for reassurance, Kathy thought, and said, "No, we believe she'd been dead some time by then."

"You're not local CID, are you? Do you think there's something suspicious about Vicky's death?"

"We just want to be sure. Did you know her well?"

"Fairly well. We'd drop in on each other after work for a drink, that sort of thing."

"Were you her doctor?"

"No. I don't think she had a regular GP."

"She had some sleeping pills beside her bed. Did you prescribe them?"

"Oh . . ." Downey colored a little, then looked concerned. "Yes, actually, I did. She was having trouble getting to sleep. Why? You're surely not thinking of suicide, are you?"

"Is that unlikely, in your opinion?"

"Yes! Vicky wasn't depressed, I'd swear to that."

"Molly Stapleton seemed to think that she was agitated and tense."

For just a moment Kathy thought she saw something in the other woman's eyes, as if she wanted to tell her something, then she seemed to change her mind and said, "Well, we all have our problems. I think Vicky was having some difficulties coping at work."

"In what way?"

"I think her boss was putting pressure on her, you know, the usual thing."

"Harassing her? Sexually perhaps?"

"I'm not sure." Anne Downey spoke carefully, choosing her words.

Kathy noticed that her coat, soaked from the rain, was dripping onto the matting on the floor, and she apologized.

"Don't worry. Give me your coat and I'll hang it up," Downey said, and handed Kathy a towel to dry her face and hair. Kathy also wiped the book and framed print. "Tisdell was taking these from Vicky's boat," she said and as she did so she noticed a single word, *Nevermore*, etched into the scrolls of lines beneath the bird in the picture. "What does that mean?"

The doctor seemed to hesitate for a moment, then said, "That's from the poem, 'The Raven,' you know?"

Kathy turned the picture over and noticed that the tape on the back had been neatly sliced open. She glanced at Downey and saw that she was staring at the cuts, then, when she realized that Kathy was watching her, quickly looked away. "Looks as if the back's been opened," Kathy said, easing it off. There was nothing behind the print. "Did she hide something here, do you think?"

"No idea."

"Are you aware that Vicky Hawke wasn't her real name? It was Gudrun Kite. Does that mean anything to you?" She studied the doctor's face. Her surprise seemed muted.

"No."

There was something slightly strange about her manner, an evasiveness perhaps, as if she felt uncomfortable talking about this. After Tisdell's bizarre outburst, Kathy felt an odd sense of alienation, as if these boat people inhabited a parallel universe of fog and secrets.

"We have to assume that Vicky was trying to hide her presence here."

Downey looked away. She was silent for a moment, then said, "You could be right. I never saw her bring a friend back to her boat. She was certainly very new to narrowboating."

"Do you know how she came to be here?"

"Not really. The mooring became vacant and she just showed up on her boat. She caused a bit of chaos when she arrived—she really wasn't used to handling a narrowboat. We felt kind of responsible for her, I suppose. We all pitched in to show her the ropes."

"What about Ned Tisdell—are you his doctor?"

"No, but he told me that he's on medication, and I've tried to keep an eye on him. He was pretty devastated when he heard the news about Vicky. Please don't be too hard on him. He's had a few problems in his life, but his heart's in the right place. Authority figures make him nervous. I think that's what that was all about, really, the way he reacted to you. But there was no harm done, was there?"

Kathy paused, imagining the reaction she'd get from DC Judd if she requested help in arresting Tisdell on suspicion. "He seemed quite irrational, saying Vicky was killed."

"He just gets confused sometimes. He was very attached to her."

"That's what's worrying me."

"You mean, was he obsessive? No, they were friends, that's all. Look, I'll check on him when he comes back, and I'll make sure he takes his pills and behaves."

Despite her misgivings, Kathy decided to let it go. She thanked the doctor and left to go aboard Gudrun's boat, *Grace*. She replaced the things Tisdell had taken, then tried calling the number that Desmond Kite had given her, but there was no answering ring. After another search for possible hidden storage places she left empty-handed, locking the doors behind her.

ON THE WAY HOME she picked up a pizza base and some ingredients at the supermarket, and after a shower set about preparing a meal. As she worked she recalled the things that Ned

Tisdell had said to her, trying to remember his exact words. What did "the mark of the beast" mean? She thought she'd heard the term before but couldn't recall the reference. It sounded occult.

She fired up her laptop and googled the phrase, coming up with a long list of Web sites apparently devoted to it. She opened one and read.

The prophecies concerning the Mark of the Beast are about to be fulfilled, and those who worship the Beast and receive his mark will face God's wrath. The Beast is Satan himself, and his mark is a physical sign that the bearer is his worshipper. This truth is made plain to us in the Book of Revelation, 13:16–17, as follows:

"He causes all, both small and great, rich and poor, free and slave, to receive a mark on their right hand or on their foreheads, and that no one may buy or sell except one who has the mark or the name of the beast, or the number of his name."

Kathy shook her head, dismissing it as Tisdell's raving, then read the second paragraph again, *a mark on their right hand*, remembering the sticking plaster on Gudrun's hand. Then the oven timer beeped that her pizza was ready, and she shrugged, closed the computer, and went to fetch a knife and fork.

SEVEN

A SUBDUED SENSE OF crisis pervaded the team during the following week, and not just in the old Georgian terrace on Queen Anne's Gate where they were based but throughout the whole of Homicide and Serious Crime as rumors circulated of desks being cleared, familiar faces disappearing, restructurings being implemented. It was as if the first shocks of a long-forecast storm had finally arrived, in flurries of suddenly convened meetings and urgent demands for reports and analyses. D.K. Payne and his team of task auditors were everywhere, querying everything, leaving a trail of muttering detectives and tearful civilian staff in their wake, and behind them, mostly unseen but always felt, the intimidating figure of Commander Lynch loomed large.

And with all this going on, a sheaf of urgent memos clutched in his free hand, Brock was irritated to get a phone call from someone he'd never heard of, who claimed to be a friend of a friend. The Indian accent misled him, and he was about to snap that he was quite happy with his phone plan and hang up when he caught the name Andy Harris, and listened more closely. He had to ask the caller to repeat his own name a couple of times before he finally got it, Dr. Chinmay Chandramouli.

"I'm sorry, Chief Inspector, I think I've got you at a bad time." The voice was brisk.

"No, it's all right. How exactly can I help you?"

"I'm a fellow of your old college, Trinity. The Master would have rung you himself, but he was called away suddenly to Geneva—something about the Large Hadron Collider—and I'm speaking for him. He'd be extremely pleased if you'd accept an invitation to come up and dine with him."

"Really?" Brock was astonished.

"Yes. May I ask, has Inspector Kolla briefed you about her visit to Cambridge at the weekend?"

"Ah, yes." Brock's heart sank.

"I was tutor to both Freyja and Gudrun Kite during their time with us. We're all shocked by this latest disaster to hit Professor Kite's family. He is in a very bad way, and when Andy contacted us we were able to persuade Desmond to come and live at the college, at least for a while, so that we can keep an eye on him. May I ask if there have been any developments regarding Gudrun's death?"

"It's in the coroner's hands, Dr. Chandramouli. There appear to be no grounds for suspecting anything other than an unfortunate accident."

"I see. There has been a great deal of discussion at the college about the deaths of the two girls, of course. One of our fellows is Professor Iwan Bronikowski at the Institute of Criminology, over at Sidgwick Avenue. You may know of him? He has been informing us about investigative procedures and recent developments in forensic science."

Brock had an image of elderly dons at high table mulling over the finer points of DNA analysis and the law and he stifled a groan.

"Of course, Iwan isn't a practitioner like yourself, and several of us feel that it would be invaluable to have a practitioner's insights. The Master is especially keen."

Kathy had warned him, but he hadn't expected this kind of approach. "Dr. Chandramouli . . ."

"Chinmay, please."

"Chinmay, I think DI Kolla explained to Professor Kite that Freyja's death is outside our scope. I have no information about it and can't intervene—"

"Oh no, no, we quite understand that. And we're not asking for any special favors with regard to the investigation into Gudrun's death. No, what we're concerned about is Desmond's mental health. He's quite obsessed about Freyja's death and we feel we need to be better informed in order to reason with him and help him come to terms with it. I have spoken to the chief constable here—a Sidney Sussex man, incidentally—and he thinks it could be a very good idea. He feels, as we do, that a Scotland Yard officer like yourself could add considerable weight to our efforts."

I'll bet he does, Brock thought.

"If you can spare the time."

"That could be a problem." But part of Brock's mind was turning over the possibility. It had been years since he had been back to Cambridge.

"A weekend? Next weekend?"

"I'm sorry. At the moment it's impossible for me to leave town."

"Ah . . . Well then, might I come down to London and buy you lunch, as quick as you like, and talk over a few thoughts?"

Reluctantly Brock agreed and they fixed a time for the following day.

"Thank you so much," Dr. Chandramouli said. "The Master will be so pleased."

LATER THAT SAME DAY Kathy took a phone call in the room she shared with DI Bren Gurney at the back of the building, with its view through a tall sash window into a fern-filled courtyard. It was the pathologist, Sundeep Mehta.

"I've just had the toxicology results back for Gudrun Kite, Kathy."

"That was very fast."

"Yes, I got the impression from Brock that he wanted this cleared up quickly, so I applied a bit of pressure. They confirm my opinion from the postmortem, that cause of death was carbon-monoxide poisoning. She had ingested a moderate amount of alcohol and a rather heavy dose of benzodiazepine—the sleeping pills, presumably—but not enough to kill her."

"Enough to knock her out?"

"Possibly. But no physical signs of foul play."

"Okay. There was one thing I noticed, a sticking plaster on her right hand. It looked fresh."

"Yes, as was the wound it covered. A neat incision into the flesh between the thumb and index finger, just over a centimeter deep, made immediately pre- or postmortem."

"*Post*mortem? Are you saying someone cut her after she was dead, and applied a dressing?"

"Well, in theory it's possible. There was little sign of hemostasis, you see, the first stage of healing, which begins immediately after a cut."

"What caused it?"

"I've no idea. Did you notice anything sharp she could have cut herself with—scissors, a kitchen knife?"

Kathy remembered a sharp knife in one of the kitchen drawers, but there had been no sign of blood, nor was there a bloody tissue or dressing wrapper in the waste bin. Perhaps Gudrun had flushed them down the toilet.

She thanked Sundeep and asked for a copy of his report, just for the record.

THE REPORT WAS LYING on her desk the next day when she returned from getting a coffee, and Mickey Schaeffer was standing over it, reading. He looked up. "Hi. I'm trying to find the Weston file. You don't have it, do you?"

"No, not me. Maybe Bren."

"Okay." His eyes dropped to Sundeep's report again. "Who's Gudrun Kite?"

"The girl on the canal boat. Vicky Hawke was an assumed name. She'd taken someone else's identity."

"Really? Why?"

"I don't know."

He was looking at her keenly, as if trying to make her out, and she felt herself becoming irritated under his examination.

"Do you still think she was murdered?"

She shrugged. "Doesn't look like it. The postmortem report confirms the pathologist's suspicion—carbon-monoxide poisoning."

"I didn't think we were still involved."

"We're not. I was just curious."

He raised an eyebrow. "Well, I wouldn't let our task auditor find out. You know, the review team gave Brock a pasting over our handling of this—a catalog of errors, they called it."

She didn't know, and she wondered how he did. "Who told you that?"

"DKP. A warning."

It took her a moment to work it out—D.K. Payne, the task auditor. Why had Payne warned Mickey and not her?

The conversation annoyed her, and after Mickey left she phoned DC Judd at Paddington—"Just to check you got my report about the dead woman's identity," she told him.

"Yes, thanks, ma'am. It's all gone off now to the coroner."

"Accidental death, then?"

"That's our conclusion."

"How about the stove? Did you get an engineer's inspection?"

"Yep. Definitely dodgy—incomplete combustion and a leaky flue. He said it was an accident waiting to happen."

"I see. But still, there's something odd about this case. Why did she hide her identity like that? Did you follow that up?"

There was a moment's silence. "People do that all the time. They want to get out of the life they're in and start again with a clean slate."

Kathy could hear the defensiveness in his voice. "That's right. So we need to know what was making her previous life so uncomfortable that she felt the need to do it. I think this makes a thorough forensic examination of the boat essential now, don't you?"

She heard the suggestion of a suppressed sigh of impatience down the line.

"With respect, ma'am, no, I don't. And I know my inspector wouldn't support such a request. Our budget is under a great deal of pressure here."

"Yes, of course, and I sympathize, but all the same, I will put it in writing." She took a note of his inspector's details and rang off.

Later Bren Gurney returned to his desk, and she asked him, "Do people refer to the task auditor as DKP?"

"First I've heard of it, why?"

"Mickey Schaeffer called him that. What do you think of Mickey?"

"He's all right. We're going to the England–Wales match together next weekend."

Rugby chums, Kathy thought.

"Why?" Bren asked. "Is there a problem?"

"No, I just realized that I know nothing about him. Usually you know everyone's story within a week or two. Is he married?"

"Separated, shared custody of a boy. Mickey's bringing him along to the match. Why, interested?" He grinned. "Time you settled down, Kathy."

"Not with a married guy I have to work with. No, I just wondered what made him tick."

"Comics," Bren said. "He collects old *Eagle* comics. Got an outstanding collection apparently. Spends his free time scouring the flea markets and secondhand bookshops."

"Really?" Kathy tried to picture it, but couldn't.

"Anyway, tomorrow's his big test, isn't it? For you too, and for all of us."

Operation Intruder. Kathy felt a surge of unease. The new commander had given it the highest priority, despite the short notice, and she would be in the thick of it. Bren was right, Brock's team would be on trial.

"I wish I was going in with you, Kathy, but Mickey won't let you down, I'm sure of it."

"He'd better not."

EIGHT

BROCK HAD ARRANGED TO meet Dr. Chandramouli at a small restaurant in Soho, not far from the churchyard where he'd said good-bye to Commander Sharpe. He remembered Sharpe's hint that he could tell Brock a few things about his successor, Lynch, and he wished now that he'd gone along for that drink. But he remembered how Lynch's creature, D.K. Payne, had called him away, almost as if he could sense the possibility of rebellion. Brock shook his head, annoyed at feeling infected by the general paranoia.

The mathematician arrived, a tall, aristocratic-looking Indian with an easy charm and long flowing silver hair. Ominously, he was carrying a briefcase.

"I'm so delighted to meet you, David. I can't tell you how appreciative we all are that you were able to make time to see me."

"I hope it's not a wasted journey for you, Chinmay."

"I'm sure it won't be."

"How is Professor Kite?"

"Oh . . ." Chandramouli pursed his lips, shook his head. "He's in a very sad place at the moment. Debilitated by grief. And one can't help feeling that all those years immersed in dark Norse sagas haven't helped. We have been trying to persuade him to get professional help, but he is intransigent, quite intransigent.

We are concerned about the possibility of suicide, and are trying to keep a very close eye on him."

They ordered from the menu, both regretfully refusing the
wine list, and Brock said, "My colleague, Inspector Kolla, did
say that he made her think of a gloomy old Viking patriarch."

Chandramouli nodded. "He gives the impression of being
arrogant and remote, but the older fellows, who knew him when
he first joined us, remember a sensitive, cheerful young man. He
was only thirty-four when he was made a fellow, having published the brilliant first volume of what was planned to be a
comprehensive, ten-volume history on the Norse epics. Sadly,
thirty years later, only one other volume has eventuated, long
delayed, to rather disappointing reviews."

"Tell me about the girls, Freyja and Gudrun."

"That's the other thing that distresses us a great deal, that
two such talented young graduates of ours should have died so
tragically."

"You were tutor to both of them, you said?"

"I was. I saw them more or less weekly throughout their un-
dergraduate and postgraduate terms. Freyja was the more outstanding of the two—a first in her undergrads, then a master's with
us, a Fulbright to MIT for a doctorate, then a couple of years
working in the States before she returned to a job in Cambridge.
Gudrun followed in her footsteps: a computer science degree,
an upper second, then an MPhil in our Computer Laboratory
and off to London. Both very likeable young women. Freyja
was a fine athlete, mainstay of the college women's hockey
team, and also passionate about ethical issues. One summer,
for example, she worked in an orphanage in Mumbai, and then
the next year she went to South Korea to rescue bears from
bear-bile farms. And very attractive, too, in a sporty sort of way."

He looked pensive, and Brock said, "Was Gudrun overshad-
owed by her older sister?"

"I suppose so, yes. She didn't *shine* in quite the same way. In fact, she was rather a quiet, introspective person, more comfortable with her computer than with people."

"But a competent computer scientist?"

"Oh, very. The MPhil isn't for everyone. Which is why I find it rather incomprehensible that she should have taken a job in marketing. Do you know what kind of company it was?"

"A security company."

"Really? What sort of security?"

"From what I understand, everything from CCTV and alarm systems to computer security and data protection."

Dr. Chandramouli frowned and began to speak, but was interrupted by the arrival of their meals. When the waiter left them alone again, Brock said, "Something bothered you, Chinmay?"

"Well, yes. You see, data protection was Freyja's field."

"Freyja? I thought Andy said it was quantum mechanics."

"Quantum cryptography, actually. It's to do with transmitting uncrackable encoded messages in individual particles of light, or photons. Freyja began working in that field in her master's at Cambridge, and then continued at MIT. It's the cutting-edge area for secure digital communications these days, which of course is crucial for everything from paying your bills online to protecting military secrets."

"And she was working on that in her job at the Cambridge Science Park when she returned from America?"

"I believe so, yes. I didn't see much of her in the year she died, but I remember we spoke about the holy grail of quantum cryptography—the creation of a complete-quantum-mechanical network. I got the impression she was involved in that quest in some way, although she had to be rather circumspect in what she could tell me."

"Do you know the company she was working for there?"

"Penney Solutions. It's a technology consultancy company that provides outsourced research and development to clients in a variety of fields—mainly electronics and biotechnology, I believe. It was started by one of our graduates, Philip Penney, about twenty years ago, not a huge company but one of the standout successes of the so-called Silicon Fen. The Cambridge police did speak to Dr. Penney after Freyja's death, but there was no suggestion of her research being a factor, except that she worked ungodly hours out there, which was why she was cycling home in the dead of night. Of course," he added, with a disingenuous air, "I'm sure Dr. Penney would be glad to speak to you if you so wished."

Brock set down his knife and fork and wiped his mouth with his napkin. Time to set things straight, he thought.

"Chinmay, much as I sympathize with your concern for Professor Kite, there really are only two things that I can see would help him—a good counseling psychologist, and the arrest of whoever knocked Freyja down—and I'm afraid I'm not in a position to help with either. There's no way that I can reopen a case in another police area without new evidence. I'm sorry."

Chandramouli raised his hands. "No, no, we understand. Professor Bronkowski made that quite clear to us. He's been working on a research project with the Manchester police for some years now and is familiar with police protocols. He reviewed the Cambridge investigation, and came to the conclusion that it was extremely thorough and professional. No, we were thinking more along the lines of finding some ways to help Desmond look to the future instead of the past. We've discussed a scholarship in his daughters' names, or a fund to help the victims of road accidents, but we thought you might have more creative ideas, with your background."

Brock thought that unlikely, but the mathematician's mind had moved on, as he raised his eyes to the ceiling and stroked his throat in a mannerism that his students probably imitated. "*Security* . . . that is an intriguing coincidence, is it not? I wonder if Philip Penney has heard of this company in Paddington—what was their name?"

Brock told him and he wrote it down carefully in a small notebook. "I might ask Philip. Anyway, David, I took the liberty of copying a few of the documents relating to Freyja's accident, and if you have the time to take a look at them, you never know, it might spark something. Any ideas, anything at all, would be much appreciated."

They finished their meal and when they parted on the footpath outside, Dr. Chandramouli handed Brock a heavy envelope. "And when you have a little time you must come up to Cambridge and have dinner at the Hall with us and meet the Master."

Brock said good-bye, taking the package with some misgivings.

IT WAS AFTER NINE when he got home that evening. Warren Lane and the railway cutting beyond the fence were wreathed in fog, and the muffled bang of a fog warning on the tracks echoed in the chill night air. He opened his front door and wearily climbed the book-lined stair, switching on lights, breathing in the familiar smell of old volumes with a feeling of relief. Shrugging off his coat he went to the bathroom to wash, then to the kitchen, where he prepared a roast beef sandwich and a glass of whiskey and took them through to the living room. The radiators of the central heating were ticking comfortingly, but he switched on the old gas fire that he had retained for the friendly glow of its flames and collapsed heavily onto the sofa in front of it to check his mail. When he'd sorted through the bills and circulars he was left with Chandramouli's package. He'd been mugged, he thought, in the most gentlemanly way, but mugged all the same. He was almost sure that Chandramouli had known all about Paddington Security Services, and had steered the conversation to plant the idea of a connection between the sisters' deaths in Brock's mind, so that he would feel compelled to reopen Freyja's case.

He sighed and opened the envelope and began with a summary of the police investigation that Professor Bronikowski of the Institute of Criminology had compiled. It soon became clear to him that the Cambridge police had carried out an exemplary investigation. They had gone door-to-door along the length of Milton Road, checked every CCTV camera in the city, mounted a thorough public appeal for information, and carried out an exhaustive forensic examination of the area where Freyja was killed. At the end of it, the only witness they had was the man who had raised the alarm, and his recollection of the car was useless—no make, no color, no number. After hitting Freyja it had simply vanished into the night.

The postmortem report was equally depressing, the list of injuries that Freyja's body had suffered reading like a catalog of human vulnerability. But among all the ruptured organs, smashed bones, and torn muscles there was one odd little feature that the pathologist had fastidiously recorded—the flesh between the thumb and forefinger of Freyja's right hand had been sliced open. Brock frowned at the entry, remembering what Kathy had told him about Sundeep Mehta's postmortem of Gudrun Kite. It was a small thing, an insignificant coincidence, but still.

He moved on to the other papers, the university records of the two girls, and finally, as if to remind him of where his loyalties lay, a complimentary copy of G.M. Trevelyan's *Trinity College: An Historical Sketch*.

He thumbed through the book, but his mind kept drifting off. Finally he picked up the postmortem report and read it again. It listed the contact details for the pathologist, Dr. Arthur

Morrison, and Brock reached for the phone and dialed. He introduced himself, apologizing for the late call.

"Not a problem." The voice sounded decisive, businesslike. "What can I do for you?"

"We're investigating the death of Gudrun Kite in London last week, and I believe you carried out the postmortem on her sister, Freyja, in February of this year."

"That's right. One of our anesthetists, Andrew Harris, told me the Met were involved. Are you reopening Freyja's case?"

"No, we have no grounds for that, but we want to make sure that there's no connection between the two deaths."

"It's a tragic thing. I've seen it before, families suddenly struck down by a succession of tragedies, out of the blue. The survivors are left shell-shocked, saying *why us?* I met old man Kite, and Freyja too, at a dinner at the Harrises' once. She was a delightful young woman, really special. It was a shock when she turned up in our mortuary. So, how can I help you?"

"I've read a copy of your postmortem report on Freyja, and I had a small query I wondered if you could help me with."

"Fire away."

"The injuries were very extensive."

"Oh yes. She must have been hit at speed, become entangled beneath the vehicle, and then reversed over."

"Have you ever seen anything like that before?"

"I've seen worse, but usually in different circumstances: a high-speed impact with the body crushed inside the cab. I would say this was one of the worst hit-and-run cases I've encountered."

"Among all the injuries you listed, there was one that looked a little different, an incision in the right hand, between thumb and index finger. Remember that?"

"Hm . . . vaguely. Right hand?"

"Yes, a clean cut. Did you have any idea how that could have been caused?"

"I don't think the question was asked, really. It was such an insignificant injury among all the others. There could have been any number of sharp pieces of metal or glass involved."

"Could it have been inflicted postmortem?"

"Postmortem? What do you mean? In the hospital?"

"No, at the accident site. I'm asking because Gudrun had a very similar incision in her right hand when she was found. It seems an odd coincidence."

"Well . . . I don't know what to suggest. And your pathologist reckons it was done postmortem?"

"He thinks it's a possibility. He couldn't find any signs of hemostasis."

There was a lengthy silence on the line, then Morrison cleared his throat and said, "You're not suggesting . . . You know that nonsense about serial killers leaving a signature on their victims is just a Hollywood myth, don't you, Chief Inspector?"

"Yes, so I believe."

"They wouldn't be that helpful, or stupid."

"No. All the same, you might like to check if you've had any other cases with such a wound. And perhaps I could ask our pathologist to speak to you, compare notes."

"Fine. I'll dig out my records and photographs tomorrow."

After he hung up, Brock tried Kathy's number, but it went straight to voice mail and he hung up. She would be asleep by now, he guessed, as he should be. He looked at his watch; he might get three hours.

NINE

KATHY'S ALARM WOKE HER at two thirty a.m., its shrill buzz
breaking into a troubled half-sleep of uneasy dreams in which
the rosy-faced dead girl on the narrowboat was somehow lying
asleep in the fast lane of a motorway in the path of thundering
traffic. Kathy stumbled to the bathroom and had a quick shower,
gulped down a cup of tea and some toast, and put on her short
black dress—the one with a hint of bling around the collar and
hem—dark tights, and high heels. She did her makeup, not
sparing the mascara and lipstick, put on her best earrings and
necklace, and combed her blond hair back into the bob she'd
had done at the salon the previous evening. She stared at her
reflection in the mirror, added a touch more lipstick, and decided
it would do. She had to look good, for Jack Bragg, the Butcher,
was back in town.

She put on her coat and took the elevator down to her car in
the basement of her high-rise and drove in to Central London, to
the garage beneath West End Central police station, where she
reported in, earning a couple of wolf-whistles on the way, and
drew a Glock 33 subcompact pistol and some .357 SIG ammu-
nition.

Jack had once been a menacing presence in the London under-
world, the leader of a clutch of vicious extortionist and strongarm

thugs who had terrorized businesses across the East End and gone on to develop an extensive drug- and gun-running network across the south of England. After a series of brutal murders, his gang had been broken up and Jack forced to flee the country, leaving his wife Patsy in charge of his assets, including their big house in Kent and his casino, Fantasyland, just off Leicester Square, through which he had laundered his illicit cash and, it was said, bribed and corrupted a number of useful public officials.

Although Jack had fled, probably to the Philippines, he had not forgotten London, especially when he learned that Patsy had divorced him and taken up with Sergei Romanov, who was now making a great deal of money operating Fantasyland twenty-four hours a day, seven days a week. The Metropolitan Police had not forgotten Jack either, and had been patiently awaiting his return. Intelligence that he had slipped back into the UK had now been gathered—not by the old methods of informants or whispers on the grapevine, but the new way, using a computer program developed for the US military to collate information from social networking sites, financial transactions, IP network logs, satellite navigation equipment, and mobile phone traffic. This had been achieved by a team of specialists, designated Unit 12, within the Met's new Digital Security Task Force, known as DiSTaF. They had deduced from their intercepts and computer modeling that Jack was planning to take revenge on Romanov and his ex-wife, murdering them both and plundering the casino. For over a month Unit 12 had digitally sensed Jack assembling his team. Patsy had been moved to a safe house under constant police guard, and twenty-four hours ago Unit 12 had decided that the casino hit would occur around dawn on the following day, sending Homicide and Serious Crime into urgent preparations, with Brock's team as the lead unit of what had been dubbed Operation Intruder.

DS Mickey Schaeffer was looking dapper in a tuxedo. He eyed Kathy approvingly. "Got your gun?"

She opened her shoulder bag. He was wearing his in a holster beneath his dinner jacket, one of the new Glock 22s, three ounces heavier and twenty-six millimeters longer than Kathy's model. "We have different ammo," he said. "Not good."

He was tense, fingering his bow tie.

"I don't think we'll run out," she said with a smile.

"How can you be so calm? You ever meet Jack?"

"No. You?"

"In my first year in CID we found someone who'd upset him. He'd chopped her into little bits and stuffed her inside a couple of old sacks used for cow manure. I still get the nightmare."

They caught a cab to Fantasyland, and entered arm in arm, looking as if they'd been out on the town all night.

The gaming rooms were relatively quiet, a few bleary-looking couples yawning, a gaggle of young women from somewhere up north—Manchester by the sound of it—still buzzing on pills and alcohol, a couple of more serious gamblers with expressionless faces. Kathy had an earpiece hidden beneath her hair, through which she heard the operation controller checking the arrival of armed response units in the surrounding streets. Together, she and Mickey made their unhurried way from room to room, checking the layout against the plans and photographs they'd memorized, and mentally recording the faces of guests and staff. A camera in Kathy's bag was also transmitting pictures to control.

A shriek drew them back to the gaming tables, where one of the Manchester women had spilled her drink over the roulette wheel and was now giggling hysterically. They watched as a big, stony-faced security man moved in to steer her away to a seat while the croupier fussed over the table with a box of tissues.

More staff appeared, and Kathy noticed the security man check his watch and walk away.

After a few minutes the controller's voice sounded in Kathy's ear. She listened, then turned to Mickey and murmured, "Someone inside the building is taking a call from Jack on a mobile."

There was no one in that room using a phone and they hurried out to the bar, then into another gaming room and simultaneously noted the big security man standing on the far side with a hand raised to his cheek. As they moved toward him he wheeled around and pushed the exit door open behind him, at the same time hitting a fire-alarm button on the wall. The alarm immediately began to scream as he disappeared through the door. They followed, running, through the door and down a corridor, around a corner, Kathy talking to control as they went. They came to a stair, a long flight, with the man halfway down.

"Hey!" Mickey shouted. "Police. Stop! Stay where you are!"

The man looked back over his shoulder, then began racing down the steps three at a time. Mickey, ahead of Kathy, was faster, and before the man reached the bottom he launched himself at him and the two fell in a struggling heap. As she ran down after them Kathy saw the man jerk his arm out from beneath Mickey, a knife gripped in his hand. She jumped onto him, stamping on his wrist with a heel, and he gave a scream. She pointed her gun at his face and he froze, staring up at her.

"You all right, Mickey?"

"Yeah." The DS struggled to his feet.

There was something unexpectedly fearful about the security man's expression, Kathy thought, almost panicky. He gulped, the Adam's apple leaping in his throat. "We gotta leave," he croaked.

"What's that?"

He hesitated for a moment, teeth clenched as if trying to prevent himself from speaking. Then he gave an odd kind of whimper and said, "There's a bomb."

"Where?"

He shook his head. "Two minutes."

Control was speaking urgently in Kathy's ear. They could see the images of the man but not hear what he was saying. Kathy told them, then said to Mickey, "Take him outside. I'll make sure the place is clear."

He began to protest but she turned and ran back up the stairs, along the corridor, through the door. Most people had left the gaming room, a straggler scooping up betting chips. She shouted at him to get out and then saw the Manchester girls still fooling around in the next room, shrieking with laughter, refusing to move. She ran to them, grabbing the arm of the one who'd spilled her drink. "There's a bomb," she cried. "Get out NOW!" She bustled them to the door, stumbling on their high heels, then down the stairs, across the hall, out into the sudden cold of the street. One of the women started complaining that she'd left her purse behind and began walking back toward the front door with its lurid flashing lights. Kathy grabbed her arm and hauled her back. "Come ON!" she yelled. "We need to cross the street." She saw men running toward them, recognizing Brock and someone else—the new commander. She heard the howl of a fire engine, and then a tremendous blast hit her back and knocked her flat onto the ground.

TEN

SHE THOUGHT SHE MUST be underwater, because all she could hear was the muffled sound of her own breathing. She raised a hand to her face and felt the mask. Scubadiving then. She struggled to remember, but nothing came to her. Then she opened her eyes and saw a head looming over her, blurry, then coming into focus, a familiar face—Bren. He was mouthing something to her, but she couldn't hear a thing. He vanished and she closed her eyes again. She felt the sway of her body in the current.

She woke again to a dream, hearing the distant squeal of women's voices, from Manchester surely, demanding dirty leprechauns.

After a while she was aware that the swaying had stopped and everything seemed very quiet. She tried opening her eyes and there was Bren once more, looking down at her.

"Kathy! You're awake!"

Why was he talking with his mouth full of cotton wool? He vanished again, and she blinked up at dazzling light. Raising a hand to her face she found that the mask had gone, but that there was soft padding covering her forehead.

"Hello." A young man was looking down at her.

"Hello," she replied.

"What is your name?" he asked politely.

"Kathy. Kathy Kolla. Detective Inspector Kathy Kolla."

"Good. Do you know what day it is?"

What a stupid question. "Wednesday." Then she remembered getting up in the middle of the night. "No, Thursday. What happened to my dress?"

The young man grinned and shone a flashlight into her eye.

"Thirsty," she mumbled, her mouth seeming filled with rancid dust from the explosion, and tried to struggle upright.

WHEN SHE EVENTUALLY INSISTED that she was all right, the doctor gave her some painkillers and told her to go home and rest. Bren had brought her some police overalls and a pair of running shoes, because her little black dress and high heels were beyond repair. It seemed she had been remarkably lucky, just a few scrapes and bruises and some lingering deafness, though there was still a risk of concussion. They had all been very lucky, with no fatalities and only a couple of significant injuries. They left the Manchester girls in casualty still laughing, one with an arm in a sling and another with a bandaged head, texting home about what a blast London was, and how their trip had been pure dynamite.

"What's a dirty leprechaun?" Kathy asked Bren.

He grinned. "Some kind of Irish cocktail. Why, you want one? Let's get you home first." He checked his watch.

"You in a hurry?"

"There's a debriefing in an hour."

"Forget about home."

"You sure?" He looked at her doubtfully. "You took a hell of a bang."

"I need to be there, Bren."

BROCK MET THEM AT the police station, concerned for Kathy, and when she had assured him she was okay he led the way to the assembly room, where Mickey was still in his dinner suit, a disheveled James Bond, face flushed, lapping up the attention as Commander Lynch leaned in close to hear him explain a detail. Kathy stayed at the back of the packed room, still feeling slightly disoriented, but suddenly the commander was advancing on her, the crowd parting in front of him, and he was shaking her hand. It was the first time she had seen him up close, and she felt the power of the man, fierce, stocky, rocking forward on the balls of his feet as if to gouge the truth out of her. But his voice was soft, almost gentle. Was she all right? He regretted that they would have to take her through it all again after the debriefing.

She had expected them to get a dressing-down, for Jack Bragg had not been caught and a sizeable chunk of a West End city block was a smoking ruin, but instead Lynch seemed remarkably sanguine. There had been no fatalities and the exercise had been a decisive demonstration of the powerful new digital surveillance techniques of Unit 12, which had accurately pinpointed Bragg's attack. It was just unfortunate that they hadn't been able to figure out that his intention wasn't to rob the casino but to destroy it. And they had an arrest, thanks to the nimble footwork of DI Kolla and DS Schaeffer. There were muted cheers, and then a few puzzled looks when Lynch announced, almost as an afterthought, that Ashur Najjar, the arrested security man, would be questioned by a special team.

As the meeting broke up Kathy and Mickey were led away to an interview room where Lynch and a man from Unit 12 were waiting. Kathy looked around to see if Brock would be joining them, but apparently he wasn't required. There was a large TV screen at one end of the room on which they began to replay the film made by the little camera in Kathy's bag, working through it in painstaking detail, step by step, image by image, identifying each of the people inside the casino. After a while it occurred to Kathy that they were looking for a second accomplice, perhaps the one who had brought the bomb. As they came to the point where they saw Najjar speaking into his cell, Kathy felt her heart begin to thump, her breathing speed up. Then she was aware of Lynch studying her.

"All right, Inspector? You can be excused if this is too stressful. How about you, Schaeffer?"

"No," Mickey said confidently. "I'm fine, sir."

"Me too," Kathy said.

"You sure?" Lynch smiled at her, but it was a cold smile, and it suddenly struck her that he didn't like her. Was that it? Or perhaps didn't trust her? Why would that be, when he didn't know her? Had she made some unspoken mistake? Or was it because she was too close to Brock? Was he out of favor?

They continued, right up to the end, a blur as Kathy hustled the Manchester girls out of the building.

"Right," Lynch said finally. "Got enough for now, Darryl?"

The Unit 12 man had said almost nothing so far, concentrating on making notes and diagrams. Now he pushed back the glasses on his nose and nodded. "Yep."

Yep? She hadn't come across this example of the new breed, or anyone else from DiSTaF for that matter. He reminded her of the bird in the print on Gudrun's narrowboat, with his black clothes and gelled hair and dark-framed glasses, and she wondered if he'd gone through police academy or spent any time on the beat, or if he'd been plucked straight out of a computer science lab.

Without another word Commander Lynch got to his feet and left the room. Darryl gathered up his papers and followed him. Mickey grinned at Kathy. "We did well."

Kathy wasn't so sure. "Why aren't we interviewing Najjar?"

Mickey shrugged. "Ours not to question why, Kathy."

LATER SHE PASSED ZACK, their civilian computerroom opera-
tor, working at his screens. He called after her, "Hi, Kathy, how
you feeling now?"

"I'm fine."

"Where did they take you to check you out after the blast?"

"Accident and emergency at UCH."

"That's what I thought." He looked puzzled. "So why did
they take your prisoner to a private clinic in Richmond?"

"Richmond?"

"Yeah. Was he badly hurt?"

"No, not as far as I know. Just shaken up, like the rest of us.
Are you quite sure?"

"It came up on the computer, an acknowledgment that he'd
been checked in to the Pewsey Clinic, Richmond, for emergency treatment. Here, I'll show you . . ."

He tapped away for a few minutes, then looked up with a
frown. "It's gone. It's not here any more."

"What kind of clinic is it?"

Zack pulled up its Web site. An image showed a house overlooking the river. "Drug and alcohol rehab, that's what they're
advertising. Had he overdosed or something?"

Kathy thought back, picturing the security man's walk, his
reactions in the stairwell. "No, he seemed to be functioning
normally."

"Well, I don't know . . . I didn't imagine it, Kathy. It was there,
and now it isn't."

ELEVEN

THE FANTASYLAND BOMBING HAD shaken the team out of their preoccupation with the office review, and the following day there was a mood of excitement in the office. The papers were full of the case, and people stood around, comparing the photographs and reports, but no one, not even Brock, knew what was happening to the arrested security man. Finally, in the late afternoon, when he had heard nothing, Brock phoned Lynch's office and was informed that, following intensive questioning, it had been decided to release Ashur Najjar without charge. When Brock exploded, Lynch's assistant explained soothingly that Najjar would be closely monitored, in the hope that he would lead them to Bragg, the real target of the operation. When Brock asked who had been detailed to shadow him, he eventually came to understand that the monitoring would be entirely electronic, carried out by Unit 12, and would not involve physical surveillance as such. Having made clear his dissatisfaction at the lack of consultation, he rang off, feeling edgy. He went over to his office window, looking out over the roofs across the street to the bare branches of the trees in St. James's Park beyond, then turned and fiddled with his new coffee machine, and buzzed Kathy and asked her to come up.

When she arrived she spotted the new machine immedi-ately. "That's neat," she said, going over to examine it.

He explained that it had arrived unexpectedly in the post, a surprise birthday present from his son in Canada. The recent shock of discovering that he had a son, by his ex-wife who had left him and London almost thirty years before, still lingered, and when Kathy asked how John was, now that he'd returned home, his answer was vague.

"Fine, I think. He was making noises about maybe coming back to the UK, but I told him that the way things are we'd be better all moving over there. Anyway, how are you today?"

"Good."

"Are you sure?" He looked at her with concern, seeing the signs of strain in her face. "That was some explosion. I don't know how more people didn't get hurt. You're looking a bit pale."

"I'm grieving for my outfit."

"Ah yes, we'll have to do something about that."

He poured their coffees and they took them to the table on which an unmarked file was lying. As they sat he pointed to it and said, "Take a look."

She opened it and spread out two photographic enlarge-ments, each of a right hand with the flesh between thumb and forefinger sliced open. "Gudrun Kite?" she said.

"That one is. But you'll see that the other cut is a bit bigger, less careful."

She looked more closely. "Ye-es. But very similar. Whose is it?"

"Her sister's, Freyja. That picture was taken at her post-mortem, eight months ago. They're both postmortem photo-graphs."

As Kathy examined them, he told her about his meeting with Chandramouli and conversation with the Cambridge pathologist. "Neither he nor Sundeep can account for it," he said. "They haven't seen it before." He noticed a worried expression on Kathy's face and said, "Something the matter?"

"It was something one of the other boat owners said to me, a bit of a crackpot; he said that Gudrun died because she had the mark of the beast, and when I googled the phrase I found a quote from the Book of Revelations saying that the mark of the beast—of Satan, that is—was on your right hand."

Kathy looked at her own right hand, the pad of flesh on which a pen or a javelin might rest, feeling uneasy. "You don't think it could be the signature of a killer, do you?"

"I've been trying to resist that idea. Anyway, they're not our cases, and I don't think, in the current climate, that this is enough to justify our involvement, although there is another coincidence. Apparently Freyja, like Gudrun, was working in the field of security, for a Cambridge company called Penney Solutions, though from what I can gather they're a very different kind of outfit from Gudrun's Paddington firm.

"I asked Zack to run a quick check on the two companies to see if he could find a connection between them." He reached for a second file on his desk and handed it to Kathy, who scanned the notes inside.

Paddington Security Services, PSS, was registered as an approved contractor by the Security Industry Authority, and offered a range of services, from the installation of CCTV and other security systems to "information protection, storage and retrieval, image processing, and data mining." Zack had identified a list of clients, from retail chains and transport companies to government agencies, including the Home Office and Ministry of Defense, and noted that they were backed by the financial resources of the Harvest Group, a private equity investment company in the City.

Penney Solutions sounded equally impressive, if less glossily commercial. With eighty employees and specialist consultants, it was one of the high-tech companies that had spun off academic research at Cambridge University to offer research and development services to corporate and government organizations, and had also carried out joint projects with a similar American company at MIT. Their areas of expertise included the development of innovative biomedical engineering, solar energy devices, and wireless communication technology.

"It doesn't say that Penney Solutions works in security."

"No, but according to Dr. Chandramouli, Freyja was working on new ways to encrypt information for data security, which I suppose could be relevant in any of those areas they mention."

Kathy read on. Zack had drawn up a list of Penney Solutions's clients, but there were none that had appeared on the Paddington list. She closed the file. "It's all rather inconclusive, isn't it?"

"Yes. And of course we've been warned about wasting our time on other people's cases when we have so much more urgent business of our own to attend to, like catching Jack Bragg. Even if we aren't permitted to interview our own suspects."

"Ashur Najjar?"

"Yes. They've let him go." He gave her the details and she told him about her conversation with Zack concerning the Richmond clinic. Lynch's assistant had said nothing about a clinic, and as he sipped his coffee Brock became increasingly angry. How was it possible to run an investigation when the process was being compartmentalized, information withheld? The truth was that he wasn't running it, Commander Lynch's office was.

Kathy interrupted his brooding thoughts. "I still feel uncomfortable about Gudrun Kite's death. It bothers me, leaving it unresolved. Why was she hiding her identity? Why was she working at Paddington Security Services? I've been thinking . . .

I may take another trip up to Cambridge this weekend. Nothing official, just to see how Professor Kite is coping."

Brock felt his frustration fade. "Funny," he said. "I was thinking exactly the same thing. Would you mind a fellow traveler?"

Kathy smiled. "No. Of course not."

TWELVE

THEY MET AT KING'S Cross in time to catch the nine fifteen to Cambridge. Kathy had removed the dressings and her hair covered the bruised area on her temple. Brock seemed subdued, and as the express sped northward across the flat country he said nothing while Kathy reread the material that Dr. Chandramouli had provided. After a while she looked up.

"I expect you'll want to meet Andy Harris?"

"I think not."

"He said you were great friends."

Brock raised a skeptical eyebrow.

"He said you were a great fellow, a splendid cricketer, and a solid batsman . . ."

"Did he now."

". . . with an eye for the girls."

Brock made a choking noise. Eventually, after a long pause, he said, "I did have a girlfriend for a while. Nice girl, a nurse. Then Andy Harris whispered in her ear that I preferred boys and took her off my hands. Sneaky little bastard."

Three-quarters of an hour after leaving London they stepped out onto the station platform on a bright crisp morning, very different from the fog-shrouded evening of her last visit.

They caught a cab into the city, the driver obviously eager for conversation.

"Trinity, is it? Regular visitors are you?"

"No," Brock said shortly, then added, "It's been a long time."

The driver glanced at him in the rearview mirror and said with a knowing gleam, "A student here, were you?"

"That's right."

"I dare say you'll notice a few changes."

One of these became apparent when they approached the narrow streets of the city center, where stainless-steel posts blocked the route. An electronic tag in the taxi signaled for them to sink into the roadway and the car moved on. "Your digital revolution," the driver ruminated. "It's everywhere now, isn't it? When you were here the students probably climbed into college over revolving spikes after the gates were locked for the night; now they get in with a swipe card. Makes the world seem not quite real, know what I mean?"

"Yes," Brock said, "I know exactly what you mean."

He was staring out of the window with a puzzled frown, and Kathy said, "Different from what you remember?"

"Yes, he's right, it doesn't seem quite real. The buildings are familiar, but not the same. I remember them as a bit scruffy, knocked about by time, but now they seem so immaculate and clean, almost artificial." Then, under his breath, he murmured, "A mistake to come back."

The cab stopped outside the Great Gate of Trinity and they paid the driver and walked toward the door beneath the statue of the founder, King Henry the Eighth, and in to the window of the porters' lodge inside. Brock, so it seemed to Kathy, had something of the same air of trepidation he might have felt when he first arrived there at age nineteen.

The porter came out, adjusting his bowler hat. "Welcome

back, Mr. Brock. Dr. Chandramouli told me to expect you and Ms. Kolla. I'll take you to his room."

"Where is it?"

"Nevile's Court, sir."

"Let's go by way of New Court."

"Of course."

They emerged from the gatehouse into the broad expanse of Great Court, where the porter chatted to Kathy, pointing out its features—the Tudor fountain in the center where the students had once washed, the chapel and dining hall, the Master's Lodge—and continued through an archway into another court, with gothic gables and a large tree in its center on a circular lawn. Brock paused for a moment, staring up at a window.

"Memories, sir?" the porter said.

"Ghosts," Brock replied.

They crossed this court into a cloister leading through to Nevile's Court. The porter continued his commentary—Christopher Wren's Library, the room where Lord Byron lived with his pet bear—and brought them at last to staircase L, where Dr. Chandramouli had his room, a pleasant study with a large window overlooking the court. Kathy took in the shelves of books, the computer, the whiteboard covered with incomprehensible symbols, and came to a framed photograph hanging over the fireplace, of two men standing together in front of the fountain which they had just passed in Great Court. One of the men looked Indian, and Kathy peered closer, to see if it was Chandramouli.

"That's my inspiration," he said to her. "Srinivasa Ramanujan, from Tamil Nadu like myself. He was almost entirely self-taught, yet by the age of seventeen he had arrived at a host of new results in number theory and other areas of advanced mathematics, and in 1912 sent some of them to three academics here at Cambridge. One of them was the other man in the picture, the great G.H. Hardy of this college. He invited Ramanujan to Cambridge, where he astonished the other mathematicians, was made a fellow of Trinity, contracted something deadly—probably tuberculosis—and in 1920 died at the age of thirty-two, leaving behind a mass of extraordinary results."

Chandramouli wasn't what Kathy had expected of a mathematician. With his flowing leonine locks and smooth charm she could imagine him hosting a popular-science series on Channel 4. He sat them down and poured coffee, and said how much he and his colleagues appreciated their visit and were looking forward to joining them for dinner that evening.

"Well, to business then," the mathematician said. "I've arranged for you to meet Philip Penney out at the Science Park, as you suggested, David, and then lunch with Desmond Kite. And Professor Bronikowski would like to show you their new facilities at the Institute of Criminology this afternoon. Is there anything else you'd like to do?"

"That sounds fine."

"I'd like to talk to you about the two women," Kathy said. "I know their academic records, but I don't feel I know their characters. How did they get on together, and with their father?"

Chandramouli thought for a moment, then said, "Let me tell you a little story. The first time I met Gudrun she was still at school, while Freyja was my student here. One day Gudrun came knocking on my door, demanding to see me. It transpired that Freyja had mentioned to her that another student was plagiarizing her work, but she wasn't particularly bothered and didn't intend to report it. Gudrun, however, was incensed, and so came storming in here in her school uniform to demand that I do something about it." He chuckled at the memory. "You see? Freyja was so confident in her own talent that she wasn't troubled by someone else's cheating, whereas Gudrun, the younger, plainer, and less gifted of the two, was ferocious in defense of her sister. That was the way they were—unusual, I thought. I have two children of my own, and their relationship is very different." He gave a rueful smile.

"I see," Kathy said. "And interesting that Gudrun came to you, someone she didn't know, to complain, rather than to her father."

He frowned. "Perhaps. What's your point?"

"I'm wondering why Gudrun hid her life in London from her father—her address, the name she was going under, where she worked. I'm wondering if she was hiding from him."

"Oh . . ." Chandramouli looked mildly shocked, as if the idea hadn't occurred to him. "Surely not. I assumed that there might have been an abusive boyfriend somewhere in the background, something like that?"

"Or an abusive father? I must say, Professor Kite came across as a fairly intimidating figure when I met him."

"He was in a state of shock . . ." The tutor looked uncomfortable, shooting a glance at Brock as if for support, but Brock said nothing, listening impassively. "He's much calmer now, and you'll have the chance to make a clearer judgment today, but I must say that I've never heard any suggestion of such a thing. They always seemed to be a rather harmonious family, at least until Desmond's wife, Sigrid, died."

They finished their coffee and Chandramouli led them out to the river meadows on the Backs behind the college to where he had parked his car. They set off around the north of the city toward Milton Road, where they pulled in at the place where Freyja had died. It was a straight stretch of two-lane road, with a line of solid semidetached houses set back on either side. Chandramouli pointed out the witness's house, its upper-floor bedroom windows visible over a front hedge.

"It was three o'clock in the morning. Apparently the man suffers from insomnia. He was lying awake in bed when he heard the sound of a crash and got up to look."

"I wonder if he's in," Kathy said. "What was his name?" She checked through their documents. "William Copley—Bill."

They knocked on the front door and after an interval heard the shuffling of feet from inside. An elderly man wearing a cardigan and slippers opened the door, peered out at them, said, "Not today, thank you," and began to close it again.

"Mr. Copley?" Kathy said quickly. "We're from the police. Can you spare us a few minutes?"

He looked dubious, asked to see her identification, and reluctantly let them in.

"It's about the accident you witnessed out in the street last February."

"What, again?" He sighed. "I'm almost sorry I reported it now, the amount of my time it's taken up. We even had a reenactment out there, held up the traffic, actors, everything. They didn't take this amount of trouble when our Paul was killed on his motorbike. But I haven't seen you before. What's going on now? Have you found them, the ones that did it?"

"I'm afraid not. We weren't involved in the original investigation and it would really help us to picture what happened if we could see the view you had from your bedroom window."

He gave another exaggerated sigh of forbearance. "I suppose so."

He led the way upstairs and along a small landing to a doorway, through which he peered, then said, "Wait here," and disappeared inside. Chandramouli edged forward and took a quick look through the narrow opening, then turned back and whispered with a chuckle, "He's making the bed."

"Come in then," Copley called to them, and they filed in.

"Bed . . . window . . . view . . ." He pointed to each in turn, and they crossed the room to look down into the street.

"Over there. The front hedge is a bit higher now than it was then."

"You're absolutely certain there were two people in the car?" Kathy asked.

"Oh yes. That's what the reenactment was all about, to make sure I could have seen them both, and I did, one on each side at the front, big fellows, moving about in the light of their headlights."

"When you first described what you saw you thought that one of the men was holding a weapon in his hand, didn't you?"

"Yes, the one on this side of the car. But when they made me think about it I realized it was probably a torch. There was a kind of glint, you see."

"A glint?"

"Yes, of light. Probably he switched it on."

"But the car headlights were still on?"

"Yes, yes."

"Could the glint have been something else, maybe the light from the headlights reflecting off something shiny?"

Copley puffed out his cheeks and frowned, pondering. Then he shook his head. "No, no, we went over this so many times. I'm not going to change my story now. It'd make me out to be a fool."

"Not at all, Mr. Copley. We all know how hard it is to be quite sure what we remember seeing, especially at night. But just for the sake of argument, is it remotely possible that the man was holding a knife?"

His eyebrows shot up. "A knife? First I've heard of that one. Where did that come from? Was she stabbed?"

"It's just something we needed to check with you. Is it possible?"

"Well, he was definitely holding something. Yes, I suppose it's possible it was a knife. The idea never came up before."

When they returned to the car Chandramouli was bursting to know what was on her mind, but Kathy refused to be drawn.

Soon the entrance to the Cambridge Science Park came up on their left. As he turned in, Chandramouli explained its history: set up by Trinity College in 1970 as the first science park in the UK, and now perhaps the most successful. They passed landscaped parking areas surrounding modern buildings with names that ended in hi-tech-sounding syllables like "sys" and "synx" and "pharma." At one of these, a two-story glass and steel pavilion, they pulled into a visitors' parking space and followed the mathematician to doors emblazoned with Penney Solutions's logo.

Dr. Philip Penney was exactly what Kathy imagined a middle-aged geek to be—big glasses, long hair, dressed in jeans and desert boots and rolled-up shirtsleeves, and with an infectiously enthusiastic light in his eyes.

"Come," he beamed, leading them into a conference room with a floor-to-ceiling glass wall looking out across parkland to other similar buildings tucked among the trees, people strolling and jogging along a winding path beside a small lake. They took seats around a glass-topped table supported on a spidery metal structure that might have come from a Mars probe.

"Chinmay explained that you wanted to talk to me about Freyja Kite," Penney said. "I was very sorry to hear about her sister. Must be hell for their old man. But does this mean that Freyja's death is still being investigated?"

Brock answered, "With a second tragic accident coming on top of the first, we want to be absolutely certain that there's nothing more to it. The Cambridge police did a very thorough job investigating Freyja's death, but we'd like to be clear about one or two things. Could you tell us what Freyja was working on at the time of her death?"

"Simply, new ways of keeping digital communications secure. It's an absolutely critical field at the moment, whether we're talking about hackers breaking into confidential government databases, or cybercriminals trying to steal from your bank accounts, or hostile governments accessing military and commercial secrets." His eyes shone with the light of a prophet.

"Most people aren't aware of it, but there's a silent war going on out there, with tens of thousands of crooks, spies, and mischiefmakers intent on disrupting the flow of information upon which our whole way of life depends.

"At present, messages on the Internet, for example, are secured by a process called public key encryption, which scrambles them through a mathematical function that is easy to run forward but difficult to reverse. It's reasonably secure, but given enough computing power, a determined hacker can crack it. Freyja was working on an alternative system, called quantum key distribution, QKD, which guarantees absolute security."

"That sounds pretty important."

"Oh, it's huge. Of course, we're not the only ones working on this. There are teams beavering away all around the world. Freyja was working on a specialized commercial application that looks promising."

"So when you heard that she'd been killed, weren't you concerned that it might have had something to do with her work?"

"I've got to confess, that was the first thing that came into my head. But when I thought about it, it made no sense. A rival, a competitor, would want to steal her work, not bump her off. We checked all her computer files, her work records, and they were intact. Believe me, we are very security-conscious here—we have to be."

"Perhaps the people who knocked her down were hoping she was carrying her work with her?"

"Well, they would have been disappointed. We have strict policies on that sort of thing, and when we checked we found no missing or unauthorized copies of her files. And I just don't believe it. To murder someone on the offhand chance that they'd be carrying a saddlebag full of secrets? It would be far too clumsy and dangerous. Easier to have waited until she got home and went to sleep, and then break in and rob her, don't you think? And anyway, they'd be far more interested in what was going on inside her head. They'd have tried to bribe her or entice her away to a far better-paying job with them."

"Hm." Brock nodded in agreement, then said, "Have you come across a company called Paddington Security Services?"

Penney frowned at the sudden change of direction. "Should I have?"

"Were they involved in the project that Freyja was working on?"

"I really couldn't say."

"Why not?"

Kathy watched the way Penney shrugged and half turned toward the view through the glass wall. The atmosphere in the room seemed to have changed in some indefinable way, as if a familiar background sound had suddenly fallen silent.

"It was an off-the-shelf job, in which we were part of a consortium of specialist consultants—subcontractors, if you like—commissioned to resolve individual features of the project. We weren't necessarily aware of the other members of the consortium."

"Who commissioned you?"

Penney gave a tight little smile, regretful but firm. "I'm sorry, I can't divulge that. We sign strict confidentiality agreements with our clients and consultants, to protect both them and us. As I just explained, there's a war going on, and the enemy thrives by discovering the connections between the people working against them. Then they target the weakest link and so penetrate the whole network. Confidentiality is an essential part of our defenses. But why are you interested in Paddington Security Services?"

"Freyja's sister Gudrun was working for them at the time she died."

"Ah, I see, and you wondered if there was a connection. Sorry I can't help."

Dr. Chandramouli, who'd been listening to this with a puzzled frown, chipped in, "Oh, come on, Philip. You can at least confirm that you've never heard of them, surely."

Penney turned to him and Kathy saw that the friendly, rather unworldly geek had changed into something else, a man who didn't like having his decisions questioned.

"Not even that, Chinmay. Sorry, that's the world I have to live in." He reached into his pocket suddenly and pulled out a phone, consulted the screen and said, "I'm afraid I'll have to bring this to a close." He extended a hand to Brock. "I wish you the best of luck, Chief Inspector."

Dr. Chandramouli looked troubled as they made their way back out to the car. As they buckled up he said, "I really must apologize, David. I don't know what to say. Philip has always seemed to me to be a very obliging chap. But that was extremely rude, hustling us out like that, simply refusing to help."

But Brock seemed unfazed. "Not at all, Chinmay," he said. "I thought Dr. Penney was quite helpful, under the circumstances."

"Really? Well . . . You may not thank me for the next arrangement I made for you. When Andy Harris heard you were coming up he practically twisted my arm off to get you to have a beer with him. I'm sorry, but if you'd rather not, I'll give him a ring and say you can't make it."

Brock gave a sigh, then said, "No, that's fine."

"Oh good. When I told him we were coming here he suggested the Plow in Fen Ditton, not far away."

They drove out to the highway at the end of Milton Road and followed it south across the River Cam into open farmland, where they turned off onto a country road that took them into the village of Fen Ditton, where Chandramouli drove to the parking lot of the Plow. Andy Harris was waiting for them in the bar, greeting them effusively, Brock looking wary, Kathy thought. They took their drinks to a table at a window looking down a sweep of lawn toward the river and Harris immediately plunged into reminiscences of student misadventures.

Thinking that her presence might add to Brock's obvious lack of enthusiasm, Kathy started a conversation with Chandramouli, and asked him whether the Kite girls' unusual names were Swedish like their mother's.

"Old Norse, I think," he said. "Typical Desmond to name them after Valkyries or something. He has a rather one-track mind."

Outside, pale autumnal sunlight glinted on the surface of the river, ruffled by a cold wind. A rowing eight suddenly flashed across their view, the oarsmen straining, faces red with effort. Chandramouli started talking about the races, the Bumps, that were held on this stretch.

As he was talking, Kathy saw Dr. Harris pointing toward the river and made out the words *canal boat*. She turned to hear what he was saying and he said, "Yes, Kathy, I was just telling David why I thought it would be appropriate for us to meet here. After your visit, Desmond was telling me that you'd got mixed up, saying that Gudrun was living on a canal boat, and it reminded me of the last time I saw Freyja, not long before her accident. It was here. Someone at the hospital was retiring, and a group of us came out here for a farewell lunch, and I was sitting like this at the window when I saw Freyja walking down across the grass toward the river, where there was an old houseboat drawn up at the bank. There was a man with her, and I assume they must have been having a drink in the other bar. They were talking intently, and when they reached the boat he got on board and waved good-bye to her.

She turned and came back up to the pub, but I didn't see her again."

Kathy said, "Do you remember what he looked like?"

"No, that didn't register, I'm afraid, but I remember the boat, one of those old-fashioned canal boats with a name painted on the side. I do remember that—*Venerable Bede* it was called. Rather splendid, I thought."

Kathy stared at him. "Are you sure it was Freyja, not Gudrun, that you saw?"

"Oh, definitely Freyja. No doubt about that."

He turned back to Brock, talking about boats and the river, but Kathy was thinking of her encounter with Ned Tisdell on the towpath of the Regent's Canal. Then Brock's phone started to ring.

HE HAD BEGUN TO warm to Andy Harris. The years had rubbed the awkward corners off the young man he had known, who had been too ambitious, too competitive, to be a comfortable companion. Now he had found his balance and seemed absurdly glad to meet up with Brock again. Then Brock's phone rang, and his heart sank when he checked the number and heard Commander Lynch's voice.

"Brock? Where are you?"

"Cambridge, sir."

"I need you. Where's Kolla?"

"She's . . . here too."

"What? Are you two having a dirty weekend?"

"Sadly, no, sir."

"Don't fucking *sir* me. What are you doing in Cambridge?"

"Having a weekend off."

"Not any more. Get yourselves back here. There's work to be done."

Brock hung up with a frown and Andy Harris said, "Problems?"

"Yes." Brock looked at Kathy. "Seems we're needed urgently in London." He turned to Chandramouli. "I'm sorry, Chinmay. It looks as if we won't be able to stay for dinner after all."

"That is a shame. Will you have time for a sandwich with Desmond Kite before you leave?"

"Yes, I'd like to see him. But I'll have to send my apologies to Professor Bronikowski."

"Of course."

DESMOND KITE WAS CERTAINLY brighter, Kathy thought. The shambling hermit had been transformed into a tragic hero from one of his own sagas, a figure of great but frail gravitas. He received them in his college room in Great Court, focusing his attention on Brock, whose hand he shook with a bony claw.

"I'm so glad you've come," he said, his voice deep, sounding as if he might be welcoming a fellow knight to the halls of Valhalla.

"I'm sorry for the reason that brings us here," Brock said, and Kite gave a somber nod of his head in acknowledgment.

"If the immense resources of the Metropolitan Police can be brought to bear upon the deaths of my children, then I am sure justice will prevail."

Oh dear, Kathy thought, *Andrew Harris was right, he's living in another world.*

Kite was showing Brock a framed photograph of two girls, his daughters at school age.

"Gudrun had a tendency to be bullied at school," he said loftily, "but Freyja always protected her. It was already apparent that Freyja was extremely bright. A born mathematician." He pronounced each of the syllables of "math-e-mat-i-cian" distinctly, as if it was a word from an exotic foreign language.

"Gudrun too," Brock prompted.

"Well . . . computers. She was competent, apparently."

Kathy and Chandramouli stayed silent in the background as the two older men sat facing each other and Brock asked Kite to tell him more about Freyja. And when he eventually ran out of superlatives, Brock asked him what she had told him about her work at Penney Solutions.

"Oh, it was far too esoteric for an old history man like me to comprehend. She tried to explain it to me, how two particles of light, remote from one another, could nevertheless be connected in some mysterious way, so that if you did something to one, you did it also to the other." He gave a dry bark of a laugh. "And they say that my Nordic sagas are fanciful!"

Then Kite leaned forward to Brock and fixed him with a mischievous smile. "She called it Huginn and Muninn."

When Brock asked him what that meant, he spelled out the words and said imperiously, "I'm sure that's not beyond your powers of research," as if Brock were a student who needed a little goading.

Eventually they finished their conversation and left Kite to his books. Chandramouli drove them to the station. "You must come back when you have more time to revisit old haunts," the mathematician said, and it seemed to Kathy that Brock seemed regretful now at leaving the city.

When they were on the train Kathy got out her iPad and connected to the internet. After ten minutes, during which Brock stared out of the window, lost in thought, Kathy looked up and said, "Right. Norse mythology 101. The god Odin had two ravens, called Huginn and Muninn, who sat one on each shoulder. Every morning they would leave Odin and fly all over Midgard, returning at dusk to whisper in his ears all that they had seen and heard, and in this way Odin kept himself marvelously informed of all that was going on in the world."

"Surveillance? Spies?" Brock said. "Spy technology?"

"Sounds like it, doesn't it? Cryptology, code-breaking, that's what Freyja was into. And Gudrun had a print of a raven hanging on the wall of her boat."

"How do you know it wasn't a crow?"

"No, it was definitely a raven, because inscribed at the bottom was the word *Nevermore*, which is the refrain . . ."

". . . from the poem 'The Raven,'" Brock said. "All right, what else?"

"Norse mythology 102. Freyja was the name of one of the major goddesses, and was associated with love, beauty, fertility, and gold. Gudrun, on the other hand, was human, and made the mistake of marrying King Atli, who murdered the whole of her family. In revenge, Gudrun killed her two sons by Atli and served them up to him at a feast, then told him what she had done before setting fire to his hall and killing him and all his court. Kind of makes you wonder what Desmond Kite thought of his two girls, doesn't it?"

"And what they must have thought of him—Gudrun especially. Find anything else?"

"Yes. Your friend Andy remembered that the canal boat that Freyja went down to at the Plow was called the *Venerable Bede*. I know that boat—it's currently moored next to Gudrun's on the Regent's Canal. Its owner is Ned Tisdell, and when I went back there last Saturday I found Tisdell coming out of her boat carrying a book and that raven print, which he said belonged to him. I've just looked him up on the PNC. Four years ago he was released from Belmarsh Prison after serving three years for assault on an employee at a pharmaceutical research laboratory in Essex. According to a summary of the case, several staff disturbed a group of intruders who were attempting to release test animals, and in the subsequent melee a laboratory technician was stabbed by Tisdell. In mitigation, his defense disclosed a history of mental instability and failure to take prescribed medication."

Brock said, "So we need to investigate Tisdell, and Paddington Security Services, and we need a proper forensic examination of Gudrun's boat."

"The local police have already turned me down on that. It is still their case."

"Then it's time we made it ours. I'll see to it."

Kathy had another thought. She got back on to the PNC and typed in Anne Downey's name. She had a nagging feeling that the name should have meant something to her, and the database provided the answer—Aaron Downey, her son, aged three, had been abducted during a visit to the local supermarket with his grandmother. Within four days the perpetrator, a known pedophile, had been located and the little boy rescued, but not before he had suffered serious abuse from which he later died. Kathy read through the details, feeling sick, trying to work out what difference this information made. She thought of those four narrowboats moored alongside each other, the Stapletons, Downey, Tisdell, and Gudrun Kite, all with a dark shadow in their past, something to hide or escape from.

THIRTEEN

THE TRAIN DREW IN to King's Cross and they caught a taxi to New Scotland Yard, where they were directed to the basement.

At first Kathy thought they must have been sent to the wrong room. It was deserted, but there were the signs everywhere of recent activity—overflowing waste baskets, lists and diagrams scrawled on whiteboards, coffee cups, notepads, the remains of sandwich lunches, the smells of sweat and coffee. In the middle of all this debris was a wall display of maps, aerial photographs, the plans of a house, and photographs of both the house and a woman, about Kathy's age.

"Looks like you, doesn't she, Kolla?"

They turned at the sound of Commander Lynch's voice from the doorway. He came in, a hamburger in one hand, coffee in the other, kicking the door shut behind him. "Recognize her?"

Kathy shook her head, but Brock said, "It's Jack Bragg's wife, isn't it?"

"Patsy Bragg, correct. And that's her house, Oakdene, on the edge of Knoll Park outside Sevenoaks." He took a big bite of the burger and continued talking as he chewed. "Very comfortable, very private. Jack must have thought about it a lot over the past six years, living in his shithole in the Philippines, thinking of his lovely wife in their stockbroker mansion, screwing his former lackey Sergei Romanov in his four-poster bed.

"Yesterday we tracked Ashur Najjar to the grounds of Oakdene, where he appears to have taken up residence in one of the oak trees in the garden, from which he can observe the house and front drive." Lynch pointed to a red cross that had been marked on one of the aerial photographs. "We've got a police car parked outside the front door, but Patsy hasn't been there for three weeks; she's staying at a secure address until we catch Jack. But now we think it's time for her to go home." He took another bite. "Well, not her exactly. Someone who looks like her."

Brock looked at him sharply. "If you're thinking of DI Kolla, I'd say she's suffered enough at Jack Bragg's hands. He nearly blew her to kingdom come. It's someone else's turn to play the bait."

Lynch grinned. "Very gallant, Brock. What does DI Kolla have to say?"

Kathy looked from one to the other, then said, "Maybe you could tell me what you have in mind, sir."

"Sensible answer. After dark, Mrs. Bragg's substitute will arrive at Oakdene in a taxi. She'll pay off the cab, and approach the front door. The officer in the police car will go to her and they will stand talking under the light on the front porch, so that Najjar can clearly identify her. Then she will open the door and go inside, while the officer returns to his car. Najjar will then phone Jack, who will make his way to Sevenoaks and attempt to get to the house, where we will catch him."

"You make it sound simple," Brock objected. "Where's Jack now?"

"We don't know, but he's not at Oakdene. We've been scanning the area with infrared cameras, and Najjar is the only human being in the vicinity of the house."

"Is Najjar armed?"

"Very probably, but he won't take a potshot at Mrs. Bragg at the front door, because he'll need to check with Jack first, and Jack will want to do this job himself."

"What if there's a bomb in the house, like at Fantasyland?"

"There isn't. We've done a thorough sweep." Lynch was obviously getting irritated by Brock's questions. He turned to Kathy. "We've spent the last eight hours planning this in every detail. We'll infiltrate an armed officer in through the back door of the house, which Najjar can't observe. In the suitcase you'll be carrying when you arrive, you'll have a weapon, body protection, and communications. But it will never come to a personal threat to you. The perimeter of the grounds will be secured by an impenetrable cordon of armed officers, a ring of steel. Jack will never get near you. When you get inside the house you'll go upstairs, draw the curtains, and put on the bedroom light, then return downstairs and wait there, in darkness, so there's no chance anyone can take a shot at you. You leave the rest to us. This is the best chance we'll ever get to nail Jack Bragg. Will you do it?"

Kathy hesitated. "I'd need to see Patsy Bragg, study the way she walks."

"Sure. We've got her here, waiting to meet you. She's brought clothes for you, and we've got a makeup artist ready."

Brock said, "You're planning on doing this tonight?"

"Sooner the better. Kathy's perfect for this. What do you say? Are you up for it?"

Kathy nodded. "Yes. Yes, of course."

"Good. We'll get you briefed."

He turned away to pick up a phone and deliver a stream of orders to someone. While he was talking, Brock spoke to Kathy. "I don't like this one bit."

"That's because you weren't involved in the planning."

"And why the hell wasn't I? What was it Dr. Penney called

himself—a subcontractor? That's what we are, subcontractors, not given the whole picture, just called in at the end for a bit of dirty work."

"Right." Lynch turned back to them. "Let's take you to meet Patsy."

He led them down the corridor to a room at the end that had been turned into an improvised dressing room, with a rack of clothes on hangers, a mirror, make-up laid out on a table, and several women who turned to consider Kathy. She recognized Patsy Bragg, noting the similarities in their height and build.

"So you're my double," Patsy said, coming over. She was obviously keyed up, nervous.

"My name's Kathy. Do you think I'll do?"

Patsy bit her lip, considering. "Yeah, I guess you might. What do you think, girls?"

One of the other women nodded. "No worries. We'll have to fix your hair."

Lynch frowned impatiently. "How long will that take?"

They checked their watches. "We'll have her ready by seven."

"All right. We'll leave you to it. Come on, Brock."

While they worked on her, Kathy got Patsy to walk around the room and talk to her. Patsy told her that she had met Ashur Najjar many times at Fantasyland and she was sure that he would recognize her. Kathy got her to mime the scene of arriving in the taxi, talking to the policeman, and opening the front door. She had a way of cocking her head when she was thinking, and of flicking through her keys, that Kathy thought she might be able to use. Kathy was intrigued to know how Patsy felt about this operation, in which her husband might be captured, hurt, or even killed. She got her answer when the girls had finished with her hair and makeup, and she was pulling on Patsy's chic Katherine Hooker coat.

"Damn!" Patsy said. "You *are* me." She looked troubled. "I

hope you don't find out why I haven't been able to eat or sleep since I heard he was back."

"What do you mean, Patsy?"

"For the first three years we were married, I thought Jack was an ordinary sort of bloke—a bit rough, but basically a normal bloke. I'd heard that he had this nickname, 'Butcher,' but he said it was a joke, because his dad had been a butcher in Whitechapel, and Jack used to help him in the shop. Then one day Mr. Lynch showed me photographs of what Jack had done to the Aaron brothers, because he wanted me to help him put Jack away. He said Jack had used a cleaver and worn a butcher's apron, which he'd left at the scene, so people would know. I didn't believe it, but when I told Jack, I saw from his expression that it was true. Later he admitted it. He said it was necessary for his reputation, for people to be frightened of him, to know what he'd do to them if they upset him. And I've upset him, good and proper."

"Well," Kathy said, "hopefully we'll get him this time. So Mr. Lynch has been after Jack for some time then?"

"Oh yes, he goes way back. He was an inspector then. Jack nearly killed him once."

Well, Kathy thought, that makes things a bit clearer.

As she gathered up the handbag and keys, Patsy said, "I don't know how long you're going to be in there, but if you get hungry there's frozen meals in the kitchen freezer and drinks and snacks in the pantry. Help yourself."

"Thanks."

The two women stared at each other for a moment, as if at their own reflections in a mirror.

"Better you than me, honey," Patsy said, and walked away.

Lynch returned and they had a final briefing before Kathy was led to the underground car park, where a taxi with a plainclothes police driver was waiting for her. When she got in Lynch leaned in to give her some parting words. "Don't worry, it'll be a piece of cake."

"Yes, sir," she said, and smiled reassuringly at Brock, standing behind Lynch's shoulder looking worried.

Brock stepped close to her and said, "You really sure you want to do this?"

"Yes, I'm okay."

"Well . . ." he said reluctantly, and reached into his pocket. "Take this."

Kathy felt him press a small object into her hand, and looking down she saw the sort of small pepper-spray canister that could be bought over the counter in the USA. She laughed. "Where did you get this?"

"I got some for Suzanne."

Kathy's eyes widened. Would Suzanne really need this in the Sussex country town where she lived? "But I'll have a Glock."

"All the same, keep this in your pocket."

If things went wrong it would be useless, she knew, but she was touched, picturing him, a senior police officer, buying illegal imports on the Web to protect his partner.

ON THE DRIVE DOWN to Sevenoaks, speeding down the A20, rain glittering in the headlights, Kathy exchanged a few words with the driver, then sank back into the seat in silence, trying to prepare herself for what lay ahead. Her fingers felt inside the pocket of the coat and closed around Brock's gift, like a good luck charm.

They turned off the main road into a succession of country lanes, until they slowed at an opening in a high brick wall, and swung in through the gates. Kathy heard the crunch of tires on gravel and looked out through the window at thick undergrowth and the outline against the night sky of black branches, among which Ashur Najjar was supposedly perched. *Bragg must be paying you well*, Kathy thought, *or have you very frightened*.

They drove past the police car and came to a stop near the front door. Kathy got out and stood by the cab window, back straight, poised as Patsy would have been. She took her time opening Patsy's purse and handing over some notes. The cab driver murmured, "Good luck then," and the cab began to move while Kathy turned toward the front door. As she approached, a light sensed her and came on, and at the same time she heard the cop get out of the patrol car and call, "Mrs. Bragg?"

She turned, letting the light shine directly on her, and smiled at the man as he approached. He asked her if everything was all right and she said, "Well, I damn well hope so," tilting her head and gesturing in that way Patsy had.

"I'll be here if you need me," he said.

"Thanks." She fished in Patsy's bag for the keys, flashed a Patsy kind of smile at the patrol officer and turned to the door, feeling her back naked to a sniper in the woods as she carefully inserted the correct key, stepped inside, and drew a deep breath.

"Anybody around?" she called.

A dark shadow moved in the gloom ahead. "Right here, ma'am, PC Lister."

"I'm going to put a light on." She reached out to where Patsy had told her and felt for the light switch. "Wow, this is nice."

"Yes." PC Lister nodded. "Very tasteful, Lutyens maybe, or even Voysey. Not what I expected for Butcher Bragg."

Kathy looked again at PC Lister, standing there in his body armor cradling a submachine gun. "All quiet then?"

"Absolutely."

"Well, I'll go on upstairs and switch this light off."

"Right. I'll be down here in the living room, through that door there."

Kathy made her way up the oak staircase, treading silently

on thick carpet, listening to the solid beat of a grandfather clock's pendulum somewhere down in the hall. In the master bedroom she switched on the lights and closed the curtains. She took off Patsy's good coat and laid it on the four-poster bed, then opened the suitcase and took out the Kevlar vest, the headset, and the pistol and put them on. She looked around, taking in the details, and noticed a bottle of perfume on a dressing table. She sprayed a little on her wrist and sniffed it, expensive and very nice, then put more on her neck and returned down the stairs to join PC Lister. Through her earpiece she heard background noise, then a female voice telling her that Ashur Najjar had made a phone call to a number in Stanmore, on the far side of London. "That puts the target at least an hour away. You can relax."

"Did you get that?" Lister asked as Kathy came into the living room.

"Yes."

"Nothing to do but wait. At least it's comfortable in here. Not like for poor old Najjar out there."

Kathy sat, listening to a fresh shower of rain pattering on the windows. The pistol, tucked into her waistband, cut uncomfortably into the small of her back. She tried to ease it around without success, then pulled it out and laid it on the coffee table at her side.

"Have you eaten tonight?" Lister asked.

"No, I didn't get a chance."

"Me neither. I had a look in the kitchen, but couldn't find anything."

"There's frozen meals in the freezer and stuff in the pantry," Kathy said. "You stay here, I'll take a look."

"There's a nasty smell out there. Reckon something's gone bad."

Kathy made her way out to the hall again, her eyes now used

to the dark. When she reached the kitchen she realized what Lister had meant about the smell. She opened the freezer compartment of the fridge, momentarily dazzled by the light, and found joints of frozen meat, but no meals. She closed the door, looking around for the pantry, and came upon a utility room. The smell was stronger here. There was a toilet inside, and when she lifted the lid she gagged, seeing a dark mass inside the bowl. She dropped the lid quickly and pressed the flush, then turned back to the kitchen. The pantry was on the other side, but she could find no sign of the drinks and snacks that Patsy had described.

She gave up and returned to the living room. PC Lister was stretched out on the leather sofa, as if he'd fallen asleep. Kathy began to say something, then stopped, noticing a black stain spreading out from the sofa across the pale carpet.

Then an arm came around her from behind and a hand gripped her throat tight. "Hello, Patsy, darling," a hoarse voice whispered in her ear. "Long time."

She tried to struggle, but the grip on her throat tightened, lifting her almost off the floor, knocking her headset off. The hand was gloved with chain mail, she realized: a butcher's glove.

"Ah, that perfume," Jack Bragg murmured. "Takes me back. Shame it has to end this way." He raised his other hand in front of Kathy's face to show her the meat cleaver. "I'm wearing my dad's old leather apron. He'd be proud."

"I'm . . ." she croaked.

"You're what? Sorry? I'd like to hear it, doll, but I'd better not hang around. Chop, chop. I'll start with the legs." He kicked her feet out from under her and as she fell awkwardly onto the carpet he came down on top of her. He knelt on her back and the mailed hand closed around her mouth and nose. Kathy, squirming helplessly, dug her fingers into the pocket of Patsy's tight jeans and closed on Brock's little present. She desperately tried to tug it out, fumbling with the smooth tube, then rammed her thumb on the button as she raised her hand, filling the air around them with a spray of choking gas.

"AARGH!" Bragg gagged, jerking backward, and as Kathy began to wriggle out of his grip he brought the cleaver down. She twisted her head away and felt a blinding explosion of pain in her left shoulder, followed by chaos—searing gas, pain, a hammering at the door, Bragg screaming at her—and then a sudden silence.

It seemed an age, a few seconds probably, before they came pounding in. Lights came on, men shouted, Kathy raised her head and saw PC Lister, his head almost severed from his poor slack body. Someone was talking to her, demanding an answer, "Where is he?" Then a shout from the kitchen, "Back door's open!" She heard the sharp crackle of gunfire.

FOURTEEN

KATHY OPENED HER EYES and saw a familiar figure, Brock, sitting reading a newspaper. He looked up and smiled at her. "Hello," he said.

She tried to reply, but her throat was gummed up and she couldn't swallow. He seemed to understand, and reached toward her with a plastic cup. It was only then that she realized that she was lying in a bed. She took a sip of the water and he said, "How do you feel?"

"Dunno," was all she could manage. She looked around, taking in the curtain rails, the signs on the wall, the drip. "Hospital?"

"Yes. You've had an operation on your shoulder."

She struggled to think what that was about and had a sudden memory of being crushed on the floor. When she tried to flex her muscles she found that her right hand worked all right, but her whole left side seemed to be paralyzed. She looked down and saw the bandages and straps.

She gazed back at Brock, who nodded and said, "Bad fracture. Your vest saved you."

"Butcher," she mumbled.

"Yes."

"We got him?"

He shook his head, a look of disgust on his face. "He slipped out the back door and disappeared into the night. So much for the ring of steel."

Now she had it, the whole sequence clear in her mind. "But how did he get in?"

"He was already there. He had a cubbyhole in the cellar, probably been there for several days waiting for Patsy to come back."

"Taking food from the kitchen, not flushing the toilet. But I thought Ashur Najjar phoned him in Stanmore?"

"Najjar must have phoned somebody else, who then used another phone to relay the message to Bragg. Najjar tried to shoot his way out. They killed him."

"Oh God . . . what a screw-up. Is Lynch angry?"

"Furious. So am I. It wasn't done right. You should never have been put in that situation. That was his responsibility."

"Patsy told me that he and Bragg go way back. Sounds like a personal thing. She said Bragg almost killed him once."

"Yes, well, maybe that's clouding his judgment. Anyway . . ." he put a smile on his face, ". . . you're going to be all right."

"Your little toy saved me. That stuff's horrible." She paused, stroking her bruised throat, feeling again the grip of the mailed fist. "He was convinced I was her—even at the end, he screamed he would come back and get me. I'd used some of her perfume, you see. He recognized it right away. That's how he knew, in the dark, that I was Patsy." She stared down at the drip disappearing into the dressings and whispered, "PC Lister . . ."

"Yes. They've told his wife."

A vivid image came into Kathy's mind and she turned sharply away and was sick before she could reach the bowl.

PALE LIGHT WAS LEAKING into the sky as Brock returned to New Scotland Yard. Commander Lynch could only spare Brock a couple of minutes, his PA informed Brock, in a tone that suggested he should know better than to barge in without an appointment, even at dawn. He waited until Lynch's door opened and D.K. Payne came out, clutching a sheaf of files. Payne nodded grimly back at the door, and Brock got to his feet and marched in.

Lynch's head was down, scanning a document. He said, "Yes, Brock?" without looking up.

"I've just come from the hospital. DI Kolla is in recovery. The doctors are satisfied with the way her operation went."

"Good, good. I'll try to get down there later."

He was clearly exhausted, but Brock, furious, plowed on. "I'm not happy that she was put in that situation."

Lynch looked up slowly. "Nobody's happy. We lost an officer."

"There'll be a major incident inquiry, I take it."

Lynch's eyes narrowed. "I'm working on an operational review now."

"But you were acting as senior investigating officer. The SIO can't review his own . . ." the word *debacle* came into his mind, ". . . case."

"I do what I'm told, Brock," Lynch said, anger clearly bubbling to the surface. "As will you." He glared at Brock for a moment, then snapped, "Sit down."

Brock sat.

"While we're on the subject of doing what we're told," Lynch continued, "what were you and Kolla doing in Cambridge yesterday, exactly?"

Brock took a deep breath, resenting this change of subject. "We spoke to the father of Gudrun Kite, the young woman who was found dead on a boat on the Regent's Canal last week."

"That's Professor Desmond Kite, of the same Cambridge college that you attended?"

Brock hesitated, wondering how the hell he knew that. "Yes."

"Who else did you meet?"

"People who knew Gudrun Kite and her sister Freyja, who died in an accident in Cambridge earlier this year."

"To what purpose?"

"I wanted to assure myself that there was no connection between the two deaths."

"And did you *assure* yourself?"

"No. There are aspects of both cases that merit further investigation, in my opinion."

Lynch rammed back in his chair, staring bleakly at Brock. "Last Friday week you attended a Strategic Review Tribunal at which DI Kolla's conduct regarding the Gudrun Kite case was held up as a prime example of wasteful and regressive police practice. Now you're spending your weekends together trying to justify her bungling, and at the same time impress your old college chums that you can do what the local cops could not."

"No, I—"

But Lynch spoke over him, raising his voice. "You have a reputation, Brock, for being stubborn and intransigent, for keeping your head down and going your own way, for not being a team player, and for encouraging these traits in your subordinates."

Brock held himself in check. "There should have been more consultation on the Bragg case."

Lynch slapped his open palm down angrily on his desk. "You weren't here, Brock! You were in fucking Cambridge!"

For a moment they glared at each other, then the steam seemed to go out of Lynch. "Go away, Brock," he said wearily.

"I've got things to do. Go away and figure out how we can catch Jack Bragg now."

"I should have thought that was obvious," Brock said.

Lynch blinked at him, as if wondering if he'd misheard. "What are you talking about? He could be anywhere by now, on a plane back to Manila for all we know."

"No. He still thinks that was Patsy in the house. As he left he yelled that he would come back and get her. So put out a press statement that Patsy Bragg was attacked in her home last night but has survived and is recuperating somewhere safe, anywhere but that hospital—it's a disaster waiting to happen."

"Why?"

"There are a dozen ways in and out. We can't secure it, and if he tries anything there will be casualties."

Lynch looked thoughtful. "Richmond."

"Sorry?"

Lynch waved his hand carelessly. "There's a private clinic in Richmond we use sometimes. It's a possibility. How far have you thought this through?"

"Not far. But we also need to move DI Kolla out of that hospital. As long as she's there both she and everyone else in the building are in danger."

"All right." Lynch looked at his watch. "Come back at noon and we'll see what we can come up with."

Brock walked the few blocks back to his office at Queen Anne's Gate. He thought about trying to get an hour or two's sleep, but he felt jittery and unsettled, and ended up making himself a cup of strong coffee from his new machine and sitting by the window thinking, watching improbably pink fluffy clouds float over St. James's Park. Lynch's barbs about Cambridge had got under his skin, and the worst of it was the possibility—no, probability—that Lynch was right, that the Kite girls' deaths were simply two sad accidents, and that the visit to Cambridge had been a quixotic diversion, a foolish attempt to salve his pride after his mauling at the tribunal.

He finished his coffee and decided to go back to the hospital, by way of the Regent's Canal.

He parked his car against the railings overlooking the triangular basin of Little Venice, and walked over the bridge to the steps leading down to the towpath of the western branch of the canal. Smoke was drifting up from the flue of one of the boats at which a jogger was stretching with one foot on the gunwale. He looked up as Brock approached, and called out, "Hello. Can I help you?"

Brock introduced himself, showing his ID.

"Oh, yes, we spoke to Inspector Kolla," the jogger said, offering his hand. "I'm Howard Stapleton, from *Roaming Free*, here. That's *Grace*, where the accident happened."

Brock nodded admiringly at Stapleton's boat and they chatted for a few minutes about its performance, Stapleton coming alive when Brock asked about the engine.

"Beta 43 horsepower diesel, with a six-horsepower hydraulic bow thruster."

"Really? How does that work?"

Stapleton enthusiastically explained, then answered Brock's questions about the other boats.

"What about Ned Tisdell's boat—*Venerable Bede*, isn't it? Which one is that?"

"Oh, it's gone, I'm afraid. He took off a couple of nights ago, without a word to anyone. Just like Ned, that was—unpredictable, impulsive."

"You've no idea where he went?"

"Not a clue. Could be anywhere by now. He might have said something to Anne Downey." He pointed to her boat, and Brock saw a light glowing at a curtain in one of the windows.

"Thanks, Mr. Stapleton." Brock gave him a card. "Maybe you could let me know if Mr. Tisdell comes back. There's something we need to check with him."

Dr. Downey answered his knock, coming out onto the stern to speak to him. She was wearing an old green jacket, folding her arms against the chill, but didn't invite him in. No, she said, she didn't know where Tisdell had gone, and couldn't remember exactly when he'd left—perhaps last Tuesday or Wednesday?

As he thanked her and walked away, Brock wondered why she had been so defensive.

Kathy was asleep when he got to the hospital. He spoke to the police officer on duty at her door, then went in and sat by her bedside for an hour, but when she still slept on he decided to return to his office, picking up a sandwich and cup of tea at the snack bar on the way out.

THERE WERE THREE OF them sitting at the meeting room table: Lynch, D.K. Payne, and a woman Brock remembered seeing at a conference some time before. She was dressed in black, had a sharply cut helmet of gray hair, and was staring at him through stylish scarlet-framed glasses.

"You know Superintendent Russell, Brock?" Lynch said. "Suzy, this is DCI Brock."

They shook hands and Brock sat down, trying to work out which branch she was from. Payne had a laptop open in front of him, Russell an iPad, and Lynch a clipboard, filled with notes.

"I think we're getting somewhere," Lynch said. "Following your suggestion, Brock, we've been sketching out a possible scenario. Suzy, will you?"

Special Branch, Brock remembered suddenly. She'd been with Special Branch.

She spoke in short, precise sentences, describing the leaks

that might be made to the press, the information mislaid in the hospital, the hints given to Patsy's relatives, all designed to lead Jack Bragg to the clinic in Richmond.

"How will the clinic feel about that?" Brock said at last.

"They'll be fine," Russell said confidently. "They're old friends of ours. The place is very secure. Neither they nor DI Kolla will be in any danger."

"I'm sorry?" Brock said, wondering if he'd misunderstood. "You're surely not suggesting that DI Kolla be placed in this clinic?"

"Of course." Superintendent Russell gave him a patient smile.

Lynch broke in. "Think about it, Brock. Kolla is at risk now, and also needs continuing medical attention. The safest place for her is the clinic."

"Used as bait again!" Brock exploded, rising to his feet. "She's been through this twice now with Bragg. That's enough!"

"Sit down, Brock. Just think it through. It makes no sense to send Kolla off somewhere else, risking confusion and greater danger to her. As far as the Butcher is concerned, she *is* Patsy Bragg. That's the one strength we have. You pointed that out yourself."

Brock listened as they spelled out the details, down to the bottle of Patsy's expensive perfume that Kathy would give to the ward sister when they moved her out of the hospital.

When they'd finished he said, "I want to record my objections to this plan. DI Kolla has been through two traumatic experiences in the past week. She's in no condition to participate in another operation, or even to be asked for her consent."

"Objection noted," Lynch said curtly. "Now let's get on with it."

"It might reassure DCI Brock if he stayed close to DI Kolla, at least during her transfer to Richmond," Suzy Russell said, with a sympathetic smile to Brock.

BROCK MADE HIS WAY back to the hospital where he found Kathy awake, eating a light lunch, a little color in her cheeks.

"You're looking better," he said.

"I'm okay, just tired. I can't believe how tired I feel. But how am I going to give you a game of gin rummy with only one hand?"

Brock smiled, remembering when he'd been the one laid up in hospital and she'd come in to play cards and chess with him.

"So, they're moving me, are they?" Kathy said.

"How did you know?"

"DCS Lynch came in to see me a couple of hours ago. He told me they were thinking I'd be safer at the clinic at Richmond where they took Ashur Najjar after the bombing."

Brock frowned—Lynch had given no indication that he'd already spoken to Kathy. It was infuriatingly typical of the man, to needlessly keep information to himself. Brock had read somewhere that it was a symptom of borderline personality disorder.

Kathy said, "I think the Met must have some arrangement with them. Lynch said rich foreigners worried about their safety often go there for their treatments. The security is very tight, he said, the windows all bulletproof glass etcetera. And the medical facilities are wonderful. Sounds okay."

"I've just come from a meeting with Lynch about this, but he didn't mention he'd discussed it with you. I told him I opposed the idea."

"Did you? Why?"

"They're using you as bait again, hoping that Jack Bragg will follow you there."

He watched Kathy blink, holding herself together as she took that in.

"But all the same . . ." she said slowly, ". . . if he really thinks

I'm Patsy, he's going to do that anyway, wherever I am. Better that I'm somewhere safe, no?"

Brock nodded unhappily. "Yes, it does make sense I suppose. And I'm coming with you to make sure it *is* safe."

"And I really do want to nail that bastard," she added.

FIFTEEN

BY THE TIME THEY'D wrapped Kathy's head in bandages and strapped an oxygen mask to her face, there was little chance that she could be identified. She seemed more groggy than before, Brock thought, having been given a sedative for the journey. He escorted the gurney along the corridor to the elevator, then down to the ground floor to a rear entrance where an ambulance was waiting. They stepped out into the driveway and were caught in a dazzle of flash. A voice called out, "Chief Inspector Brock! You're running the hunt for Jack Bragg, aren't you?"

Brock waved them away, and another voice shouted, "Will you confirm that's Mrs. Bragg with you?"

"No comment," he said, moving between them and the gurney.

"How is she, Brock? How extensive are her injuries? Just give us a word."

"Did he use his cleaver?"

"Is she disfigured?"

He'd been set up, he realized as he jumped into the ambulance. This was why Suzy Russell had suggested he escort Kathy, so that the press couldn't avoid making the connection between the figure on the gurney and Patsy Bragg. He flicked out his phone and called Lynch.

"We've just left the hospital. The press were waiting for us at the back entrance. They'd been tipped off, hadn't they? Why the hell didn't you tell me?"

"It was meant to be a surprise, Brock. All part of the plan. Don't worry, you played your part perfectly."

"I'm not some actor in a second-rate cop show. I'm a police officer trying to protect a wounded colleague."

"I know what you are, and you're being pompous. Don't worry, everything's under control. Did Kolla give the perfume to the nurse?"

"Yes."

"Good. Now she can relax. There's nothing more she needs to do except get better. The food is excellent at the clinic, I'm told."

When he hung up Kathy raised a hand to remove her mask and said, "Is everything all right?"

Her voice was faint, barely audible above the noise of the engine, and she looked exhausted. "Yes, of course," he said brightly. "Everything's under control."

She nodded and closed her eyes. "How's everything else going?"

He told her about visiting the canal basin and finding that Tisdell had gone, but he wasn't sure that she heard.

ACCORDING TO THE BOOKLET on Kathy's knee, the Pewsey Clinic occupied Pewsey Hall, a mansion built by Robert Pewsey on the banks of the Thames at Richmond in 1840. Pewsey had made a fortune trafficking opium from the East India Company's poppy fields in Bengal to the British trading houses in China, and had built Pewsey Hall after being inspired by a visit to the Royal Pavilion in Brighton, putting a Mughal dome over the front door and miniature minarets at its four corners. It had subsequently been extended by the only one of his six sons to survive

India, and then gone into a period of decline. In 1995 it had been purchased by a private consortium of medical specialists and converted into the Pewsey Clinic, one of whose specialities was the treatment of addiction to the products of the poppy which had paid for the building in the first place.

After the bandages had been removed from her head, Kathy had showered in her room with private bath, been given fresh pajamas and slippers, had consultations with a doctor and a physiotherapist, and now sat in a luxurious bathrobe at the window of her room, sipping a glass of freshly squeezed orange juice, looking out across a swath of perfect lawn toward the river. To the right, her view was framed by the high hedges of the maze designed by Robert Pewsey on his deathbed, and to the left a copse of trees beyond which the tip of Eel Pie Island was visible. The thick glass of the windows insulated her from any sound outside, and she felt suspended in time, waiting for something to shatter the bubble.

She had finally persuaded Brock to go back to his work. He had been anxious, suspicious of the security arrangements that had been explained to them by the head of security at the clinic. When the man had said that it was against the clinic's policy for patients to be armed, and that it was in any case unnecessary, Kathy was afraid for a moment that Brock might lose his temper. Instead he had phoned Lynch again, who had ordered him to do what he was told. Kathy was relieved when he finally agreed to leave.

The day faded and lights came on in the grounds outside. There was a knock at the door and she was offered a menu for her dinner. She gave her order and after a while an excellent meal arrived. As she ate she thought that this must be what it was like to travel first class, swaddled and protected. After her recent shocks it made her feel deeply relaxed, and she surrendered to an overwhelming sense of exhaustion. When they took away her tray she went to bed. A nurse came in to ask her if she needed something to help her sleep, but she was already slipping into unconsciousness.

SHE AWOKE TO THE sound of a deep throbbing, more a visceral vibration than a sound, that seemed to come from the building itself. She sat up in bed, feeling disoriented, trying to remember where she was. A hospital. She felt a momentary tremor of panic, then took a deep breath and forced herself to relax. Her broken shoulder ached and her throat was parched. She could still taste the foul dust from the Fantasyland bomb. She felt a sudden need for a drink, something fizzy and sweet, like Sprite, to take away the taste, and remembered a machine somewhere in the corridor. She got out of bed, slipped on the bathrobe and limped to the door.

The lights in the corridor were dimmed, and the place seemed strangely unfamiliar. She walked in the direction of the nurses' station where she'd seen the drinks machine, but could find neither, and it occurred to her that she was mixing up the two hospitals. Surely in this place you would just ring for room service.

The throbbing sound was still there, but fainter now. She turned a corner and saw a male nurse coming toward her, an identity card clipped to his pocket. When they were close, Kathy looked at the man's face just as he turned his eyes to her, and she froze in shock. The nurse had the face of Ned Tisdell. He too looked startled. He opened his mouth as if to say something, then broke into a run, disappearing around the corner while Kathy just stared after him.

She told herself that it was impossible; Ned Tisdell belonged in a different world entirely, the Gudrun Kite case, nothing to do with Jack Bragg. It was like watching *Julius Caesar* and having Hamlet stroll onto the stage. Besides, this man's hair was different, neatly combed, and he was cleanly shaved. But she was sure that he had recognized her, and had panicked when he saw her.

The lights in the corridor suddenly came on full, and a small red bulb mounted on the wall began to flash. She turned back the way she had come and bumped into a nurse.

"Mrs. Bragg!" the woman cried. "You should be in your room!"

She grabbed Kathy's good arm and steered her quickly toward her door.

"Please," Kathy said, "do you have a man working here called Tisdell, Ned Tisdell?"

The nurse shook her head. "Not to my knowledge. Now please, wait in your room."

"What's going on?"

"Nothing, I'm sure. Just a security alert." She switched the light on in Kathy's room and looked around, checking. "There we go. Someone will be here shortly."

She'd hardly finished speaking when a security guard appeared and the nurse departed. Kathy asked him what was happening.

"Suspected intruder in the grounds, ma'am. Not to worry." He fiddled with his earpiece.

"Listen," Kathy said, "can you do a check for me? Find out if there's someone who works here called Ned or Edward Tisdell?"

"Yeah, I can do that, when this is over."

"You need to do it now." She saw the look on the man's face. "I'm a police officer, right?" The man looked uncertain. "I'm almost sure that I saw someone in the corridor just now who is known to us, and I'm sure he doesn't belong here. Could you please check?"

He shrugged and reluctantly spoke into his radio. It was some time before he could persuade the person at the other end and came back with an answer. No, there was no one of that name on the clinic's staff.

Kathy was aware of the throbbing vibrations returning, and realized that it was the sound of a helicopter. The guard moved over to the window, cautiously pulling back the blind, and they saw a dazzling light beaming down from the sky, illuminating the lawn. He listened for a moment to his earpiece and said, "They think he's hiding in the maze." As he spoke, Kathy watched the searchlight move over the hedges, the throbbing of the helicopter's rotors very loud now. Dark figures scurried across the lawn. To Kathy it all seemed remote and unreal, so that when the guard turned to her with a grin and said, "They've got 'im," she felt nothing but a vague sense of anticlimax.

"Are they sure it's Jack Bragg?" she asked, but the guard hadn't been briefed on the identity of the intruder.

"Whoever it is, everyone sounds really happy."

"YES, IT'S JACK BRAGG all right," Brock said when he arrived soon afterward. He had booked himself a room in a nearby hotel, he explained, and had dashed over as soon as he heard the helicopter. "No doubt about that. We can all relax."

But Kathy didn't feel relaxed. She just sat there on the edge of her bed, staring down at her one good hand gripping her bathrobe, as if trying to hang on to reality.

"How are you feeling, Kathy?" Brock was looking at her with concern. "How's the shoulder?"

She said, "Something's not right, Brock."

"How do you mean?"

"Just before the alarm sounded I went out into the corridor to get a drink, and I met a man in a nurse's uniform. It was Ned Tisdell."

"Ned Tisdell? You mean from the canal boat?"

"Yes."

"But . . ." Brock hesitated, then said cautiously, "Surely that's not possible, is it?"

"That's what I told myself. But I'm sure it was him."

Brock sat beside her on the edge of the bed and put a reassuring hand on her good arm. "You don't look well, Kathy. Shall I call a nurse?"

"No, look . . ." It felt such a struggle to get the words out.

Brock said, his voice immensely patient, "Do you remember me talking to you about Ned Tisdell in the ambulance as we brought you over here?"

She looked at him in surprise. "No. I was feeling a bit sleepy, with the painkillers."

"Yes. Well, I talked to you about him, and then you came here and had a meal and went to sleep. Don't you think it could have been a dream, your mind replaying what I'd told you in the ambulance?"

"No, it wasn't a dream. I was out there in the corridor; one of the other nurses found me just after Tisdell ran away, and she brought me back to my room. Look, I know it sounds weird, and I've tried to tell myself that I was wrong, but I wasn't. You see, he recognized me, and looked as surprised as I felt. He began to say something, then turned on his heels and ran away."

"He was in a nurse's uniform?"

"Yes, with an ID card clipped to the pocket. He looked neater than before."

"Okay, so you bump into a nurse in the corridor who looks a bit like Tisdell. He's surprised to see you wandering around in the middle of the night and begins to say something, then the alarm sounds and he has to hurry back to his station."

Kathy took a deep breath. The effort of trying to explain, to convince him, was overwhelming. "I've been wondering if it's possible that there was some connection between him and

123

Bragg. Maybe he got involved with someone from Bragg's gang while he was in prison. Maybe he did jobs for them when he got out, and heard that Bragg was coming back to the UK, and Gudrun discovered something and Tisdell had to kill her . . ."

She ran out of steam, seeing the expression on Brock's face, knowing how far-fetched it sounded.

"Tell you what," Brock said, "I'll do some checks, here in the hospital, and into Tisdell's background."

He would do it, she knew, so that he could reassure her that she was mistaken. But surely it *had* been Tisdell; she had looked into his eyes and knew that it was him. And yet, she hadn't been herself at all, half doped with sleep and pills. "Thanks," she said, defeated. "So what was it you told me about him in the ambulance?"

"That his boat has gone from the canal basin. It seems he disappeared three or four days ago."

SIXTEEN

COMMANDER LYNCH WAS REENERGIZED, like a man from whose shoulders a great weight had finally been lifted, bouncing on the balls of his feet, slapping people on the shoulder, *laughing* for goodness' sake. Brock watched this transformation with interest and some relief; perhaps the earlier, darker Lynch was an aberration after all, the effect of a man under extreme pressure.

Operation Intruder wasn't finished, however. With considerable relish Lynch was outlining the new trails to be followed, to round up Bragg's contacts in Stanmore and all the other people who had helped him to get into the country and sheltered him once he was here. Commander Sharpe would never have done this, Brock reflected, taking over the whole operation himself. Serious Crime had dozens, hundreds of cases as important as this one on its books. What was Lynch trying to prove? Who was he trying to impress?

Brock's phone buzzed. He saw that it was Sundeep Mehta calling and turned away from the briefing to take the call.

"Brock! I've had trouble getting through to you. You're very busy, I hear."

Brock could hear the shriek of a saw in the background, and had a sudden image of a skull being cracked open. "We've had a bit of excitement, Sundeep. Is there a problem?"

"Something rather curious, my man." Sundeep liked to affect a ripe accent when he had something juicy to impart.

"Oh yes?"

"We did the PM on Ashur Najjar this morning."

"Yes?" Sundeep was spinning it out, toying with him, and Brock didn't have time. He could see Lynch moving on to a street map of Stanmore and talking about phone intercepts.

"I got a very *snooty* phone call from someone in the Home Office telling me that I was to give it top priority."

"Because it was a police shooting, I suppose?"

"That's what I assumed. But he did ask me—no, *order* me, in the nicest possible way—to accommodate another doctor at the PM, but not a pathologist."

"Oh? What was he?"

"He didn't say, but I looked him up—he's a cardiac surgeon!"

"Why? Did Najjar suffer from a heart condition?"

"I wish I could tell you, my man. When we opened the thoracic cavity he stepped up and said he had instructions to remove the heart, just like that! I was flabbergasted. I phoned back to this fellow at the Home Office and he confirmed it, said the heart was needed for special study, wouldn't say why. So I had to stand back while our friend removed it, weighed it, and put it in a cold storage container he'd brought with him. I didn't get a chance to look at it at all. Then he just observed us, saying not a word, while we carried on with the postmortem. What do you make of that?"

"Had Najjar been shot in the heart?"

"No. Two bullets passed through the lower abdomen and one—the fatal shot—hit his head."

"Could they have wanted it for a heart transplant?"

"No, no, it was far too late for that. I guessed it must be part of some kind of research program, but I haven't been able to find any reference to such a thing. And why was the man so uncommunicative?"

Brock could imagine Sundeep in the pathology suite, trying with mounting frustration to tease information out of the surgeon.

"Let me know if you hear anything more," Brock said. "I'm in the middle of a meeting—'fraid I have to go."

"Well, I feel like putting in a formal complaint. It's most irregular. He did promise to send me a report on the heart, but still, it was *my* postmortem."

Odd, Brock thought as he rang off. He returned his attention to Lynch, who was setting out his strategy for the follow-up operations.

KATHY WAS TAKEN FOR another X-ray, then another session with the doctor who had seen her when she checked in to the Pewsey Clinic. Dr. John Partridge was a youngish man with a brisk, confident air and the sort of considerate bedside manner that one might expect in an expensive clinic. He removed the dressing on her shoulder and examined her stitches. Bragg's cleaver had penetrated the fabric of her protective vest and given her a deep flesh wound about ten centimeters long, as well as snapping the collarbone. Kathy glanced down and saw that the whole of her left shoulder was swollen and purple.

"The resetting of the bone has been successful," the doctor said. "Clavicle fractures usually heal well. You should have full union of the bone within four months, full mobility in six, and full strength in nine, all being well."

"I can't wait that long."

He smiled. "We'll keep your arm in a sling for three or four weeks to allow initial bone and soft tissue healing, after that there'll be a regime of therapeutic exercise."

A nurse replaced her dressing, fitted her sling, and returned her to her room. She was feeling better today, her head clear, appetite back.

She had a succession of visitors—Brock, Lynch, someone from Human Resources, and then someone she didn't know, a woman dressed in a smart black suit, with a sharp haircut, and scarlet-framed glasses.

"I'm Superintendent Suzy Russell, Kathy," she said, offering her hand. "I head up a new unit you may have heard of, the Digital Security Task Force. The acronym is DiSTaF—my idea." She gave a little smile.

"We've been helping Commander Lynch on the Bragg case, and I just wanted to meet you personally to thank you for the part you've played, and commiserate for all you've had to go through."

"Thank you, ma'am." Kathy was impressed—she seemed very confident, intelligent, focused.

Suzy Russell went on, asking her how she felt, whether she was being looked after, what she needed, listening to Kathy's answers with an empathy that made Kathy warm to her. She had a flat Midlands accent that made her sound practical and down-to-earth.

"I've also inherited this place for my sins," Russell added with a raised eyebrow, looking around the room. "The Met has had a role in the security of Pewsey for some time, simply because of the kind of patients who come here—the rich and famous—and the kind of unwanted attention they can attract. We've had to be a bit more proactive than just sending the local safety officer round to advise on locks and alarms. So I was concerned to hear that you'd seen an intruder in here while they were rounding up Bragg last night."

Kathy was disarmed by the way she said it—that Kathy had

seen an intruder, not just *imagined* she'd seen one, which had been everyone else's reaction.

"Yes, though everyone seems to think I must have got it wrong. I certainly was a bit groggy."

"Oh, we've got to take it very seriously. This man you recognized, Ned Tisdell, tell me about him."

"I only met him the once, by his canal boat near Little Venice, though he made a pretty vivid impression." She described the circumstances, and her later discovery that he had a record.

"Yes, I've got a copy of it." Russell took a file from her shoulder bag and took out Tisdell's police mugshot. "This is him, right?"

"Yes."

"Well, he's certainly not on the staff here. You noticed an ID card, didn't you? That's what bothers me. Did you happen to see the name on the card?"

"Sorry, no."

"The thing is, he would have needed that card to get through the security scanners to enter this place. But we've checked the scanner records and every entry is accounted for. To bypass the system he would have had to use some pretty sophisticated electronics."

"I see."

"There is one other alternative." Russell took a second photo from her file and showed it to Kathy. "This guy is on the staff here, and was on duty last night. He remembers meeting a patient in the corridor just before the alarm went off. To me he looks a bit similar to Tisdell. What do you think? Take your time."

Kathy stared at the picture. The resemblance was there, similar features but smartened up. "It does look a bit like him."

"The corridor lights were dimmed, weren't they? Do you think it's possible you were mistaken?"

Kathy's heart sank. "I suppose," she said heavily. "I suppose it's possible. I'm sorry."

"Don't worry." Russell briskly tucked the file back into her bag. "It's easily done. Better safe than sorry. Now look, you've been through a lot. You need to relax for a while and forget about work. Later on, when you're recovered, I want you to come and see me and I'll tell you about DiSTaF. I'm looking for people like you. But in the meantime, put your feet up and immerse yourself in a good book. Tonight, order yourself a glass of Moët before your dinner."

Kathy laughed. "I wish."

The superintendant departed, leaving Kathy feeling slightly bothered. Russell had been sympathetic and direct, and the explanation she'd offered for Kathy's false sighting of Tisdell was entirely plausible. Yet she couldn't shake off the vague sense that she had been very smoothly manipulated.

LATER, MICKEY SCHAEFFER AND Pip Gallagher, another detective from Brock's team, came to see her, carrying flowers, grapes, and her laptop. They spoke about how upbeat the atmosphere in the office was now, and how Lynch seemed like a changed man.

"They should have broken both the bastard's legs," Mickey said.

"What, they broke Bragg's leg?" Kathy said.

"Yes!" Pip cried. "Poetic justice, eh, after what he did to you?"

"No one's told me anything," Kathy said. "He put up a fight, did he?"

"Yeah," Mickey grinned. "He got a bit roughed up. He's in . . ." He stopped suddenly, bit his lip, then went on, "He's still in treatment."

Kathy looked at him. "What were you going to say, Mickey?"

"Nothing."

"He's not *here*, is he?"

Mickey frowned at the floor.

She stared at him in disbelief. "He is, isn't he?"

Pip said, "Is he, Mickey? I didn't know that."

"No one's supposed to know," Mickey conceded reluctantly. "I only heard it by accident. They figure this is the safest place. Don't worry, Kathy, he's in the secure wing. He can't get to you."

Kathy felt a sudden heave of panic. She took a deep breath, fighting down the nausea. More deep breaths. *Slowly*, she told herself. *Slowly*.

"Kathy, I'm sorry." Mickey sounded worried. "Just forget I told you, please."

"Forget!" she exploded. "Christ, Mickey, I'm not gaga. You think I shouldn't know a thing like that, that I'm locked up in the same building as the man who wants to chop me into cubes?"

"Kathy, Kathy . . ." He held up his hands. "Take it easy. It's all under control."

"That's what they said about the ambush at his house. Does Brock know this?"

"I shouldn't think so."

"Then how the hell do you know?"

"I told you, I overheard—"

"Bullshit! Who told you?"

Mickey sighed. "Kathy, if you tell them I told you it'll cost me my job. You've got to calm down, there really is no need to panic. I'll sit outside your door all night long if you want."

"Drop dead, Mickey."

He got to his feet, head down. "Yeah. Sorry."

They watched him leave, closing the door softly behind him, then Pip said, "Oh, shit. Do you want me to tell Brock, Kathy?"

Kathy took another deep breath, feeling the anger and panic subside. "No, better not. I don't want to lose Mickey his job"

When she was on her own again, Kathy studied the building plan mounted by the door of her room, showing the fire escape routes, and identified an extension to the main house marked *Secure Area*. It contained a cluster of individual rooms labeled *Ward S*, along with a larger suite called *Laboratories*. She went for a walk down the corridors and eventually found the place where a pair of doors gave access to the secure area. They were locked and bore a sign *Access for authorized staff only*. There was a scanner to one side of the doors, and a pair of cameras covering the area.

She returned to her room, powered up her laptop, and typed the name of the clinic into Google Earth. She studied the aerial view that came up on the screen, the house in its parkland setting beside the river and the precise geometric figure of the maze in which Bragg had been trapped. The closest part of the house to the maze was the secure wing, served by its own access road branching off the entrance drive. It would have been a short hop to bundle Bragg straight in there from the maze—or had he been processed somewhere else first and then brought back?

She zoomed out to take in more of the surrounding area of Richmond and Twickenham, and noticed a number of jetties and piers along the river where small craft and narrowboats were moored, most noticeably at Eel Pie Island, where there was a crowded boatyard.

She was interrupted by a knock on the door and a nurse came in carrying a tray on which stood a tall flute of champagne. "Compliments of Superintendent Russell," she said with a smile.

"Wow," Kathy said. "I must have done something right." She closed the laptop awkwardly with her one good hand and took the glass. "She mentioned that you have a secure wing here. I bet they don't get this sort of treatment."

The woman laughed. "Oh, I don't think it's that sort of secure—it's more for special patients who need complete privacy. But I've never worked there, they have different staff. Give me a ring if you want a refill."

Not reassured, Kathy sat by the window sipping her drink thoughtfully, then opened her laptop again to see what she could find out about DiSTaF. The Metropolitan Police Web site gave it a short entry, describing it as a specialist support unit. Its mission statement included the formulation of strategies for accessing and securing digital communications of all kinds for the Met, the acquisition and development of new digital technologies, the support of criminal investigations, and the shaping of digital policy. Kathy didn't see how she could contribute much to any of that, but still, it was flattering to be asked, or at least hinted at being asked.

In any case, she thought with a sigh, according to her doctor she wasn't going to be in a position to do much about it for months.

SEVENTEEN

THE FOLLOWING DAY KATHY told Dr. Partridge that she wanted to leave. He shook his head.

"Not yet. It's a nasty fracture and I'm concerned that a bump might mean we have to reset it. Aren't we making you comfortable enough here?"

"It's very comfortable, thanks, but I'm impatient to get home."

They compromised on one more day.

Brock visited soon after. They took a walk out into the grounds and into the maze, where a taped-off area of ruined hedges showed evidence of Bragg's capture.

"Have you seen him?" Kathy asked.

"No. So far Lynch has kept him under wraps."

"I heard he was hurt."

"Yes. Nothing too serious, unfortunately."

"I even heard a rumor that they were holding him here."

"Here? No." Brock frowned. "No, that can't be right."

"No, well, I suppose Superintendent Russell would have told me, but it did make me wonder, her coming out here."

"Suzy Russell? She came here?"

"Yesterday. She called in to wish me well. She seemed quite concerned about my imaginary sighting of Ned Tisdell."

Brock frowned, staring at the broken shrubs, then said, "As soon as they're satisfied with you here, Kathy, Suzanne wants you to go down to Battle and stay with her for a bit. Get out of London—fresh air, fresh scenery. What do you say?"

"That's kind of her. I remember the last time she looked after me, convalescing, and it did me good, but now I just want to go home."

"Well, the offer stands."

They strolled across the lawn and Kathy looked down the slope to the dark water of the Thames. "So we don't know where Tisdell has gone?"

"No."

"I've been watching the river from my room, waiting for his boat to appear."

Brock put his hand under her good arm and steered her back toward the house. "Change of scene, Kathy, that's what you need, as soon as you're fit to leave."

"Tomorrow," she said. "I'm checking out tomorrow."

And so she did, the following morning at ten thirty, as soon as Dr. Partridge had given her a final once-over and a list of things to avoid. "Don't go jogging, or try to drive, or travel in a crowded train, or get hopelessly drunk any time in the next month. Protect your shoulder like a newborn baby."

She smiled. She liked him. "Thank you, Doctor."

"Make an appointment on your way out to come back and see me in two weeks."

She did so and got them to call her a cab, leaving the Pewsey Hall grounds with a sense of intense relief. She gave the driver her home address in Finchley, but asked him first to drive along the river, stopping at the succession of piers and moorings she had seen on Google Earth. At each one she got out and checked the boats, asking anyone she saw if they remembered seeing a narrowboat recently, with the name *Venerable Bede*. Nobody had, and she was on the point of giving up when they came to the footbridge across to Eel Pie Island, where she could see the crowded boatyard.

She walked over to the island, her overcoat buttoned tight around her, limp left sleeve tucked into the pocket, and worked her way along the shore. Most of the boats were small leisure craft, but among them were scattered the long thin forms of narrowboats. She checked each of the elaborately painted names, but didn't see the one she was looking for.

At a boathouse she saw a man working on an outboard motor. He straightened, wiping his hands on an oily towel as she asked her question.

"*Venerable Bede*? He owes me money. You a friend of his?"

Kathy showed her police ID and he gave a grim smile. "In trouble, is he? Yeah, I thought as much when I saw him. I should have made him pay in advance but he said he needed to get some cash and I was soft-hearted. Gave him some diesel too."

"What name did he give you?"

The man consulted a thick date book of wrinkled pages. "Tisdell, Ned Tisdell. That mean anything to you?"

"Yes. So when was he here?"

More checking in the date book. "Arrived last Friday afternoon, then disappeared during Sunday night. When I arrived at dawn on Monday morning, *Venerable Bede* was already gone."

The day before yesterday, Kathy thought. "Any idea which way he was heading?"

The man shook his head. "He arrived from downstream." He pointed to the east. "But where he went, I've no idea. If you find him, tell him I want the seventy pounds he owes me."

As she returned to the taxi Kathy thought about the timing. Tisdell had arrived on Friday, after the Fantasyland explosion but before the ambush at Bragg's house, so there could be no way that he could have expected to find "Mrs. Bragg," or Bragg himself, at the Pewsey Clinic. And yet he was there, Kathy hadn't been imagining it. He had recognized her and fled, taking off on his boat into the night. The thing was incomprehensible. What did Tisdell have to do with Bragg? It seemed that only Tisdell could tell her that.

She made one more stop on the way home, at her local bookshop in Finchley, where she bought a guide to the inland waterways of the UK. She saw that there were two ways by which the *Venerable Bede* could have made its way from Paddington to Eel Pie Island: either west along the Regent's Canal to the junction with the Grand Union Canal at Hayes, then east to the River Brent and its connection with the Thames at Brentford, not far from Eel Pie Island; or, alternatively, eastward along the Regent's Canal to its end at the Thames on the other side of the city at Limehouse, the longer route. But where would Tisdell have gone now? He could have continued up the Thames to Oxford, and then north on the Oxford Canal to the Midlands, or back along the Grand Union to Leicester and the north, or down the Thames to Limehouse and into the River Lee system. And if he didn't want to be spotted, if he hid the name of his boat and didn't stop at a registered mooring, it was hard to see how, long and slow though he was, she could track him down.

Kathy sat at the window of her flat on the twelfth floor of her high rise, staring out at the familiar view across the city. Somewhere out there, below the lowering gray clouds, within that endless crust of buildings, the *Venerable Bede* might still be lurking, tucked into an unobtrusive canal basin perhaps, or chugging slowly out toward open country. She tried to picture it, the dark paintwork, the small windows, something stacked on the roof at the stern end—what was that? A couple of rusty fuel drums, she remembered, and beyond them a shapeless pile of stuff trussed up beneath a bright blue tarpaulin. A very bright blue tarpaulin that should be visible from the air . . .

She got on the phone to Zack's cell.

"Kathy! How are you? We've all been worried about you."

"Much better now, thanks, Zack. I'm back home, taking it easy. Listen, there's a little job you might be able to help me with. I'm trying to trace a boat that's somewhere on either the Thames or the Regent's Canal or the River Lee. I haven't got much to go on, but it's just possible that I could identify it from an aerial shot, and I wondered if you could access film that the helicopters of the Air Support Unit may have shot during the past seventy-two hours."

"Shouldn't be a problem. Could be a big job sifting through it all though."

"I've got nothing else to do. Could you send the relevant stuff through to my computer? Just those three waterways, nothing south of the river."

"What case number do I put it down to, Kathy?"

"Oh . . . do you have to?"

Zack laughed. "No, don't worry, I won't let D.K. Payne-in-the-butt find out what you're up to, whatever it is."

"Thanks, I'll owe you one."

THE FIRST DOWNLOADS ARRIVED on her computer the following morning and she immediately began to work through them. They were dated from the previous weekend and were mostly close-range clips from the helicopters' cameras of crime scenes in action—tracking a speeding car, searching open ground around which a couple of patrol cars were circling, observing a fire, a traffic pile-up, a crowd scene. There were occasional shots of the Thames, but none at all of the Regent's Canal, and no sign of a narrowboat with a blue tarpaulin on its roof. She kept working through the day and in the late afternoon, as she was about to take a break, came across a night sequence in which an infrared camera followed the white blob of a running man across a black screen. The picture jumped abruptly to the same figure running across a scene brightly illuminated by the helicopter's Nitesun searchlight, toward some sort of geometric pattern laid out on the ground. It was the Pewsey maze, Kathy realized suddenly; she was witnessing the cornering of Jack Bragg. She saw other figures running toward the maze, and watched as they all converged. Then the clip came to an end.

She rubbed her eyes and went out to get something to eat. When she returned she loaded up the film shot on Monday and Tuesday, working more quickly now as she skipped quickly through long sequences in which there were clearly no signs of a waterway. By midnight she couldn't focus any more, and went to bed.

She woke to find more downloads from Zack, and went back to work, trying to ignore her growing feeling that this was a waste of time. She finished the Tuesday film, then Wednesday, skimming faster and faster, then stopped for a quick lunch before moving on to the last set, taken the previous day, Thursday. The weather changed in rapid time across her screen, from dark morning to gray afternoon, brightening suddenly toward evening. Now the camera was gazing down at the towers of Canary Wharf, glinting in a golden light from the west. The view moved on to the broad shimmer of the Thames as it curled around Limehouse Reach, and panned over the enclosed pool of Limehouse Basin carved into its northern bank. This marked the eastern end of the Regent's Canal, she knew, the basin like a kind of mouth clamped onto the flank of the river. Kathy froze the image. Three long marina jetties lined with boats extended into the green waters of the lagoon, the most westerly jetty harboring the long pencil forms of narrowboats. One of them, tightly tucked into the pack, displayed a blob of blue at one end. Kathy zoomed in to the limit of legibility, and saw two shapes like fuel drums behind the blue rectangle. She checked the time on the image—it had been taken just twenty-four hours previously.

She shouldn't drive, of course, but her car was an automatic and she wasn't going to get anyone else involved, not until she was more certain. Slipping on her coat she made for the door, pausing at the last moment to grab her phone, a camera, and her extendable baton and stuff them into her pocket.

She headed south into the city, driving cautiously with her one good hand on the wheel, then east along Commercial Road to Limehouse, where she turned into the streets surrounding the basin. It took her a while to park and make her way down to the waterfront between the flanks of smart new apartment buildings that had been built around the old dock. The narrowboats were in front of her, ranged perpendicularly along each side of the jetty she had seen through the helicopter's lens. She hurried down the line, checking each boat, their names and roofs, and came to a halt at the end. No blue tarpaulin. The *Venerable Bede* wasn't there.

There was a marina office beneath one of the apartment blocks and Kathy went inside to inquire. An elderly man wearing a boating cap was sitting behind the counter, talking to someone on the phone, a leisurely conversation by the sound of it; he waved to acknowledge Kathy but kept on talking. She took out her police ID and thrust it across the counter. The man's eyebrows raised, he looked at her again, then said, "Anyway, love, have to go." He put down the phone. "How can I help you, officer?"

"A narrowboat by the name of *Venerable Bede*. I have information it was here yesterday. What can you tell me?"

"Hm . . ." The man consulted his computer, slowly pressing keys. "*Venerable Bede*, registered owner Edward Tisdell?"

"That's it."

"Arrived Tuesday evening, five ten, through the Limehouse Lock from the river; left two hours ago, at two fifty."

Kathy cursed herself for not phoning here before she left. "Where did he go?"

"No idea, sorry. He wouldn't have gone back out to the Thames or I would have spotted him." He pointed to a side window that gave a clear view of the lock on the short neck of canal connecting the basin to the river. "But there are two other ways out."

He took Kathy over to a large wall map and pointed to a corner of the basin. "That's the end of the Regent's Canal, and over on this side is the entrance to the Limehouse cut. He could have taken either, around Central London one way or out to the Lee Valley the other."

"How far could he have gone?"

"Not so far on the Regent's Canal—there are several locks on the way. You might catch up with him at Johnson's Lock or Mile End Lock with a bit of luck. No locks the other way till north of Bow, so he'd have got much farther."

Kathy was aware of the light beginning to fade in the late afternoon sky, and decided to go for the shorter bet, on the Regent's Canal. She thanked the man and ran back to her car.

The GPS took her to Stepney, where Ben Jonson Road crossed the canal, her view blocked by the high walls on each side. She drove up onto the pavement where a footpath led down to the canal side, overlooked by new apartment buildings on both banks. Ahead of her the canal passed through Johnson's Lock and continued into the distance between banks of trees still carrying the last of the red and golden leaves of autumn. There was a chill in the motionless air, and patches of mist were beginning to form over the surface of the water. There wasn't a boat in sight.

She headed north, to Mile End Road, from which she should

be able to see the next set of locks, and parked on a side street. From the bridge she could look down on the canal toward a weir and set of lock gates. In contrast to the road, roaring with evening rush-hour traffic, the canal, seen through the iron railings and half-shrouded now in fog, seemed eerily silent and secretive. And deserted. Kathy gave a sigh of resignation. The Lee Valley, then, although it would be dark by the time she got there, and her chances of finding him then seemed slight.

As she was about to turn away, a movement caught her eye, and she looked down to the water directly below the bridge and saw the prow of a boat slowly emerge from the shadows. Gradually its length appeared, a narrowboat, and spread across its roof a blue tarpaulin. Kathy felt a buzz of excitement. There was a figure standing at the tiller as the stern came into view, a man, Ned Tisdell, guiding the boat toward the lock.

Kathy ran back to the side street on which her car was parked and followed it down to the towpath alongside the canal. The *Venerable Bede* was ahead of her, steadily chugging toward the black lock gates. On the other side of the water the new buildings of the Queen Mary London University campus were brightly lit, but on this side the canal ran alongside the comparative gloom of Mile End Park, and Kathy jogged down to a clump of trees not far from the lock and watched as Tisdell maneuvered to the bank.

It was an elaborate process, Kathy realized, to take a boat through the lock, especially if, like Tisdell, you were on your own. Having tied up at the shore he walked to the lower gates and put his weight against the long balance beam of the paddle to open them. He returned to the boat and steered it into the lock and tied it up again, then climbed out and closed the lower gates. He was carrying some kind of tool, she saw, a windlass, which he took to a pedestal near the upper gates, inserted it, and began to turn. Kathy heard the rush of water as the lock began to fill to the level of the upper reach, lifting the boat slowly up to the new towpath level.

Kathy wondered what to do. If she approached him on her own he might turn violent, and she was in no state to fight back. Yet she had no grounds for calling for assistance—he would deny having been in the clinic and she wouldn't be believed. Yet she couldn't just let him slip away into the night. She needed answers, and it seemed to her that the only weapons she had were surprise and persuasion—and, if worst came to worst, the ASP baton in her pocket.

She watched Tisdell heaving on the upper beam to open the gate, and while he was engrossed in doing this, she ran out from her cover to the stern of the boat and dropped down into the well. The rear doors were open and she slipped inside.

EIGHTEEN

KATHY WAS BECOMING FAMILIAR now with the interiors of narrowboats, and the way in which their owners adapted them to fit their lifestyles. She had expected Tisdell's to be as chaotic and disorganized as he had appeared, but the opposite was the case. In fact, the more she took it in—the table set for a single meal, the clothes hanging on a rack to dry, the computer on a small workbench—the more she got the impression of an obsessive neatness and symmetry underlying everything. She worked her way down the length of the boat, checking cupboards and storage chests as she went. Around her she heard the groans of the boat as it settled at the new level in the lock, and then felt the throb and lurch as Tisdell began to move it forward into the canal, followed by silence as he cut the engine and tied the boat up once again so that he could go back to close the upper gates.

She had returned to the living area at the stern, and was searching under the cushions of the built-in seating along one side when she heard his feet thump on the steel plate and his sudden shout, "What the fuck?"

She looked up and saw him standing at the bulkhead staring at her, the bent steel bar of the windlass gripped in his hand. Then he must have recognized her, for he took a sharp breath and went pale, and put out a hand to steady himself against the door frame.

"What do you want?" he croaked. "You've come to arrest me, haven't you?"

"Not necessarily," Kathy said, speaking more calmly than she felt. "Depends what you have to tell me. Come in and sit down. We need to talk."

Remarkably, Tisdell complied, edging over to a chair and sitting down, still gripping the iron bar. His body gave off a rancid smell of sweat from his exertions at the lock.

"Let's start with the Pewsey Clinic," Kathy said. "What were you doing there?"

He gave a little grunt and fixed her with a defiant glare.

"Do they do animal experiments there? Were you back to your old tricks, Ned?"

"No!" The denial was explosive and seemed credible.

"Okay, what about Jack Bragg? What do you know about him?"

She was met by a look of total incomprehension. "Who?"

"Well if it wasn't for animals or Jack Bragg, what were you doing there?"

"They do the devil's work."

"What sort of work?" She stared at his face, trying to interpret the tangle of calculation and madness. Then she lifted her right hand, showing him the pad of flesh between thumb and forefinger. His eyes widened immediately. "The mark of the beast, Ned? Do they have something to do with it?"

He didn't reply, mouth tight.

"And how did you get in there? How did you get through the security?"

Again he didn't answer.

"I could arrest you for trespassing."

The resistance seemed suddenly to drain from Tisdell. His

shoulders sagged and he shook his head wearily. "Yes," he whispered. "Why don't you?"

Kathy still couldn't read his reactions. They seemed inscrutably childlike, as if he were responding to a wholly different framework to her own.

The light had almost gone now and Kathy could hardly make out his expression. She looked around for a light switch when there was a sudden thump at the rear of the boat. Tisdell started and rose cautiously to his feet. He moved to the stern doors, pushed them open, and looked out. He gave a shout, "Hey!" and came flying backward into the room to land in a heap at Kathy's feet. She looked down and saw his face covered with dark blood, and as she took this in she heard the slam of the doors closing and the rapid clatter of metal against metal. She ran to the doors and found them locked, and as she stood there rattling the handle she gulped a sudden lungful of diesel fumes. She coughed and turned back to Tisdell's prone body on the floor.

"Ned!" She tried to cradle his head, seeing the deep gash above his right eye, and felt inside his mouth for his tongue to stop him choking. He gave a splutter and a groan, and his face was suddenly lit up by a flash of light and a tremendous roar. Kathy turned to see flames running down over the portholes in a blazing cascade, and more rushing across the floor toward them. She leaped to her feet, grabbed Tisdell's arm, and tried to drag him away from the approaching fire, at the same time feeling her lungs burn with scorching smoke. Tisdell inhaled it too, and responded with some deep instinct that sent him scrambling to his feet. Together they ran down the tube of the boat away from the flames and smoke to the bedroom at the bow. Tisdell pushed ahead of her and tried to open the bow doors, but they too were jammed tight from the outside. He threw his shoulder against them hopelessly, then turned back and stared at Kathy. She closed the bedroom door, aware as she did so how light and flimsy it was. Even as she formed the thought she saw trails of smoke creeping under the bottom edge. She grabbed a blanket from the bed and packed it against the foot of the door.

"Is this Bragg's gang?" she demanded.

Again that blank look on Tisdell's face, turning to open-mouthed panic as flames reflected in his wide eyeballs. Kathy turned to see dribbles of fire running down over the window. The tarred roof would be alight, she guessed. She could feel the heat growing around them. They would be roasted alive inside this metal pressure cooker.

"Where's that steel bar you had?" she asked urgently, but he just shook his head, gazing at his empty hands. He'd dropped it somewhere, too late now. She looked around desperately and could see nothing of any substance that she might use to break the heavy window. Then she remembered the baton in her pocket. She tugged it out and pressed the release button for it to telescope out, and swung it hard against the glass. There was a loud crack and a jagged star appeared. She swung again and again, and the glass splintered and burst. She kept hacking at it until the frame was clear.

"Now," she panted. "Get yourself through there."

"I can't," he wailed. "It's too small. I'll get stuck."

"Only one way to find out. Hands above your head."

She pulled a stool beneath the porthole. Tisdell mounted it and gingerly pushed his arms through the opening, then his head, his shoulders, and then he was stuck. She heard him scream and imagined burning tar showering down on his head as she pushed at his backside. And then suddenly he kicked her in the chest and burst through, plummeting out onto the flickering surface of the dark canal.

Kathy slipped off her coat, stepped up onto the stool, and tried to work herself through the opening with her one good arm raised above her head, but even as she did it she realized it wouldn't work—she would have to take the other arm out of its sling and lift it vertically alongside the other. She hesitated, biting her lip in anticipation of the pain, then raised her hand. An excruciating jolt shot through her as she ducked her head and threw herself at the hole, squirming through and out into space. A shock of freezing water smacked her and she surfaced spluttering, good arm flailing, and went down again. Then she felt someone grab her by the collar and pull her up. It was Tisdell, swimming strongly now, pulling her through the water away from the burning boat. She did what she could to help, kicking and beating at the water with her good arm while the other dragged helplessly at her side.

Then they were at the bank, a dark spot beneath a clump of trees, and Tisdell was trying to haul her up over a stone curb and onto the grass.

"Quick, quick," he was gasping. "Gotta move, gotta hide."

He was right, of course, but all she could think about was the terrible pain in her shoulder that flared with every movement.

"Whasamatter?" he gasped as he half dragged, half carried her toward a clump of bushes.

"Collarbone . . . broken."

"Fuck."

They collapsed together into a dense rhododendron bush and crawled into the darkness. Gasping they turned and saw, through a screen of dripping leaves, the boat burning like a giant Roman candle in a tower of flame.

After a few minutes they heard the howl of fire engines, and Tisdell said, "We've got to get away from here. Can you walk?"

"Of course I can bloody walk," she snapped, teeth chattering now with cold. "There's nothing wrong with my bloody legs." Then she added, "Thanks, Ned. I don't think I could have made it to the bank without you."

"Don't mention it," he mumbled. "You got me through that window."

They clambered out onto the grass and began to move away across the park, Tisdell running, Kathy trying to keep up, gasping as every step sent an intense stab of pain through her shoulder. Finally she was reduced to a walk toward the figure of Tisdell waiting impatiently in the far shadows. When she reached him she saw that he was whispering hoarsely into a phone, in an argument by the sound of it.

When he hung up she said, "How much farther?"

"To the end of the park. Just a little way."

It seemed much farther than that. They came to an embankment and had to go right down to the canal towpath to cross beneath the railway, then on across another long stretch of parkland to go under a road bridge and into yet another park.

"Nearly there," Tisdell panted. He pointed to some industrial buildings ahead and they emerged out onto a bridge over the neck of a branch waterway coming off the Regent's Canal. "The Hertford Union," he said. "Connects to the Lee Navigation at Hackney Wick."

He was peering out into the foggy darkness, and Kathy, following his eyes, thought she could make out the dim shape of another boat moored a little way off.

They went down to the towpath and approached the vessel cautiously, Tisdell looking over his shoulder and all around before he stepped up onto the stern and tapped at the door. As he held out his hand to help her, she made out the name painted on the side of the boat: *Aquarius*. The door opened and Anne Downey stuck her head out. She nodded at Tisdell and turned to look at Kathy, her expression full of doubt and misgiving.

Downey stepped back to let them in, then went back out to

look around before shutting the door firmly and turning to stare at them. "Tell me what happened, Ned," she demanded.

He told her as best he could, stumbling from one incident to another, and several times she impatiently stopped him and made him explain more clearly. Finally she said, "So how did they find you?"

"I don't know."

Downey looked from one to the other, the two of them standing there shivering in their wet clothes. "You must have led them there," she said to Kathy.

"No."

"She's hurt, Anne," Tisdell said.

She held up a hand. "How did you find Ned?"

Kathy took a deep breath and spoke in a rush, feeling as if she might pass out before she was finished. "I broke my collarbone in a police operation last Saturday night, and was taken to the Pewsey Clinic for treatment. While I was there I bumped into Ned in the corridor. I couldn't figure out what he'd be doing there, and when I told the others they insisted I must have imagined it, but I knew I hadn't. So when I left the clinic I went down to the river and discovered that his boat had been moored at Eel Pie Island. It was gone by then, but I spent a couple of days searching through camera footage until I spotted the boat at Limehouse Basin. So this afternoon I drove down there and then followed the Regent's Canal until I caught up with him. I wanted to find out what he'd been doing at Pewsey, and what he had to do with Gudrun Kite's disappearance."

She came to a stop, then mumbled, "Can I sit down?" She half fell onto Downey's sofa, wincing as the pain bit again.

Downey, implacable, said, "You must have told somebody where you were."

"No." Kathy shook her head. "I didn't call anyone."

"Then they were tracking you."

"Who?" Kathy burst out angrily. "Who is this *they*?"

"Where did you leave your car?"

"Near the Mile End Road bridge over the canal."

"What about your phone?"

"I lost it in the boat."

There was silence for a moment, the two women staring at each other, then it was broken by Tisdell.

"Anne, she saved my life. I wouldn't have got out of that boat without her. You have to help her. Can't you give her some painkillers or something?"

The anger and mistrust in the doctor's eyes faded a little and she sat down beside Kathy and said, "Show me."

They eased Kathy's top off and Downey carefully removed the dressing on her left shoulder. She sucked in her breath, frowning. Kathy looked down and saw that the stitches had burst open, and pieces of white bone were visible in the gaping wound.

"Who did this?" the doctor asked.

"A killer called Jack Bragg." She looked carefully at the doctor's face, which showed no reaction. "You know of him?"

Downey shook her head, then got up to fetch her medical bag. "Should I?"

"Well it's a hell of a coincidence that Ned turned up just as we were capturing Bragg in the grounds of the clinic."

Downey pulled on surgical gloves. "But that was Sunday night. You said you got this on Saturday night."

Kathy explained how they'd laid a trail for Bragg to follow to the clinic, after he had attacked her.

"Sounds as if it's the clinic that's brought you all together, not Bragg," Downey said, and Kathy thought that made sense. Downey told Tisdell to fetch a cup of water then peeled some pills from a foil and handed them to Kathy. "Take these and I'll do what I can to clean you up. But you're going to need some serious work done on this shoulder."

Kathy clenched her teeth as Downey dabbed at the wound, then, as she applied a fresh dressing, Kathy said, "Ned told me he went to the clinic because they do the devil's work there. What did he mean by that?"

Anne Downey met her eyes for a moment, then looked away.

"Is this to do with Gudrun Kite's death?" Kathy asked. "I want to find out what really happened to her. I've met her father, who's devastated by her disappearance, especially since he lost his other daughter, Freyja, in a hit-and-run accident earlier this year. But . . ." she paused, reading the expression on Anne Downey's face, ". . . you knew that, didn't you?"

Downey said nothing.

"Listen, you just said I need my shoulder patched up again, so I'd have every reason to go back to the Pewsey Clinic. Perhaps I could help find what you're looking for there. But I'd need you to tell me what that is. Why are you being so damned cagey?"

The doctor hesitated, then said, "I just don't know what to say to you, Inspector Kolla. I think I'll have to get advice from someone more experienced in the ways that you people work." She frowned, taking out her phone, then said, "Strictly speaking you shouldn't drink with those pills, but after what you've been through we might make an exception. Ned, give Inspector Kolla some whiskey while I make a call." She got up and went through the galley to the other end of the boat, closing the door behind her.

She was away a long time, during which Kathy gratefully gulped down a large Scotch. Tisdell had pulled off his sweater and arranged it and Kathy's top in front of the wood-fired heater around which they sat, soaking up the warmth. Finally the door opened and the doctor returned. She sat down facing Kathy, looking grave.

"I'm going to trust you with something precious, something you must agree to tell no one about. Will you promise?"

"Anne, how can I—?"

"Promise!" the other woman insisted, and Kathy, seeing that she had no alternative if she wanted to pursue this, nodded. "Yes, all right, I promise."

Downey opened her right hand, and Kathy saw that she was holding a credit card. She handed it to Kathy, who turned it over and shrugged. "A Visa card? So?"

"It's not a Visa card, although it looks exactly like one. It's what Ned used to enter the clinic. It's programmed to clear you through their security systems without leaving any record of your entry. With this, you can get into any part of the building."

"How did you get hold of this?" She looked at Downey. "Was it Freyja? No? Gudrun then, the computer whiz, she made it for you, didn't she?"

The doctor didn't reply, but Kathy was sure she'd hit the mark. "All right, so what would I be looking for?"

"There's a secure area there. The card will get you inside. We believe that they carry out certain procedures there."

"Operations? Like what?"

Downey hesitated, then shook her head. "You may find evidence there of unusual medical procedures performed on animals, and humans—documentation, films."

"And?"

Another hesitation. "One of the doctors there, a surgeon, came from South Africa, where he was working in the prison service. There was a scandal—he'd been carrying out experimental procedures on the convicts. It was covered up and he left the country and came to work at Pewsey."

Kathy stared at her, a queasy feeling in her stomach. "Not Dr. Partridge?"

"No. His name is Viljoen, Carl Viljoen."

"And how do you know this?"

"My friends are good at uncovering secrets on computers."

"I see. You'd better tell me how I can contact you." But again the doctor shook her head.

"Someone will get in touch with you when you leave the clinic. It's best you forget that you've seen me, or Ned. You can't drive. I'll call you a cab to take you there. But we'd better move your car—they'll be checking all the vehicles in the area. Do you still have the keys?"

Kathy felt in her pocket. They were still there. She unfastened the car key and said, "Where will you take it?"

Downey thought. "Your place would be best. Where do you live?"

Kathy told her. "Just leave it in the front and put the key in my mailbox." She also still had her wallet in the pocket of her jeans and she tucked the Visa card inside it, and Ned helped her to pull on her top, then an old green Barbour jacket that Anne Downey gave her. They stepped out of the boat onto the towpath and Downey pointed to a gap in the buildings lining the canal.

"Go up to the street. The cab will pick you up there. Do you have money?"

Kathy nodded and they shook hands.

"Good luck," Downey said. "Whatever happens, don't let them get that card."

"How shall I return it to you?"

"Just destroy it when you're finished."

"There's someone I need to call," Kathy said. "Can I borrow your phone?"

Downey shook her head one last time. "I'm sorry, Inspector, you're on your own." She turned on her heel and Ned Tisdell followed her back to her boat.

THE TAXI ARRIVED AFTER ten minutes and drove Kathy across the city to Richmond. She stepped out at the front entrance to the Pewsey Clinic with a deep sense of foreboding. The onion dome loomed above her in the darkness, mocking her with its absurd self-confidence. The bizarre architecture now seemed like camouflage, a mask for a secretive institution where the wealthy—and the police—brought their secrets.

As the crunch of the taxi's wheels on the gravel drive faded into the fog, the door opened and a man in the uniform of the clinic's security staff said, "Why, Mrs. Bragg, what a surprise."

Kathy began to correct him, then stopped and said, "I've had an accident with my shoulder. I'm afraid I'm going to need some help."

The man peered beyond her into the darkness, then said, "Dear me. You'd better come in."

A nurse was called and took her into a consulting room, where she looked in consternation at the state of Kathy's clothes as she helped her peel them off.

"What on earth happened to you?"

"A stupid accident," Kathy said. "I slipped and fell in the park, into a pond." It sounded ludicrous.

"There's a smell on your clothes, of burning . . ." The nurse removed the dressing and stared in horror at the state of Kathy's shoulder. "Heavens! I'll call Dr. Partridge. Don't move." She rushed out of the room. Kathy sat motionless beneath the bright fluorescent light, feeling overwhelmed by a reaction of weariness.

PARTRIDGE MUST HAVE LIVED nearby, for he arrived in less than fifteen minutes. By then Kathy was more presentable, wiped down and dressed in a hospital gown. He examined her shoulder, then checked the rest of her. There was an extensive graze on one arm, and an angry sore on the other. He peered closely at it.

"Is that a burn?"

Kathy shrugged and the doctor gave her a look of concern. He checked her eyes, then probed her scalp.

"I don't think I hit my head," she objected. "I'm fine, really."

He took no notice, scrutinizing. "Well," he said at last, "I really don't know what you've been up to, Mrs. Bragg."

"I'm not . . ." she began, then swallowed. Her throat felt scorched from the fire. She started again. "Is Mr. Bragg still here?"

"Mr. Bragg?"

"Yes, I heard that he was here too, in the secure wing."

Partridge looked at her. "We need to give that shoulder another X-ray. Come along."

"Couldn't you check the computer?" Kathy said over her shoulder as the nurse led her away. "See if he's still here?"

After they'd taken the X-ray Kathy sat alone for a while, until Partridge reappeared with a woman in a white coat, an anesthetist. "We're going to have to do some more work on that shoulder, Mrs. Bragg. We'll give you something to help you relax."

Kathy began to object, but Partridge leaned over her and murmured, "Mr. Bragg is not now, nor ever has been, a patient at Pewsey, Mrs. Bragg. Now just breathe deeply and relax."

She felt a prick in her hand and, after a brief moment of resistance, surrendered to the feeling of calm that enveloped her.

NINETEEN

BROCK WALKED DOWN TO his local newspaper stand and took the Saturday morning paper to the café next door, where he ordered a breakfast of poached eggs on toast and a pot of tea. It had been another frantic week and he was glad to have the weekend off. He scanned the front page. There were more allegations of illegal phone hacking, more WikiLeaks revelations, a stabbing murder in Streatham, and a fire on a boat on the Regent's Canal— see page six for details. He turned to page six. Students at Queen Mary London University at Mile End had called emergency services to a fire on a canal boat moored opposite the campus. By the time the fire department arrived the fire was so intense that the boat was reduced to a burned-out shell. Investigators were trying to determine the cause of the blaze and could not yet identify the owner or confirm whether anyone had been on board the vessel, which was described as a fifteen-meter-long narrowboat.

Brock wondered if Kathy had read the report. He hadn't seen her since she had been released from the Pewsey Clinic— when was that? Tuesday, he saw her, four days ago. He pulled out his phone and dialed her mobile, and got an odd message about the number not being "in service." Her home phone invited him to leave a message, which he did, asking her to call him. Then he rang the office and spoke to the duty officer, who did a quick search and came back with the contact details of the police investigating the narrowboat fire. They couldn't tell him much more than was in the newspaper report. Forensics were scouring the ashes inside the boat but so far had found no human remains. It was suspected that an accelerant had been used to start the fire. So far there was no indication of who the boat had been registered to. Brock left his number and asked to be kept informed of progress.

Kathy woke to see sunlight glimmering around the edges of unfamiliar venetian blinds. No, they were familiar, she remembered now: the Pewsey Clinic. She tried to sit up and found that her left arm was bound firmly to her side and thickly wrapped in some kind of bandaged padding. When she reached with her right for the glass of water on the cabinet beside the bed she saw that there was a dressing on the burn on her forearm. She wondered what else they knew about her by now.

There was a button beside the glass and she pressed it. In a moment a nurse appeared.

"Good morning, Mrs. Bragg. How are we feeling this morning?"

Without waiting for a reply she was clipping Kathy's fingertip to a machine and taking notes of the readings.

"Did we sleep well?"

"Mm, thanks. What time is it?"

"Almost midday. Are we hungry?"

Yes, she was hungry.

"Something light to start off? Omelette? Smoked salmon? Dr. Partridge looked in earlier but decided not to disturb you. I'll let him know you're awake now."

She opened the blinds and Kathy realized that she was in her old room, and remembered her sense of foreboding when she arrived.

"Where are my things?"

"Your clothes are being cleaned, and your wallet and keys are in the bedside drawer there, but you didn't seem to have brought anything else. We didn't find a phone or handbag."

"No, I came over in a bit of a rush."

"Would you like me to contact anyone for you?"

Kathy thought about that. She imagined Brock's consternation if she told him where she was, his need for explanations, and the possible stir he might create at headquarters. That was what bothered her most, that Payne and Lynch would get to hear of her misadventures with Ned Tisdell and put a stop to her investigations before she'd found out more about Anne Downey's claims. "No, it's all right. A bit of peace and quiet will do me good."

The afternoon passed slowly. Dr. Partridge came and expressed satisfaction with the operation he'd performed the previous evening, but warned her that her collarbone could tolerate no more challenges. "Next time," he said, "you'll be permanently disfigured." He contorted his shoulder to give an impression of the hunchback of Notre Dame.

She watched a little TV, then got out of bed and found she was steady enough on her feet. Through the window she watched branches swaying in the wind, but inside the clinic everything was quite still. She sat on the seat by the window and thought about Ned Tisdell and Anne Downey, and tried to imagine what they and Gudrun Kite had been up to. Not long before her accident, Freyja Kite had met Tisdell in Cambridge. They had both previously been interested in animal welfare—was that what this was really about? Anne Downey's talk of mysterious procedures on animals and humans? She would have to check if Downey's name was known in that connection.

They brought her an evening meal, and afterward the nurse came with some pills—antibiotics and something to help her sleep. She palmed the sleeping pill and swallowed the rest, then went to bed.

Some time after midnight she got up and arranged a pillow and a cushion from the window seat to imitate her sleeping figure in the bed. She shrugged on a dressing gown and took her wallet from the bedside cabinet, with the Visa card inside, and cautiously opened the door. The corridor was deserted, the lights dimmed. She followed the route she had previously taken to the door of the secure unit without meeting anyone, swiped the card at the scanner and pulled on the door. It opened silently, then closed behind her as she moved quickly away down the corridor inside.

There was a different atmosphere in here. The air was cooler and tinged with a chemical smell, as if the area was served by a separate air-conditioning system, and the surfaces were harder and more sterile, plastic-sheet flooring instead of carpet, no artworks on the walls. To Kathy's right were the doors to the four individual bedrooms she had seen on the building plan, each with a small vision window and security scanner lock. She looked into the first room, and by the faint glow of a night-light made out an empty pillow. She moved on, peering through the second window, and then she froze, seeing Jack Bragg sitting on the edge of the bed, fully dressed, one hand gripping an aluminum crutch. He had been staring at the floor in front of him, as if deep in thought, but now, almost as if he had registered her presence on the other side of the door, he began to raise his head and she ducked away, heart pounding. She moved quickly to the next room, then the next; they were both empty. Across the corridor she saw a door to what she remembered from the plan was a larger room, and at the same moment she heard a woman's voice from somewhere farther down the corridor, then another replying. They seemed to be coming her way, and she quickly swiped her card across the scanner in front of her and pushed open the door.

The room was in darkness, and colder than the corridor. She closed the door silently and stood by the vision panel. Two nurses walked past outside. When they had gone she took a deep breath, tasting a sharp chemical tang. Looking around she saw in the dim light from the door panel that she was in what appeared to be an operating theater, with large lights suspended over two steel tables. There was a bench down one side of the room, and across the far end she made out the handles and doors of a row of stainless-steel cabinets, each with a small panel of glowing digital symbols with the same reading, 3°C. They reminded her of something, somewhere she'd been, and then it came to her— Sundeep Mehta's pathology suite, the cadaver room.

She went over to the cabinets and tugged on the handle of the first. It opened with a soft pneumatic whoosh to reveal a long storage container inside. It was big enough to contain an adult corpse, much larger than was needed for its present occupant, which appeared in the poor light to be a small child curled up on its side, its body shockingly covered in dark hair. Like a monkey. Then she realized that it was a monkey, a small dead primate.

With an unsteady hand she closed the container and went to the next.

A man's voice made her jump. It sounded so loud that she thought he must be there in the room with her, but when she spun around there was no one. He gave a laugh, and she realized that he must be standing right outside the door. She shrank back against the wall until she heard his voice move away, then went over and peered cautiously out, seeing two men, big bulky figures with shaved heads, now standing outside Jack Bragg's room. Dressed in black leather jackets and jeans, they didn't look like clinic staff, but it seemed they had some kind of authority, for one of them swiped a pass across the door scanner and they went into Bragg's room.

After several minutes the door opened again and they reappeared with Bragg. One of them, a barrel-chested man with a battered boxer's face, had a supporting hand on Bragg's arm as he struggled to walk on his crutch, while the other, with a bodybuilder's thick neck, followed with Bragg's bag. They began to move back along the corridor the way they had come, toward the mortuary where Kathy was hiding, but then Bragg said something and pulled his arm out of the man's grip and turned to go the other way, toward the connecting door to the rest of the clinic. The two men exchanged a glance then took hold of him again, steering him back, protesting, along the corridor.

Kathy waited a couple of minutes, then, when no one else appeared, she slipped out. She paused to look into Bragg's room to check that it was empty, then continued to the security doors. She swiped the panel and pulled the door open, and stepped out, straight into the path of a nurse, who jumped in surprise and stared first at Kathy, then at the security door closing behind her.

"Mrs. Bragg! What are you doing?"

"I couldn't sleep. I thought a walk would help."

"But what were you doing in *there*?"

"Oh, I just noticed that the door was partially open and I was curious. Nothing to see though."

The nurse looked at her doubtfully. "We'd better get you back to your room. Come along."

Kathy obediently walked beside her and tried to say good night at the door of her room, but the nurse insisted on coming in, frowning as she took in the cushions arranged beneath the bedclothes. She told Kathy to sit in the armchair by the window and left the room, returning in a moment with a security man and another man Kathy didn't recognize—a doctor, going by the white coat and stethoscope. They stared at the bed, then came over to Kathy. The doctor looked hard at her.

"How did you get into the security area, Mrs. Bragg?"

Kathy registered a South African accent.

"Is that what it is? I didn't know. I just felt like a walk and came to a door that wasn't quite closed and I went in. I looked around, but it was chilly in there and I came back out and bumped into the nurse."

The doctor felt her pulse, smelled her breath, examined her eyes and fingers, checked her dressings.

"You were given a sedative at nine thirty, yes?"

"I was given some pills, yes."

"But you couldn't sleep?"

"No. I had some pain in my shoulder, but not enough to call a nurse. And I wanted to make a phone call."

"There's a phone beside your bed."

"Oh, right. Well I'd like to make that call now, please."

"To your doctor?"

"No, a friend."

"Wait," he said, then got to his feet with a nod to the guard, and left the room.

"It's urgent," she called after him, but he didn't look back.

Kathy took a deep breath and went over to the window. Nothing was visible in the darkness outside. She paced back across the room, then, when she was alongside the bed, quickly picked up the phone and began keying in Brock's home number, but immediately the guard was at her shoulder, tugging the phone out of her hand and cutting off the call.

"Just be patient, Mrs. Bragg," he said.

The doctor appeared at the door. "We're giving you a new room. Come."

They made their way along the corridor, and Kathy realized that they were heading toward the security area. When they reached its door she said, "No, I don't want to go in there."

"It's all right," the doctor said soothingly. "This is where we can give you complete care and rest."

She wanted to tell him that she had already seen one outcome of that complete care and rest in the cold cabinet, but he had moved behind the guard, who was holding her good arm tightly. She said, "Please let go of me," and suddenly, surprisingly, he did release his grip and at the same time she felt a sharp prick in her upper arm. She looked down and saw the doctor's hand withdraw the needle from the fabric of her gown, and immediately she began to feel dizzy. "No . . ." she mumbled, and felt her knees buckle.

TWENTY

BROCK SPREAD THE SUNDAY papers across the breakfast table while Suzanne, sitting opposite him in the thick robe she'd bought him last Christmas, sipped her coffee.

"Who made that phone call during the night?"

"Don't know. It only rang a couple of times. Private number." He picked up a slice of toast and munched on it.

"You don't think it could have been Kathy?"

He looked up at her. Sometimes it was uncanny the way she read his mind. "I did wonder."

"Anything in the papers about the canal boat?"

He shook his head. "I'll try her number again."

He felt Suzanne's eyes on him as he dialed, still without success. He left another message on her home phone and got that same strange reply from her mobile number. "What does 'not in service' mean?"

He reached for a drawer in the wall unit and fished around for an old address book in which he had the number of the superintendent of Kathy's high-rise. "Jock," he said, "David Brock here, Kathy's boss. Good morning. I haven't been able to contact Kathy for a few days. She's not answering her phone. Have you seen her?"

"Not recently, but her car's parked outside in the fore-court."

"How long's it been there?"

"Since yesterday morning. It wasn't there on Friday."

"So she returned home Friday night?"

"Must have."

"Okay, thanks. Would you let me know if you see her?"

He put down the phone and Suzanne said, "She probably needs a bit of time on her own, after what she's been through."

THE FOLLOWING MORNING, MONDAY, Brock held his weekly workload review meeting with his team at Queen Anne's Gate. He had received a cryptic message from Commander Lynch to make space for possible unspecified surveillance operations that might arise during the week, and he went through their case list, briefing Phil, the action manager, on priorities. When they had finished, Brock spoke to Bren Gurney, asking if he had heard from Kathy.

"Not since she left the clinic," Bren said. "I got the impression she just wanted to drop out and recover after what happened."

"Did she talk about going away?"

"Not to me."

Later he phoned Kathy's friend Nicole Palmer, who worked in criminal records, but she hadn't spoken to Kathy since Thursday. At lunchtime he was sharing a plate of sandwiches with Phil, going over his figures, when he got a call on his cell. It was Jock, from Kathy's block of flats.

"She's just come in, Mr. Brock," he said, sounding hesitant. "Car dropped her off. I wasn't sure whether to ring, but you asked me to let you know."

Brock felt a great wave of relief, somewhat surprised to realize just how anxious he'd been. "That's good, Jock. I appreciate it. I'll give her a ring."

"Thing is . . ."

"Yes?"

"Well, she's not her usual self."

"How do you mean?"

"Reckon she's drunk as a skunk."

"What?"

"Three sheets to the wind."

"Drunk?"

"Aye, unsteady on her feet. And she asked me how Trudy was today."

"Trudy?"

"My old cat. It's over a year now since she died."

Brock remembered. Jock's cat had been killed by someone trying to intimidate Kathy, its mangled corpse stuffed into her mailbox. No matter how much she might have had to drink, there was no way that Kathy would have forgotten that.

"I think I'd better come over, Jock."

"I think maybe you should."

WHEN HE GOT TO Finchley, Jock was waiting for him in the lobby and accompanied him up to the twelfth floor. Brock rang the doorbell of Kathy's apartment and they waited. He knocked and still there was no response.

"Maybe she's in the shower," Jock suggested doubtfully.

"Have you got your master key?"

Jock took a bunch of keys out of his pocket and inserted one in Kathy's door.

She was lying sprawled on the sofa, wearing an old green jacket that Brock hadn't seen on her before. He went over to her and registered how pale and still she was, her eye sockets dark with shadows like bruises. Her clothes looked freshly laundered and the bandages and straps on her left arm were clean. He knelt beside her and put his cheek to her nostrils and was relieved to feel the coolness of a breath. He could smell no booze, but there was an unmistakeable antiseptic odor about her.

"Kathy," he said, and gave her a little shake.

She murmured softly but didn't open her eyes.

"Is she all right?" Jock said.

"She's sleeping." Brock stared at her pinched features, thinking. Finally he got out his phone and rang Sundeep Mehta's cell number.

"Sundeep?"

"You're lucky you got me. I'm between rooms."

"You're busy?"

"It's Monday, old chap. Monday is always busy. The Grim Reaper works overtime on weekends. What's the problem?"

"It's Kathy. She disappeared for a few days and now she's back and she's passed out. I think she's been drugged."

"Call an ambulance."

"Yes, I could do that."

There was a moment's silence, then the pathologist said, "But you thought of me instead. Why?"

"Something's going on here that I don't understand, Sundeep. I'd value your insights."

There was a sigh, then, "Where is she?"

"At her apartment in Finchley."

"I'll be at least an hour. Are you sure you shouldn't call an ambulance?"

"I will if there's any change. Thanks, Sundeep."

"Give me the address."

When he rang off Brock turned to Jock and asked him to bring Sundeep up when he arrived. "I'll stay with her, Jock.

Thanks for your help. Oh, incidentally, the car that brought her here, did you get a look at it?"

"A black Merc, tinted glass. But I didn't think to get its license-plate number, and I couldn't see the driver. I was more concerned with helping Kathy."

While he waited, Brock gazed around the room. It didn't look as if Kathy had been there for days—the congealed plate in the sink, a bowl with a couple of wrinkled apples, a curdled bottle of milk in the fridge, a copy of last Thursday's newspaper. Kathy's laptop was on the table in front of the window, surrounded by pages of scribbled notes, a London street atlas, and a guidebook to the inland waterways of the UK. He began to examine the notes. They appeared to be working through a series of recent dates, listing times with London place names against them, with the most recent on top, the final entry being for the previous Thursday, *16:12.33–16:13.07, Limehouse Basin.* At the bottom of the pile the earliest sheet contained a cell phone number. Brock dialed it.

"Hello?"

He didn't recognize the voice at first. "Who is that?"

"That you, boss? This is Zack."

"Zack . . . What did Kathy phone you about last Wednesday?"

There was a hesitation. "I heard you were asking about her, boss. Is she all right?"

"I sincerely hope so, Zack. So what's the answer?"

"She, er, asked me not to mention it to anyone. She wanted me to get hold of surveillance tapes from the ASU helicopters for her."

"What was she looking for?"

"A boat, she said. She wanted shots of waterways, to see if she could spot it."

"And did she find it?"

"No idea, boss. Sorry, I wanted to tell you . . . Is she in trouble?"

"Just keep this to yourself, Zack. What job did you assign it to?"

"None. I did it on the quiet."

"Let's keep it that way."

Brock rang off and turned to see Kathy stirring on the sofa. He went to her, helped her to sit up, and fetched her a glass of water. She gulped it down.

"Oh," she said, blinking, looking around. "Home. Just a dream."

"What was, Kathy?"

"Cold . . . dark."

"You feel all right now?"

"Mm." She nodded, closed her eyes and the glass fell from her hand, tipping water across Brock's lap.

He propped Kathy up with cushions and was rubbing himself down with a tea towel when the doorbell rang. Sundeep stared quizzically at his wet trousers.

"Small accident," Brock said. "She woke briefly. Very groggy. Come in."

Kathy began to come round again as Sundeep was taking her pulse. "I haven't had one of these in ages," he said cheerfully. "A live patient, I mean. Maybe I've lost the knack." He gently lifted her eyelids, examining her pupils, then made her follow his moving finger. After a series of other tests he asked her if he could remove her top. She mumbled, "Okay," and Brock helped him. The pathologist carefully examined her skin, pointing to several tiny red marks on her right arm, and opened the dressings to examine the wounds beneath.

When he'd finished he sat back. "She's recovering from heavy sedation. She's had a number of injections, and been dressed for some minor burns and abrasions, I'd say professionally."

"By a doctor?" Brock was thinking of Anne Downey.

"Or a nurse or paramedic." Sundeep gazed at Kathy thoughtfully. "I'd like to take some blood and run toxicology tests."

"Yes," Brock agreed.

"Don't mind me," Kathy murmured, eyes still closed.

"She's on the mend." Brock smiled at her.

"Stabbed in the back," she whispered.

"What?"

She winced and eased her shoulders. Sundeep got to his feet, walked around behind the sofa, and got her to lean forward so that he could examine her back. He found a small dressing beneath the left shoulder blade, which he peeled away to reveal an angry red puncture.

"Another injection?" Brock asked.

"Looks like it. A big one. Like an epidural, but not quite in the right place." He got a new dressing from his bag and applied it, then took some blood samples from her good arm. He asked her about allergies and tried to get her to tell him what had happened.

"Jack Bragg," she said, eyes still closed. "Broke my shoulder."

"And after that?" Brock urged her, but she shook her head drowsily.

"Give her time," Sundeep said. "She needs to sleep. I'll give you some antibiotics and painkillers for when she wakes up."

"These injections," Brock said, "how old are they?"

Sundeep shrugged. "They look fresh to me. The last twenty-four hours."

Together they helped take Kathy through to her bedroom and got her into bed, then Sundeep left. Brock took out his phone and put a call through to the contact number he had for the investigating officer of the narrowboat fire.

"I was about to phone you, sir," the man said. "I think we may have a name for that boat. Wondered if it meant anything to you."

"*Venerable Bede*," Brock said. "Owner Ned Tisdell."

"Right! How did you know?"

"Just a guess. How did you find out?"

"A marina manager at Limehouse Basin phoned us to suggest the name after he heard about the fire. He said that boat was moored in the basin for three nights last week, leaving on Friday afternoon at two fifty, which could have placed him at the Mile End Lock at about the right time. He also told us that a female police officer called at his office later that afternoon looking for the boat. Mean anything, sir?"

"Yes, that would have been one of my officers. We wanted to speak to the boat owner about a suspicious death."

"I see. So the officer didn't find the *Venerable Bede* then?"

"No. Is there any other identification for the burned-out boat?"

"It conforms to the registered dimensions of the *Venerable Bede*'s license, but otherwise no."

"No trace of Tisdell?"

"We're satisfied now that there are no human remains among the debris. We think that the owner must have moored the boat and left it for a while, during which vandals set it on fire."

"Vandals?"

"Yes, there's been a spate of break-ins and vandalism of boats on the Regent's Canal in recent months. We've got a pretty good idea who the culprits are. We think this is one attack that got out of hand. Our informant at Limehouse Basin remembers that the boat was carrying drums of fuel on its roof, and possibly cans of paint, and the fire department thinks that's what caused such an intense blaze. If the boat wasn't insured, Tisdell is probably happy to keep out of the way and let us dispose of it. I see he's got a record, by the way."

"True enough. So, case closed then?"

"Looks like it."

Brock phoned Bren at Queen Anne's Gate, and gave him an outline of what had happened. "Put out an alert for Tisdell, will you, Bren? Hospitals, airports—and see if we can get a fix on him through his phone or credit card." He hung up and went back to Kathy's bedroom, where she was lying, dead to the world.

"What have you been up to, Kathy?" he murmured. "Why couldn't you let me know?" She had been convinced that she'd seen Tisdell at the Pewsey Clinic, he guessed, and determined to track him down to prove it. So where had she been since Friday night?

He took up his phone again and rang Suzanne at her shop in Battle, and told her what had happened. She was just about to close up for the evening and said that she'd come straight up to London, but Brock suggested she wait until the morning. "I'll stay with her tonight," he said, "make sure she's okay. There's not really enough room here for three of us."

He waited by Kathy's bedside, checking every few minutes to make sure that she was still breathing, so still was she. Finally he got up to make a cup of coffee and when he returned Kathy opened her eyes.

"Hi," she said faintly. "Have you come to visit me? Did the nurse let you in?"

"You're at home now. You've had a rough time. How do you feel?"

She swallowed painfully and winced as she moved her left arm. "This damned thing hurts." Her voice was stronger now, but hoarse.

"Yes, I've got something for that."

He fetched a glass of water and helped ease her up into a sitting position against her pillows. There was a little more color in her face and her mind seemed more alert. Brock gave her some of Sundeep's pills.

"How long have I slept?" she croaked, squinting at the closed curtains, the bedside light. "Is it Thursday night?"

"It's Monday night, Kathy."

"What?" She looked at him incredulously. "No . . . that's not right."

"I'm afraid it is," Brock said. "What's the last thing you remember?"

She frowned, thinking. "The clinic . . . then I came home. Wednesday? Thursday?"

"You came home from the clinic last Wednesday. Nicole phoned you on Thursday, but nobody's seen you since then. We were worried about you."

She took a deep breath and stared up at the ceiling. "I remember being back here, in the apartment. Bored."

"You were trying to track down Ned Tisdell's boat, from the ASU film that Zack got you."

"Oh yes . . . Yes!" Her face brightened. "When I left the clinic I got the cab to stop on the way home at mooring places on the river nearby." She bit her lip with the effort of remembering. "I found out that Tisdell's boat had been moored at Eel Pie Island on the night that they caught Bragg—the night I saw Tisdell in the clinic. You see? I was right! He *was* there!"

"Well done," Brock said gently. "So when you got home you started looking for him on those aerial shots."

"Yes. I remembered that his boat had a blue tarpaulin on its roof. It took me ages, but eventually I spotted him at Limehouse Basin. So I went down there. He'd already left a few hours before, so I played a hunch that he had gone back up the Regent's Canal. Ooh . . ." She paused and closed her eyes, rubbing her forehead.

"Headache?" Brock asked.

"Yes. Just suddenly came on."

He waited until she relaxed again and sank her head back against the pillows with a sigh.

"You found him then, at Mile End Lock."

"Did I?" Her breathing seemed to have become more labored.

"Yes. There was a fire. You burned your arm."

"Oh . . ." She gulped. "Don't know, but I can taste it."

"What?"

"The smoke . . . burning paint . . . it's in my throat. I can't get rid of it."

"You don't remember the fire?"

She shook her head, face creased as if in pain.

"There's plenty of time," Brock said soothingly, although his chest was tight with impatience.

A little later Sundeep phoned. "I've got some preliminary results."

"That was very quick," Brock said.

"I took the samples in myself and stood over them while they did the tests. They're only generic profiles at this stage, but they should be accurate enough. She's been given a cocktail of sedatives. We've identified propofol, plus a benzodiazepine . . ."

"Rohypnol?" Brock said.

"Something like that, plus something else, a beta blocker, probably propranolol. It's used to treat anxiety and panic, but currently there's research going on to see if propranolol can be used to erase the memory of trauma, if it's administered immediately after the event."

"To wipe out a memory?"

"Yes."

"Does it work? Is it permanent?"

"We don't know."

When Brock finished the call he saw that Kathy had slipped

175

back into sleep. He switched off her light and went back to the living room and watched the evening news. He felt hungry but didn't want to leave Kathy alone, and phoned Jock, who said he could order in some takeout. While he waited he switched on Kathy's laptop and checked its record of recently opened documents. In Google history he found that she had been searching the British Waterways Web site, and looking up references to the Pewsey Clinic, and newspaper reports on Jack Bragg. And that was the thing, he thought later as he sat chewing his tandoori chicken—what the hell did those things have to do with one another?

He felt tired, and dozed off for a short while on the sofa before blinking suddenly awake. Getting to his feet, he washed the dishes in the sink and began taking a closer interest in his surroundings. He remembered his first visit to this apartment—how many years ago?—the Marx Sisters case, the first time they'd worked together, when he'd felt obliged to visit her to apologize in person for doubting her integrity. He had brought a bunch of flowers—blue cornflowers—a gesture which she had quite rightly treated with withering contempt, although she was only a sergeant and he a chief inspector. He smiled at the recollection. He had realized then that she was someone special, someone he would have to take account of, and she hadn't disappointed him. In fact, he realized, she had reinvigorated his career, bringing a new freshness and dynamic to his life. Was that why he hadn't seriously thought about quitting along with Sharpe and the others? Because life without Kathy would be too dull?

In all those years she didn't seem to have accumulated much, he thought, looking around, compared to the stuff that had ended up in his place. Was that because she was too single-minded about her job, or because she was on her own? He examined the collection of CDs in the cupboard. All the Norah

Jones albums were there. "There are times when only Norah Jones will do," she'd told him once. He picked the first, *Come Away with Me*, and slipped it into her CD player.

He stood at the window, listening to the title track, looking down at the ribbons of lights threading out across the city. Her laptop was on the table in front of the window, and he wondered about emails. It was pure chance that he'd seen Zack's number on the desk and found out about her search for Tisdell's boat. What might there be in her emails? Perhaps Tisdell had tried to contact her. All the same, he felt guilty clicking on the icon and opening up her mail.

Junk, a magazine subscription reminder, several emails from her friend Nicole (one with recipes, another coyly recommending a dating site a friend had used, a third suggesting a theater visit), more junk. He almost missed jgreenslade@mcgill.ca.

Hi Kathy,

How are you? Are you sure the old man liked his coffee machine? I thought it was a good idea of yours, but his letter of thanks finally arrived this morning (doesn't he like emails?) and it seemed very formal and cold. Am I wasting my time? I wish I could chat to you on the phone, but I can never catch you in, and I don't like to call your cell in case you're in the middle of a crime scene or something. The first snow fell last night and I thought of you. You've got to come to Montreal for Xmas! You'd love it.

Don't work too hard,

John.

Brock felt his face burn. Kathy had been keeping up a correspondence with his son! Well, why shouldn't she? And it was she who had suggested the coffee machine for his birthday. *The old man . . . formal and cold.* He hadn't meant to be. He just hadn't found it easy, coming to terms with an unknown adult son. And what sort of email was this anyway? A love letter?

He took a deep breath and stared out of the window into the darkness. What business was it of his?

He closed down the laptop and tried to concentrate on Norah Jones.

TWENTY-ONE

SUZANNE ARRIVED EARLY THE next morning, carrying a bag full of groceries, health drinks, muffins, and coffee. Brock, who had slept uncomfortably on the sofa, had heard Kathy cry out from time to time during the night, but now she seemed to be well rested and alert, and mobile enough to go to the bathroom and wash up.

She returned and sat with them at the table, which Suzanne had cleared and set for breakfast. Kathy shivered and Brock picked up the old green Barbour jacket slung across the back of a chair. "Is this yours?" he said.

She stared at it. "No. I've never seen it before."

"You were wearing it when you came home yesterday." He felt in the pockets, but there was nothing there. For some reason it seemed familiar, but he couldn't place it.

Suzanne went to find Kathy a sweater, and Brock, munching a muffin, said, "When we spoke last night, you said the last thing you could remember was going to Limehouse Basin to find Ned Tisdell."

Kathy nodded.

"You had your car with you?"

She frowned, thinking. "Ye-es . . . yes, that's right, I drove out there."

"And then?"

She stared at the wall, sipping her coffee. "Um . . . It was late afternoon. I drove north, I think."

"Following the Regent's Canal."

She nodded.

"To Mile End."

"Really?"

"There's a lock there. It was getting dark. On one side of the canal there were university buildings, and on the other a park. You found Tisdell's boat moored just past the lock, remember?"

She screwed her forehead in concentration. "I'm not sure."

"There was a fire, Kathy. Last night you said you could still taste it."

She swallowed. "Yes."

"Tisdell's boat was on fire. Remember?"

"Yes." Her voice was a whisper.

"Did you see who did it?"

Kathy put her cup down carefully and raised both hands to her face. "Not sure." She shook her head, breathing in short gasps. Suzanne returned with a thick sweater and wrapped it around her shoulders, giving Brock a warning look.

"Was Tisdell on the boat? Did you try to help him?"

Kathy began rubbing her bound arm. "I can't remember, Brock. I just can't remember!"

"It's all right, Kathy," Suzanne said. "Just relax, eat your breakfast. It'll all come back to you when you're good and ready."

But Brock wasn't so sure about that.

THEY HAD AGREED THAT Suzanne would stay with Kathy until she felt well enough to travel to Battle, where she could recuperate and hopefully recover her memory. Brock left them to go back to Queen Anne's Gate, stopping on his way out to ask

Jock if there were any cameras around the apartment building. Jock said he didn't think so, but as Brock drove out of the front parking lot he came to a crossroads with traffic lights, where he spotted a camera mounted on one of the poles.

When he got to the office he found Zack and handed him a note of the location of the camera and the times and vehicles he was interested in. Zack nodded and handed Brock an unfamiliar form to fill in.

"What's this?"

"New procedures, boss. DKP. He seems to be keeping a particularly close eye on me all of a sudden."

Brock grunted and scribbled his signature across the form.

"The case number, boss?" Zack pointed to the box.

Brock hesitated, then put down the number for Operation Intruder.

"Is Kathy okay?" Zack asked.

"Yes, she's fine. Just needs to take it easy."

Brock went up to his office, his heart sinking at the sight of an enormous stack of papers waiting in his in-box. He hesitated at the coffee machine for a moment before switching it on, then took off his jacket and set to work. His secretary, Dot, came in soon after with more files for his attention.

"What's going on, Dot?" he complained. "I turn my back for a few hours and I'm inundated with paper."

"It's the new regime," she said, "to make us all more lean and efficient. How's Kathy?"

"She's had a rough time. Suzanne's taking her down to Battle to recuperate."

"She wasn't . . . interfered with, was she?"

"No, but she's lost her memory of what happened to her."

"And I suppose you slept on her sofa last night, keeping an eye on her."

Brock looked at her in surprise. "How did you know that?"

She raised an eyebrow, looking pointedly at his crumpled clothes. "You should keep a fresh shirt in the closet here. Shall I pour your coffee?"

"Thanks, I'd appreciate it."

"And Mr. Payne has requested an urgent appointment. Wouldn't say what for."

Brock groaned, checked his watch. "In an hour?"

"All right. I'll bring in some flowers. Cheer the place up a bit." She returned ten minutes later with a large vase of oriental lilies, voluptuous blooms with pollen-laden stamens. Brock eyed them with surprise, then got back to his paperwork.

When the task auditor arrived, looking spruce in a sharp suit and high-collared gleaming white shirt, he looked around Brock's office with an appraising eye and went over to the window. "Great view up here, David."

David? Brock gritted his teeth. "Yes. I'd offer you coffee but our machine's broken."

A grin formed on Payne's mouth, as if he expected things to be broken up there. "Don't worry. I won't take much of your time. See you've got a bit of paperwork to catch up on."

He took a seat and opened the file case he was carrying. "I just wanted to ask you to persuade your team to follow due process, David. I've been trying to impress the point on them, without much success."

"Due process?"

"Yes—specifically, charging resources to the correct cost centers. A number of your team seem to be using Intruder as a bottomless well to pay for unrelated activities."

He drew some papers out of the case and handed them across to Brock, who flicked through them. They were photocopies of request sheets from Bren to the UK Border Agency and Zack to the Air Support Unit, citing the Intruder case number.

"So?"

"As far as I'm aware, these were not activities sanctioned by the Intruder resource manager."

"I authorized them," Brock said.

Payne looked puzzled. "Does Commander Lynch know?"

"Not yet."

Payne took a deep breath. "Can you tell me what activities these relate to?"

"I'll discuss that with the commander."

"'You'll find that difficult at the moment, David. Mr. Lynch is very much tied up with new developments—you've probably heard whispers from the other team commanders."

Brock hadn't.

"And he really doesn't have time for trivia. So it would be much easier if you could clarify it for me."

Brock considered him for a moment. Payne gazed back, then frowned suddenly, snatched a tissue from his pocket, and sneezed explosively.

"Sorry," he gasped.

Brock pushed a box of tissues across the desk at him and said, "DI Kolla was badly injured during the attempt to arrest Bragg at his home, as you well know."

Payne sniffed. "Yes, of course."

"Later, she was receiving treatment at the Pewsey Clinic on the night Bragg was arrested. That night she identified what she thought was an intruder in the clinic, although I and everyone else thought she must have been mistaken. When she returned home she made some further inquiries and succeeded in establishing the intruder's identity. That's what these requests relate to. It's an ongoing matter."

Payne gave another violent sneeze.

"Are you all right?" Brock asked.

"Hay fever," he muttered, looking accusingly at the lilies. "But DI Kolla is on sick leave."

"Yes. She's a very dedicated officer. Don't worry, I'll let you know if we foresee any major resource implications."

"I shall have to check this with the Intruder budget."

"Of course." Brock got to his feet and showed Payne to the door. After he'd gone Brock said to Dot, "Nice flowers. Did you know he suffers from hay fever?"

She gave a little smile. "I think I heard something. Was there a problem?"

"Not at all." Then he added under his breath, "Lilies that fester smell far worse than weeds."

Later Brock got a call from Zack. "That CCTV check you asked me to make, boss?"

"Yes?"

"Mr. Payne has put it to the end of the line. They tell me it could take a week."

Brock swore under his breath.

"Oh, and you left some papers down here. I'll send them up."

Brock couldn't remember any papers, but an envelope arrived soon after. He opened it and tipped out three photographs. The earliest, taken at eleven sixteen on Friday night, showed Kathy's car being driven through the crossroads, though it wasn't possible to make out the driver. The other two showed a black Mercedes saloon with dark tinted windows passing through the junction at one ten on Monday afternoon and again five minutes later on its return, its license plate clearly visible. There was also a handwritten note in Zack's writing; the car was registered to the Pewsey Clinic in West London.

A MOTORCADE OF MAROON Rolls-Royces was drawn up at the front doors when Brock arrived. He parked unobtrusively further down the drive and watched an elderly man wearing an Arab keffiyeh being helped slowly out of the clinic and into the lead car, while a large group of relatives looked on. When the cars moved off Brock went to the entrance and asked to speak to the director, showing his police identification. After a ten-minute wait he was shown into an office where a man seated behind a large antique desk was reading from a document in front of him, an expensive-looking gold fountain pen poised in his raised fist. The man set the pen down carefully and came around the desk to shake Brock's hand. He looked magisterial, the sort of clinic director that international invalids would feel reassured by, but he also appeared puzzled.

"Detective Chief Inspector Brock? Vernon Montague. I don't believe I've had the pleasure."

"I work for Commander Lynch in Homicide and Serious Crime Command."

Montague's face didn't betray whether the name meant anything to him.

"I'd appreciate your help in clearing up a small matter."

"Oh?"

"A colleague of mine, Detective Inspector Kathy Kolla, was a patient here last week, under the name of Bragg."

"Ah yes. During the *drama*." He raised an eyebrow. "Pewsey isn't usually the setting for such events, but of course we're happy to assist the police in any way we can."

"I believe she returned here a couple of days ago."

Montague's look of bemusement returned. "Really? She dropped in on us, did she?"

"No, I mean she was admitted as an inpatient here for a second time."

The director hesitated, considering Brock. "Is that what she told you? Is this some kind of personnel matter? A compensation claim?"

"No, no, nothing like that. The fact is that DI Kolla has completely lost her memory of what happened to her between last Friday evening and yesterday afternoon. I'm trying to find out. She appears to have had some kind of medical attention during that time, and I think it's possible that she came here."

Montague shook his head doubtfully and returned to his desk, where he stabbed the keyboard of his computer. "No," he said decisively. "She hasn't been back, either as an in- or out-patient, since she was discharged last Wednesday."

"I see." Brock rubbed his beard, frowning. "That is odd . . ."

"Sorry we can't help," Montague said, getting to his feet again.

". . . because she was dropped off at her flat in Finchley at one ten yesterday by a car registered to the clinic. This is its number." He placed a note on the desk. "Maybe you could find out how that came about."

Montague's eyes widened marginally. He picked up the note and read it. After a long pause he said, "Wait here," and marched out of the room.

Brock waited. After five minutes a secretary came in and asked if he would care for a coffee. He said yes. He drank it slowly, and waited some more. Finally the director swept back in, followed by a man in a white coat with a stethoscope tucked into its pocket. They drew up chairs in front of the desk and sat facing Brock.

Montague spoke. "It appears that Ms. Kolla's second visit, to which you referred, was unplanned and unexpected, and its details have not yet been entered into the computer. This is Dr. Partridge, who treated her on both occasions. John?"

Dr. Partridge cleared his throat, his posture stiff like a witness giving evidence in a courtroom. "Kathy arrived here unaccompanied at about eight o'clock last Friday night. I was at home at the time, but the duty nurse phoned me immediately and I came straight in, arriving perhaps fifteen minutes after she presented herself. She appeared to be in a state of shock, largely incoherent, her clothes soaked through. She couldn't explain what had happened to her, and when I examined her I found that she had several fresh abrasions on her arms and legs, some bruising to her head and elsewhere, and, most disturbingly, that she was no longer wearing the support for her injured left arm and that her collarbone fracture appeared to have been aggravated, as a result of which she was in considerable pain. We cleaned her abrasions and arranged for her to have an X-ray, from which it was obvious that the fracture would have to be reset. We did that and kept her here until yesterday morning, when she insisted on discharging herself. I arranged a car to take her home."

"Were you happy with her condition when she left?" Brock asked.

"I was concerned about her mental confusion and the possibility of concussion, and I wanted her to stay longer, but I would say we'd done as much for her as we could in the time available. I advised her very strongly to give her left arm and shoulder complete rest for at least a month, and to follow the recovery program we set out for her previously."

"What drugs did you give her while she was here?" Brock took out a small notebook and clicked a ballpoint.

"Sedative, antibiotic, painkiller . . ."

"What drugs specifically?"

Partridge glanced at Montague, and said cautiously, "I'd have to consult my notes."

Montague was more forceful. "No, I'm afraid not. Dr. Partridge has already told you as much as we can share with a third party—more than we should, in fact. Of course, if Ms. Kolla wants to come in and speak to him herself, he'll be happy to see her. Is there anything else?"

"How did she get here on Friday evening?"

Dr. Partridge said, "The nurse told me that a taxi dropped her off at the front door. That's what the security officer who opened the door for her said."

"Is he here?" Brock asked.

Partridge shrugged. "Night shift."

"You can phone and speak to him this evening when he's on duty," Montague said magnanimously. "And now, if that's everything . . ."

"Inspector Kolla reported seeing a man by the name of Ned Tisdell here in the corridor of the clinic on the night we arrested Jack Bragg on the grounds."

"Yes, she mentioned it to one of our security guards," Partridge said, "who told me that Kathy had insisted he check our records, but they found no mention of that name."

"Would you mind checking again for me, Mr. Montague?" Brock said. "It could be important."

Montague reluctantly went back to his computer and did a search. "No," he said finally. "No one of that name."

Brock showed them a copy of Tisdell's police photo, but they both shook their heads. "Well, thanks for your help," he said as they rose to their feet. "I've heard quite a bit about Pewsey over the past couple of weeks. I hadn't realized before about your connection with the Met. I wonder if I could have a quick tour?"

Montague stopped short. "A tour?"

"Yes. I'm interested in your facilities."

Montague blinked at him, and Brock waited.

"Very well," Montague said at last. "Dr. Partridge had better get back to his work, but I'll have my PA take you around."

Brock was shown out to a seat in the entrance hall, where he waited until a smartly dressed young woman with an identity tag around her neck came to him and introduced herself as Emily, Mr. Montague's PA. She showed Brock around the facilities of the general clinic, many of which he had seen from his visits to Kathy, before they came to the doors to the secure wing. Brock pointed to the warning notice and said, "What's in there?"

"That section is off-limits to guests. It contains the laboratories, operating theater, and high-level care suites."

"Is that where they held Jack Bragg?"

"Jack Bragg the gangster?" Emily looked startled. "He certainly wasn't held here, Chief Inspector."

"Ah, just an ugly rumor," he said. "Can we go in?"

"We don't normally allow visitors, but the director did tell me to give you every assistance, so . . ." She smiled and swiped her card and they went inside.

Staff were changing the bed linen in one of the rooms, and Emily said, "We've just had a very distinguished client from one of the Gulf states stay with us."

"I think I saw him leave. Everything go well?"

"Oh yes. It invariably does. The level of care here is extremely high."

She took him to the laboratories and imaging rooms, all immaculately ordered, and on their return Brock pointed to a pair of doors with circular vision panels.

"That's our secondary operating theater."

Brock peered through the window and asked to be let in to the deserted room. For some reason it felt to him more like a morgue than an operating theater. He noticed what looked like four chilled cadaver storage drawers at the far end of the room.

"Do they ever experiment on animals at the clinic?" he asked.

"I believe they did once, but not any more."

Brock went toward the stainless-steel drawers, stooping to look at their digital temperature readings.

"Oh, you'd better not touch," Emily said, but he was already pulling open the first drawer, then each of the others in turn, all empty.

"Looks like your success rate can't be that invariable if you need four body cabinets," Brock murmured. He smiled at her look of consternation. "So, is there anything else I should see?"

"No," she said hurriedly. "You've seen everything now."

As they made their way back to the entrance hall, Brock caught a momentary glimpse through an open office door of the director, Montague, haranguing someone, gesturing with a pointed finger. For a second Dr. Partridge was visible, his face as white as his coat, shaking his head.

THAT EVENING, BROCK DROVE down to East Sussex, to Suzanne's small house just off the main street of Battle. Kathy seemed more herself, Suzanne told him at the front door, although she was still agitated at not being able to remember what had happened to her in those blank days. "I told her to put it out of her mind," Suzanne said. "It'll all come back when it's good and ready, I said. Do you think that's true, David?"

"Sundeep has been pestering the experts, but nobody seems to know."

"Can't they give her an antidote or something?"

"Apparently not. As you say, we just have to let things take their course. Where is she?"

She was sitting with Suzanne's two grandchildren in the room overlooking the back garden, playing gin rummy with one hand. They finished their game and the children went off to do their homework while Suzanne opened a bottle of wine and went to the kitchen, leaving Brock and Kathy to talk.

"How are you feeling?"

"The arm's a bit sore, but mainly I'm feeling angry, because I still can't remember anything of what happened. It's like a bit of my brain has been stolen. What did I do in those three days? What was done to me?"

"I've made a start. We got the license plate on camera of the car that dropped you home yesterday. It was registered to the Pewsey Clinic, so I went there and spoke to the director, Vernon Montague. You've met him?"

"No, I don't think so."

"He thinks he's a better actor than he is. His first reaction was that you might drag them into some kind of compensation claim, then when I told him you'd completely lost your memory he denied that you'd been there. Then I told him about identifying their car and he discovered that you had been there after all. Your doctor was called in, Partridge, and he said you turned up on their doorstep in a taxi at eight on Friday night, soaking wet. We're trying to trace the taxi now. Ring any bells?"

"Friday night?" Kathy frowned, shaking her head. "I don't remember."

"About two hours after Ned Tisdell's boat was reported on fire."

"I caught a taxi to the Pewsey Clinic and was there for almost three days and I can't remember a thing?" Kathy rubbed her head in frustration.

Brock had gone to Mile End that afternoon and taken photographs of the burned-out boat and its surroundings, and he now downloaded the images onto Kathy's laptop and showed them to her.

"That's the *Venerable Bede*?" she said, astonished. "It's completely gutted. Nobody could have survived that."

"According to Partridge you were soaking wet when you arrived at the clinic, although it was a dry night. Could you have gone into the canal?"

Kathy closed her eyes with a groan. "I don't know . . . I just don't know."

"It's all right, Kathy. Don't worry, we'll work it out. There were no human remains on the boat, and we've got an alert out for Tisdell. We'll get there in the end."

"I don't understand any of this, Brock—Tisdell and Bragg and the clinic. And Gudrun . . . I had a dream about her today. After Suzanne gave me lunch I lay down and had a sleep, and I saw her. I was in her boat, and it was very dark. I was desperately searching for her, and I came across four steel drawers. I opened one and there she was inside, laid out, bright pink, dead."

"Four steel drawers?" Brock murmured.

"Like in Sundeep's mortuary. I suppose it was all mixed up in my mind."

"There's a secure area at Pewsey. Did you ever go in there?"

Kathy pondered. "I remember noticing it on the fire-escape plan in my room, and wondering what it was all about. But there's a security door that only staff can pass through."

"Yes."

"There was something else. That old green jacket I was wearing when I came home. I remember that Anne Downey had a similar one."

Now Brock remembered the doctor standing at the back of her boat in a shabby old coat, arms folded. "Yes. We should get hold of her too."

Kathy sighed. "But what's the point, if I can't remember anything?"

LATER THAT EVENING, BROCK got a text message from headquarters. Team leaders were to cancel their appointments for the next day and attend a briefing with Commander Lynch at eight a.m.

TWENTY-TWO

THE ATMOSPHERE WAS MILITARY, Brock thought, with a large map of the southeastern counties projected on a screen facing them, the enemy positions marked with circles and code numbers. Staff officers scurried around supplying the demands of the senior planning team, who sat beneath the map with their heads together, while the junior officers waited, studying the individual briefing pouches they had each been handed on arrival.

"All right!" Lynch barked, and everyone sat up to attention, the room abruptly silent. "Thanks in large part to intelligence which has been gained from the interrogation of Jack Bragg in the last few days—and nights—we are now in a position to execute over two hundred arrest warrants in eight locations in and around London."

There was a murmur of surprise across the room—at the scale of the operation and that they had been able to get such information from Bragg.

"This will be one of the biggest operations mounted by the Met in recent years. The range of offenses we shall be pursuing is extensive, including drugs, firearms, extortion, corruption of public officials, and fraud. Each of your teams has been assigned a series of targets and you will be working in close cooperation with borough commands whose briefings you will be attending later this morning. The raids will commence at oh-two-hundred hours tonight. This is, hopefully, the final stage of Operation Intruder."

They broke up to be briefed on their individual roles, Brock and Bren sitting down in a corner of the room with one of Lynch's planners. As they got to the end Brock became aware of Lynch standing silently at his shoulder, observing. When he looked up, Lynch nodded his head and Brock got to his feet. They went to a table where cups were set out for coffee and helped themselves.

"What's this about Kolla?" Lynch said.

Brock gave him a summary of Kathy's disappearance, and Lynch shook his head.

"She didn't strike me as that stupid."

"She was trying to prove a point," Brock said. "No one believed her when she said that she'd seen Tisdell at the Pewsey Clinic the night Bragg was captured. Now it seems she must have been right, yet the clinic denies any knowledge of him, and how could he have got in without a pass?"

"The fact that his boat was in the neighborhood doesn't prove anything."

"There's no possibility that he was working for us, is there?"

"*Us?* Of course not. You tell Kolla that she's on sick leave and to stop this nonsense. And you concentrate on Operation Intruder."

"How did you get Bragg to talk?" Brock asked. But Lynch was moving on to one of the other tables.

OPERATION INTRUDER WAS MILITARY in its execution too, in the coordination of many different units, the precise timing of their actions and the overwhelming effectiveness of their results.

By dawn the following day Brock's team, exhausted but elated, had carried out seven separate house raids within their area and made eighteen arrests without injury to anyone involved. As similar results came in from the other teams and the first sensational reports appeared in the media, stories began to circulate about the extraordinary performance of Commander Lynch over the past week, his tireless attention to detail, his ability to go without sleep for long periods, and his almost superhuman drive. By the time the scene-of-crime and interview teams moved in to mop up and the scale of the victory became apparent, military nicknames began to attach themselves to him in both the ranks and the press reports—Monty, Napoleon, or Stormin' Fred, according to taste. After the arrests and interviews came the court appearances and a blizzard of paper, all managed with similar efficiency, although exhaustion was now setting in. By Saturday afternoon the ranks were thinning out, skeleton crews taking over, and Brock began packing up. He folded the camp bed in his office on which he'd caught short spells of sleep during the previous days and, feeling soiled and weary, made his way out into the cool evening air and walked around the corner to St. James's Park station and caught the underground to Blackfriars, and then a train on the suburban line out to Dulwich. When he got home he phoned Suzanne, had a long scalding shower, changed into fresh clothes, packed a few items into a bag, and got into his car and set off for Battle.

Suzanne opened the door to him with a hug. "How are you?" she asked, examining his face critically.

"Exhausted. You?"

"Happy to see you."

He lowered his voice. "How are things?"

She rocked her open hand, nodding back over her shoulder toward the sitting room, where he found Kathy on the window seat overlooking the back garden. She looked up with a smile of what seemed like relief and got to her feet, eager to hear what had been going on in London. He gave her a quick account, making light of it and getting her to smile with descriptions of the reactions of their team to the operations—Phil the action manager imperturbable as always, Bren taking care to ensure the supply of emergency hamburgers and tea, and Pip eager to make use of her recent firearms training.

"And Mickey?" she asked.

"He was seconded to the planning team, Kathy. He seems very interested in the new Digital Security Task Force."

"He's ambitious," she said.

Brock tried to read her expression. "I'm hoping he'll tell us what DiSTaF's all about. Anyway, more important, how have you been?"

"Oh, I feel okay, except that I still don't know much about what happened in those three days. It's like trying to remember a dream; I get random snatches, but when I try to pin them down they fade away into darkness." She shook her head in frustration and he noticed the nails of her right hand were bitten short.

"I've been given strict instructions to get you to counseling as soon as possible," he said cheerily, and watched her gloomy nod. "Anyway," he patted her arm, "there's more color in your cheeks." He felt vaguely guilty, as if he'd abandoned her here, as if they'd all been swept off course by Lynch's obsessive campaign against Bragg and by the wider winds of change of which it seemed somehow a symptom. And looking at Kathy, preoccupied and unconsoled, he felt as if he'd let her down, had betrayed the instincts that had always underpinned their relationship. "We'll talk about things tomorrow," he said. "But for now, let's see what Suzanne's got to drink."

Kathy smiled. "We made a special trip to the liquor store for you."

"But not for me alone, I hope."

THE NEXT MORNING THEY took a walk up to the ruins of the abbey and then on down to the meadow beyond, across which the Norman army had struggled in 1066, on an autumn day much like this perhaps, with the threat of rain and squelch of mud underfoot.

"Every morning I wake up hoping that I'll be cured, and my memory will have come back, but all I can get are fragments, and some of them don't make any sense at all—that image of Gudrun lying in a steel drawer, for instance; it keeps coming back, but it feels unreal, just like a dream."

"You said she was in one of four stainless-steel drawers."

"Yes."

"I saw four drawers like that at the clinic, in a room they use as a temporary mortuary. But it was inside the secure area of the clinic—someone would have to have taken you through the security check. Do you remember that?"

Kathy frowned. "Something . . . Just when you said that I had a sudden picture of Butcher Bragg standing in a corridor, supported by two men in leather jackets. But that doesn't make sense either. That must have been a dream too."

"Tell me about the other things you remember."

"Going to Limehouse Basin and talking to the man there, then standing on a bridge somewhere, looking down through railings at the canal, Tisdell's boat . . ."

"You can remember his boat?"

"Yes, but not going onto it. The next thing is sitting in a taxi, shivering with cold and my arm feels terrible, and I'm ashamed because I've made the seat wet and I think the cabbie will be mad."

"You were on your way to the clinic. Can you remember anything about the cab?"

He watched Kathy's brow crease with concentration. "A minicab? I don't remember a glass panel divider like in a black cab."

"And inside the clinic?"

"Ah . . ." She gave a violent shake of her head. "It's so damned frustrating."

"Don't worry," he said. "It'll come back to you."

He took a different tack. "Let's go back to the beginning," he said. "You're a detective faced with a confusing story about two sisters who, within nine months of each other, die apparently accidental, unrelated deaths. What other explanation are you considering?"

Kathy took a moment to focus, reluctantly he thought, on what he was asking. In the silence he heard a crow screech in the trees up ahead.

"Freyja was a brilliant mathematician, working on some cutting-edge project to do with the security of communications. Then she was murdered."

"Why murdered?" he objected softly.

"Because why else would Gudrun take on a false identity to infiltrate a company that specializes in security of communications?"

"Does it?"

"You should see their setup, all hidden scanners and restricted access."

"But we don't know of any connection between Paddington Security Services and Penney Solutions in Cambridge."

"Freyja must have told Gudrun about it. In any case, Ned Tisdell makes the connection—he met Freyja in Cambridge and then Gudrun bought a boat to park right next to him in Paddington, a stone's throw from their offices. And now they've killed him too."

"You think so?" But Brock was thinking that there had been no sightings of Tisdell since the fire on his boat.

Kathy said, "The thing I don't understand is what this has to do with the Pewsey Clinic."

"Three murders, Kathy? Who on earth could be responsible?"

Kathy sighed, plunging her free hand deeper into the pocket of the green jacket she'd somehow acquired. "I've absolutely no idea."

Of course there were other, much more likely and less melodramatic explanations, Brock told himself. Tisdell might have met Freyja at the Plow in Fen Ditton by accident. Perhaps he had then been introduced to Gudrun and the two of them had hit it off—both rather solitary misfits by the sound of it. Perhaps Gudrun had gone to Paddington to be with him, hiding her identity to escape from her father, or because there was some other threat to her that they hadn't discovered, a jealous boyfriend maybe. And the deaths of the two sisters were far more likely to be the tragic accidents that everyone assumed them to be, with Ned Tisdell now probably having moved on to some other corner of the country.

But there was a kind of fierce determination in Kathy's account that Brock didn't want to dismiss or argue with at this stage, so he said, "How could we move forward then?"

"Establish a connection between Penney Solutions and Paddington Security Services and learn more about Freyja's work. Dr. Penney was very evasive, wasn't he?"

"Yes, and that is a problem. The work they do there is commercially sensitive and he doesn't want any information leaking out to competitors. The Paddington people are probably the same, and we have no grounds for forcing them to open up their books. In any case, Freyja's work would probably be unintelligible to us." He came to a stop, rubbing his beard as he pondered. "But there is somewhere we might go for help."

"Oh?"

"DiSTaF. Isn't that what they're supposed to be concerned with, digital security? Suppose I take this to their boss, Suzy Russell, and see what she can make of it?"

Kathy thought about it. "She might be interested. She was certainly concerned about the possibility of Ned Tisdell having got into the clinic. And she invited me to go and see what DiS-TaF was all about when I felt better."

"Did she?" Brock looked shocked. "Sounds as if they're trying to poach my whole damned team."

Kathy smiled. "Would you go through the commander?"

"Lynch has got too much on his plate at the moment, and he's also made it very clear that he doesn't want to hear any more about the Kite girls. No, I think a direct approach to Russell would be best."

AND SO, BACK AT his office the following morning and having dealt with the immediate priorities on his desk, Brock made a call to Superintendent Russell's office and found himself offered an appointment for a snack lunch within the hour. Her office was a short cab ride away, in a sleek glass and steel office building so new that there were still pieces of protective tape on the stainless-steel handrail by the front door. A young man standing by the reception desk, designer-stubbled and looking more like a fashion model than anything more functional, showed him to the lift and took him up to the top floor and into some kind of lounge room furnished with contemporary sofas the same scarlet color as Suzy Russell's glasses. She arrived a moment later, and shook his hand warmly.

"We'll get a bit of peace and quiet up here. Fancy some

lunch?" She gestured to a sideboard on which was laid out a platter of food. On the wall above was hung a huge enlargement of an etching of a cross-section through a building, which Brock recognized.

"Jeremy Bentham's Panopticon," he said.

"Ah, you recognize it."

The building was circular, Brock recalled, six stories high with prison cells ranged around the perimeter all facing in toward a tower in the center from which they could be observed. "1791," he said. "The perfect machine for control by surveillance."

"Or just the possibility of surveillance," Suzy Russell said, smiling. "That was the real stroke of genius. There might not even be anyone in the tower. Just the possibility would be enough to maintain control."

Brock filled a plate of delicate morsels which he had trouble identifying. Russell poured them glasses of mineral water and led the way out to a balcony on which stood a small table and two chairs.

"Like you," she said, "I prefer to be located in an annex away from headquarters. Although I can't boast a private pub in my basement." She shot him an arch smile that seemed almost flirtatious. Had she been investigating him? He knew that the eccentric little Victorian bar installed in the basement at Queen Anne's Gate by the previous owners was known to a few people in Homicide and to property services, but surely not beyond.

"Well," he said, admiring the view across the rooftops toward the Millbank Tower, "we certainly don't have anything like this."

"It's a little suntrap up here," she said, "even on an autumn day. I come up here to think. So what did you want to talk about?"

"Thanks for seeing me at such short notice, ma'am . . ."

"Suzy, please. And everyone calls you Brock, am I right?"

Brock nodded and told her about the Kite sisters.

"You think their deaths may be linked to Freyja's work in Cambridge?"

"Both have the appearance of tragic accidents, but I don't like coincidences, and Gudrun hiding her identity to work at the Paddington security firm smacks of something less innocent going on. But without anything more concrete, my hands are tied."

"How might we help?"

"I'd like to know if Paddington Security Services is involved in any way with the project Freyja was working on. If they are, that would make the possibility of coincidence highly unlikely."

Russell was taking notes on her iPad. "I've heard of Penney Solutions. They've got a reputation as a highly successful, innovative company. Surely if there was any question of Freyja's death being linked to their project they'd be keen to have it investigated?"

"When we spoke to Dr. Penney he seemed preoccupied with keeping their work secret. He refused to discuss what other companies they had links with. Perhaps he felt we were the wrong people to talk to, and perhaps he was right. But I imagine you have the expertise, and the levels of security, to reassure him that what he might tell you will remain confidential."

"Hm, maybe. But I know people in this area are very nervous about industrial espionage. You've discussed this with Fred Lynch, I assume?"

"The commander is up to his neck in the Bragg cleanup, as you know, Suzy, and this is way below his radar. I really just need to know if it's worth pursuing any further. If it is, I'll talk to him again."

Russell chuckled. "Let me sniff around. But if it comes to a direct approach to Penney Solutions, I'll have to inform Fred."

"Fair enough," Brock said. "Thanks, I'm grateful."

"Well, maybe you can do something for me. DS Mickey Schaeffer—Fred has been impressed by his work on the Intruder task force, and Schaeffer has put out feelers to join DiSTaF. How would you rate him?"

"Competent, hard-working, intelligent. But has he got the technical background for you?"

"He has a computer science degree."

"Does he?" Brock wasn't aware of that. "Well then . . . yes, he might be right up your alley, although I'd be sorry to lose him. DI Kolla said you'd spoken to her about having a look at DiSTaF. You're not going to steal my whole team, are you?"

She smiled. "Don't worry, I was only thinking about those two, and Kolla, for all her operational flair, doesn't have the IT skills I'd need."

"Thank goodness for that."

"But she could acquire them. You wouldn't want to hold her back, would you, Brock?"

Brock wasn't sure what the truthful answer to that would be, so he swallowed the last of his lunch and left.

TWENTY-THREE

A COUPLE OF DAYS later Bren Gurney knocked on Brock's door. He had been covering Kathy's desk while she was away, checking her mail.

"I've got rid of most of the stuff, but I wasn't sure what to do with these," he said, handing Brock a file.

The top item was a sheaf of papers stapled together, the cover sheet a memo from the telecommunications section which said only that they were attaching their response to Kathy's order of the sixteenth. The second page was a copy of Kathy's request for telephone records and respondents' identification for a cell phone number in the name of Vicky Hawke. The form had been stamped *Non-urgent*, with D.K. Payne's signature beneath. This was followed by five pages of phone records and a list of names and addresses.

"Ah," Brock said. "Have you had a look at this?"

"Yeah. I assume that's Gudrun Kite, not the real Vicky Hawke."

"Yes. Kathy got her cell number from her father."

"Right. He's on the list of callers, along with the company she worked for in Paddington."

Brock scanned the names. There was the mail-holding address in Crouch End and a couple of people from the canal boats—Anne Downey, Ned Tisdell. His eye stopped at a name he didn't recognize, Oliver Kovacs, with an address in Watford against which had been written *does not exist*.

"Should I send these through to Kathy?" Bren asked.

"Leave them with me, Bren. I'd like Kathy to forget about work for a while."

"Sure."

"By the way, did we get anywhere with tracing the taxi that dropped her at the clinic?"

"Oh, I'm not sure. I haven't checked. Sorry, with all the rest that's been going on . . ."

"Of course, and it's probably way down the priority list."

"I'll get after it."

Later that afternoon Brock was checking through his inbox and came upon the fire department report on the fire on Ned Tisdell's boat. He scanned it, then read it again more carefully. He was consumed by an uncomfortable sense of things left unresolved, and decided to pay another visit to the Paddington canal basin. When he got there he noticed changes as he stood on the bridge over the canal and looked down on the row of narrowboats, several of which were unfamiliar. Gudrun Kite's empty *Grace* was still there, and next to it the Stapletons' *Roaming Free*, from whose flue stack a column of white smoke curled up into the evening air. As he descended to the towpath and drew closer to the boats he saw light gleaming from the windows of *Roaming Free* and heard a sudden gust of laughter. He stepped up onto the stern and knocked on the door.

"Hello?" Howard Stapleton opened the door and stuck his head out, recognizing Brock. "Ah, Chief Inspector!"

"Is this an awkward time, Mr. Stapleton?"

"No, no, not at all. Come on in."

Brock followed him down the steps and into the warm body of the boat, seeing Molly Stapleton up ahead, sitting with a young woman he didn't recognize, both holding glasses of wine.

"We're just having a glass of wine with Debbie," Howard Stapleton said. "You know Debbie Rowland, from *Jonquil*, two boats along? And this is her little boy, Ethan. This is a very important Scotland Yard detective, Ethan. Say hello."

A small boy got up from the floor where he'd been playing with a model car and stood to lopsided attention in front of Brock, offering his hand to shake. Brock took it and introduced himself, getting the impression from the cheerful grins on the adults' faces and the empty bottle on the galley bench top that the party had been going for a while.

"I'm interrupting you," Brock said.

"Not at all." Stapleton checked his watch. "Are you off duty? Join us in a glass."

Brock smiled. He wanted them to relax, and said, "You're right, I am off duty. I was just passing and saw your lights on. So, yes, a glass of wine would be very welcome."

"We're debating about heading up to Manchester for the winter," Molly Stapleton said. "I have a sister up there, so if the canals freeze over we'll have an alternative refuge for Christmas."

"I hadn't thought of the risk of getting frozen in," Brock said, taking the glass Howard offered him.

"Oh yes, you have to plan for the winter. You don't want to get trapped out in the fens or somewhere," Molly said. "Is this about Ned Tisdell's boat catching fire? We read about it in the paper. We couldn't believe it."

"The local police think it was vandals," Brock said.

"Dear heavens, have things got as bad as that? Maybe we should head north."

"But you're looking into Vicky's death, aren't you?" Debbie Rowland asked. "Have there been any developments?"

"No. A report has gone to the coroner and, subject to his

findings, the case is closed. Accidental death. No doubt there will be recommendations about the safety of those heaters."

"That was so tragic." Debbie spoke with a wistful look at her glass, which Howard was topping up.

"Did you know Vicky well?" Brock asked. "I should say Gudrun, since that was her real name."

"Yes, that was really weird, wasn't it? I thought I knew her quite well—we all did—and yet we had no idea she was using a false name. But I always thought it was a bit strange that she was so savvy about computers, yet she was working in marketing. I mean, I'm a Web site designer and I've done a few courses, but she was way beyond that. She helped me once when I had a problem; she could do the most amazing things."

"Did she say much about her job?"

"Only that she hated her boss and would like to bankrupt him." Her jaw dropped. "Oh my god, she wasn't doing anything like that, was she? Sabotaging him or something?"

"Not as far as we know." He sipped his wine and smiled at Howard Stapleton. "Nice wine." He didn't want this to sound like an interrogation, although he was thinking that Debbie Rowland was someone they should have spoken to before now. "I get the feeling that she was making a break from whatever problems she'd had in the past," Brock said, "and was glad to make new friends like you three, in the boating world."

"Yes, yes," Debbie agreed, wistful again. It seemed to be her default mood.

"And Anne Downey and Ned Tisdell," Brock added.

"Oh yes, she was really close to them."

"Was she?" Howard looked surprised and slightly put out.

"Yes. I think Ned was a bit of a lost soul, like her, a bit damaged, you know? And Anne was like a mother figure to her. Vicky told me her own mother had died—was that true?"

"Yes, a couple of years ago. Did she speak about her father?"

"She said he was remote and unapproachable."

"We haven't heard from Ned or Anne since they left," Howard said.

"I might have a pretty good idea where Ned is," Debbie said.

"Really?" Brock said.

"If he's lost his boat and doesn't have anywhere to stay, he'll probably have gone to Anne for help."

Molly Stapleton leaned forward and said with a mischievous look, "They weren't an item, were they, Debbie?"

Howard looked shocked. "What! No, of course not. Anne would never have been interested in someone like Ned."

But Debbie said, "You know, I did wonder about that. She was very protective toward him, wasn't she, and they were kind of secretive, the two of them."

"But Ned wasn't . . ." Howard groped for the word.

"A perfect gentleman like you, darling?" his wife said sarcastically. "Perhaps Anne preferred something a bit less predictable."

Howard choked. "Well, he was that all right."

"And where would Anne be now, I wonder?" Brock said to Debbie.

"Could be anywhere," Molly said.

"No," Debbie said, "I bet she's still in London. When I asked her where she was moving on to next she said she'd be staying in London for a while; she had unfinished business, she said. You should check with British Waterways or the Environment Agency, although there are lots of private moorings—sorry, I'm telling you your job, aren't I? I mean that's what you do every day, isn't it, finding people?" Debbie thought a moment. "There was one place she mentioned once, when we were talking about places to stay. She said it was a quiet spot, where you could usually rely on a mooring. Over in the East End—Hackney Wick, near the Olympics site."

Brock nodded. "I believe Gudrun—Vicky—had a friend called Oliver Kovacs. Know anything about him?"

Howard said, "Oh, you mean Ollie, over on the other bank, the houseboat from hell. Ollie Kovacs is the mad old bloke who lives there." He pointed out through the side window to the ramshackle structure across the water. "Hardly a friend of Vicky's though, surely. He's as likely to throw something at you as speak to you."

"I did see her over there once," Debbie said. "I meant to ask her about it. It gives me the creeps, that place. I'll bet it's got rats."

Brock thanked them and got up to leave. At the door Howard Stapleton pointed to the riverside restaurant farther down the far bank. "Ned Tisdell worked over there. Maybe they have a phone number for him. Ask for Ricci, the owner."

Brock returned to the road bridge over the canal and crossed to the street running above the other bank. On one side were rows of expensive Georgian terrace houses, with sparkling paintwork and security cameras at the front doors, while on the canal side leafless trees spread their branches over the houseboats attached to the bank. He walked to the restaurant where a sign proclaimed *Ricci's* in stylish red neon. The lights were on but there were no diners yet at the tables as he pushed open the door and took in a deep breath of Italian cooking. A young man with a shaved head and haughty poise came to ask him if he had a reservation.

"Is Ricci in?"

"Who shall I say?"

Brock showed him his police ID and the waiter raised a vaguely scandalized eyebrow, as if ready to protest his innocence. "Hang on."

Ricci Ragonetti, as he introduced himself, was a short, plump man with a brisk manner. "Detective Chief Inspector? This must be something important."

"I'm wanting to speak to Ned Tisdell. I'm told he worked for you, and I wondered if you could tell me where I might find him."

"Ah, about his boat, is it? That's a bad business. We've had some cases of breaking and entering and vandalism along the canal, but setting fire to property is beyond a joke. Yes, Ned worked here off and on for a couple of months. He had a talent in the kitchen—vegetarian food of course, he's a vegan, and his pasta puttanesca was something special. But he was difficult, a bad timekeeper, sometimes turning up late or leaving early because he had other business to attend to. Then, two weeks ago, he didn't show up at all. His boat was gone, and that was that."

"No idea where he might be now?"

Ricci shook his head.

"What was this other business he was involved in?"

"I got the impression it was some kind of club. He talked about having to go to a meeting. But he wasn't what you'd call a great communicator, our Ned."

Brock thanked him. "That smells good; wish I could stay."

"Hey, wait there."

Ricci bustled away then returned with a carrier bag in which Brock saw a plastic tub. "What's this?"

"We do frozen meals for special customers, and this is one of Ned's dishes—tofu and spinach cannelloni. You try it. You'll see what I mean about his cooking."

It seemed that everyone along the canal wanted to offer him their hospitality.

"I shouldn't accept it, but I will," Brock said. "Many thanks."

"Don't mention it. Have you spoken to old Ollie?"

"No—should I?"

"Ollie Kovacs, bit of a hermit, lives in a tumble-down houseboat just along from here. Ned quite often called in there after work, took him leftovers. It's possible Ned may still be in touch with him."

"Thanks, I'll try him."

"Be careful, though, he hates coppers."

When he got back onto the street Brock took out his phone and called Kathy's number. She sounded cheerful, saying she'd spent the day helping Suzanne in her antiques shop while her assistant Ginny was off. "It was a relief just to be doing something useful, and good to feel tired after being on my feet all day. We're in the kitchen now, preparing dinner. So how are things with you?"

He told her about the list of Gudrun Kite's phone calls and his detour to the canal after work. "It seems both Gudrun Kite and Ned Tisdell used to visit a character living in a houseboat on the other side of the canal by the name of Oliver or Ollie Kovacs. Does that mean anything to you?"

"I remember Howard Stapleton pointing out a ruined houseboat."

"That's the one, I think. I'm on my way there now. So he wasn't interviewed?"

"He may have gotten a knock on the door, but I doubt it. The investigation, such as it was, never got that far. Can I help?"

"No, you enjoy your dinner."

He exchanged a few words with Suzanne, busy with making something complicated and Moroccan, then rang off and continued to a gate in the railings with a small, almost illegible sign reading O.K. tied to it with a clumsy twist of wire, and, in the uncertain light from the streetlight, cautiously followed a broken flight of brick steps down the canal bank to Ollie Kovacs's houseboat. At least, that was what he assumed it was, although in the shadowy darkness it looked more like a pile of abandoned tarpaulins. When he reached the foot of the bank, however, with the sound of lapping water coming from somewhere close to his feet, he was able to make out a glimmer of light coming from around the frame of an old door half hidden beneath a flap of canvas. There was also a tremor of sound coming from the door, the faint anguished wail of a trumpet, something he recognized. He paused, then had it—Miles Davis of course, one of the early albums.

The sound immediately cut off when he rapped on the door. There followed a long wait before the door opened a little way and the head of an elderly man peered out, blinking suspiciously through horn-rimmed glasses.

"*Miles Ahead*, I think," Brock said mildly. "Am I right?"

The eyes stared at him for a long moment. They reminded him of the child Ethan's large, innocent eyes. As he grew accustomed to the light Brock made out a straggly gray beard, a huge bald dome of a head and bushy eyebrows. The eyes moved down to examine Brock's clothes and fixed on the plastic bag with Ricci's logo.

"What's that?" The voice was a growl, but beneath the two syllables Brock felt he detected education.

"It's Ned's tofu and spinach cannelloni."

"Ah . . ." The bushy eyebrows rose. "What do you want?"

"A few words."

"About?"

"Ned. You're Ollie, am I right? I'm Brock. Just a few minutes of your time, Ollie. Ned would like you to have the cannelloni."

As if he'd uttered a password, he watched Ollie step back and, stooping to get through the low door, Brock moved inside, into what seemed to be an improvised lean-to tilted precariously against the side of a very old wooden shed, with small square windows and elaborate faded lettering along its exposed side. In the dim light of a single dangling bulb, he saw that the lean-to was filled with a chaotic jumble of old junk—obsolete machinery, paint pots, plastic baskets of clothing and blankets—and among it all he made out a mattress on a brass bedstead and a wicker basket from which a large old gray dog was observing him balefully.

"Well?"

Brock saw that a crude doorway had been hacked into the flank of the shed, giving access into what appeared to be an inner room, lit by a warm orange glow.

"Shall we go inside?" he suggested.

Ollie looked a little surprised by this, but then shrugged and led the way. Brock found himself inside the belly of a narrowboat, but one unlike any he'd seen so far. It was lined with wide timber planks, whose brown varnish had turned dark with age. A big and battered cast-iron kitchen range stood against one wall, a coal hod at its side, and a fat black metal flue rising to the ceiling. The fumes of burning coal took Brock back to his earliest childhood, before the Clean Air Acts put an end to coal fires. The space was lit by several paraffin lamps, whose warm light showed a rickety old table and chairs, threadbare carpets, and an assortment of old photographs hanging on the walls, along with horse brasses, a braided whip, and an assortment of ancient tools. The photographs showed stoic men in flat caps, waistcoats, and large boots, and women dressed in long dresses and strange head coverings like nuns.

"Canal people," Ollie said. "From the same time as this boat."

Brock picked up the educated vowels again, beneath a rougher veneer, and the tone of a teacher. "Really? This was an old narrowboat, was it?"

"This was the passenger packet boat *Princess Louise*, which worked the Grand Union Canal from the 1880s."

"That's amazing," Brock said, turning around and seeing other compartments disappearing down its length. "You have no inkling of this from the outside."

"What was your name again?" Ollie tugged suspiciously at his beard.

"Brock." He beamed at Ollie and scratched his own beard, as if in solidarity.

"And you're a friend of Ned's?"

Brock handed him the bag. "Here." He unbuttoned his coat and sat down carefully on one of the chairs. "I'm trying to contact Ned. I haven't been able to reach him since his boat was vandalized."

"Vandalized!" Ollie scoffed, sitting down facing Brock. "You know better?"

"That was attempted bloody murder!"

"*Attempted* murder? So he is still alive?"

Doubt returned to Ollie's face. "So how do you know Ned?"

"I want to help him, Ollie."

This was the wrong answer, Brock realized, watching the doubt deepen in wrinkles on the man's forehead as he looked more closely at Brock's clothes, and then clear suddenly in an explosive, "You're a cop, aren't you?" He rose to his feet. "You're a fucking cop!" For the briefest instant his eyes darted down the length of the boat, as if to check something, to make sure something wasn't visible perhaps, or that a door was closed, or maybe for a weapon.

"Yes, I'm a cop," Brock confessed calmly.

"Well you can clear off!" His voice had risen to a shrill pitch. "Get off my boat!"

"I want to help, Ollie," Brock repeated. "I work with Detective Inspector Kathy Kolla, who saved Ned on the night his boat was burned. Did Ned tell you about Kathy? She's laid up now, badly injured, and I need to know what's going on."

Ollie looked momentarily perplexed, as if having difficulty absorbing this, and Brock went on, "And I want to know about Gudrun."

There was a beat and then the reply, "Gudrun? Who's Gudrun?" But Brock was sure he'd seen recognition in those big childlike eyes.

"She called herself Vicky. She lived in *Grace* across the other side of the canal there, and she used to visit you, before she died. That's how Kathy got involved in this, trying to find out what happened to Gudrun. Can you help us, Ollie?"

Ollie abruptly slipped on an air of helpless bewilderment that Brock found unconvincing. "They were both good to me, Ned and Vicky, bringing me food and stopping by to have a chat, that's all. They were good souls. But I don't know what they were mixed up in! I live a quiet life. I don't get out much." He shrugged. "You're wasting your time talking to me, Mr. Policeman."

Brock eyed him for a moment. "Think about it, Ollie—two serious accidents in houseboats on this canal. We don't want a third, do we? This old boat would go up like a bonfire. Here, this is my card, phone me any time. Tell Ned to contact me."

As he got to his feet, Brock noticed some battered old paperbacks discarded under his chair, and he pulled a couple of them out—a well-worn volume of *The Basic Writings of Bertrand Russell* and *Noam Chomsky: A Life of Dissent*.

He nodded at Ollie as if approving his taste, and made for the door. As he pushed it open a gruff voice behind him muttered, "*Milestones*, not *Miles Ahead*."

WHEN HE GOT HOME, Brock slipped a frozen meal into the microwave, opened a bottle of red, and switched on his computer. Kathy phoned him as he was typing in *Oliver Kovacs*.

"How did it go with Ollie?" she asked.

"A character. Very cagey, said Gudrun and Ned were just passing acquaintances, but there was more to it than that. I think he knows where Ned is, or at least has heard from him since the fire. But Ollie's very hostile to the police."

"That's understandable," Kathy said. "I've been looking him up."

"You've beaten me to it. What do we have?"

"He got a degree in sociology in the sixties and was in Paris during the student riots in 1968. In 1972 he was arrested briefly outside the Atomic Weapons Research Establishment at Aldermaston during the CND Easter march, and again in 1984 during the miners' strike, protesting against the Thatcher government. On that occasion he was injured by a riot squad policeman who hit him a bit too hard with his stick."

"Any lasting damage?"

"No mention of that, although he tried unsuccessfully to sue. That was the end of his police record, although I wouldn't be surprised if Special Branch or MI6 had more. He's published a number of articles on politics and socialism and was a member of several left-wing groups until about ten years ago, when he seems to have retired from all that and gone quiet."

"What does he do for money?"

"Don't know. Family probably. His father was Sir Oliver Kovacs, merchant banker."

They talked about the canal people for a bit longer and then Brock asked Kathy if she'd remembered anything else about her missing days.

"No, nothing. I went to a shop in town today that sells herbal medicines, and got a bottle of pills for memory—ginseng and stuff. I know what you're going to say, but I'm desperate. I feel like I've had a partial lobotomy."

"A copy of the fire department report on the fire on Ned's boat came in this morning. The only thing I noticed that we didn't already know was that the handles on both sets of doors into the boat, fore and aft, had been chained and padlocked, on the outside. Ollie was right: It was attempted murder."

He heard Kathy's intake of breath, and said, "Sorry. I shouldn't have mentioned it."

"I don't want to be treated like an invalid, Brock. I want to know everything. Maybe it'll help bring things back."

"Yes, of course."

He hung up, closed down his computer, and contemplated his dinner, wishing he'd hung on to Ned's cannelloni.

TWENTY-FOUR

KATHY WOKE WITH A cry, opening her eyes to darkness. She was in a boat, a coffin on the water . . . She struggled to take a deep breath, expecting to choke, but instead, in a whirl of panicky sensations, she recognized the smell of tagine spices and abruptly remembered where she was. The relief she felt immediately began to dispel the dream, so that she had to concentrate to capture it before it vanished. The rattle of chains—that's what had shaken her awake. She couldn't remember ever having dreamed a noise before. It had been very vivid, echoing though the darkness in the boat, and it had made Ned panic. His terror had galvanized her. She'd pulled out her ASP and used it to smash a window and then forced him to climb through. How he'd wriggled and squirmed, including one painful kick in her chest. Then the agonizing struggle to get herself through with her bad shoulder, and out, tumbling into the sudden shock of cold water . . .

But all that had happened after the rattling chains, she realized, after the dream ended. A flood of excitement filled her. This was a memory, not a dream. And it didn't end there. She forced her mind back to the water: the terrifying glare of fire on the dark surface; the gulping vomit of foul canal water as she fought to swim, one-handed, in her clothes; Ned grabbing her hair, her shirt, hauling her up the bank.

What next? She felt almost as breathless, lying there in bed, as she'd felt running through the darkness—toward what? And then Anne Downey's face was in front of her, looking so worried and severe. Anne Downey and her boat. Now she had it. She sat up in bed, heart pumping, feeling a scary mixture of elation and fright.

In the kitchen, by the light of the full moon glowing in through the window, she made herself a cup of tea. On the pegs she saw the old jacket she'd arrived home in—Anne Downey's coat. She pulled it over her shoulders and sat at the table and made herself go through it all again, step by step, right up to the taxi ride, the consternation at the clinic, the arrival of Dr. Partridge, stripping off her wet clothes, X-rays . . . then nothing, not a thing, until Jock was helping her through the door of her own apartment.

There was something else, a strange detail that itched at the back of her mind. Then it came to her. She went upstairs again and opened her wallet, and found a Visa card that wasn't hers. She examined it closely. It had a number and valid expiration date, and a cardholder's name, *A. Black*. She had a clear image of Anne Downey putting it in her hand, but couldn't remember why.

ON HIS WAY INTO work Brock received a text message:

Mtg Commander Lynch earliest. Contact me. Carol (secy).

He phoned her and arranged to go straight to headquarters. The matter was extremely urgent, was all she would say.

When he arrived at Carol's office she gave him a long considering look that he'd seen before, on the faces of court officials when a convicted man was brought up for sentencing.

"Morning," he said brightly.

She returned his greeting with a cool smile then knocked on the inner door and put her head inside. "DCI Brock is here, sir."

There was an indistinct growl from inside, and Carol stood back to let him in.

Lynch looked up at him, face rigid, as the door closed softly behind him. Brock wondered what he'd missed. Had one of his team shot an unarmed civilian, or sold the details of the Bragg story to the press? Why hadn't anybody warned him?

He walked forward toward the desk, Lynch saying nothing, just staring at him with that same look. There was an empty chair facing the desk, but Brock didn't take it. He stood beside it and said, "Sir?"

Finally Lynch spoke. "Why did you go behind my back and ask Superintendent Russell to undertake a private investigation for you?"

Brock initially felt relieved. Was that all? He wondered which part of Lynch's question to begin with.

"Knowing how busy you are, sir, I didn't want to bother you until I knew the result of Superintendent Russell's investigation."

The nostrils flared, the face, previously very pale, became slightly pink.

"Yes, I am busy, Brock." He put his hand on a high pile of papers beside him on his desk. "I have two hundred and eight suspects under arrest from the biggest police operation in six years and all my officers are working one hundred and ten percent on the follow-up investigations—all of my officers except one." He pointed a finger like a pistol barrel at Brock. "You, apparently, have time to indulge yourself in a little private matter which I have previously *explicitly* told you to drop."

"Sir, I've been pulling my weight during the present crisis, working the same long hours as everybody else, and my team has performed well. But I believe there are grounds for considering the deaths of Freyja and Gudrun Kite as murder, and the fire-bombing of Edward Tisdell's boat as attempted murder, and I—"

Lynch stopped him with that same gesture he'd used before, slamming his hand down on his desk. "You don't listen, do you, Brock? You just don't listen!" He was shouting now, his face growing a deeper red. "This is sheer, bloody-minded insubordination, and I will not have it!"

Brock was beginning to feel annoyed. Lynch was no doubt under tremendous pressure, but this was sounding like paranoia.

Abruptly the shouting stopped, and Lynch spoke in a quieter, more menacing voice. "This is your warning, Brock, a formal caution. You step out of line once more, *once more*, and you'll be out of here, out of your cozy little nest in Queen Anne's Gate, so fast your ass won't scrape the footpath. Now go away."

HE HADN'T BEEN LONG back in his office when a call came in for him from Suzy Russell. After Lynch's tirade, she sounded reassuringly brisk and sensible.

"Brock, we've completed a check on those two firms, about as far as we can without talking to them directly. Nothing much on Paddington Security Services: One of their employees was arrested for downloading kiddie porn four years ago and their books were audited by the Inland Revenue two years ago, but otherwise nothing interesting. Regarding Penney Solutions, there have been rumors of them being the subject of industrial espionage, possibly by the Chinese. Did Dr. Penney mention anything like that to you?"

"He said they were always on the lookout for espionage."

"Yes, it's a huge potential problem at the moment, and the Chinese are prime suspects for much of it. And, from what we were able to find out, Freyja's work was concerned with protecting data and internet traffic—just the sort of thing they'd be very interested in. But it's a big jump from that to possible murder. That isn't the Chinese style at all, they'd want to be low key and invisible. They might try to lure Freyja to work for one of their front companies, or try to bribe her, or hack her computer, but not assassinate her."

"Maybe they hired contractors."

"Hm. Anyway, industrial espionage is one of our main areas of concern, and we'll keep this one on our radar. But you said that the key thing from your point of view was to find a connection between the two firms, and that we haven't been able to do. As far as we know, there's nothing to link them."

"Oh." Brock felt a sag of disappointment.

"Sorry." There was a pause, and then she added, "I had a meeting with Fred Lynch yesterday about other matters, and I mentioned your approach. It would have looked odd if I hadn't."

"Ah yes. He just called me in about it to tell me off."

"Ouch."

"I hope this won't cause a problem for you."

"No." She laughed. "I can handle Fred."

That's more than I can, Brock thought. He realized that he'd never come across another fellow officer with whom he felt he had so little in common. By comparison, Sharpe's regime seemed positively benign, as he had predicted. It made Brock wonder what made Lynch tick.

"Well, thanks for your help anyway."

"Any time."

His next caller was Mickey Schaeffer, asking for a private word.

He came into Brock's office looking pleased with himself but also a little guilty. He accepted a cup of coffee from Brock's machine, which he examined briefly with a few compliments, and then they sat down.

"The thing is, boss, I really enjoy working in your team, but you probably know that I've got a computer science degree, and if possible I'd like to build on that."

Brock nodded.

"Well, following the whole Bragg operation I've had an approach from the new DiSTaF unit, and I think they can give me some opportunities to do exactly that."

Brock went through the motions. He would be very sorry to lose Mickey, he said, but he could understand his desire to transfer and, if he ever wanted to come back, the door was open.

Mickey looked relieved. "I just think this is the future, boss."

An hour later Bren knocked on his door.

"We traced the cab that took Kathy to the clinic that night, Brock. It was called to a street address in Old Ford Road in Globe Town, by a cell phone owned by Anne Downey."

"Ah." He took the street map that Bren gave him and saw that the address was next to the place where Old Ford Road crossed the Regent's Canal.

"Do you want me to find out where she is now?"

Brock shook his head, still studying the map. The address was also near the place where another canal, the Hertford Union, branched off to the northeast, out to Hackney Wick. "No, Bren. I've just had a bawling out from the commander about this case. We are under strict orders not to touch it."

Bren's big face wrinkled in a frown, the same look that Brock had seen when watching him play for the police rugby team, facing an oncoming pack. "Why would he do that?"

"It's a waste of our time, apparently."

"Don't we have any discretion to decide that?"

"Not any more. So, we'll leave it alone."

"What about Kathy? Might this not help her get her memory back?"

"Let's hope so. I'll talk to her."

Bren hesitated, expecting more, but then he said, "Okay. Let me know if you need a hand."

KATHY WAS ALONE IN Suzanne's house, getting ready to go out for the day. She had promised herself a visit to the coast, to Bexhill-on-Sea, where her parents had taken her one summer as a child, and, with a clear sky and a mild breeze coming in from the Channel, she had looked up the train times—Battle to Crowhurst and West St. Leonards, then along the coast to Bexhill. She would probably be disappointed going back, she guessed, but a little nostalgia was allowable, wasn't it? They would come suddenly into her mind from time to time, her parents, often at unexpected moments, inspired by an old song on the radio, the sight of an ancient Bentley like her dad's, a taste of her mother's favorite Rose's lime marmalade. And the memories were always bittersweet, for they belonged to an earlier time, a time of innocence, before her father's disgrace and suicide.

The house phone rang, Brock perhaps. She picked it up, but a woman's voice spoke.

"Mrs. Bragg? This is Marele from the Pewsey Clinic."

Kathy was astonished. How had they got this number? And why did they keep calling her that? She answered carefully, "Yes, Marele?"

"Dr. Partridge has asked me to phone you to arrange for you to come in to the clinic for a consultation. Can I arrange a car to come and pick you up?"

"What, today? I have an appointment with him next week."

"He wants to see you earlier, because of a problem with your medications. Dr. Partridge says it's important."

Kathy thought about it. Perhaps this was to do with her memory loss. Maybe the medications were aggravating it.

"Yes, all right. I'm down in Sussex at the moment, near the coast. I suppose I could get a train up to town . . ." The timetable was lying in front of her.

"Where does it come in?"

"Charing Cross."

"I can arrange a car to meet you there and bring you out to Pewsey."

"That would help." Kathy was impressed. Perhaps her dark reflections on the clinic had been misplaced. She checked the timetable. "I could catch the train that gets in at eleven-oh-three this morning."

"Let's see . . . Yes, Dr. Partridge will be free for you at twelve. Someone will meet you at Charing Cross, under the clock. I'll give you a number in case you need to contact us."

When she rang off Kathy thought, *Oh well, nostalgia can wait*. She might go on from the clinic to her apartment to pick up a few things she needed. She checked her watch and set about getting ready. But how had they known to contact her at Suzanne's home number? Brock, she thought. They must have phoned him.

IT WAS A PLEASANT journey, up through the Sussex and Kent countryside, and then across the southeast suburbs into the city. At Charing Cross she threaded her way among the crowds toward the clock suspended under the balcony, where she spotted a man in a black leather jacket holding a piece of cardboard on which the name MRS. BRAGG was printed.

"Hello," she said.

He nodded at her and led the way out to the front. He had the build and battered looks of a boxer, and there was something disturbingly familiar about him, but she couldn't place it. The waiting car was a black Mercedes with tinted windows.

The man held the passenger door open for her, then went around to the driver's side. As she worked the buckle of the seat belt she was aware of him getting in beside her, and then of a sudden sharp prick on her right thigh. She looked round quickly and saw the needle, and just had time to think, *Oh no*, before the vehicles and people milling around outside the windshield blurred and faded away.

SHE WOKE GENTLY, AS after a very restful sleep, to find herself sitting in a comfortably solid padded chair in a well-appointed living room. She made to rub her face, but found that her right hand was fastened tight to the arm of the chair with a leather strap. Her left arm was also immobilized in the same way, as were her legs. She looked around the room, thinking that she recognized it, the dark timber door in front of her and the molding, the tasteful fabric of the curtains, the plump leather sofa . . . The plump leather sofa on which PC Lister had been lying with his throat cut.

Kathy swallowed bile. Her eye went down to the carpet, where a rug lay across the place where his blood had spread. What was she doing here? A flutter of panic rose in her chest and she thought she might throw up.

"You awake?"

She twisted in her seat to see a man sitting behind her in an armchair. He put down the newspaper he was reading and came across to examine her face, the straps. He was the man who had met her at Charing Cross, the boxer.

"I need a drink of water," Kathy said, voice croaky.

He went out and returned with a cup of water which he held to her mouth. She gulped it down, coughed, and said, "I'm not Mrs. Bragg. I'm a police officer. My name is Detective Inspector Kathy Kolla. I can give you a phone number to—"

"Shut up," he said, bored, and went back to reading his paper.

After a while he got to his feet again and wandered out. Kathy tried to ease her right wrist out of the strap, but it was too tight. The man returned after ten minutes with a sandwich in his hand, and stared at her impassively as he chewed.

"Have you met Mrs. Bragg?" Kathy tried, but he just walked past her to his chair, and a large TV on a unit to her right came to life with a sports channel. After perhaps an hour the man's cell began to play a tune and he switched the TV off.

"Yep . . . Yeah . . . Okay."

The TV came on again, and when Kathy tried to speak to him he turned the volume up. After a little while he switched it off and went to the window, staring morosely out as if expecting someone. Suddenly he straightened and moved quickly to the door, closing it behind him. Kathy heard the crunch of wheels on gravel, the muffled sound of voices in the hall.

Then the door in front of her swung open and Jack Bragg came limping into the room. Behind him, like a medieval torturer's assistant displaying the instruments, a man with the physique of a bodybuilder was holding a leather apron and a meat cleaver.

TWENTY-FIVE

IN A FOLD OF hills on the Kent-Sussex border, Brock pulled into a parking lot in front of a barn bearing a sign reading *Coggins Lakes*. He made his way around to the entrance to the barn and went inside. To one side was a small café, on the other a bait and tackle shop, and in front of him a counter at which a ruddy-faced man looked quizzically at the way he was dressed, in suit and tie.

"Afternoon. Not here for the fishing, sir?"

"No. I've come to meet one of your regulars—Mr. Sharpe?"

"Ah, Dominic, yes, he's here, at North Lake."

The man produced a map showing a string of small lakes. "Probably at swim number eight or nine—those are his favorite spots." He marked the place with a cross and traced the path that Brock should follow. Brock thanked him, wondering what a "swim" was.

He set off on a woodland trail. The air was still, pleasantly warm in the sun, and the valley silent apart from the twitter of small birds and the distant murmur of a tractor. He skirted one lake, then another, seeing isolated anglers motionless among the trees that lined the shores. On the hillside beyond, a cluster of conical coast house roofs stood out against the sky.

The former commander, wearing boots, coat, and hat, was

sitting in a folding chair at the water's edge, surrounded by a surprising array of angling gear, intently studying a patch of dark water a little way off.

"Any luck?"

Sharpe swung round and jumped to his feet. "Brock, good to see you."

He moved with a sprightly energy, his face fresh with healthy color, not at all the gloomy, gray-faced specter he had become toward the end. Brock imagined him in those interminable meetings at headquarters, dreaming of afternoons by the lake just like this.

"What are you after?"

"Carp or wels catfish. Carp mainly. I caught a forty-two-pounder last week."

"Good heavens, a monster."

"Oh, the catfish go up to seventy-five, would you believe."

Perhaps this was the perfect pastime for an old copper, Brock thought, both hunter and executioner, with not a lawyer in sight to get in the way.

"I'm stiff from sitting here," Sharpe said. "Let's take a walk."

"You're looking really well," Brock said, stopping himself with difficulty from saying "sir."

"It'll take me a while, so I'm told, to really disengage, but I must admit I haven't missed a thing. You should try it." He shot Brock a shrewd glance. "According to all the press reports, Fred Lynch has been achieving miracles. So how are you finding the new regime?"

"Exactly as you predicted, Dominic." There, he'd used the first name. He'd called him Dominic once before, when things had been getting a bit fraught, but it felt unnatural, vaguely improper.

"Tell me all." He gave a greedy little lick of his lips. "Strictly between these four hills, of course."

So Brock told him about Lynch's obsession with Bragg, his

need to micromanage everybody's activities, and his budget stringencies.

"Oh, the budget I can understand," Sharpe said with a benign smile at a passing cloud. "Not of his making. Severe pressure from above."

"He believes that the cuts are an opportunity to move faster toward some radical new form of policing."

"What kind of new form?"

"I'm not sure, except that it will be heavily into information and communications technology."

"Ah! Suzy Russell!"

"Yes. You know about her?"

"Of course. Have they made DiSTaF public yet?"

"Yes, it's up and recruiting, and seems to have played a key part in tracking Bragg."

"Lynch and Russell have been grooming each other for a while now. That's where your vision of the future is coming from. You'll find that Suzy Russell's budget is protected—except that you won't, because I'll bet it isn't published. I got a glimpse of it once, DiSTaF's five-year budget plan, and it was pretty impressive. She's persuaded a lot more people than Lynch that she's the future."

"I see."

"As for Bragg . . ." Sharpe paused, gazing across the lake to where another angler could be seen wrestling a large fish ashore. "Well, blow me down. Geoff Warrender! And I was sure my swims were the only viable ones at this time of year. The damned man'll be impossible now."

So there was a downside to anglers' paradise. Brock waited while Sharpe stood there, shaking his head in disbelief.

"Yes, Bragg's been the focus of everything since Lynch took over, almost as if he's turned the whole command into a vehicle for some personal campaign."

Sharpe nodded, refocusing. "Interesting. There was a rumor, years ago, when Lynch came up for a promotion, that he was connected in some way with Bragg."

"Connected?"

"Mm. Not corruptly, necessarily, and I doubt there'll be anything on the record, but something . . . maybe personal? I don't know."

They strolled around a copse of wintry silver birch, talking, exchanging information, until there was nothing more to say. When they got back to Sharpe's fishing spot they shook hands.

"Sorry I couldn't give you anything more concrete, Brock. My advice is, keep your head down. These storms will pass."

Brock nodded and said, "So what do you do with forty-two pounds of carp?"

Sharpe made a face. "I usually throw it back. Taste's pretty foul, Penny can't stand it, refuses to cook it. The dogs love it, of course."

"WHO THE HELL IS this?" Bragg stood in front of Kathy, glaring down at her.

The boxer frowned. "Er, it's your wife, Mr. Bragg."

"No it's not!"

"I am a police officer, Jack," Kathy said calmly, although the sound of his voice was sending panic signals thumping through her. "My name is Detective Inspector Kathy Kolla. I advise you to release me immediately."

Bragg rounded on the boxer, who backed away a step, holding up his hands. "I just did as I was told, boss. She met me at Charing Cross, blond lady, just like you said."

"You searched her?"

The boxer shook his head.

"Well do it now!"

Kathy held Bragg's eyes as the boxer groped her, handing her wallet to Bragg, who swore again as he opened it and saw her ID. He thought for a moment, then waved the third man over and took the cleaver from him. Then he moved to the side of Kathy's chair and pulled the little finger of her right hand flat against the arm, positioning the blade over the knuckle. "Who's your boss?"

"DCI Brock, Homicide and Serious Crime."

"And who's his boss?"

"Commander Lynch."

Bragg stared at her. "Bastard!" he swore softly, spittle dribbling down his chin. Kathy had the impression he wasn't referring to her. "What are you doing here?"

"I was here in the house when you came back that night, impersonating your wife. You broke my collarbone with that . . ." She stared at the cleaver suspended over her hand.

"No, it was her, I recognized her perfume."

"I found that upstairs in your bedroom when I arrived, and helped myself."

For a long moment Kathy held her breath, watching the anger burn in his eyes. Then he muttered, "Go on."

"They sent me to the Pewsey Clinic, hoping you would try to get to me there. I was registered as Patsy Bragg . . ."

"That bastard!" Bragg repeated.

". . . so when the clinic phoned me this morning and asked for Mrs. Bragg I just said yes. How did you get my phone number? Someone at the clinic gave it to you?"

But Bragg wheeled away, thrusting the cleaver back at the other man.

The boxer said, "What'll we do, boss?"

"I need to think," Bragg muttered. "I'm going to take a swim. Put her in the cellar."

"Let me come to the pool," Kathy said quickly. "Maybe I can help you work this out."

Bragg looked at her, then shrugged. "All right." He nodded to the others. "Carry her down in the chair."

The pool room was a lavish space, with a twenty-meter pool, a bar, lounge chairs, and gym equipment with a view out over the garden. They heaved Kathy in and set her up against one wall. She felt both vulnerable and absurd on her throne. When Bragg came in, wearing trunks and a white robe, he barked, "Move her to the edge and tip her in if she gives any trouble." Then he threw off the robe and dived in.

As Kathy watched him furiously plowing up and down the length of the pool she tried to work out what had happened. Why was Bragg here? Surely not on bail. Had he escaped from custody? And wouldn't they then at least come and check his home? She tried to think of some angle she could use, but all she could think of was his impulsive anger and violent paranoia. He finally came to a stop and, as he stretched to haul himself up the steps, she noticed something that made her think.

He wrapped himself in the robe and took a towel from the boxer and rubbed his head. Then he threw the towel back at the man and said, "Sorry, love, you're going to have to disappear."

"That's not a good idea," Kathy said.

"Best I can come up with." He went over to a table and picked up a pack of cigarettes and a lighter. He lit up and began to murmur to the boxer, who leaned close to him to listen.

"How did you get that mark on your back?" Kathy said loudly.

Bragg paused, but didn't turn round.

"It was at the clinic, wasn't it? Did they tell you what they'd done to you?"

He turned and stared at her. "What are you talking about?"

Kathy saw the hint of angry suspicion in his eye and wondered how far she could push this. "They did it to you while you were under, didn't they? And it hurt for a couple of days, didn't it?"

He took a step toward her, his expression torn between irritation and doubt. "How do you know that?"

"Because they did it to me too."

"So? It was an injection, that's all."

"Hell of a big needle. Like an epidural, my own doctor said later, when he had a look at it, only in the wrong place. Directly behind the heart."

Bragg stiffened and like a reflex his hand came up to his heart, as if to reassure himself that it was still beating. "Go on. What did your doctor think?"

"He couldn't figure it out. But I'll tell you something else. Remember your mate Ashur Najjar? He was hurt when you bombed Fantasyland, and taken to . . . where do you think? The Pewsey Clinic. Then he was released, and they followed him here and supposedly shot him dead right out front here."

"What do you mean, *supposedly*?"

"I've seen the postmortem report. The shots weren't fatal. But when the regular pathologist opened him up, another doctor, one brought in specially, insisted on removing his heart." She watched Bragg's eyes widen. "It was taken away. No one's seen it since."

As a hastily woven conspiracy theory, Kathy thought it painfully thin, and yet it had the ring of improbable truth, because of course much of it *was* true.

"You're making this up." Bragg had fixed her with a mad stare. Without looking away he said, "Bennie, throw the witch in the pool." The boxer took a step forward.

"I wish I was making it up, Jack," Kathy said quickly. "You see, I think that you and I, like Ashur, have seen too much. I think it would suit a few important people if we both suffered fatal heart attacks in the not too distant future. Don't you?"

Bragg glared at her for a moment, then stretched out his hand to the boxer. "Give us your knife." The man took a long flick-knife from his pocket and handed it over. Bragg took it and the blade sprang open. He advanced on Kathy, walking round behind her so that she couldn't see what he was doing. She winced as she felt the cold blade slide down the back of her neck, then there was a sudden rip of cloth as Bragg sliced down through her sweater and shirt to expose her back. In a mirror on the far side of the pool she watched him stare at her back, then raise his eyes to the ceiling and give an angry roar. "Freddy! I'll kill you!"

Freddy? Freddy Lynch? Kathy said, "You know Fred Lynch, do you, Jack?"

"Know him?" he bellowed. "He's my treacherous little fucking brother!"

TWENTY-SIX

AS HE WAS DRIVING back up to London, Brock's phone rang. There was background noise on the line and he didn't recognize the caller's voice. The man repeated his name. "Desmond Kite, Chief Inspector."

"Oh, Professor Kite, how are you?"

"I, er, I'm hoping that I can have a few moments of your time, sir." The voice was weaker and more hesitant than Brock remembered, and the "sir" at the end seemed uncharacteristically humble.

"Fire away."

"I wonder if you could spare me a few minutes today or tomorrow for a brief meeting? I'm on my way to London now."

"By train?"

"Yes. We're due into King's Cross in half an hour. I could get a taxi to your office . . ."

Not a good idea, Brock thought. "I'm on the road at the moment. What if I meet you at King's Cross?"

"Well, yes, that would be excellent."

"Get yourself a cup of tea in the café by the Euston Road exit, and I should be with you not long after you get there, traffic allowing."

"Very kind of you, sir."

WHEN BROCK WALKED INTO the café he saw Kite, looking very elderly now, a gray muffler wrapped around his neck, hunched over a cup and saucer. They shook hands and Brock sat down opposite him.

"Can I get you something, Chief Inspector?" Kite looked around vaguely.

"I'm fine. How can I help you, Desmond?"

Kite lowered his head, as if having to summon all his strength to begin. "Concerning Gudrun . . . I've been feeling very guilty about her. Is it really true that she gave me a false address in London?"

Brock nodded.

"She must have hated me." He said it in a hollow, desolate voice, then took a deep breath as if to pull himself together. "I've been very slow on the uptake—Gudrun's death, living on a boat under a false name—I just refused to take it all in. I always favored Freyja, you see, and I realize now how hurtful that must have been to poor Gudrun. And I suppose it was even worse after Freyja died. I mourned her too fiercely, and pushed Gudrun away." He nodded his head slowly. "She must have hated me."

"No, I think Gudrun was hiding for a different reason. I think she may have been trying to find out what had happened to her sister, and preferred to keep her identity secret."

"So you do think there was something suspicious about their deaths?"

Brock hesitated. "I honestly don't know. Officially both cases are closed, but I am keeping an open mind. I know you need some resolution in this, and I'll do what I can." Brock thought of Lynch and felt how inadequate his words were.

Kite nodded. "Thank you. There were two things that I

wanted to do in London, apart from seeing you. I wanted to visit Gudrun's boat."

"Of course. You will be her next of kin, I assume?"

"Yes."

"It's still at the same mooring, and I have a key." Brock handed it over and described where the boat was. "And the other thing?"

"At Gudrun's funeral a woman spoke to me briefly after the service. She said that she wanted me to know that Freyja and Gudrun were brave girls, that I should be very proud of them, and that they had died for what they believed in. At the time, my mind in turmoil, I didn't really take it in, but I was struck by the strength of her feeling. I didn't know who she was, but afterward the funeral director identified her from the book that people signed at the door of the chapel. Her name was Anne Downey."

"I see. And she mentioned Freyja as well as Gudrun?"

"Yes, as if she knew them both well. And then I wondered if she had been at Freyja's funeral too, and when I looked in Freyja's book of mourners, sure enough, there was Anne Downey's name. Now I want to find her and ask her what on earth she meant, what she knows. Have you any idea how I can contact her?"

"I'd be interested to hear her answers too," Brock said, thinking this over. "I don't know where she is, but if she's still with her boat, there's somewhere we might try."

THEY WENT OUT TO Brock's car and headed east, out through Finsbury and Shoreditch to join the Old Ford Road. They stopped at its bridge over the Regent's Canal, and looked along its length in both directions, and along the Hertford Union Canal where it ran into the Regent's. It was around here, Brock thought, that Downey had put Kathy in a taxi to the Pewsey

Clinic, wearing her jacket. There were a few boats to be seen, mostly small pleasure craft, but the only narrowboat wasn't Anne Downey's. All the same, they knocked on its window and asked its skipper if he'd seen the *Aquarius*, but he couldn't recall it.

Old Ford Road continued east, roughly parallel to the Hertford Union, and Brock worked his way along, turning off from time to time down the side streets that led to the canal. Streetlights were coming on now, the afternoon light fading and the damp air seeming to thicken, as if ready to condense into fog. They crossed under the A12 into Hackney Wick and an area of factory and warehouse sheds, beyond which they caught glimpses of cranes and the glow of high-intensity lights at the Olympics site. After several wrong turns they came to the canal, on its final stretch before it ran into the Lee Navigation waterway. Halfway along its length was a lock, taking boats down to the lower level of the Lee, with an assortment of small boats on this side of it, but no narrowboats. Brock parked the car and they found a flight of steps leading down to the towpath, and began to walk into the gathering mist.

They reached the lock, and Kite pointed at the small boats. "These aren't the right type, are they?"

"No." Brock stared along the canal bank toward the Lee, seeing nothing resembling a narrowboat. "Looks as if my guess was wrong."

"What's that?" Kite said, pointing to the glimmer of a light in a dark hole in the canal bank opposite, beyond the lock, overgrown by trees and hemmed in by old brick industrial buildings.

"I'm not sure." The only immediate way across was the beam on top of the lock gates, or else to return to the car and find a bridge farther back, but by then it would be dark.

Brock said, "Wait here, Desmond. I'll take a look."

The beam was about a foot wide, split in the middle where

the two gates came together. Brock stepped up onto it and began to walk steadily across. He jumped down on the far side and turned to look back at Kite, and was startled to see him standing unsteadily on the first gate, arms outstretched like a high-wire acrobat. Brock held his breath as Kite reached the middle, and stopped. Brock saw his eyes stray to the long drop on the downstream side, and the lanky figure began to sway. Now his arms were windmilling and Brock could see exactly what was going to happen, the figure toppling down and disappearing under the dark waters of the Lee. He jumped back onto the beam and ran to Kite, grabbing hold of an arm and hauling him along the gate by sheer force of will.

"Ah," Kite said, as he staggered onto dry land. "That was rather exciting."

The remains of an old towpath ran along this side of the canal, its concrete slab broken and overgrown with weeds, the smell of decay and stagnant water heavy in the air. They picked their way around bits of rusty metal guttering and broken timber pallets, and came to the area of dark shadow they'd seen from the other side. It appeared to be a short quay, a length of canal dug back into the bank to provide access to an industrial building from which a broad canopy extended out over the water to provide for covered loading. And beneath the canopy, moored against the abandoned factory wharf, lay a narrowboat, hidden from both the air and the land, a light glowing from a porthole. They made their way carefully toward it.

It was the *Aquarius*, the name picked out in ornate blue and silver letters. Brock saw the sudden doubt appear on Kite's face as he made out the name, as if having second thoughts about what Anne Downey might have to tell him about his daughters.

"Come on," he said gently, and took Kite's elbow to help him up onto the stern. They heard music, the faint jangle of a harpsichord, Bach perhaps, or Scarlatti. The older man gripped the tiller to steady himself as Brock tapped on the door.

The music fell silent, then Anne Downey's face, cautious, appeared at the door. Recognizing Brock, she looked hostile, then surprised as she recognized Kite.

"Dr. Downey," Brock said, "you know Desmond Kite, I think. May we come in?"

She looked at Brock coldly. "I've got nothing to say."

"Please . . ." Kite said hesitantly, as if he hadn't had much practice at begging. "For a grieving father's sake, would you give us a few minutes of your time, Doctor?"

She frowned reluctantly. "I'll speak to you alone, Professor."

"David is my friend," Kite said, putting his hand on Brock's arm. "We were at university together." Brock tried not to show his surprise, but he supposed it might almost be true. Kite continued, "I know that he's as determined as I am to see justice done for Gudrun and Freyja. I really would like him to hear what you have to tell me."

Anne Downey gave a sigh of resignation and reluctantly opened the door to them. As he straightened at the foot of the steps, Brock saw that Ned Tisdell was farther down the boat, sitting tensely at the dining table, where it looked as if they had been preparing an evening meal together.

"I've never been in one of these," Kite said, looking around wonderingly. "It's very snug, isn't it? A great deal more comfortably appointed than a Viking longship, and yet of similar proportions, one might say. I wonder if Gudrun . . ."

His voice tailed away, and Anne Downey answered his unspoken question. "Yes, she used to refer to her boat as her 'longship.' I think she liked to think of herself as a Viking maiden from the sagas you used to read to her and Freyja."

"She told you about that?" He looked wistful.

"Yes, and about taking them to the Viking Ship Museum in Oslo, to see the Gokstad ship."

"Ah . . . So you knew all the time, did you, that she was Gudrun Kite, not Vicky Hawke?"

Downey looked at him sharply, as if she'd misjudged him. "Um, come and sit here at the table, Professor. This is Ned Tisdell."

Tisdell was staring at Brock, then turned to Downey. "You shouldn't have let them in, Anne. You know what Oll—"

"They won't be here long, Ned," she interrupted quickly. "What was it you wanted to ask me, Professor?"

"At Gudrun's funeral you told me that both of my girls had died doing what they believed in. I want to know what you meant by that. What were they mixed up in?"

Downey took a deep breath. "What I meant," she said slowly, "was that their lives, although cut short, had been useful and productive."

"No," Kite insisted, with a sudden decisiveness that took them all by surprise. "No, you meant more than that. Why did Gudrun have to take on somebody else's identity and not tell me, her own father? She even hid where she was living from me."

"Perhaps she just needed time to be alone, and anonymous."

"But why? Why would she hide from me? What had she got herself involved in?"

Downey shook her head and turned away. "I'm sorry, I can't help you."

Brock, who had kept silent up to now, said, "Come on, Anne, it's not that difficult. Gudrun took someone else's name because she didn't want certain people to know that she was Freyja's sister. Isn't that it?"

Downey said nothing, so Brock continued, "And she didn't want them to know that because she was trying to find out who was responsible for her sister's death. Yes? Am I right?"

Still Downey refused to speak, Ned Tisdell staring at her all the while as if willing her to silence.

"Well, let me suggest a possibility, then. Perhaps she suspected that one or both of the men in the car that knocked Freyja down worked in London for Paddington Security Services, and she came down here to try to get some evidence against them. Could that be it? Was that what she was doing? Hacking into their personnel files? Pumping their colleagues for proof that they'd been in Cambridge that night?"

Anne Downey gave an impatient shake of her head, and Brock wondered which bit he might have got wrong. He decided there was nothing he could do but press on. "Did they find out and threaten her? She told you all about it, didn't she? So why the hell didn't she—or you, for that matter—go to the police?"

Downey gave an exasperated sigh, as if she couldn't believe this.

Brock, casting around in his mind for leverage, said, "How did she make the connection to the Paddington company? Were they involved with one of the other firms at the Cambridge Science Park? I know they're not involved with Penney Solutions."

Downey raised her eyebrows in mock surprise. "Oh really?"

"Yes, we checked. There's no connection."

Downey gave a bitter snort. "Oh, brother, you people really are pathetic." She stared at his puzzled expression and said, "You don't know that Penney Solutions and Paddington Security Services have the same owner?"

"No, that's not possible. I had a high-level check done on the two companies."

She laughed. "High-level check! Then they're keeping you out of the loop, aren't they? Paddington is wholly owned by the Harvest Group, which also owns a controlling fifty-five percent of Penney."

Brock blinked. Why hadn't Suzy Russell mentioned this? "The Harvest Group?"

"Venture capitalists. They invest money in speculative new technologies."

"All right . . ." Brock was trying to make sense of this. "So there is a connection. But why would Gudrun have suspected the Paddington people of being involved in her sister's death?"

Downey shrugged, looking as if she regretted saying what she had. "I've no idea. What about you, Ned? Did she say anything to you?"

Tisdell shook his head.

"No," Brock growled. "You know more than this. You both knew Freyja, didn't you? You went to her funeral, Anne, and you, Ned, took your boat up to Cambridge and met her on the grounds of the Plow at Fen Ditton, near the science park. You two have been involved in this from the beginning. Hell, they tried to kill you too, Ned, setting fire to your boat. Come on, you'll have to do better than that. What's really going on?"

Downey and Tisdell exchanged a look, but said nothing.

"Very well, I'll have to arrest the pair of you as accessories both before and after the fact, concealing evidence relating to the deaths of Freyja and Gudrun Kite."

"Oh God," Tisdell groaned, cradling his face in his hands.

Anne Downey looked at him anxiously, then turned to Brock. "You work with Kathy Kolla, don't you? Let me speak to her. I trust her, she saved Ned's life."

"All right." Brock took out his phone and dialed Kathy's new cell number, then handed the phone to Downey. She listened for a moment, then frowned. "There's no reply."

Brock tried again without success, then rang Suzanne's home number. When Suzanne answered he asked for Kathy.

"She's not here, David. She left me a note to say that she had to go up to town this morning. I would have expected her to be back by now. I tried to ring her, but had to leave a message."

Brock hung up. He turned to Anne Downey. "That night she rescued Ned, you called a cab to take her to the Pewsey Clinic. Why did she decide to go there?"

"It was her idea. She had damaged her broken collarbone again getting Ned out of his boat and she needed more help than I could give her. She thought they would be the best people, since they set the bone originally. Also . . ."

"Yes?"

"Well, I hoped she might be able to find out more about the clinic. But when I couldn't contact her afterward I assumed she hadn't been able to."

"I don't understand. She'd already spent several days there before. How did you expect her to find anything out this time?"

"I . . . I gave her a pass card so she could access the secure area."

"You what!" Brock stared at her in disbelief. "A pass card . . . Is that how Ned got into the clinic that night?"

"Yes."

"So Kathy was right, he was there."

Anne Downey nodded.

"How did you get hold of a pass card?"

"I can't tell you that," she said, a note of her earlier defiance creeping back.

"Listen, Anne. They kept Kathy in that clinic for three nights, and when she came out she was drugged to the eyeballs and couldn't remember a thing. She still can't—they wiped her memory with drugs."

Downey looked shocked.

"So what the hell's going on in there? What were you trying to find out?"

"I . . . Oh God . . ." The doctor put a hand to her mouth. "The clinic is also owned by the Harvest Group. I worked there for a couple of months in the general ward the year before last. That's how I got involved in this. I was doing routine work with patients on rehab, but I became aware of some odd things going on. There was a secure area that only a few staff could access, and they just said there were patients with special needs in there. But they also kept animals at that end of the clinic—we never saw them, but there was a smell sometimes, and occasionally you'd hear something, pigs, I think, screaming."

"They were doing animal experiments?"

"I assumed so, maybe organ transplants—liver, kidney, and spleen transplants have been successfully carried out from pigs, and pancreas cells for diabetics. Xenotransplantation, it's called. There were rumors among the staff, but nobody really knew. Then I met Ned by chance, because of our boats. We had moorings next to each other out at Alperton on the Grand Union. When I told him I was working at Pewsey he told me he knew about the place from his friends in animal liberation, who believed that unlicensed experiments with animals had been going on there for some time."

She stopped as Ned suddenly jumped to his feet. "Did you hear something?"

They listened, then Anne smiled sadly at her friend. "Poor Ned. After the attack on his boat he's been a bag of nerves. I'm surprised he can even stand being cooped up inside here."

"About Pewsey," Brock said.

"Yes. Ned's friends had a blog about animal rights issues, and Ned wrote a piece about Pewsey based on what I'd told him. Then Freyja Kite got in touch with him, and said she was interested in what was going on there too, and could we meet. So Ned and I went up to Cambridge in his boat, and Freyja told us about her research."

"So this was all about animal liberation, was it?" Brock said.

"No," Anne said, "Not at all . . ."

Her words were lost in a deafening crash of noise as the doors at both ends of the boat were smashed open and dark figures came pounding in. Brock recognized the familiar gear and began to rise from his seat but was abruptly forced back down by a strong hand on his shoulder. One of the men strode forward to the end of the table and said, "I am a police officer. I have a warrant to search these premises and I require you to identify yourselves. You . . ." He pointed at Anne, whose eyes were wide with shock.

"I . . . My name is Anne Downey. I'm the owner of this boat. What—"

"You!" The man pointed at Ned.

"Officer," Brock said. "I am Detec—"

"Shut up!"

Ned, trembling and stumbling over his words, gave his name. Two of the uniforms moved forward and handcuffed both him and Anne Downey.

"You two are under arrest on suspicion of illegal entry of restricted premises and obstructing the course of justice. You are not required to say anything, but anything you do say . . ."

He finished the warning and turned to Brock. "And you are?"

Brock carefully drew back his jacket and took out his wallet, showing the man his police ID. The man flinched. "Sir."

"What's your name, Inspector?"

"Leith, Derek Leith, sir; same command as you, assigned to Operation Intruder."

"Can I see your warrant?"

The inspector handed it over. It was dated four days previously, and had been signed by Commander Lynch.

"I was in the process of questioning these two people when

you arrived, Inspector," Brock said. "I'd like to finish what I was doing."

"I'm sorry, sir. I have explicit instructions to prevent them communicating with anyone until they have been placed in custody."

"And where will that be?"

"I'll take them to the Stratford station." The inspector turned to Kite. "You are Professor Kite?"

"Yes."

"I'm instructed to advise you to go straight home, sir. Someone will contact you."

Kite looked shaken. "I see. Yes, very well. But . . . aren't they to be charged with murder?"

"Not at this stage." He turned back to Brock. "You came with Professor Kite, sir?"

"Yes. My car is back at the bridge."

"One of my men will escort you both back there. Now, if you please."

Brock turned to look at Anne Downey. She stared at him, then at Kite, and said softly, "You bastards."

TWENTY-SEVEN

JACK BRAGG HAD A local doctor, it seemed, a tubby little man who gave every impression of being terrified by his patient. He examined the mark on Bragg's back gingerly, as if fingering an unexploded bomb. Then he came and had a look at Kathy. If he thought it odd that she was tied to a chair, he didn't say anything.

"Mm, a little unusual, Mr. Bragg, certainly. You haven't asked the doctor who treated you at the clinic? Would you like me to speak to him?"

"Not until you figure out what he's done. She thinks . . ." he nodded in Kathy's direction, ". . . that they've injected us with something to give us a heart attack."

"Hah!" The doctor's laugh turned to a cough as he caught the fury in Bragg's eyes. "That may be a little far-fetched."

"How can we find out?"

"Um, well, we might do a CAT scan, or an MRI, and make sure there's nothing odd going on in there."

"Do it."

The doctor fumbled his phone and made arrangements for an immediate MRI at a local clinic. "Her too?" he asked Bragg.

"No. Just me."

They hurried out, leaving Kathy still tied to the chair by the pool, with the boxer watching her. His name was Bennie, Kathy had gathered, the body builder was Troy.

"Nice try," Bennie said. "Trouble is, when he finds out it's a load of bullshit he's going to be very angry with you."

Kathy, feeling a chill in her stomach, knew that he was right. "That's why you need to let me go, Bennie. You don't want my blood on your hands. Cut the ropes and tell him you had to go out for a few minutes, and I must have had a blade up my sleeve."

Bennie thought that was quite funny, stretching his mouth briefly in a smile before he turned and ambled across to a newspaper lying on a bench. He had a slightly unsteady gait, bumping into a chair on the way, as if one fight too many had upset his sense of balance.

BRAGG AND THE DOCTOR returned after an hour, looking grim. One glance at Bragg's face told Kathy that the little speech that she'd prepared to persuade him to spare her would be pointless.

Bennie got to his feet, a look of anticipation on his face. "Okay, Mr. Bragg?"

"No, it's not okay." He glared at Kathy. "You were right." To the doctor he said, "Show her."

The doctor, who had a large envelope in his hand, came toward her and pulled out several prints from the MRI scan.

Kathy, startled and wondering if this was some kind of game they were playing with her, looked at the sheet he held in front of her. It showed the ghostly forms of what looked like ribs and soft organs, and in the middle of them a small, sharply defined white lozenge, about the size of a grain of rice.

"There appears to be an implant," the doctor said, sounding shaken. "Immediately behind the left ventricle of the heart."

"A time bomb!" Bragg roared. "A fuckin' poison capsule waiting to dissolve! Just like you said."

Kathy was stunned. This was crazy. It couldn't be right—she'd made it all up!

"I imagine you must have the same thing," the doctor said to her. "Of course, we don't know what's in it exactly . . ."

"Don't be stupid," Bragg said bitterly. "It's not going to be bleedin' vitamins, is it? This is murder by stealth. Now I understand why they let me out, so I can go home and have a quiet heart attack in my own bed and everybody'll be happy. Well, you're just going to have to take it out, Doc."

"Impossible."

"What?"

The doctor wrung his hands. "I'm sorry, Mr. Bragg, but I couldn't possibly do something like that. It's in just about the most inaccessible part of your body, right next to your heart. It would require major surgery, an operating theater, a highly skilled surgeon, postoperative care . . ."

Bragg pondered for a minute. "Well, we'll have to go to where we can get all of that. Troy, get the guns. You can go home, Doc. Not a word to anyone, okay?"

"Yes, yes. I'll leave you the scans, shall I?" He dropped them on a table and scampered off.

Bennie, standing at his shoulder, said, "What about her?"

"We'll take her with us. They may need to practice on someone else first. Untie her and kill her if she tries anything."

WHEN BROCK AND KITE reached the car their police escort waited until they drove back to the main road, heavy with rush-hour traffic. Brock said, "They knew your name, Desmond. I think you'd better explain."

"Yes, of course. I should have been open with you, but I wasn't sure. They said to keep it to myself, you see."

"Who did?"

"A senior police officer, a Superintendent Russell. She came to see me a couple of days ago."

"In Cambridge? When?"

"Er, Tuesday it was."

He'd had lunch with Suzy Russell on Monday, and he'd spoken to her on the phone earlier that morning and she'd said nothing.

"Go on."

"She explained that they now had convincing evidence that Freyja and Gudrun's deaths were not accidental. They had specific evidence that two people who knew the girls—Dr. Anne Wood and Ned Tisdell—were involved in their murder. Both people were in hiding, and the police couldn't trace them. However, she suggested that if I came to London and started asking after them they might agree to see me, and then the police could act. So that's what I did."

"Did she tell you why they would have been involved in the girls' murder?"

"They're involved in industrial espionage, she said, stealing industrial secrets that Freyja was working on."

"So how did the police find the *Aquarius* just now?"

"I led them there. Superintendent Russell told me to leave my phone turned on, and they'd know where I was."

"I see." Brock pulled in to the curb and sat for a moment, thinking. Finally he said, "I'd like you to turn it off now, Desmond."

"Why?"

"Superintendent Russell has told me a very different story. I don't think she's been entirely frank with either of us. And I'd like to know the rest of what Anne Downey was going to tell us before the squad arrived. Did she strike you as a guilty witness?"

"She was very hostile, they both were."

"Yes, and frightened and suspicious. But guilty of murder?"

Kite hesitated, then said, "I'm not sure that I can judge . . . When we were talking to her I tried to imagine it, and I couldn't."

"That's what I was thinking."

Professor Kite hesitated for a moment, then drew out his phone and turned it off. "What now?"

"I'm going to take you to see a man who I think knows what Anne knows—maybe more. All these people seem to have a great distrust of the police, and are very reluctant to talk to me, but he may be prepared to say more to you."

They drove on in silence, back through Central London toward Paddington. When they reached the canal basin, Brock drew to a stop and they got out and went over to the railings.

"Over there is Gudrun's boat, *Grace*, and next to it *Roaming Free*, that one with a herb garden on the roof." Brock pointed, Kite peering through the mist. "It's owned by a couple, the Stapletons, who were friendly with Gudrun. Farther down is *Jonquil*, owned by Debbie Rowland, another friend. You might like to speak to them, but I don't think any of them have the answers you're looking for. However, down there is someone who might."

Kite followed his direction. "What, in that wreck?"

"It's a houseboat, of sorts. The man's an eccentric, name of Ollie Kovacs, with a history of involvement in radical causes, and Gudrun used to visit him. I think he knows something. Why don't you try and find out? When you're finished go over to Gudrun's boat and give me a ring from there."

They shook hands. "Good luck."

"Where will you be?" Kite asked anxiously.

"I've got a little job to do. Don't worry, I won't be far away."

FROM THE TENTH FLOOR the ground was barely visible, wreathed in patches of mist in the twilight gloom. Brock turned from the view through the glass wall and went over to the reception desk where a young woman was talking on the phone. She ignored him as he studied the business cards displayed on the desktop. He selected one, *Steve Budd, Business Manager,* and when she finally hung up and favored him with a blank smile he said, "Steve in?"

She blinked. "Steve?"

"Steve Budd." He held up his police ID. "I'm Dave, from Superintendent Russell's crew."

"Oh, yes." She picked up the phone.

"Tell him I'm a bit pushed for time," Brock added, and wandered back to the window. There was a Christmassy feel to the view from up here, he thought, the streetlights glimmering through the tinselly fog.

"Dave?"

Brock wheeled around. A short, pugnacious-looking man was peering at him uncertainly. "Steve," he said forcefully, sticking out his hand and taking the other in a tight grip. "They sent me over to have a word. Where can we talk?"

Budd showed him into a meeting room and Brock unbuttoned his overcoat and sat down with a grunt. "Gudrun Kite's father's in town. Just wanted to warn you, in case he tries to make contact."

"Ah." Budd's face cleared. "Yes, they told me he might come. Don't worry, I know my lines. He's not going to make trouble, is he?"

Brock sighed wearily. "You never know, do you? He's a bitter old man who's convinced that his daughters were murdered and that the cops are covering it up."

"Whoa." Budd blew out his cheeks, raising his hands as if to fend off trouble. "Don't ask me, Mr. Kite, sir. I know nothing. Far as we're concerned she was Vicky Hawke, an excellent employee."

"That's the way," Brock nodded.

"You don't think he'll go to the press, do you?"

"We'll look after it. But you've got nothing to worry about, have you?"

"Our people don't like publicity."

"Harvest, you mean?"

Budd gave a fretful sigh, then shrugged. "Anyway, the police should be happy. From what I read in the papers everything's going brilliant, isn't it?"

Brock nodded. "Oh yes. Brilliant."

"Well then, you'll just have to keep Gudrun's old man off our backs, won't you? Was there anything else?"

"No, that's all." Brock got to his feet.

"All right then." Budd showed him out to the elevator. "See you around, Dave."

WHEN HE REACHED THE street Brock checked his phone, but there was no message from Professor Kite. The air was colder now. He imagined the two men huddled together in the ruined belly of the *Princess Louise*, elderly scholars interrogating each other for the truth.

The DiSTaF office block seemed quiet, the lobby deserted apart from the same fashionable young man lounging behind the desk. He snapped upright as Brock pushed through the door, alerted perhaps by the look on Brock's face.

"Sir? Can I help you?"

"Superintendent Russell," Brock growled.

"She's not in, sir."

"Really." Brock began walking to the elevators.

"Really," the man repeated. "And you can't use the elevators without a pass . . . sir."

Brock turned back to him, and saw his smirk. He stomped back over to the desk and pushed his face too close to the other man's. "Where is she?"

"Um . . ." The man winced, tilting his head back. "She's out with the others. They're all out celebrating."

"Where?"

"I could contact her if it's urgent."

"Where?"

He cleared his throat. "Tiles, Buckingham Palace Road."

"Thank you."

Brock drove slowly along Buckingham Palace Road until he spotted the place, a wine bar and restaurant, and turned off into a side street and parked his car half up on the sidewalk with his police pass visible on the dash. From the restaurant on street level he was directed downstairs to the private party in the basement bar.

From the volume of laughter and chatter they had been there for a while, a couple of dozen of them, all young and casually dressed. They turned to look at him as he moved among them, eyeing him over the rims of their wineglasses as if trying to work out what he was doing there. One called out, "Looking for the men's room, pal?" He could see no sign of Suzy Russell.

"Brock!"

He turned and saw Mickey Schaeffer coming toward him, a puzzled look on his face. "Boss, hi. Can I help you?"

"Hello, Mickey. I was told Superintendent Russell was here."

"She was, but she got a phone call just a couple of minutes ago and had to leave."

"Ah. What's the occasion?"

"Operation Intruder, boss. A bit of a celebration. Everybody seems very happy with the way it's gone. Can I get you a drink?"

"No thanks, Mickey. See you later."

Mickey followed him to the foot of the stairs. "Boss," he said, voice lowered, "how's Kathy doing?"

"Not too bad. Convalescing."

"With your friend in Battle, yes? Bren told me."

"Yes, that's right." Mickey was looking thoughtful, and Brock added, "Why, is there a problem?"

Mickey seemed about to say something, but then someone from the party called out to him and he shook his head and turned away.

COMMANDER LYNCH'S SECRETARY CAROL had been installed at headquarters at the same time as Lynch himself, displacing Commander Sharpe's secretary Lillian and completely rearranging her room within an afternoon. No one was very sure where she'd come from, and the word was that she was not given to idle chat, was fiercely loyal to Fred Lynch, and was filled with a sense of her own self-importance. On the previous occasions they'd met, Brock had formed the impression that she didn't like him. This time he was sure of it.

"No, Chief Inspector, you may not speak to the commander." It was said with satisfaction.

"It's extremely urgent."

"Send an email."

Brock took a deep breath. "I need to speak to him now. He's not answering his cell."

She fixed him with a bleak glare. "He is at an important function, if you must know, and has turned off his work phone."

"He has another phone?"

"Why don't you go and talk to Mr. Payne. He may be able to help you."

Brock left, seething. When he got back to Queen Anne's Gate he told his secretary Dot, who wasn't surprised.

"She's a bitch, everyone says so. Leave it with me. I may be able to get hold of his personal cell phone number."

"I'd appreciate it, Dot. And I'm expecting a call from Professor Desmond Kite. He hasn't rung this number, has he?"

"No. There's a heap of other messages on your desk, none critical."

Brock went reluctantly into his room to face the in-box. After thumbing through the pile of documents and files he pushed them aside and turned to his computer. The Web site for the Harvest Group described their operations:

> *From our offices in London, Palo Alto, and Singapore, we have supported innovative companies for over twenty years, helping to develop groundbreaking technologies with a potential for global growth. We focus on the fields of electronic technology and life sciences, making investments ranging from seed funding to large-scale development capital for market-ready products.*

Brock wondered what market-ready products Paddington Security Services and Penney Solutions had developed that would have interested Suzy Russell.

TWENTY-EIGHT

BENNIE THE BOXER BROUGHT the car to a halt on the drive at an acute angle to the front door of the clinic and they got out, Bragg leading, then Kathy, with the two men behind her, the hard muzzle of a gun pressed into the small of her back. She tried to see an opportunity to get away or warn the people inside, but at the same time she felt irresistibly drawn to the disaster that was about to happen, the angry psychopath exploding inside the secretive clinic.

One of the clinic's security men answered the door. "Why, Mr. Bragg . . ." he began, then choked as Bragg grabbed his throat, propelling him backward into the deserted hallway.

"Where's the boss?" Bragg demanded.

"Mr. Montague?" The man croaked, his eyes slipping sideways toward a door marked *Director's Office.*

They marched toward the door and burst through into a secretary's office, where Bragg gathered up the shocked woman behind the desk and continued toward the inner door bearing the nameplate *Vernon Montague, Director,* which he kicked open.

Montague was sitting behind his large oak desk, holding up a color brochure which Dr. Partridge, standing by his side, was explaining to him. They simultaneously lifted their eyes to the intrusion as the six people burst in and crowded forward onto the large Indian carpet in front of the desk.

"Phones," Bragg barked, and his two helpers moved quickly around the room, removing cell phones and making the guard and the secretary sit on the floor, while Bragg locked the doors they had come through. Kathy watched the reactions of the two men behind the desk, Dr. Partridge wide-eyed and shocked, while Montague, after initial outrage, seeming to recover more quickly. There was a moment, as Bennie began to search him, when the two men exchanged a brief look, some kind of acknowledgment that Kathy couldn't quite interpret.

Then Montague's eyes met hers. "Inspector Kolla," he said coldly, "would you mind explaining what's going on here?"

Before she could answer, Bragg stepped between them, reaching across the desk and grabbing the director's tie and hauling him forward. "Montague, you piece of shit!" he roared. "What have you done to me?"

Montague made a choking sound and Bragg released him, slapping him hard, twice, across the face as he rebounded back into his chair. Bragg turned to Dr. Partridge. "Who are you?"

"I'm . . ." Partridge swallowed, coughed, glancing with alarm at his boss, whose face had turned purple. "I'm a doctor, Partridge is my—"

"Well, look at these, *Doctor*!" Bragg bellowed, and drew a rolled envelope from inside his jacket and emptied its contents, the MRI scans, onto the desk in front of him. "What do you make of them, eh? A professional opinion?"

Partridge fumbled with them hesitantly. "Um . . . medical scans?"

"Yes, yes!" Bragg said impatiently.

"Upper body scans. I . . ." He stopped, his eyes focusing on something on one of the sheets.

"Yes?"

"That looks like . . ." He glanced at Montague, then at Bragg.

"What? A pacemaker? A baby? A fucking flying saucer?"

The room was utterly silent for a long moment, and then Partridge whispered, "An implant."

Bragg gave out a manic scream. "YES!" He was breathing heavily, bouncing from foot to foot, and both men behind the desk cringed back in alarm. "AND WHO PUT IT THERE, DOCTOR? YOU?"

Partridge shook his head wildly. "No, no. That's not my field."

Bragg drew back, straightening, breathing in, becoming still, his sudden immobility more frightening than his previous manic agitation. Then he reached under his jacket to the waistband of his jeans and drew out a very large handgun. He cocked it slowly, leaned forward across the desk, and pressed its nose into Montague's forehead. "Who put it there, Montague?"

Montague licked his swollen lip. "Our senior surgeon, Carl . . ." The second name was lost in a hoarse choking cough.

Bragg pointed to the phone on the desk. "Get him in here."

"He's not at the clinic. He's probably at his rented rooms in Harley Street, or—"

"Phone him. Get him here NOW."

Montague picked up the phone with a shaking hand.

"On loudspeaker," Bragg demanded, and they listened to the buzzing notes as Montague dialed.

"Vernon!" A suave voice, discordantly oblivious and relaxed, filled the room. "How are you?"

"Carl. Something of a panic, actually."

"Really?"

"Where are you?"

"On my way over to the clinic. The new trial, remember? What's the problem?"

"The . . . implants. A spot of bother."

"You don't sound yourself, Vernon. What kind of bother?"

"Can't explain over the phone. Be as quick as you can, okay?"

"Be there in ten. And take it easy. I'm sure we can deal with it."

"Good," Bragg said as the line went dead, easing back on his heels. "That answers my first question. Now the second. Who did you do it for?"

"What?" Montague gazed up at him blankly, an angry red mark on his forehead where the gun muzzle had been pressed.

"You heard. Who did you do it *for*? Who was your client? Who paid your expensive fees?"

Montague's eyes flicked momentarily toward Kathy, and Bragg gave a nasty laugh. "Come on, Montague, I want documentation—files, contracts, letters of instruction, invoices, records of payment. It's all here somewhere, isn't it?" He looked around the room. "Or is it outside in the office? Do I have to tear the place apart? No, I've got a better idea—you'll tell me where it is."

This was a new Bragg, horribly jocular. He fixed Montague with a leery grin for a moment, then turned and began wandering around the room, his gaze roaming over the bookcases, the oil painting of an Alpine scene above the fireplace, the carriage clock on the mantelpiece, as if he were playing a children's party game. Finally he settled on the secretary kneeling on the floor. He lifted his gun and pointed it vertically down at the crown of her head. "So where is it, Vernon?"

Montague's mouth opened, then shut, then opened again. "There's nothing here," he croaked. "Our confidential papers are kept elsewhere."

"This will make a terrible mess of your carpet. Inspector Kolla, tell them how many people I've killed in my long and illustrious career."

Kathy had been easing herself into a position where she

might throw herself at Bragg, but now she froze as all eyes turned to her. "I've no idea. A dozen?"

"Oh." Bragg looked mortified. "A few more than that."

The secretary was staring up at the gun. Bragg smiled down at her. "I'll count to five. One . . ."

"Please!" Montague cried.

"Two . . ."

"No!"

"Three . . ."

Montague gave a final strangled cry: "But I can't!"

"Four . . ."

There was a moment of stillness, and then the secretary said in an unnaturally calm voice, "There's a safe behind the bookcase in the corner over there. I know the combination."

Bragg beamed down at her. "Good girl."

He walked back to the desk and, as he passed, lashed out suddenly with his fist holding the gun. Montague screamed and toppled backward, clutching his face. Bragg continued to the corner and followed the secretary's halting directions to swing back the bookcase and open the safe. "Switch more lights on, Bennie," he barked. "I can't see a fucking thing over here." He began rifling inside, pulling out folders, examining them and tossing them to the floor until he found what he was after. He held up a blue file. "Project Raven," he said with a snarl.

Something distracted him through the tall windows facing out to the drive, and Kathy turned and saw the headlights of a car approaching.

"Bennie," Bragg said, "we've got a visitor. If it's Carl bring him in. If it's anybody else tell them the place is closed down for quarantine."

"Right." The boxer hurried out and returned a few minutes later escorting a tall, lean man whose hairless head gleamed pink. Kathy had a sudden vivid recollection of him standing over her, touching her broken shoulder with the tips of his fingers. He was staring now at Vernon Montague standing behind the desk, clutching a handkerchief to his nose, his white shirt splashed with blood. Then he turned his attention to Jack Bragg, his eyes pausing for a moment at the file in his hand.

Bragg put down the file, picked up the MRI scan from the desktop and walked over to the surgeon. "Hello, Carl. You remember me, don't you?"

"Oh yes."

"You stuck an implant in my heart, didn't you?" He waved the scan in Carl's face.

Carl glanced at the image and said calmly, "Not actually *in* your heart, Mr. Bragg. Close by."

"What's in it?"

"Didn't they tell you? It's nothing to worry about."

Kathy saw a red gleam grow in Bragg's eye. Carl saw it too, and added quickly, "A microchip, that's all. Something to tell us where you are."

"A time bomb, more like."

"No, no, nothing like that." The surgeon's attempt to shrug off the idea with a careless smile, as if it were absurd, didn't sound entirely convincing.

"Well, now you can take it out again."

"No, that's not possible."

"NOT POSSIBLE?" Bragg roared, and his free hand went for the man's throat. "You'd better make it possible, Carl, or I'll put an implant in you, a nine-millimeter implant."

"It would be difficult," Carl gasped. "That's the point, you see, to make it difficult to remove. Didn't they explain all this to you? It would be a . . . life-threatening operation."

Bragg stared at him, nostrils flaring. "But you've done it before, haven't you?"

Carl gave a nervous shake of his head. "No."

They were all staring at Bragg, waiting for his reaction as he pondered. "Then you'd better have a practice run." He nodded at Kathy. "On her."

"I really wouldn't advise it . . ."

But Bragg wasn't listening to him any more. He turned to the secretary sitting on the carpet. She looked pale and stared back up at him with frightened eyes. "Who else is in the building tonight?" he demanded, and she told him. It was a quiet night at the clinic, with just four patients and two nurses on duty. Evening meals had already been served and the kitchen staff had gone.

He snapped orders to his two men, who went out, returning soon after with the nurses and several cell phones.

"Right," Bragg said. "Time to get to work, Carl."

"Neither of these nurses has adequate theater experience," Carl protested, but Bragg waved him away.

"You and the doc over there will do it. Bennie will go with you, and watch every move you make."

"I think this is a bad idea," Kathy said.

"Who cares what you think?" Bragg waved at the boxer to get on with it.

"No, really. We should wait and get this done by a proper heart specialist. Someone who doesn't have an interest in you and me ending up dead on the operating table."

Bragg stared bleakly at her. "We don't have time for that. But don't worry, if you end up dead on the operating table I'll kill Carl here and take your advice."

Bennie gripped her good arm and waved his pistol at Partridge and Carl. "Lead the way, doctors."

As they walked down the deserted corridor Kathy heard the two men in front arguing quietly.

"We can't do this, Carl," Partridge was saying.

"Shut up and let me think."

"But at the very least you'll need an anesthetist!"

"Looks like that's your job, John. I think you'll discover all kinds of unexpected talents when there's a gun pointed at your head."

They reached the doors to the secure area. Carl swiped with his pass and they moved on through. Something—a different smell perhaps—awakened a memory in Kathy's mind. It came back to her now, entering this corridor, the room on the left from which she'd watched Bennie and the other man helping Bragg to leave, the four mortuary cabinets in that room, in one of which she was probably going to end up.

They reached the operating theater and Bennie waved them inside. When the door closed behind them, Carl turned to him and said, "Well? What do you want us to do?"

He said it in a respectful tone, as one might speak to a manager rather than a threatening thug, and for the second time, Kathy felt she had completely misunderstood the relationship between the rest of them and Bragg's two bodyguards.

"Just wait," Bennie said. He took his cell phone from his pocket and stepped back out into the corridor.

Kathy looked at the two doctors, trying to decipher their expressions. "What's going on?" she said.

"We have a slight *probleem*," Carl replied, drawing out the Afrikaans word, and turned away with a look of disgust.

After several minutes asking questions that the other two refused to answer, Kathy fell silent as the door opened again and Bennie looked in, pocketing his phone, and waved to Carl to join him outside. Dr. Partridge was left looking deeply troubled, and Kathy tried again.

"John, you're my doctor, for God's sake," she said softly.

"I don't need to be reminded of that," he snapped.

"Well, act like it. Bragg is a psychopathic killer and we need help. Get out of my way."

He shifted, refusing to meet her eyes, and Kathy stepped

quickly forward to the phone fixed to the wall. She fumbled it clumsily with her one good hand, and began pressing the buttons. Then another hand, much bigger than her own, closed around hers and tugged the phone away.

"Don't be stupid," Bennie murmured in her ear. "Go and sit down over there and do what you're told."

Kathy did so, aware of Carl whispering urgently to John Partridge. Finally Partridge said, "You're sure?" He sounded frightened.

Carl nodded, patted the other man's arm and said, "Pre-op, John."

Partridge hesitated a moment, then disappeared into another room that opened off the theater. When he returned he was carrying a needle. Kathy felt Bennie close his fist on her broken shoulder and she froze as Partridge came toward her.

"You're a doctor," she said. "I don't agree to this. You can't go ahead with it."

Partridge, looking sick, shook his head, avoiding her eyes. She felt the sharp stab of the needle in her arm.

TWENTY-NINE

BROCK'S PHONE PURRED ON the desk at his elbow. He picked it up and immediately recognized Desmond Kite's voice. He checked his watch; it was after seven, almost three hours since he'd left the professor at the canal.

"David!" Kite sounded slightly breathless.

"Are you all right, Desmond? How did you get on?"

"I'm fine, very well, yes, excellent." Not just breathless but excited, almost elated, Brock thought, trying to interpret the tremors and unexpected changes of pitch in the other man's voice.

"Was Ollie Kovacs any help?"

"Oh yes, oh indeed. I was doubtful at first, profoundly skeptical in fact, but he showed me evidence, chronologies, scientific data, correspondence even—much of it illegally obtained, I regret to say, but convincing, oh yes, very convincing."

He drew a deep breath before continuing in a rush. "In the end I was completely convinced. I only wish that Freyja and Gudrun could have told me. I might surely have been able to help them, talk to the right people. But they probably thought that I'd be taken for a crank, one of those stupid old men who bore their colleagues to death with their pet theories. No, that wasn't their way. They didn't want to whisper to people of influence, they wanted to shout to the world, to tell everyone what was going on."

Brock was becoming alarmed at the rising note of what sounded like hysteria in the old man's voice. "Desmond, why don't I pick you up and you can tell me all about it over dinner?"

"No, no time for that now. I have Superintendent Russell with me. I am anxious to persuade her to go on the record, but she is understandably reluctant. I would like you to speak to someone more senior—the commissioner or chief constable or whatever he's called. I want them to order her to talk, or else speak on her behalf. It has to be someone in authority, David. If they want to save her, they must tell the world the truth."

"Superintendent Russell is with you now?" Brock frowned. "Let me speak to her, will you, Desmond?"

"Very well."

There was a scuffling sound, then Suzy Russell's voice, tense. "Brock? He's got a bomb—"

She was cut off abruptly and Kite spoke again. "I'm completely serious, David. Perhaps for the first time in my life."

"Desmond, where are you?" But before he'd finished the sentence the line went dead.

He grabbed the internal directory and found the number he wanted, asking for a trace on Kite's phone. Almost immediately the answer came back that it was turned off and couldn't be located. He checked who was still in the office and found that Bren Gurney and Pip Gallagher were in the lobby, on the point of going home. He told them to hang on, then grabbed his coat and went out to Dot's office. She too was about to leave. "Sorry," she said, "they won't let me have Lynch's private number."

Brock swore and took the stairs at a run. In the lobby Bren

was phoning his wife Deanne, canceling dinner, while Pip was asking if she should draw a gun. Brock told her that wouldn't be necessary, thinking that a Viking battle-ax might be more appropriate.

PIP DROVE THEM TO the canal basin in record time while Brock explained the background.

"It's a bluff," Bren said in his imperturbable Cornish burr. "Where would he have got hold of a bomb?"

They pulled into the curb just beyond the gate in the railings with its barely visible sign, *O.K.* Below them the bulk of Ollie's boat formed an irregular black shape against the faintly luminescent glimmer of the canal surface, but no lights were visible on board. Brock led the way down the brick stairs, hard to make out in the misty dark. They switched on flashlights, picking out fresh marks on the mossy steps, as if someone had recently slipped or dragged something across them.

When they reached the boat they stepped in under the canvas awning and Brock tried the door. It was locked, and he nodded at Bren, who burst it open easily with his shoulder. Brock called out, his voice dying into the silence. The atmosphere inside was thick and musty, heavy with odors of moldy fabric and paper, fried food, and something else, sharper and chemical, gasoline perhaps or a solvent of some kind. They split up to search.

It was Pip who called out eventually, from a small room at what must have been the stern of the original *Princess Louise*. It was fitted out as a workshop with wooden workbenches down each side, stained and scored with use, and rows of ancient tools hanging on hooks from the walls. One of the benches was covered with the oily cogs and sprockets of a dismantled bicycle derailleur gear, but it was the other that had attracted Pip's attention. On it lay several coils of electric cable, a cluster of thin metal rods, and a couple of car batteries, together with an old wooden box with rope handles. Inside it lay two fat tubes wrapped in what looked like brown greaseproof paper.

Bren took one look and murmured, "Oh Jesus."

"Is it what I think it is?" Pip asked, and Bren nodded.

"Those are blasting caps," he said, pointing to the metal rods. He peered inside the box. "And this looks like dynamite. I didn't think they made this stuff any more. How old is it, I wonder?" He stuck his torch right inside the box and looked for a long moment, then drew back with an intake of breath. "They're sweating." He turned to Brock. "We need the bomb squad."

"Yes." Brock was thinking. "So where have they gone?" He went over to the porthole on the side facing the canal and looked out at the row of narrowboats opposite. He recognized *Jonquil* and *Roaming Free*, both with lights in their windows, and there was Gudrun's boat, *Grace*, in darkness. Yet . . . He looked more closely. "See that boat over there," he said, "the second one along? Is that a light in one of its portholes, toward the left?"

"Yes," Pip said confidently.

"Not just a reflection in the glass?"

"No, a crack in the curtains, definitely."

Brock left Bren on the street above Kovacs's den to meet the explosive ordnance disposal team they'd called, and set off with Pip across the bridge to the other side of the canal. The portholes on *Grace* were blanked out with dark curtains, but close to a glimmer of light could be seen in places around their edges. Brock continued to *Roaming Free*.

As he stepped up onto the stern he heard voices raised inside. It sounded as if the Stapletons were having a domestic. He tapped on the door and the arguing stopped abruptly. Howard Stapleton pulled the door open. "Yes?" he demanded sharply, then peered more closely. "Oh, Chief Inspector . . . sorry. Can I help?"

"A quick word, Mr. Stapleton, with you both."

Stapleton showed him in and he nodded to Molly. "Sorry to bother you, but I wonder if you've been aware of any recent activity on *Grace* next door?"

They looked at each other, then shook their heads. "Why, has there been a break-in?"

"I'm trying to trace Gudrun's father, who's in London at the moment, and I thought he might have visited her boat."

"Oh, no, I don't think so."

"Tall man, about six-two, in his seventies, lean build, thinning white hair, wearing a brown overcoat, gray scarf?"

They looked blank.

"What about Ollie Kovacs, in the houseboat across the canal? Seen him lately?"

"No," said Howard.

"Yes," Molly said. "I noticed him crossing over this way on the bridge, um, about an hour ago."

"You didn't see where he went?"

"Well, no, the phone rang just then, my sister in Manchester . . ." She shot a quick hostile glance at her husband. The source of the dispute, Brock guessed.

"Was he carrying anything?"

She frowned. "Yes, actually, he was, a rather weird-looking carpet bag from what I could make out—the fog was settling around then."

"But you didn't see the man I've just described?"

She pondered, then shook her head. "There were other people on the bridge, but Ollie was the only one I recognized and I didn't pay them much attention. What's this about? Has Ollie been up to something?"

"It's possible that there's been a gas leak on *Grace*, and I'm going to have to ask you both to put your coats on and leave for a while."

The Stapletons looked startled.

"There's another detective outside, DC Gallagher, and I want you to give her your cell number so that we can contact you when we have the all clear. She'll be evacuating the other boats too."

It took some further repetition and discussion before Brock was able to bustle them out onto the towpath, where Pip Gallagher was escorting Debbie Rowland and her small boy toward the steps up to the street.

When the towpath was clear, Brock went to *Grace* and knocked on the stern door. There was no reply, although he could make out a chink of light through the keyhole. "Desmond," he called, "it's David Brock. Open the door, please."

The silence dragged out for a long minute, and then there was a rattling of bolts and the door opened a thumb-width. Brock could just make out one of Kite's eyes, glittering and watchful, roaming around to see who was there.

"It's just me, Desmond. There's no armed response teams, no assault squads, not yet. There's still time to sort this out quietly, the way Freyja and Gudrun and your wife would be telling you to do if they were here."

"You guessed I'd be on Gudrun's boat." He sounded pleased, as if Brock had vindicated his choice.

"Yes."

"And have you done what I asked?" Kite's voice had become stronger, Brock thought, more apocalyptic. "Have you spoken to your superiors?"

"Not yet. I want to talk it over with you first. I want to hear what Ollie told you, then I can offer my advice."

"That won't be necessary, David. I don't want you to delay any longer."

"You've only just met Ollie Kovacs, Desmond. Are you really sure that you can believe what he said?"

"I told you, David, he showed me evidence, incontrovertible evidence."

"What, the names of your daughters' killers?"

"They were simply subcontractors. The real murderers were those who ordered their deaths."

"And who were they?"

"I know who they are, and the whole world will know when Superintendent Russell's superiors go on the record with the truth."

"Oliver Kovacs is a crazy old crank with a long history as a troublemaker, supporting lost causes. He'll tell you whatever it takes to make you play his game. Is he in there with you?"

"No."

"So he's run away somewhere, leaving you to do his madness for him and take all the blame for the carnage. Did he really give you some dynamite?"

"Yes. It's beneath the seat that Superintendent Russell is sitting on. It's connected to detonators and a battery. I have a switch in my hand, so you must tell your people to be very careful."

"Did he explain how dangerous it is? It's not used much any more because it's too unstable. Its shelf life is about a year. After that it begins to sweat, and the slightest knock can make it explode. How many sticks did he give you?"

"Plenty. You can't understand how liberating it feels, David, to finally *act* after all these years, to do something real and meaningful and just."

"He saw that need in you, Desmond, and he's playing you for a fool. You surely can't honestly believe that Superintendent Russell is in any way responsible for the deaths of your girls?"

"Oh, but I do, David. I believe precisely that. And you will too. You ask your superiors, ask them about Project Raven."

"I've never heard of it."

"You will, and if they want to save Russell, they must make it public. She must confess. And Brock, I will only negotiate through you. If anyone else comes within fifty meters of this boat I shall make an end of it."

"And what if they don't agree? What if she refuses to confess and they don't cooperate?"

"Then she and I shall die here, in Gudrun's longship."

Like a Viking warrior, Brock thought, as he stepped back down onto the towpath. He tried Lynch's number again, and when he still got no reply looked up another, for Assistant Commissioner Diana Fisher, head of Special Operations.

"Ma'am, DCI David Brock. I have an emergency I need to discuss with you urgently." He heard the murmur of conversation and laughter in the background.

"Brock? You're with Commander Lynch, aren't you?"

"Yes, ma'am. I can't get hold of him, so I've rung you."

"Well, he's standing right next to me as it happens. I'll hand you over, shall I?"

Lynch spoke, an angry growl. "Brock? What the hell do you want?"

"Superintendent Russell has been taken hostage by the father of Gudrun Kite, the girl in the canal boat. We believe he has a bomb."

Lynch spluttered, "What!"

"He thinks that she was responsible for his daughters' deaths, and wants a public confession. He says it's to do with Project Raven."

There was a silence, then Lynch said quietly, "He used that term, did he?"

"Yes."

"Where are you?"

Brock told him and hung up. Across the canal he could see the lights of the bomb-squad vehicles flashing in the mist.

LYNCH ARRIVED IN A police patrol car, at speed. Brock stepped forward to the curb and opened the door for him, catching a whiff of wine on his breath as he shouldered past. They stood together at the railings looking down on *Grace*, and Brock quickly described in greater detail what had happened and what steps he had taken. "I've put out an alert for Oliver Kovacs," he added.

"What do the CBRN boys say?" Lynch grunted.

"The sticks are dynamite, at least five years old and dangerously unstable. There's no indication of how many there were, but if two were left behind we have to assume Kite has a good number. They say they're going to remove the two sticks over there, but they want the whole area evacuated, all the terraces on both sides of the canal, and roadblocks set up."

Lynch nodded. "Do it."

Brock spoke into his phone. When he was finished he turned back to Lynch. "Kite says he'll only negotiate through me. He says he'll blow the boat up if anyone else goes within fifty meters of it."

"What about an approach from the other side, from the water?"

Brock shook his head. "It's a steel hull and the windows are covered. Even if they could get a clear shot he says he's holding the detonator switch."

Lynch swore under his breath. "All right, we'll negotiate. What does he really want?"

"He seems to hold the Met responsible for his daughters' deaths, and Superintendent Russell in particular. He wants a full public statement accepting blame from a senior Met officer, preferably the commissioner."

"Well, he's not going to get that. Any close family members we can use?"

"No."

"How old is he? Late seventies? He'll get tired and run out of steam before long."

"I don't think he will."

"Well, you'll just have to talk him out of it."

"If I'm going to negotiate with him, I need to know what it is that we're trying to hide. I need to know the truth."

Lynch gave him an angry glare. "The trouble is, Brock, I'm not sure I can trust you with the truth. I'm not altogether sure whose side you're really on."

Brock said nothing, looking steadily back at him until Lynch turned away with a snort of disgust. "Oh, for God's sake."

Brock waited, silent, until Lynch turned back, glanced quickly around, then began to speak in a rapid undertone, so that Brock had to lean closer to hear. "Project Raven is a surveillance program, currently under development by a consortium of high-tech companies under contract to the Home Office, with the Met as the lead user."

"Surveillance?"

Lynch hesitated again. This was like drawing teeth, Brock thought, or coaxing a rat out of its hole.

"Yes. Microchip implants."

"In humans?"

"Yes, yes, I know, it sounds sinister, but it isn't really. These days people get implants for all kinds of reasons, and micro-chips have been talked about for years—to carry your medical records, or give security access, or take the place of your credit card. There have been pilot programs—of Alzheimer patients in Florida, for instance—and a number of proposals to chip violent offenders. It's been resisted so far, but it's only a matter of time. For law enforcement the great thing about it is that it's a form of nonviolent restraint for people we know are likely to reoffend. Just the knowledge that we know where they are at any time, day or night, anywhere in the world, will make the terrorist, the psychopath, the serial rapist, the incurable pedophile, hold themselves in check. Who wouldn't want that?"

A modern Panopticon, Brock thought.

"It's really no different from the electronic bracelets we use now for prisoners on parole, just much less intrusive, much more effective, and much, much cheaper."

"And this is what Freyja Kite was working on?"

"Yes. The breakthrough has been the development of a GPS-enabled chip that can pinpoint someone's location anywhere on the globe, but there are problems of security. You have to be certain that the chip's signal can't be cloned or hacked into. That's what Freyja was working on. Penney Solutions has been responsible for the development of the electronics."

"And Paddington Security Services?"

"They're the lead contractor, responsible for production through a manufacturer in Singapore, and ultimately for marketing and sales."

"Where does the Pewsey Clinic fit in?" Brock asked, although he thought he already knew the answer.

Lynch sniffed, as if he might pass on that one, but then said, "Obviously the medical side has to be covered. Another problem was where exactly the implant should be located in the body. In the past, the usual place has been in the back of the arm or in the soft pad of tissue between the thumb and forefinger, but an offender could fairly easily get it removed from there. So at Pewsey they developed a technique of deep-tissue implants, placing the thing inside the chest, close to the heart, where it would need major surgery to remove it."

"And there have been trials of this? On volunteers?"

"On animals—pigs, mainly, and chimps."

"And humans?"

Another pause. "Six months ago, a former close associate of Jack Bragg developed a serious heart condition and urgently needed a transplant. We obliged, using Patsy Bragg as our front. She told him she had contacts who could get him treated at the Pewsey Clinic. He was very grateful and was given a new heart. What he didn't know was that the heart came with a bug. He was still working for Bragg, running his gun-smuggling business, and after he'd recovered we tracked him all over the country and Europe, and out to the Far East, including the Philippines. That was the first live trial of Project Raven. It was a great success. Coupled with the phone and internet intercepts, it's what made Operation Intruder possible, and it's what convinced our chiefs that this is a tool we've got to have."

"But you can't go around implanting people without their knowledge."

"No, of course not. That was a one-off, and it showed us just how effective the thing is. But we're at a sensitive stage, and we have to get all the technical issues resolved and out of the way before we can go public and get the legislators on board to make this thing a reality. That won't be easy, and the usual scaremongers and civil libertarians will do their best to stop it."

Lynch's tone had changed, Brock thought, no longer offering grudging information to a difficult subordinate, but rather making an effort to convince, almost as if he wasn't entirely convinced himself.

"So who killed Freyja and Gudrun?"

"No one killed them. That was two accidents that some people have tried to turn into a conspiracy." He glared at Brock as if daring him to deny it.

"Oh no, it's more than that. The postmortems on both women recorded a neat incision in the soft tissue between the thumb and forefinger of their right hands. They'd been micro-chipped, hadn't they? And whoever killed them wanted their chips back."

"What?" Lynch shook his head with irritation. "No, no. That's just more conspiracy crap. Freyja had cuts and bruises to ninety percent of her body, and Gudrun had probably just cut herself in the kitchen. We've investigated both deaths and there's nothing sinister about them."

"We?"

Lynch looked away, then reached into a pocket and produced a pack of cigarettes. He offered the pack to Brock, who shook his head. "Nobody does now, do they?" Lynch muttered. "When I started in the force it was practically obligatory." He lit up and took a deep breath, blowing the smoke out in a column that rose up through the thickening fog. "Yes, we looked into both cases, just to be sure that Raven hadn't been compromised. There was nothing, no security breaches at Paddington Security or Penney Solutions, no missing chips. If Gudrun was trying to tie Paddington Security to her sister's death, she didn't succeed."

"You mean all the time DI Kolla was investigating Gudrun's death there was another team carrying on a parallel investigation she knew nothing about?"

"It had to be that way, Brock."

"So who carried out this investigation?"

Lynch took another long draw on his cigarette, the tip glowing red. "DiSTaF," he said at last. "Suzy Russell."

THIRTY

KATHY WAS FLOATING IN a thick fog, through which she could just make out the sound of distant voices. She groaned, and suddenly one of the voices was close, speaking quite loudly in an incomprehensible jumble of vowels and consonants into her ear. Then the fog began to clear and she recognized the voice of Carl.

"She's coming round. As you see, she's alive and perfectly well."

Kathy opened one eye to see Jack Bragg's ugly snarl inches from her face.

"Looks pretty rough to me."

"That's just the anesthetic. All vital signs are normal. The operation was a complete success. It was much easier than we expected."

"Where's the wound?"

"Here, I'll show you."

Kathy realized that she was lying on her front, and felt someone unfastening the back of her gown.

"Under that dressing."

"Take it off. I want to see what you did."

"Very well."

She felt a tug on her skin and Carl went on, "You see? Just a small incision. Only a few stitches were necessary."

"Show me the implant."

"Here it is, in this dish. So, what do you say? Shall we go ahead now? The theater is all set up."

Bragg hesitated, then said, "Yeah, all right."

The voices drifted away and Kathy closed her eye, thinking that this was probably just a nightmare, and fell asleep again.

SHE WOKE SUDDENLY AND came rapidly alert, taking a deep breath and turning stiffly onto her side to look around. She was in her old room in the Pewsey Clinic, or an identical one, and she was alone. A clock on the wall said six fourteen, and she tried to work out how long she'd been out of things. At least an hour, she guessed. Memories of the afternoon came rushing back to her—Bragg's house, the invasion of the clinic and confrontation in the director's office, and, more vaguely, hearing Carl and Bragg discussing her operation. A complete success, Carl had said. She sat up and stretched, feeling the tug of stitches in her back, but remarkably little pain, just a sort of numbness. So what was happening now? Had they operated on Bragg too? Was the clinic still under siege?

She stood up a little unsteadily and walked across to the wardrobe, where she found her clothes, including her wallet, apparently intact. No phone, of course. She began to get dressed, ears straining all the while for a sound from the corridor, but heard nothing. When she was finished she went to the door and turned the handle. It was locked. The same with the window. She wondered, without much hope, if she could try to spring the door lock with a credit card, and opened her wallet. Inside she saw the mysterious Visa card, which she still couldn't place, and she slipped it out and made to stick it into the doorjamb—but to her surprise, before it even got that far, she heard the lock click open, like a magic trick. She stepped back, assuming that someone on the other side had opened the lock and expecting them to walk in, but no one did, and so she put out her hand and eased the door open. The corridor was deserted and she stepped out, the door closing behind her. Wondering, she passed the Visa card across the lock and heard it click shut. So that's what it was for, she thought, and the memory came back of Anne Downey pressing it into her hand.

At the next bend in the corridor she heard voices from somewhere ahead, muffled as if coming from a side room. Someone said, "Careful! That hurts." It took her a moment to identify the voice of the director, Vernon Montague, sounding nasal, and she remembered Bragg's casual blow to his face.

"It's broken, Vernon. You'll look a mess for a while." That was the surgeon, Carl. "You'll have a whole new look, more rugged."

"That bastard! And why didn't those two do something to stop him?"

"You know them, Vernon. They answer to a higher authority. There, that's the best I can do."

"Thanks. So Bragg can go home now, can he?"

"Yes. We'll get him out of here."

"The sooner the better. And where's that damned file he walked off with?"

"He insisted on taking it into the operating theater with him. It's still there, don't worry. So where are our two *friends* now?"

"I think Marele took them to the kitchen to give them something to eat."

"We'll need them to get Bragg dressed. Come on, let's go and get them out of Marele's clutches."

"I'm not sure I can face her," Montague grumbled. "She thinks I was prepared to let Bragg kill her rather than give him the safe combination."

"Well, you were, weren't you? I think we were all rather

looking forward to seeing what he would do when he reached five."

"Don't."

"No, it's true. I'd bet that most of the people in that room were hoping he'd pull the trigger."

"You're sick, Carl. Truly sick."

Their voices faded into the distance, and Kathy hesitated, thinking. The file—that was the key to all of this. She drew a deep breath and continued quickly down the corridor until she came to the doors into the secure area. When she waved the Visa card they slid silently open, and she held her breath, listening, but there was no sound of anyone else inside. She stepped through and the doors closed behind her with a sigh. She looked through the windows of the four private rooms, all empty. The corridor widened at its far end into a small lobby before a pair of doors marked *Operating Suite*. Through a glass panel she could see that the lights were on, but no one was visible. She entered a spartan room of sterile surfaces, some stainless-steel equipment and a gurney covered in a sheet, and immediately saw the blue file lying on a bench to one side. She hurried over and opened the cover, quickly scanning through the contents—legal agreements, letters, performance specifications, diagrams of management structure, a fold-out critical path program, handwritten notes. She looked around to see if there was a photocopier in the room, and for the first time paid attention to the gurney, and realized that from this angle the profile of whatever was lying beneath the sheet looked distinctly human. She went over and lifted the corner of the sheet and saw Jack Bragg's face, immobile, pale, eyes blankly open, and very dead.

"His clothes are in room three."

Kathy froze as she heard Carl's voice in the corridor outside.

"He's down here," Carl said, closer now.

Kathy looked around, hesitated beside the blue folder, then opened it and tugged out a sheaf of documents from its middle and snapped it shut again. She ran through a connecting door and found herself in an operating theater.

"All right, you two get him dressed. There's a wheelchair in the theater—I'll get it."

From behind a rack of gas cylinders, Kathy watched Carl come in, look around, and go to the wheelchair folded against the opposite wall. He stooped to open it, fiddling with the mechanism, then straightened and pushed it back out to the other room. Kathy waited, motionless, until she heard Carl say, "Okay, that'll do," and heard a door thump. After a while she looked through the vision panel to the other room and saw that it was deserted, the body on the gurney gone. When she pushed open the door she saw that the file, too, was gone. She checked the corridor and, seeing it empty, ran to the fire exit at the end, swiped her card, and stepped out into the cold night.

BROCK WALKED ALONG THE towpath toward the boat, seeing the curtain flick, knowing he was being watched. He hefted the bag he was carrying onto the stern then stepped up and knocked on the door, which immediately opened a crack.

"What's that?" Kite demanded.

"Something to keep you going—sandwiches, a flask of hot chocolate."

"They're probably drugged."

"No, they're not. We wouldn't want you passing out with the switch in your hand, would we?" Brock was worried by the sound of Kite's voice—truculent and hoarse, as if he might be coming down with something. "It must be cold in there. Do you need anything? Scarves, gloves, medicines?"

"Don't play with me, David. I've told you what I want, and I want it now. The longer you delay, the more dangerous things get."

"I understand, Desmond. But this will take time. I've been talking to senior officers, and trying to make exactly that point, but the commissioner and his deputies are all out of London at the moment, and it's proving hard to get sense out of them."

"I don't believe that."

"I'm doing my best, Desmond. Just hold on there. How's your hostage?"

"Complaining, whining. She's getting on my nerves. I think I may just press this switch and have done with it."

"No, don't do that. I know how stressful this is for you. Maybe you should lie down for a bit, have a rest."

The door slammed shut with a bang.

When he got back up to the road, Lynch said, "Well?"

"Not good. He's getting rattled, sounding erratic."

"Jesus."

"The problem is, sir," Brock said heavily, "that you've told me nothing that I can use to make him doubt what he's been told. In fact, everything you've said suggests that he may well be right."

"What the hell do you expect?"

"Proof—proof that I can show him—that Superintendent Russell wasn't involved in his daughters' deaths. Maybe you should go and interrogate her team, find out what she's been up to. The last I saw of them they were sipping champagne in a wine bar. They should be nicely lubricated by now."

He turned away in disgust and was met by the hostage negotiator, who'd arrived at the scene. Brock was describing his conversation with Kite when his phone rang.

"Kathy! I've been trying to reach you. Are you all right?"

For a moment it seemed as if Kathy wasn't sure how to answer, then she said, "Listen, Brock, we need to get people to the Pewsey Clinic quickly. They've just killed Jack Bragg and they're taking his body back to his house."

Brock listened in stunned silence as Kathy described what had happened. When she finished he took a note of the number she was calling from and hung up, called Bren over to organize two teams, then rang Kathy back. He got her to go through it again, with all the details, then told her about Kite.

When they'd finished he went to Lynch, who was standing at the railings, staring down at *Grace*, a fresh cigarette in his hand.

"I've just had a call from DI Kolla," Brock said, watching Lynch's face carefully. In the hazy light from the streetlights it had an unhealthy pallor. "Earlier today she had a call from the secretary at the Pewsey Clinic asking her to go in for a checkup. She was met at the station, drugged, and taken instead to Bragg's house in Sevenoaks."

"What?" Lynch looked incredulous as, in a deadpan voice, Brock related what Kathy had told him. If the bizarre story shook him, the conclusion, that Bragg had been killed, seemed to hit Lynch like a Taser. He jerked upright and stared open-mouthed at Brock.

Brock had held back one thing that Kathy had mentioned—that Bragg had told her that Lynch was his brother. Now he said quietly, "I've sent DI Gurney with teams to both the clinic and to Sevenoaks. Maybe you should get over there."

Lynch just stared at him for a minute, as if having difficulty absorbing all this, then he seemed to pull himself together. "No . . . no, I have to stay here."

Brock nodded, deciding that Kathy's revelation could keep for the time being. "There is someone who might be able to help us with Kite. Dr. Anne Downey owns the next boat, and may well be involved with Kovacs. Superintendent Russell had her arrested this afternoon. I'd like to get her over here."

"All right. Where's she being held?"

"Stratford. DI Kolla is heading over there now to pick her up. She'll need your authorization to have Downey released into her custody."

Lynch got on the phone. When he'd finished they watched a car draw up. Several officers, all in uniform, got out, the lead being taken by a woman wearing the badge of rank of assistant commissioner. Diana Fisher, Brock guessed. She came over, introduced herself and the others, and asked if there was any change.

"Not here, ma'am," Lynch said. "But we've just been informed of another hostage situation, at the Pewsey Clinic, that may be related to this one."

"Pewsey?" Fisher looked sharply at him.

"Yes. As you know, security at Pewsey falls within Superintendent Russell's purview. We've sent a couple of teams over there to deal with it."

No mention of Bragg, Brock noticed. It sounded to him as if Lynch was trying to distance himself from Russell.

"Hm." Fisher turned to Brock. "Would it help if I spoke to Professor Kite?"

"It might." Brock doubted it, but was interested to hear what she had to say. He led her down to the towpath and told her where to stand so that she could be seen from the boat, then got up onto the stern and tapped on the door.

"Yes, David? Who have you brought for me?" The suspicious voice sounded slightly querulous now, and tired.

"This is Assistant Commissioner Diane Fisher, Desmond, one of the most senior officers in the Met. She'd like to speak with you."

"Is she armed?"

"No, no, nothing like that, I promise."

"Very well. She can come to the side of the boat, but not on board."

Brock stepped back down onto the path and watched as Fisher approached the boat.

"Good evening, Professor. We're all very distressed by what has happened here. How can I help resolve the situation?"

"I've told David Brock what I want."

"I can categorically assure you that we have no knowledge of Superintendent Russell or any other police officer being in any way responsible for your daughters' deaths."

Not that Russell was innocent, Brock noted, just that we didn't know. More distancing, and Kite could see that too. He gave a loud snort of disgust and roared, "Not good enough, madam! If you don't have the knowledge, then get someone who does!"

"Please," Fisher said quickly, "how is Superintendent Russell?"

"Extremely uncomfortable! Good night." The door slammed shut.

"Mad," Fisher said as they climbed the stairs up to the road. "Quite mad. Do we have a psychiatrist here?"

"The hostage negotiator is one. He seems to think Kite is rational."

"Nonsense!"

AN HOUR LATER, WHEN Kathy arrived in a patrol car, they were all still there, joined now by the leader of the assault team and marksmen deployed around the canal basin. Brock, seeing her white face through the windshield, hurried over and pulled open her door.

"Kathy, are you all right?"

"Pretty good," she said, but, looking at her, he didn't believe it. "Any change?"

"The assistant commissioner over there tried to reason with

him, without success." He glanced over her shoulder at the two passengers in the back seat. One was Anne Downey, the other, to his astonishment, was Ollie Kovacs. Brock looked at Kathy. "How did you find him?"

"I had a good talk with Anne. She realized that this has gone far enough. She knew where Ollie was, and we went and got him and he agreed to come and help us clear this up."

Brock stared at the hunched figure peering out of the window at the uniforms and flashing lights with a rather gratified look on his face. He wondered what on earth Kathy had said to him to make him give himself up. "Are you sure?"

"Yes."

He said to Kovacs, "Hello, Ollie."

The man turned his large head and beamed through his glasses at Brock. "Hello."

"Tell me, how did you two manage to overpower the superintendent?"

Kovacs shrugged. "She was talking to Desmond and I hit her on the head."

"And then sat her on top of some sticks of dynamite. I thought you were into nonviolent protest?"

"Sometimes desperate times require desperate deeds."

"So what do you have in mind now?"

"If you let me see Desmond, I think I can persuade him to release her, in exchange for a guarantee not to prosecute."

"Why would he agree to that?"

"We've made our point."

Kathy urged, "I think it's worth a try, Brock."

It didn't make much sense to him, but he said, "All right, I'll see what I can do."

He rejoined the knot of senior officers and told them, provoking a storm of argument which Diane Fisher finally cut across.

"We have no alternative," she said. "Suzy Russell's safety comes first."

She asked for a pad of paper and wrote out and signed a guarantee that there would be no charges brought against Kite and Kovacs relating to the abduction of Superintendent Russell, subject to her safe release, then gave it to Brock to sign as witness.

He returned to the car and handed the note to Kovacs. "All right, Ollie, it's up to you now. Don't make me sorry I'm doing this. I'll take you down there."

"No, I'll go with Kathy."

Brock looked from one to the other, then raised his hands and stepped away, watching them get out of the car and head for the steps. He went back to Lynch, standing at the railing, and together they looked down at the two figures approaching the boat. The exchange of voices, Kite and Kovacs, rose up to them indistinctly, then the two figures on the towpath stepped up onto *Grace* and disappeared inside.

The wait seemed endless, ten minutes, twenty. Lynch smoked two more cigarettes and muttered savagely from time to time into his radio while Brock's imagination conjured a scene of carnage inside the boat.

At last the stern doors opened and Kathy, illuminated by the lights inside, stepped out, followed by Superintendent Russell, unsteady, clutching Kathy's coat around her shoulders. Kathy helped her get down onto the towpath, followed by Ollie Kovacs.

"Thank God," Lynch muttered.

They hurried to the steps, the others crowding around as Russell emerged at the top, looking pale and shaken, protesting that she was all right as a couple of paramedics took her arms.

Kathy moved out of the crush to Brock's side and he grinned at her. "You did it, Kathy. But how? How the hell did you manage it?"

"Later," she said. "I'll tell you later." She looked around. "Kite is the one who needs the ambulance. Where is he?"

They heard the splutter of a diesel engine starting up and hurried to the railing. Below them thick white smoke from *Grace*'s engine wreathed the boat as it began moving slowly out into the canal.

Kathy swore softly. "What's he doing?"

In painfully slow motion, as if the elderly boat could barely raise the energy to stir, it eased out into the main channel and began to chug away, past the line of other boats, past Ricci Ragonetti's restaurant on the far bank, and on into the foggy darkness beyond.

Everyone had fallen silent, watching its progress until its lights were no longer visible, only the stubborn throb of its engine signaling its presence. Then that abruptly stopped. There was a moment's utter stillness before a sudden blinding flash of light and a stunning shock wave seared through the fog and hit the watchers on the bank.

THIRTY-ONE

BROCK WAS WATCHING ON the monitor as Kathy was interviewed by two officers from outside the command. She was describing what happened when she and Ollie Kovacs went on board *Grace*. As they stepped inside, Kathy had seen Suzy Russell sitting on a chair, arms and ankles tied with rope. Ollie immediately took Kite's arm and guided him to the galley where they could talk. While they were there Kathy examined the bomb beneath Russell's chair, unfastened the battery terminals, and removed the electric blasting cap from the stick of dynamite into which it had been inserted. She moved the cap to a safe distance and then untied Russell. During this time she could hear Kovacs and Kite talking, but couldn't make out what was being said. They then returned from the galley, Kite looking serious but not objecting to what was taking place. Russell was suffering from stiffness and cramps from her confinement and needed assistance to get off the boat and up the steps, which was Kathy's first priority. She just assumed that Kite was following them.

This account obviously didn't satisfy the questioners, who kept probing her for more detail until finally they gave up and let her go. Brock was waiting for her as she emerged from the room. "That was a load of crap," he murmured to her as they made for the exit.

"Yes," she agreed. "Have you heard from Bren?"

"He's at the clinic, implementing a search warrant. The other team caught two men leaving Bragg's house. Inside they found Bragg's body, and charged the men with concealing a homicide. Sundeep will do the postmortem first thing tomorrow, which should tell us more."

"Good," she said.

She looked exhausted, and he said, "You need something to eat. Come on."

LATER, WHEN THEY'D FINISHED their steak and fries and she looked somewhat revived, Brock poured her another glass of wine and said, "All right, what really happened?"

Kathy stared down at the red liquid for a moment, and then began her story, choosing her words extremely carefully, so it seemed to Brock. "When I spoke to Anne Downey in the Stratford jail she was very tense. I think being arrested had really shaken her, and when I told her what Kite had done she became quite distressed. I asked her if she could help me persuade him to put a stop to it, and after a while she said she had an idea. A document had come into her possession, the minutes of a progress meeting on Project Raven with annotations in Suzy Russell's own handwriting for action to be taken. It was very explicit in discussing what sorts of people might be microchipped, and if the press got hold of a copy it would be highly embarrassing for the Met, and for Suzy Russell personally. She thought we could use this to persuade Russell to reveal to Kite who had murdered his daughters. When I asked her if she was sure that Russell knew that, she said, 'Oh yes, she knows.' But she wanted Ollie Kovacs involved.

"Kovacs is linked to an outfit called Digital Anarchy. According to Anne they're a bunch of hackers and whistleblowers who try to expose government and corporate machinations that they don't approve of. Both Anne and Ned Tisdell have been trying to help them get information about Project Raven.

"Anyway, Anne contacted Kovacs and we went to see him. She persuaded him that Professor Kite's antics would turn the public against his campaign, and he agreed to use the document as she suggested. So when we went on board the boat, Kovacs showed it to Suzy Russell. It was obvious from her reaction that it was genuine. He offered to let her have it when Freyja and Gudrun's killers were brought to justice, otherwise he'd make it public. As you can imagine, it was difficult for her, especially with me standing there, but eventually she told them.

"About a year ago, there was a suggestion that there was a leak at Penney Solutions, and Freyja Kite was suspected. When she was killed, Russell got worried that there had been foul play. She discovered that two employees of the Pewsey Clinic were in Cambridge that night. She monitored their communications and came across some incriminating text messages. And at that point she stopped looking. She convinced herself that the information was circumstantial, but really she just didn't want to pursue it—it would have meant both the end of the implant program and making it public. But when Ollie Kovacs asked her directly, she admitted that she was sure that those two men had killed both girls to stop their prying into the project and betraying it to Digital Anarchy. She agreed to turn her evidence over to me and I promised Kite that I would follow it up. They're the two men Bren's team caught at Bragg's house, I think, acting as his minders. Once the clinic realized that Bragg had found out what they'd done to him, they decided that he had to be silenced."

"And you, Kathy?"

"Yes, I think I was next."

"But Kite? Why did he blow himself up?"

"He seemed in a strange state of mind, not really with us, as if he were in some faraway place inside his head. Maybe he'd been shaken apart by all that had happened, or maybe he was already crazy when I first met him that night in Cambridge a month ago. I think last night he'd made up his mind that he was going to end it all in a way that nobody could ignore or sweep under the carpet, the way we did his daughters' deaths. From that point of view it was logical to take Suzy Russell with him, but when Ollie said he wasn't going to leave without her, he relented and let her go, and then went ahead on his own."

Brock thought about that. Kathy's story had raised as many questions as answers in his mind, and he knew her too well not to have recognized the evasions at certain points, when she had turned her eyes away from his and stared at the glass of red wine.

"Well, thank God you're safe," he said. "But you know what astonishes me most, Kathy? That you had a major operation this afternoon and it hasn't slowed you down one bit."

She gave him a slightly haunted look. "Yes, that's been bothering me too."

"I think we need some independent advice." He rang Sundeep's number and they spoke for a while, then rang off. By the time the bill arrived Sundeep was back on the phone. Brock listened, thanked him, and turned to Kathy. "A friend of his, a specialist, will see you at Guy's tomorrow morning at eleven." He saw the smile of relief cross her face.

BUT FIRST SHE HAD to face Commander Lynch. They met at eight the following morning in his office at headquarters, Lynch, Brock, and Kathy, and Suzy Russell too, looking embattled and subdued. They took the offered coffee and sat around an oval table.

"This meeting will not be minuted," Lynch said. He sounded

thoroughly pissed off. "I've had a report from the rescue team. The boat was blown in half, both parts now at the bottom of the canal. They've found some human remains—a head."

He scowled biliously and cleared his throat. "There'll be an investigation into the whole operation, of course, and before long I dare say we'll be relieved of any further involvement. In the meantime, we need to act fast to salvage whatever we can from the chaos. Suzy?"

"Sir, the most important thing is that Raven must be protected. It would be a disaster for the Met if it was compromised because of this."

"Yes, but how do we do that? He could hardly have chosen a more public way to draw attention to himself. The press are all over it—they've already made the connection to Gudrun Kite's death."

"It was the action of an unstable old man driven mad by the accidental deaths of his two daughters. End of story."

"There will be pressure to reexamine Gudrun Kite's death."

"I think we should do that and make a public announcement to that effect. But at the end of the day we'll confirm the coroner's conclusion—accidental death."

Kathy stared at her in astonishment. Lynch noticed the expression on her face. "What is it, Kolla?"

Kathy said to Russell, "What about O'Hearn and Ryan?"

Lynch frowned. "Who?"

Russell sighed. "Kite was obsessed with finding his daughters' murderers, so I gave him a couple of names—Troy O'Hearn and Bennie Ryan, two security men at Pewsey. I told him that I had evidence against them, which I would pass over to DI Kolla to charge them with."

"Neither of you mentioned this in your debriefing."

"No, sir. It was a necessary deception to make him agree to release us, and it worked."

"So there was no truth in it?"

"It was circumstantial. We can't seriously pursue it. If it were true, it would make things impossible for Pewsey, and for us."

Brock was watching the emotions flicker almost imperceptibly across Kathy's face—disbelief, anger, then nothing.

"But there was a witness," Kathy said in a neutral tone, "apart from me."

Russell frowned. "Yes, Kovacs was present. He is a problem, sir. We now believe he is the link to Digital Anarchy. In the confusion last night he slipped away before we could stop him. I've issued a priority arrest order, but he hasn't been picked up yet."

"What about that document he had?" Kathy asked coolly.

"Document?" Lynch stared at Russell.

"He had a copy of the minutes of one of the Raven working party meetings. He said he would make it public if we didn't do as we'd promised Kite."

"Jesus! How would he have got hold of that?"

"The copy had been sent to Montague at Pewsey. Anne Downey used to work there. I think it probably came from her. We have her in custody, as you know."

"And what was in these minutes?"

Russell hesitated. "A lot about Raven. Nothing about the Kite girls."

Lynch put a hand to his forehead, the other tapping impatiently on the table. He badly needed a cigarette, Brock thought, and said, "We're holding O'Hearn and Ryan over the death of Jack Bragg. They have a lot of questions to answer—the abduction of DI Kolla, for instance, and how Bragg was able to move about freely. We should have plenty to charge them with. They may want to do a deal, give us information about the Kite girls."

"No!" They all looked at Superintendent Russell, who had half risen to her feet. She sat down again slowly and spoke to Lynch. "Sir, can I have a word with you in private?"

Lynch nodded to Brock and Kathy, who got up and left the room. They went through the secretary's office, followed by her suspicious frown, and out into the corridor, which was deserted.

"I hate this," Kathy said bitterly. "She's going to fix things, make Lynch do what she wants, bury the whole nasty mess. Once they find Kovacs he'll probably have a fatal accident like Freyja and Gudrun, and there'll be no stopping her."

"Then we'd better find him first, Kathy." He frowned, pondering. "What I don't understand is that if Kovacs had that incriminating document all the time, why hadn't he already made it public?"

Kathy met his eyes for a moment. "Who knows?" she said.

Lynch's secretary put her head out into the corridor and called to them. "The commander will see you now."

They filed back inside and sat down.

Lynch spoke. "It's essential that we act swiftly and decisively to clear up this mess. I shall set up an independent investigating team under my direct command to review recent events at both the canal basin and the Pewsey Clinic and recommend actions, including bringing criminal charges where appropriate.

"Neither DiSTaF, Suzy, nor your unit, Brock, can be directly involved, though of course you'll be interviewed and your input will be considered."

"Hm . . ." Russell stared at her nails. "All the same, you'll need someone on the team who understands how things work. How about Mickey Schaeffer? He's familiar with both our groups without having been involved in 'the mess.'"

Lynch raised an eyebrow at Brock, who nodded his agreement.

"DI Kolla," Lynch said, "you in particular have to stand clear of what happens now. You've been too closely involved in things since day one, as both an investigator and a victim. You're on sick leave, right?"

"Yes, sir."

"So make yourself available for interview, but otherwise stay well away."

"Sir."

When they stepped out into Victoria Street, Kathy said, "What are we going to do?"

"The first and most important thing is getting you well again, Kathy. We're going to keep your appointment at Guy's." He put out his hand to an oncoming taxi and they climbed in.

THIRTY-TWO

THE SPECIALIST LOOKED WEARY, Kathy thought, as if he'd been up half the night on an operation, and in his white coat gave the impression that he might have to dash off again at any moment. But Sundeep had said that, when it came to thoracic and cardiac surgery, he was the best there was and a personal friend.

"Sundeep said this was an unusual case, Ms. Kolla. Tell me about it."

So she did, watching his eyes widen and his face set in a determined attempt not to show incredulity. When she finished he examined her back.

"So," he said carefully, "you believe that the doctors at Pewsey implanted you with some kind of device while they were operating on your shoulder?"

"Yes, me and another man. He had a chest MRI taken later, which I saw. It showed the implant quite clearly, about the size of a grain of rice, right next to his heart."

"And where is he now, this other man?"

"On Sundeep's table. His postmortem is this morning."

The doctor blinked. "And why would the Pewsey people do that to you both?"

"I can't tell you that."

"And then they removed it?"

"That's what they told me. I'd like you to check that they didn't cause any damage while they were doing it."

"Hm . . . well, I think we'd better have you X-rayed right away."

Fifteen minutes later she was back in his room watching him examine three X-ray images on a light panel.

Finally he said, "You know, if Sundeep hadn't spoken of you in such glowing terms I'd have sent you straight upstairs to Psychiatric Services. But you were right, they did put an implant into your chest—they didn't take it out, though. It's still there."

Kathy felt her heart give a skitter as he beckoned her over and pointed it out, a small white oval against the gray shadows of her organs. "It's lodged against the pericardial sac that contains the heart, at the point where the left pulmonary artery emerges. Can't you tell me anything about it?"

"I think it contains a microchip, probably for tracking the person who's carrying it."

"Ah. But why in such an inaccessible place?"

"I believe that was the point, to make it difficult for the person to have it removed."

"Really?" He considered that, examining the films with a magnifying lens. "I have read about an experimental human microchip that was designed to emit a signal," he said at last, "drawing its energy from the pulse of blood in its host. That might be the case here.

"Well!" He turned to Kathy with a bright smile. "I thought today was going to be rather dull. How wrong I was. So what do you want me to do?"

"Take it out. Can you do that?"

"It will be difficult. There will be risks. What did this other man die from?"

"Possibly from their attempt to remove his chip."

"Then I'd better see if Sundeep can shed any light."

He dialed a number and began a long conversation during which Sundeep did most of the talking. Finally the surgeon rang off and turned back to Kathy.

"Yes, your friend appears to have died of cardiac arrest while undergoing a rather drastic piece of surgery. His implant is no longer there."

My friend, Kathy thought. She couldn't grieve for Jack Bragg, but she wished he hadn't died like that, when she was faced with the same thing.

"Please, Doctor," she said, "if you think it's at all feasible, I want it out. I can't go around with that inside me for the rest of my life."

The doctor nodded. "Let me think about it. I'll go over to the mortuary and examine the body for myself, and in the meantime we'll make some more detailed scans of your chest."

He got on the phone, making arrangements and reorganizing his appointments for the day. Then he looked up. "Did you come with anyone, Kathy?"

"Yes, my boss. He's also a good friend."

"Fine. This will be a difficult decision. You should talk it over with your family or those closest to you."

AFTER MRI AND CT scans, Kathy made her way back to the room where Brock was waiting. He got to his feet, looking worried. "It's still there," she told him as they made their way out. "They didn't remove it. They just made it look as if they'd carried out a successful operation so that Bragg would agree to it. But apparently Sundeep thinks he died of cardiac arrest, which wouldn't necessarily support a murder charge."

They had reached the main road, the traffic circulating around London Bridge station roaring past. "I thought, listening to Russell last night making her confession to Ollie Kovacs and Professor Kite, that we had really nailed it, that I would be able to open up the whole can of worms—DiSTaF, Pewsey, and ultimately Harvest. But today I see it all melting away. The stakes are too high, the people involved too senior, the potential embarrassment too great. In the end, the best I may be able to do is bring a private malpractice suit against Pewsey for putting a microchip inside me without permission, which will turn out to be . . . what? A regrettable medical error?"

They flagged down a cab, and as she stared out of the window Kathy didn't mention the thing that bothered her most. She'd lain awake the previous night thinking about the two thugs, O'Hearn and Ryan, arranging Gudrun Kite's "accident." She had tried to imagine them, two big clumsy men, one of them—the boxer Ryan—unsteady on his feet, clambering on board *Grace* without alerting the neighbors, the restless Stapletons and the vigilant Anne Downey; then opening the stern door without leaving any sign of forced entry; then making their way, shoulders stooped, in the dark, down the length of the boat to Gudrun's bedroom to fix her heater flue without waking her; and finally, some time later when she was dead, returning and slicing her hand to remove the chip, without gassing themselves in the process. She just couldn't see it. And if that was the case, might not Gudrun's death have been an accident after all, and her own and Brock's persistence just obstinacy, out of misguided sympathy for Kite? Or more than that, a perverse need to prove to Lynch and the whole new regime that old-fashioned professional instinct was better than managerial rationalism?

Brock was asking if she wanted to take the taxi to her apartment, and she shook herself and said no, she'd check her mail at Queen Anne's Gate first. She could see that he was worried about her, hear the concern in his voice.

"You'll let me know as soon as the doctor gets back to you?"

"Yes, don't worry."

"Lynch was right, you know, Kathy. The most important thing you can do is get completely fit again. Until then, forget about work."

"Okay. What about you?"

"Oh, I'll get to work on interviewing the Pewsey mob with Bren, and looking for Kovacs."

But when they arrived at Queen Anne's Gate they found D.K. Payne waiting for them. The team was being reassigned to other cases, a heavy workload in the offing.

Kathy went to her desk and flicked through her in-box. Anything of importance had been diverted elsewhere. Her internal emails were mostly get-well wishes or management circulars that she didn't bother reading. Her phone rang.

"Kolla."

"Kathy, it's Anne Downey." She was speaking in an agitated whisper, as if she didn't want to be overheard. "They've let me out on bail. The police opposed it, but my solicitor persuaded the magistrate. I've come back to the canal basin and there are police everywhere. They wouldn't let me go to my boat at first. I was wondering, could we meet? I still don't understand what happened last night and I haven't been able to contact Ollie."

Kathy hesitated, then said, dropping her voice too, "Yes, of course, Anne. But not at the canal."

"No. And I'm worried that they may be following me."

"You're a doctor, Anne. Is there somewhere you know, a hospital perhaps, where you could lose them, leave by a different exit?"

Downey thought about that, then said, "Yes, I know every way in and out of the children's hospital at Great Ormond Street."

Holborn, Kathy was thinking. "Good. There's a pub not far

from there, the Bountiful Cow in Eagle Street. I'll meet you there in an hour."

As she rang off she looked up and saw Mickey Schaeffer coming into the room. He gave her a big grin and came over and sat on the edge of her desk. "Kathy, hi. How are you?"

"I'm okay. How's life on the dark side?"

He laughed. "Oh, pretty evil. No, actually it's great, I'm enjoying the different slant on things. Still trying to find my way around, the new guy. I heard about what happened last night. You really have a talent for being in the thick of things, Kathy."

"Yes, well, I'm going to put my feet up for a while. Of course, I'll be interested to learn how things turn out."

"Sure." He looked thoughtful. "Listen, we're trying to find Oliver Kovacs before he causes any more trouble. You tracked him down yesterday, didn't you? Any ideas where we should be looking now?"

"Anne Downey had a contact number for him."

"He's not answering that any more. She says she doesn't know where he might be."

"Nor me, I'm afraid."

He nodded. "Well, I've been drafted on to the new task force to tidy up after last night, so if you do think of anything you might give me a ring. And vice versa if you want an update any time, just let me know."

"Thanks, Mickey, I'll do that."

"Take care."

THE BOUNTIFUL COW WAS a sixties pub in Holborn that had been given a stylish makeover with bright colors and cowboy movie posters. Its specialities were Bountyburgers and steaks of every variety.

"I'm a vegan," Anne Downey said.

306

"Sorry. Do you want to go somewhere else?"

"No, it doesn't matter." She looked pale and troubled.

"Let me get you something." Kathy went to the bar and ordered two glasses of wine, observing Downey in the mirror, restlessly fiddling with her phone.

"Here we are."

"Thanks." Anne Downey's hand shook a little as she raised the glass to her lips. "I feel so shocked about what happened last night. I haven't been able to sleep."

"Yes."

"Why did he do it, Kathy? Did Superintendent Russell say something?"

"She gave him the names of two men who she believed were responsible for the deaths of Freyja and Gudrun. It's what he wanted."

"But then, why kill himself?"

"It's possible it was an accident. The dynamite that Ollie gave him was old and unstable."

"Oh God." She hesitated and then said, "Who were the men?"

"Their names are O'Hearn and Ryan. They work for the Pewsey Clinic."

"I remember them. They appeared on the scene when I was there."

A waitress passed their table carrying a wooden platter on which a large steak lay bleeding. Downey looked as if she might be sick, but Kathy didn't think it was the sight of the meat.

"Anne, ever since I first met you, I've had the impression that you badly wanted to tell me something, but couldn't quite decide to do it. Am I wrong?"

Downey blinked as if Kathy had struck her. Then she lowered her eyes and said, "Do you have any children, Kathy?"

"No."

"I had a little boy. His name was Aaron."

"Yes."

"You knew about that? It wasn't a really big story, like the McCann case, although Aaron was three, the same age as Madeleine McCann when he was taken. But Aaron was found within four days and the man who took him, Colin Frewin, was arrested and charged. He'd done it before, apparently, and was well known to police. We thought at first that Aaron would recover from the terrible things Frewin had done to him, but he died three months later, of pneumonia. A charge of murder against Frewin was dropped to manslaughter, then grievous bodily harm, although everyone knew that Frewin was responsible for Aaron's death. That's how I know my way around Great Ormond Street. Aaron was there for those three months."

"It was a shocking case, Anne. I'm really sorry."

Downey shrugged. "Anyway, it's relevant. Afterward, someone who had been following the case got in touch with me. She said she'd been working as a nurse at Pewsey, and had heard rumors there that they were working on a research program into new ways of restraining repeat offenders like Frewin. So I phoned them up and said I'd love to work on something like that, and they offered me a job.

"I assumed it was a drug they were working on, some kind of chemical castration, but when they eventually revealed the fact that it was a microchip implant for tracking people who posed a serious risk, I thought it was a brilliant idea. If Frewin had been chipped the police would have known immediately that he was in the vicinity when Aaron was abducted, and they could have found him within minutes, before he did any harm.

"We were doing experiments on how the chip would work inside the body, using pigs and dogs and chimps. I'd have preferred not to be doing that with animals, but it seemed to me that the work was important enough to justify it. One of the designers of the chip, Freyja Kite, used to visit the clinic, and I got to know her. She was very intelligent and passionate about her work and I was tremendously impressed by her. But after a while I began to get the feeling that she was becoming uneasy about what we were doing. She gave hints that she didn't like the way the program was being run, and was doubtful about the ethics of some of those involved, especially the people who were financing it, the Harvest Group. Apparently the project began when they acquired an electronics company in Texas which had developed a fairly sophisticated chip for human implanting, and then stopped work on it when they came up against problems of security and privacy. Harvest decided to set up a new team to solve those problems and create something that could work in any number of commercial applications, and that's what worried Freyja. There had already been stories of some companies in the US making it obligatory for employees to be chipped for identification or for their own safety. There was talk of people in hazardous occupations—firemen, police, coal miners, soldiers—being chipped so that they could always be traced in an emergency situation. Where would it end? I think she began to believe that we were creating a monster we wouldn't be able to control.

"I didn't necessarily agree with her, but I had to admit that the whole atmosphere at Pewsey was driven by profit. I remember we had a long discussion about it the last time she came to the clinic. She was there to have herself implanted with the latest version of the chip, because she said she wanted to use herself as a guinea pig. Just two weeks later she was killed."

Downey was talking faster now, as if she were afraid she might not have time to say everything she wanted.

"About a month after that Ned Tisdell got in touch with me, saying he had been a good friend of Freyja, who had told him about me working at the clinic, and he wanted to meet me and talk to me about the work we were doing there. I thought he sounded slightly mad, said I'd think about it and reported it to the clinic director, Mr. Montague. He passed it on to Superintendent Russell, who was responsible for the police security at the clinic. She came to see me and said she knew about what had happened to my son and appreciated my commitment to the Raven project—that's what we were calling it. She went on at some length about how important it was, and how it would make the world so much safer for children like Aaron. But she was worried that there were people like Ned Tisdell who, often with the best of intentions, were trying to sabotage it. They were people with a mistaken sense of idealism, who didn't understand the harsh reality that people like me have to live through. So she wanted my help. She said that Ned and his friends were trying to get information about the project, to leak it on the Web and to the press in order to get it stopped before it was properly developed. She warned me that he was known to be a violent and disturbed man with a prison record, but if I was willing she wanted me to meet him and see what I could find out.

"So I became a spy. I met Ned and he told me that Freyja had first approached him because she'd read a blog of his about Big Brother surveillance, and had wanted to help him make public some of the things that she knew were going on in secret. I pretended to show an interest in this and we began to meet regularly and I gave him information about Pewsey that Superintendent Russell fed me.

"I grew to like Ned. He was certainly manic and obsessive, but he struck me as scrupulously honest and sincere. For instance, he insisted on telling me about his prison sentence and how he'd seriously hurt a researcher at a laboratory where they were experimenting on animals. He said he felt desperately guilty about that, especially since the man was now confined to a wheelchair and had lost his job, and when Ned had money he would secretly put small amounts into the man's bank account.

I asked him how he could do that, and he told me he had friends who were hackers, and had helped him.

"Superintendent Russell was keen to find out who these people were, and wanted me to get closer to Ned. He told me he was living on a narrowboat, so I bought one too, and moved near him, keeping an eye on him. Then one day he told me about another friend of his who had bought a boat and was coming to join us. Her name was Vicky Hawke. We became friends, and I helped her with some medical issues—a persistent rash, panic attacks, insomnia—and eventually she confided in me that she was really Freyja Kite's sister Gudrun, and she was trying to find out what had happened to her sister. At first I dismissed her belief that Freyja had been murdered, but both she and Ned were utterly convinced, and I began to wonder, especially when Ned told me that Freyja had planned to steal one of the new chips by having herself implanted. Now Gudrun wanted to do the same. She had got into the computer system at Paddington Security Services and created an authorization for herself as an employee to be implanted at Pewsey. When that was done she wanted me to operate on her hand and remove the chip so that Ned could pass it on to his friends. She had also copied hundreds of documents from Paddington Security Services onto a disc which was hidden behind a print of a raven hanging in her boat.

"I reported all this to Superintendent Russell, who was pleased. She said she wanted me to go ahead with the plan because they would be able to track the chip and trace the people involved. But she was worried about the disc falling into the wrong hands and said that she wanted me to help someone to go on board *Grace* and wipe the information from it before Gudrun passed it on.

"I agreed, and met up with the man who was to do it. He wanted me to lend him my key to Gudrun's boat and also arrange for her to take a heavy dose of her sleeping pills that evening. I did that. The next morning I found the key back in my mailbox and I left early for work, assuming that everything had gone as planned. It wasn't until I got back again that evening that I discovered that Gudrun was dead.

"Superintendent Russell tried to reassure me that it had all been a tragic accident. Her man had gone aboard as planned, but discovered the boat filled with fumes, and Gudrun dead. He'd wiped the disc and removed the microchip from her hand and then left. I tried to believe her, but I knew in my heart that she was lying. It was just too much of a coincidence after what happened to Freyja. Later I asked Ned whether he hadn't been worried that they would track the microchip when he took it to his friends, and he said of course, that was obvious, but they had a container that would mask the signal. Russell had known all along that she couldn't let Gudrun pass it on."

Anne Downey fell silent at last, sagging from the effort of her confession.

"So Superintendent Russell realized at some point that you'd changed sides," Kathy said gently.

Downey nodded. "She's offered me a deal. Find Ollie Kovacs and give evidence against him and Ned, or she'll make sure I go to prison for twenty years." She looked at Kathy hopelessly. "Can she really do that?"

Kathy hesitated, and Downey gave a bitter smile. "Yes, I thought so."

"This man that you met," Kathy said. "Was it O'Hearn or Ryan?"

"Neither. I'd never seen him before. Actually he seemed very nice. I can still hardly believe that he cold-bloodedly killed Gudrun like that. He must have known when he met me that that was what he was going to do."

"Describe him to me."

"Oh, white, probably midthirties, six foot, medium build, short dark hair, smart casual clothes. He could have been one of the young doctors at Great Ormond Street. The sort of bloke I'd have liked a few years ago. Who am I kidding? I did like him."

"Did he give you a name, a contact number to reach him?"

"No. We met in the Rembrandt Gardens next to Little Venice. He had a tote bag full of comics and I asked him if they were for his children, and he said no, his boy preferred videos and TV."

"Comics?"

"Yes, old *Eagle* comics. You remember, Dan Dare? Maybe you're too young. He said he'd just found them in a secondhand bookshop. What's the matter? Did I say something?"

Kathy felt a sudden chill. She reached for her phone and thumbed back through the photographs until she came to the ones she'd taken on *Grace* when Gudrun had just been found. Kathy selected one and showed it to Anne.

"Yes! That's him. You know him?"

"Yes, I know him." Kathy looked down at the image of Mickey Schaeffer searching a bulkhead cupboard. Actually, she was feeling that she didn't know him at all.

After Anne Downey left, Kathy waited in the bar, thinking, then rang Mickey Schaeffer's number. He sounded rushed, people's voices in the background.

"Mickey, I think I may have a lead on Ollie Kovacs."

"Really? That's great, Kathy."

"Yes. I should know more this evening, six o'clock. I'll call you then."

She hung up before he could reply.

THIRTY-THREE

AT FIVE FORTY-FIVE KATHY made her way carefully down the steps to Ollie's place, sensing—or perhaps it was just her imagination—a lingering smell of burning in the damp air of the canal basin. Beneath the tarpaulins she ducked under police tapes and switched on a flashlight, picking her way through the obstacles to the door into the old boat. It yielded to a shove, its lock broken from Bren's forced entry, and she stepped inside, switching on a light. She went to the workshop in the stern where they had found the dynamite and examined the tools lying on the bench. From her pocket she took the small video camera she'd brought with her, and placed it on a shelf above the bench, its lens pointing toward the door. Then she sat down and waited.

Ten minutes later she heard the sound of a footstep, the creak of a door, and felt a slight tremor go through the boat. Then the workshop door swung open and Mickey was standing there, wearing a black leather jacket and gloves. He glanced around the room.

"Kathy, hi. What's going on?"

She looked at his face, searching for some sign that she might have picked up before, but all she could see was the old Mickey, quiet, calm, self-possessed.

"How did you find me?" she asked.

"Huh? I tracked your phone."

She shook her head. "It's been turned off. You tracked my chip, didn't you? You've been tracking me all the time."

He looked surprised for a brief moment, then gave a dismissive shrug. "So where's Ollie Kovacs?"

"I found a witness. Someone who saw Gudrun's killer coming out of her boat that night. They got a clear view, and I showed them some pictures. They identified you, Mickey."

"You're joking."

"No, they were very convincing."

"You're crazy!"

"Mickey Schaeffer, I'm arresting you for the murder of Gudrun Kite. You know the caution."

He looked stunned. "Kathy!"

"I want you to accompany me to Paddington police station where I shall formally bring charges."

He stared hard at her, calculating. "You've got this all wrong. I think you're sick." He nodded at her arm in the sling. "You've been through so much. It's affected your judgment."

"We'll see. You were on Gudrun's boat that night, and the next morning you said nothing, and did your best to block my investigation. When did you really start working for Suzy Russell?"

"Oh, Kathy . . ."

"It won't be hard to find out."

He sighed, pulled a stool out from the bench and sat down. "She's been looking for people to join her team. When she saw I'd got a computer science degree she approached me, a couple of months ago. I didn't mention it to Brock at the time because I wasn't sure it would come off."

"Did she want you to prove yourself? Was that it?"

He sighed. "She had a problem. She needed a job done by

315

someone who was tech-savvy, but also could handle themselves, like a cop. She had a word with me."

"Go on."

"Gudrun Kite, or Vicky Hawke as she was calling herself, was being a naughty girl. She'd been downloading confidential documents from Paddington Security Services relating to the Raven project. She was going to pass them on to Ollie Kovacs and an outfit called Digital Anarchy, which would have been a disaster for Raven. Time was short. Someone had to go on board her boat that night and track down all the possible devices on which she might be storing the data and erase or remove them. So I agreed to do it.

"It was all pretty straightforward. Gudrun had taken a big dose of sleeping pills and was out for the count. I was given a key, let myself in, and carried out a sweep of the boat. She had a disc hidden behind a print of a raven, would you believe. And I took her phone and laptop and an external hard drive. That was it. Job done."

"She was alive?"

"Sleeping like a baby."

"What time was this?"

"About three."

Kathy shook her head. "No, that doesn't work. She was dead by four. How could the flue have come unstuck in that time?"

"I don't know. I got a hell of a shock when we got called out there the next morning."

"Also, you had to remove the microchip that she'd had implanted into her hand. You couldn't do that while she was alive. That's what Russell really needed, wasn't it? Someone who could make a murder look like an accident. Who better than a homicide detective? Come on, Mickey. Let's go."

Schaeffer rose to his feet and stood blocking the doorway.

"You're making a fool of yourself, Kathy. You won't be allowed to go through with this. There's too much at stake. Raven is far more important than Gudrun Kite, or you and me for that matter."

"We'll find out. Come on."

He hesitated a moment, then glanced down at a hammer lying on the bench by his side. "Where is Ollie Kovacs, anyway?"

"I don't know."

"Well, it looks like you met him here and he went into one of his rages."

Kathy watched Schaeffer's hand close around the shaft of the hammer. As he raised it she said, "Put the hammer down, Mickey."

"Sorry, Kathy," he said. "I just can't let you mess everything up." He came at her, reaching out his other hand to grab the front of her coat. As he did so she ducked, drew the ASP baton from her pocket, and hit him hard across the knees. He roared in pain, and Kathy, eyes fixed on his right hand holding the hammer, didn't see his left fist as it slammed into the side of her face. She fell to the floor, stunned, while he stood over her cursing, rubbing his leg.

"Bitch," he gasped. "You've just made this a lot easier." He raised the hammer high above his head.

"You're under surveillance," she gasped.

He hesitated a second, then smiled, "Sure."

"The camera's up there." She nodded desperately at the shelf. "It's transmitting pictures back to the team."

He turned his head and saw the lens, glinting in its hiding place, and swore softly, then dropped to his knees beside her. "Where's the team?"

Kathy shook her head, transfixed by the expression of sheer hatred on his face. He grabbed her good arm and yanked it, dragging her half under the bench. He tugged a pair of handcuffs from his jacket pocket and locked her wrist to one of the bench legs, then got to his feet, kicking her savagely in the hip.

She'd made a terrible miscalculation, she realized. The important thing had been to get him to confess on video to what he'd done, but to do that she'd put herself in an impossibly vulnerable position. What had she been thinking? That he'd go easy on a woman with a broken shoulder? That she could subdue him with her baton the way she might a callow teenager?

She watched him as he peered cautiously at the camera from one side, then the other, pulling away the boxes beside it, while she looked around her for something, anything that she could use to defend herself with. She could see nothing within reach except a coil of wire half covered in a pile of shavings and cobwebs beneath the bench. Holding her breath, she eased her left hand out of the sling and stretched it out, slowly, painfully, until her fingers reached the wire and tugged it free, revealing a slim metal tube attached to one end of the coil. She had seen an illustration of something like this before, a blasting cap, such as Desmond Kite would have used to detonate Ollie's dynamite. The bomb squad must have missed it when they cleared the explosives from the benchtop. She drew it back into her sling, closing the fabric around it.

Above her, Schaeffer gave a grunt, lifting the camera down onto the bench and peering at it. Kathy began to shift upright into a squatting position, and froze as he turned on her.

"Where did you get this?" he demanded. "Not from tech support."

He turned back to the camera and began to open it up.

Kathy eased herself shakily to her feet and placed the coil on the workbench, then, leaning over toward Schaeffer, took the detonator tube and slipped it into the belt at the back of his jacket.

"This isn't transmitting anything," he said. "This is just an ordinary video camera."

He turned and saw Kathy sprawled across the bench as she tried to reach the electric socket above the bench with the other end of the wires. "What the hell do you think you're—?"

Her shoulder was a burning agony as she jammed the leads in. There was a deafening bang, and she turned to Schaeffer and saw his mouth open in shock as he fell to the floor.

THIRTY-FOUR

COMMANDER LYNCH GROANED AND reached for the mouse. He had been sitting at his desk with his face in his hands, eyes wide, staring through his fingers at Kathy's video on his computer.

"Dear God. What are we going to do?"

Brock had spent some time thinking about that. Lynch had withheld vital information, repeatedly put Kathy in danger, and had planned to let a major felon escape justice. Brock could destroy Fred Lynch. But if he did, he would not be forgiven, and he too would probably be forced out. Alternatively, he could hold his hand, and work with a boss over whom he would now have some leverage.

"What the hell do I do now?"

So Brock, seated on the other side of the desk, proceeded to tell him. First, a glass of ex-Commander Sharpe's single malt, which had survived the change of administration. Then the list of interrogations and arrests—Superintendent Russell and her staff at DiSTaF, Vernon Montague and his staff at Pewsey, the Harvest Group.

"I can't do that," Lynch said, wincing. "Too many people are involved."

"You must. We'll draw up a plan together. The whole rotten

applecart. It was a bad idea that got out of control. If you don't act decisively now, you'll go down with them."

Lynch sipped morosely at Sharpe's whiskey. They sat in silence for a while. Then Brock said, "When's Jack Bragg's funeral?"

The change of tack threw Lynch for a moment. "Um, next Tuesday, I think."

"Mm. He said a funny thing to Kathy when he was holding her at his house in Sevenoaks. He told her that you were his little brother."

Brock watched Lynch go rigid, clutching the whiskey glass so tight it might have cracked.

"She told me. She won't tell anyone else."

"God, Brock," Lynch whispered. "Somebody warned me to get rid of you two when I took over. I should have listened to them."

Brock chuckled.

"Half-brothers," Lynch said finally. "Same mother, different fathers. Our parenting was what you'd call single-mother, multiple-partners. Jack was three years older than me, and he looked after me, kept me safe in the bad times. I wouldn't have survived without him. I suppose I hoped that the microchip would be my way of looking after him, keeping a close eye on him without locking him up."

"You were going to let him get away?"

Lynch sighed. "I owed him that. I was going to tell him that I would know every step he took, wherever he was, and he must never come back."

"But you hadn't told him."

"Not yet. We wanted him to lead us to his old cronies first. But it was impossible to control Jack." He took another sip. "You think they deliberately killed him at Pewsey? It wasn't just a failed operation?"

"Yes. I think they, or rather their bosses at Harvest, decided he was just too dangerous and unpredictable."

"Yes, that was Jack all right. So, what do you want, Brock?"

"I want the very best care for Kathy. She has to have that bloody chip removed."

Lynch nodded. "Of course."

"And I want to run my own cases with my own team without being micromanaged by you or D.K. Payne or anyone else."

Lynch took a deep breath, grunted, "And?"

"And I want you to clean up this mess."

"Raven?"

"Nevermore. That's all."

"That's all . . ." Lynch echoed gloomily. He stared at the image frozen on his screen, of Kathy standing over Mickey Schaeffer. "One-handed! She's a piece of work, isn't she? Is she all right?"

"She'll survive. So will Schaeffer, apparently, though he'll never walk again. His spine is a mess."

KATHY STEPPED INTO THE bar, feeling exhausted and desperately in need of company and a drink before she headed home. She'd just heard from the surgeon that he would operate on her in the morning, if she still wanted to go ahead with it. She said she did.

The place was throbbing with sound, laughter, music. She made for a free stool at the counter and a man in front of her turned suddenly and thumped into her left arm. She gave a pained gasp and the man saw the empty left sleeve of her coat and blinked.

"Oh hell, I'm sorry."

"It's all right." She made to move on to the bar.

"No, really, I'm so sorry."

She looked at his face, pleasant, embarrassed, a bit of a tan, perhaps an Australian accent? "It's nothing."

"But I should have looked. Let me buy you a drink at least."

"No thanks."

"I insist. I'll buy you a drink and then I must go."

She shrugged. "All right."

She sat down on the stool and he stood beside her, gesturing to the bar staff.

"What'll you have?"

"Scotch." Kathy unfastened her coat and he glanced down at her arm in the sling.

"Ouch. How did you do that?"

The question seemed so ludicrous that she laughed. "I couldn't begin to tell you."

"Long story?"

"Too long."

"A saga."

"Yes," she agreed. "A saga, exactly."

One of the barmen came over and he ordered her a double. "My name's Justin by the way."

She didn't reply, thinking about Brock, wondering about how his meeting with Lynch was going. Then she registered his words and said, "I'm Kathy."

"Hello, Kathy." He checked his watch. "What do you think is the quickest way to the British Museum at this time? Should I try for a cab or the underground?"

"A cab. But it'll be closed, won't it?"

"Oh, there's a late function that I'm supposed to be going to."

Her drink came and Justin handed over a note, waited for the change.

"Thanks," Kathy said. "Cheers."

"Cheers. You look as if you've had a hard day."

"A bit rough."

"What do you do?"

Usually she would say that she worked for the Home Office, or in human relations, but tonight she couldn't be bothered. "I'm a police officer."

"Really?" He looked again at her arm. "And you got that . . . ?"

She nodded.

"Oh dear. Are you a detective?"

"Yes."

"What, serious stuff? Murder?"

He saw the expression on her face. "Sorry. I had to ask. You see, I've just discovered a murder."

She gave him a look.

"Yes. A young man, probably about twenty. He'd been hit in the back of the neck, probably with an axe. I think it was a religious killing."

"Religious?"

"Yes, I think so. Like an execution, but extrajudicial."

Kathy couldn't decide if he was pulling her leg. "You reported it to the police?"

"Yes, of course. You have to, don't you? But they weren't very interested."

"Why not?"

"Well, he died a long time ago. About seventeen hundred years ago."

"Oh." She smiled. "You're an archaeologist or something."

"That's right."

"Where was this?"

"Near St. Albans—Verulamium—a Roman villa we've been excavating. I'm putting the date of the murder at around 304 AD."

"That's very precise."

"Well, that's when the Emperor Diocletian ordered all

Christians to be persecuted, and Alban became the first Christian martyr in Britain. I'm guessing that my man was one of his followers . . ."

Kathy let him ramble on while her mind filled with flash-backs from the boat, the slight tilt in the floor when Mickey Schaeffer stepped aboard, the sudden look of clarity in his eyes when he decided that he was going to have to kill her.

"Sorry, I'm boring you. I'll say goodnight."

"Oh, okay. Thanks for the Scotch."

He half turned away, then hesitated, looking suddenly embarrassed. "The thing is, we were saying only this morning how fantastic it would be if we could get a proper detective to help us interpret the crime scene. I mean, was he killed there, behind the stables where he was buried, or had he been brought there from elsewhere? That kind of thing. We have a forensic anthropologist helping us, but a real-life detective might notice something. And I just thought, if you're on sick leave and felt like an outing . . ."

Kathy laughed. "Well, I've heard a few lines in my time, Justin, but that's original."

He grinned back. "No, I didn't mean—"

"Actually, it does sound interesting."

"Really? Well look, I must go, but let me give you my card with my email address. Contact me if you'd like to know more."

He hurried away and she examined the card. She'd been right, an address in Sydney. He seemed all right. She smiled to herself. Time to move on.

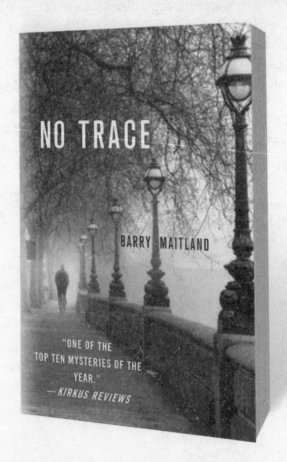